Less than Perfect

Volume 1 – Books 1-3:
Less than Perfect Secrets
Less than Perfect Friendships
Less than Perfect Christmas

Natasja Eby

ISBN-13: 9781777723491

First edition: May 2022

The characters and events portrayed in this book are fictitious. Any similarity to real persons, living or dead, is coincidental and not intended by the author. However, should you find yourself yearning for a core friend group bound tightly together by your love of music, this is purely intentional.

Cover and book design by Natasja Eby

Published by Natasja Eby
www.natasjaeby.com

DEDICATION

For all the closet musicians of the world.

ACKNOWLEDGMENTS

Thank you to Gina, Beth, Michelle, Izzy, and Nathanael. Sorry I ask the weirdest questions in life.

Meet the characters!

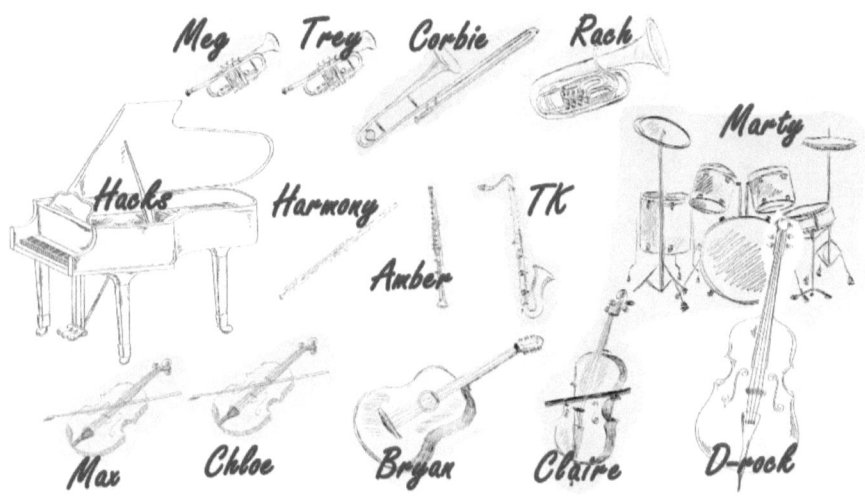

Meg   Trey   Corbie   Rach

Marty

Hacks   Harmony   TK

Amber

Max   Chloe   Bryan   Claire   D-rock

Less than Perfect Secrets

Book 1

Chapter One

Gripping the football to his body, Trey ran the last few yards to the goal line while his teammates cheered him on. Chad, one of his best friends, launched himself at Trey in an effort to tackle him. But Trey quickly dodged out of the way and leaped into the endzone.

"Yes!" he shouted as he slammed the football to the ground.

"Okay," Chad said, chuckling as he pushed sweaty hair out of his face. "I'll give it to you, that was an amazing play."

Trey grinned as some of the other guys high-fived him. It was only practice, but he knew they could pull that off in a real game. Specifically, this Saturday's game against their rivals, the Eastdale Eagles. Those guys had nothing on the Bridgetown Blackhawks.

"Job well done," Coach Hanford said as Trey ran back to him. "Go take a break. You've earned it."

"Thanks," Trey said.

He took off his helmet and headed to the bench. It was mid September and they'd just started playoffs. Saturday's game was make or break for them. But he knew they'd make it while breaking a few Eagle hearts along the way.

The warning school bell sounded, meaning they would only have 15 minutes to get ready for classes. He jogged inside, where some of the cheerleaders were hanging out by the gym.

"T!"

"R!"

"E!"

"Y!"

"Goooo Trey!" they shouted together.

He laughed, his face warming at the attention. "Thanks, ladies. Keep up that spirit at the game."

In the locker room, Trey showered and changed quickly. He looked around for Chad so he could remind him about the extra practice on Thursday, but he was nowhere to be seen. Trey shrugged it off. Chad was known to be a bit lax about the rules, but he was a mean fullback and had never let Trey down.

As Trey headed to his class, he glanced to his right and did a double take. So *that's* where Chad was. He had his hands on either side of Meg, the shyest girl in school, and was leaning far too close to her face. Meg's head was turned to the side and she murmured something that made Chad laugh. But not in a pleasant way. It sounded malicious to Trey.

"Come on, tell me you don't want a piece of this," he said as Trey crept closer.

"I don't want a piece of…whatever it is you're offering," she said barely above a whisper.

None of the other students around seemed to care or even notice Meg's intense discomfort. But when Chad firmly grasped one of her arms and leaned even closer to her, Trey decided he'd had enough.

"What are you doing?" he asked. Meg's eyes flicked up to his and he could see the quiet desperation in them.

Chad jumped at Trey's sudden appearance and the question. Then he smirked. "We're just having a conversation."

"Looks pretty one-sided," Trey said, edging closer.

"And it's finished," Meg said weakly. Taking advantage of the tiny bit of space between her and Chad, she put her free hand on his chest and pushed. But he barely budged and instead grasped her forearm.

Trey pushed Chad's shoulder hard enough to make him back up, but not hard enough to knock him over. Chad scowled, but still had a grip on both of Meg's arms.

"What's your problem, Donnelly?" Chad asked, his rough voice finally drawing the attention of others around them.

"You're the problem," Trey spat back at him. "She says she doesn't want to talk so let her go."

"Wait your turn," Chad said, pulling on Meg's arms. "You can have her when I'm done with her."

Yeah, Chad never was one for rules. But Trey had never seen this side of him before. Trey weighed his options as Meg cringed, shaking her head. She tried to free herself, but Chad's hold was so tight, her arms were going white.

"Dude," Trey said, trying to play it off. He knew Chad could have a big head, but this was ridiculous. "Just let her go. People are watching."

"You're right." With another cocky smirk, Chad let go of Meg, giving her a little push. "I'll wait till there are fewer people around to finish my conversation."

"You're disgusting," Trey said, pushing Chad again, more forcefully this time.

"Guys..." Meg put her hand up to stop Trey as the bell rang. "Just drop it, okay?"

Trey looked down into Meg's terrified hazel eyes and realized it was *him* she was talking to. Not Chad. He nodded for her sake. He could yell at Chad later.

She nodded back at him before skittering away. Chad started sauntering past, but Trey reached out and grabbed his shoulder. Chad shook him off, giving him an angry glare.

"What the hell is wrong with you?" Trey asked.

"Me?" Chad sputtered. "Why can't you mind your own business?"

Once again, Chad tried to walk past him, but Trey blocked him with his entire body. "Right now, you *are* my business. That was really uncool of you."

"I think *you're* the one who's being uncool," Chad said. "Let's get to class. Unless you want to fail again this year."

Trey's eyes narrowed. "*Excuse me?*" he said, though Chad's meaning was clear. "You're such an idiot. No wonder girls don't want to talk to you."

"That's it!" Chad dropped his backpack to the floor and put up his fists. "You can be the captain of the team, and you can weasel your way out of summer school, but you do *not* get to claim all the girls in the school."

Trey put his open hands in front of him, not willing to give into a fight. "You're being ridiculous. I don't have a claim on all the girls in this school."

"Oh, that's right." Chad sneered. "Not *all* of them, considering Lacy came running straight into my arms when you were suddenly too busy training at football camp this summer."

Trey's heart dropped to his stomach. *That* was why Lacy had broken up with him? She had said they'd simply drifted apart, that it wasn't working out. She never said there was someone else involved.

Trey grabbed the front of Chad's shirt and pulled until they were nearly nose-to-nose. "You better be lying," he gritted through his teeth.

Chad gulped hard, lifting his chin up the slightest. He was a big guy, but Trey still had an inch on him. "I'd be lying if I said she preferred you to me."

Chad may as well have slapped Trey in the face for how the insult stung. "You're supposed to be one of my best friends," he said, his voice cracking.

"Would a best friend do this?" Chad asked before swinging his fist into Trey's face.

Trey didn't react quickly enough to move out of the way. But he was fast enough to land a solid punch to Chad's gut before he was out of range. Chad wrapped his arms around his stomach, taking a quick step back.

Glaring up at Trey, Chad launched himself at him, knocking both of them to the floor. Someone nearby shouted, "Fight!" and suddenly they were surrounded by other students. Chad threw a punch that only glanced off Trey's cheek as he turned his head to the side.

Putting both hands firmly on Chad's shoulders, Trey pushed until he rolled them both over. Now, with Chad on his back, Trey straddled him and punched him soundly in the face. When he pulled back to hit him a second time, he heard his name being shouted. But that didn't stop him from getting the hit in.

"Trey Donnelly," the firm voice repeated.

A strong hand grabbed his shoulder, pulling him away from Chad. Chad scrambled up and put a sleeve to his mouth, where a drop of blood had quickly formed.

"Everybody get to class!" Mr. Carson, the normally mild-mannered science teacher, barked. As the boys began following the other lingering students, he added, "Not you two. What happened here?"

Trey opened his mouth to answer, but before he could, Chad said, "I don't know, sir. Trey just suddenly got mad and jumped me."

"That's not true!" Trey shouted.

Mr. Carson crossed his arms and stared him down. "Then what actually happened?"

For a moment, Trey was caught between the truth and wanting to protect people who had nothing to do with the fight between them. Like Meg. And yes, even Lacy. He hadn't been completely justified in trying to pummel Chad, but on the other hand, *Chad* had started the fight. Not him.

When he hesitated too long, Mr. Carson snarled, "Right. Two weeks' detention for you, Trey."

"But he started it!" Trey shouted, his frustration bouncing around the empty hallway. "I was just defending myself."

"From where I was standing, you had the upper hand," Mr. Carson answered. "Two weeks, Donnelly. *And* I'll be talking to Mr. Hanford about this. Get to class now."

Chad smirked and sauntered away. But Trey wasn't done trying to prove his innocence—or at least Chad's lack thereof.

"Mr. Carson," Trey began, "Chad really did throw the first punch. You're just going to let him go free?"

Mr. Carson blinked slowly, breathing deeply out through his nose as if all his patience for the day had already left him. "Aren't you his team captain?"

"So?" Trey crossed his arms.

"So, hold yourself to a higher standard," Mr. Carson answered. "Look, I think you're really talented and, quite frankly, I'm surprised to find you engaging physically with another student like that. Learn to accept the consequences of your actions. Now if you don't mind, I'm late for my own class and I'm handing out a pop quiz today. And I *love* pop quizzes. Two weeks of detention."

Huffing with indignation, Trey glared at Mr. Carson's retreating form. First he'd defended Meg, and then he'd kept his silence about the real reason he and Chad had been fighting, and this was his reward? Maybe his friends were right—maybe he was too nice.

♪   ♫   ♪

D-rock pushed the hair out of his eyes, glancing over at the school longingly. He should have been sitting in his chemistry class. He was probably missing one of Mr. Carson's *fun* pop quizzes right now. Instead, he was skipping class with his two friends on the bleachers by the track.

"Stop looking," Ted griped, drawing D-rock's attention. "No one's coming for us."

"Here, just relax," G said, holding out the compact cylinder in his hand.

D-rock just shook his head, not wanting to explain that he'd rather be in class than outside vaping with his friends. He'd never once tried a vape, but he knew being relaxed wouldn't bring back the marks he would miss by skipping class. At least the crisp September air was nice.

"It's not gonna kill you," G added. But when D-rock ignored him, he shrugged and took the vape back.

As his friends carried on a meaningless conversation, a consistent bass rhythm rippled through D-rock's head. It was one he'd been playing this morning before coming to school and as hard as he'd tried, he couldn't get it out. This was the reason he normally missed things in class—because his head was always in his music.

It took all his willpower not to bob his head along to the imaginary music. Ted and G were always making fun of him for something—and if it wasn't for being too sober than it would certainly be for hearing music all the time.

"D-rock."

The bassline vanished at G's irritated voice. "What?" D-rock asked.

"Can you hold these for a sec?" G held out his and Ted's vapes.

Without thinking, D-rock took them with a shrug and went back to the music. In his head, that bassline was much more complete with a guitar and drums. Maybe even a piano and…something else. Something was missing. But he didn't exactly have someone to bounce ideas off of.

"Boys!" A shrill voice rang across the empty track, causing all three of them to jump.

"It's Stringer!" G exclaimed in a hushed voice as he pushed Ted forward ahead of himself.

They clamoured down the bleachers, D-rock on their heels. The ripped hem of his jeans that extended far past his high tops caught on a step and he reached out quickly to keep from falling all the way down. By the time he'd righted himself, Ted and G were nowhere to be seen and Mrs. Stringer was standing at the bottom of the bleachers, her hands on her hips.

Resigned to his fate, D-rock dragged his feet the rest of the way down until he was face-to-face with her. Although he had a good four inches on her, his heart hammered in his chest. She was far scarier than most of the teachers at the school.

"I know I shouldn't be skipping class," he said quickly, figuring he might as well own up to it and get it out of the way.

Her dark eyes flashed. "I'm not worried about you skipping class. I didn't even know you were skipping."

"Oh." D-rock shook his head. Maybe he shouldn't have been so quick to admit that.

"It's *that*," she said, pointing to his hand.

He looked down, realizing he was still gripping the vapes tightly. "Oh no," he said. "No, these aren't mine. I wasn't even—"

"Uh-huh," she said disbelievingly. She held out her hand and D-rock dropped the vapes into it. "Oh, two! A backup in case the first one gets taken away?"

"No, Mrs. Stringer, please—"

"You know, I applaud your foresight, Derek." Mrs. Stringer's face softened, and she continued in an almost sympathetic voice. "I just wish you would apply that to your academic life instead. I'm giving you two weeks of detention."

D-rock sighed. He knew nothing would change her mind. All of the teachers already thought he was an idiot. "Yes, Mrs. Stringer," he whispered.

"I suggest you go and find out what you missed in your class," she said, her voice verging on irritated again.

D-rock nodded and stomped back towards the school. When he got close enough, he realized Ted and G had been hiding around the corner where Mrs. Stringer couldn't see them. They laughed when D-rock walked by and then G held out his hand.

The vapes. *Yeah, right.* Even if D-rock had been able to hold on to them, he would have tossed them in the trash like he wanted to do with his supposed friendships. Silently, he walked right past them, ignoring them as best as he could.

Ted and G stopped laughing and rushed to catch up to him. He brushed them off until Ted grabbed his arm and pulled him to a stop.

"Your vapes are gone, alright?" D-rock said.

"Really, dude?" Ted scowled at him. "Thanks a *lot.*"

"*And* I got two weeks of detention for you." D-rock pulled his arm back. "You're welcome."

G put up his hands. "What's the big deal? It's just detention. You lost our stuff and that was hard to get in the first place."

D-rock looked at both of his friends. Neither of them felt the least bit bad that he'd taken the fall for them, like he'd done so many times in the past. Well, this would be the last time.

"I don't want to talk to you guys right now," he said. Though if he'd been honest, he would have said he never wanted to talk to them again.

Chapter Two

It had been three days since the incident with Chad. Three days since the rumours of Trey's two-week punishment for fighting on school grounds. No one knew for sure why the fight had started or why he'd been given detention and Chad hadn't. Meg's name was never mentioned in the rumours, which made sense since Meg largely went unnoticed by the other students. But Meg had a suspicion what had happened.

She felt sick just thinking about Chad, but so far he'd left her alone. Trey had also been avoiding her but that was nothing new. Just because they'd been in almost every class together since kindergarten, that didn't exactly make them friends.

"When are you going to tell me what all the sighing is about?"

Meg looked across the lunch table at her friend Rachel, suppressing yet another sigh. The whole situation was embarrassing, and she didn't want to burden Rach with it. Rach had her own set of problems with the kids at this school.

"Do you think the boys at this school will ever grow up?" Meg asked, instead of saying what was really on her mind.

"I hope so," Rach said, one corner of her mouth tilting up. "There are only two dudes in my grade taller than me. It sucks."

Meg chuckled. Rach was 6'1" and got teased constantly for it. But at least Rach had a good attitude about it. Usually. Meg knew that the teasing got to her every once in a while, but Rach always came to school with a brave face. Meg admired her for it. She couldn't imagine being so…visible all the time.

Even the thought of it made Meg clam up all over again. Rach didn't seem to notice as she went back to her lunch. It was always a companionable silence for them. Meg liked the silence and Rach liked being with someone who was always kind to her. Their one-year difference had never bothered them.

When the lunch bell rang, they headed into the throng of students. Rach was a natural crowd-splitter so Meg stayed near her to avoid getting too close to other people. Rach stopped suddenly, reaching out to grasp a younger boy she had bumped into to keep him upright.

"Whoops, sorry, little dude," Rach said as she righted him.

Readjusting his glasses at the frames with the tips of his fingers, he looked up at her and then at Meg. "Apology accepted," he said, before moving past them.

After he was gone, Meg said, "You know Hacks isn't that little, right? He's only a year younger than you."

"Yeah, well, he has a few growth spurts to catch up on," Rach said with a smirk.

Meg smiled back at her. "Maybe when he gives his brain a rest."

Everyone knew Hacks was a brainiac who had skipped two grades and was now in grade 12. He even shared some classes with Meg, though they hardly ever spoke to each other. In fact, Hacks kept close to his group of computer science and programming friends and Meg…hardly interacted with anyone.

"See you later," Rach said as she turned down another hallway.

Well, at least there was Rach. An outcast simply for having exceptional genetics, Rach was one of Meg's best and only friends. They'd met a few years ago at band camp. And while both girls were reluctant to share their talent with the world, they still shared a love of playing music. Meg would always be grateful for that.

♪   ♫   ♪

With a heavy sigh, D-rock made his way towards detention for the third day in a row. The room was empty except for Trey, who raised his eyebrows briefly at him. But D-rock wasn't surprised to see him. Everyone had heard about Trey's fight.

Mr. Yalchin was writing on the whiteboard in large uppercase letters. THE RULES: NO TALKING. NO FIGHTING. NO ILLEGAL DRUG USE. As if D-rock was interested in any of that.

He glanced quickly at Trey sitting two rows over. They'd known each other most of their lives. They had even played together in younger grades. But Trey was from the better half of town, played sports, and was well-liked by pretty much everyone. D-rock wore thrift store clothes, had lame friends, and just wanted to get through high school in one piece.

But there was one thing no one could take away from him: his music. He had his bass. And he had even thought to bring blank music sheets with him to school. He knew he'd get bored enough to use them and his brain was always wandering to the music anyway.

As he wrote, he could practically feel eyes on him. He looked up. Nope, not Mr. Yalchin. D-rock turned towards Trey, who was staring openly at his music. A chiming sound drew their attention to the front of the classroom.

Mr. Yalchin cleared his throat uncomfortably. "I have to take a call. Behave yourselves." With that, he held up his phone and swept out of the classroom.

D-rock immediately went back to his music. He ignored Trey's glances, but couldn't ignore him when he whispered, "What are you writing?"

D-rock frowned at him. "Music."

"Well, yeah," Trey said with a chuckle. "But, I mean, what is it?"

D-rock looked down at the music, wondering why Trey would even care. "It's just music in my head. I'm writing it down so I don't forget it and I can play it later."

"You can do that?" Trey asked, his blue eyes wide. "Just…hear music in your head and write it down?"

"Sure," D-rock said, growing self-conscious. "Any musician could."

"I sure couldn't!" Trey blurted out.

D-rock stared at him and said, "Well, I did say any…*musician* could."

When Trey fell silent, D-rock went back to his music. He'd lost his train of thought and now he had to go back over the entire line just to catch up to where he'd left off. Just when he was getting back into it, Trey spoke again.

"I'm not, like…" Trey paused. "*Not* a musician."

Biting back a sigh, D-rock lifted his gaze to Trey's. "Are you saying…"

"I play trumpet." Trey shrugged. "Sometimes."

"Sometimes."

"Like every day if I get the chance." There was a hint of wistfulness in his voice that caught D-rock by surprise.

D-rock lifted an eyebrow. That sounded like…exactly what D-rock did. "Trey, you're not just *not a musician*. You *are* a musician."

Trey shrugged uncomfortably. "Okay, sure. But no one else knows. I don't play for other people."

"Neither do I," D-rock said.

Trey looked down at his hands. "But what if we did?"

"What do you mean?" D-rock asked as he unconsciously covered his music with his hand.

"You know…" Trey gestured between the two of them. "What if you and I…played together?"

"Just a bass and a trumpet?" D-rock didn't hate the idea, but… "That would be kind of weird, don't you think?"

"Nah." Trey tilted his head in thought. "But maybe we can find some other closet musicians to play with us."

"Closet musicians?"

Trey smiled. "Yeah. People like us. With no one else to play with."

D-rock didn't get a chance to answer before Mr. Yalchin came back in. But he spent the next 20 minutes thinking about it. About his bass, some drums, a guitar…a trumpet. It would only take a few musicians to make a band. But who would want to play with D-rock?

Once they'd been freed from their punishment, they both rushed out of the classroom. Trey kept pace with D-rock. Clearly the conversation wasn't over.

"So?" Trey said.

"So what?" D-rock shrugged.

"So, do you want to start a band or what?" Trey asked.

D-rock turned and looked right into Trey's eyes. "You're serious?" Trey nodded. "Aren't you kind of busy with your teams and stuff?"

Trey's gaze dropped to the floor as he shrugged. "I really love playing." He looked back up. "My trumpet, that is. But my friends…"

"They wouldn't understand?" D-rock filled in, knowing how that felt.

"Yeah."

D-rock nodded slowly, chewing on his bottom lip. "But how would we find them? And how do we know they're serious about playing and not just—" He cut himself off before he let his true insecurities show.

Trey's face broke out into a grin. "I get it. You still want to keep it a secret. I think I can figure that part out."

D-rock shook his head. If it weren't for Trey's excessive confidence, he would have turned around and given up on the idea before it even became an idea. "I guess we could put it out there and if no one responds, then that's that."

Trey's smile grew as he laughed. "Oh, we'll get a few takers. Don't worry about that." He gave D-rock a playful but hard slap on the shoulder. "We'll have our band soon enough. See you around."

With a confused smile, D-rock said, "See you."

Trey watched D-rock walk away before reluctantly heading to the back field. He wasn't exactly ready to give up sports just yet. But thinking about playing his trumpet with another musician? It sparked a fire in him that football just didn't have.

Not to mention that Coach Hanford had already benched him for Saturday's game for getting into a fight with a teammate. Yet for some reason, he was still being forced to attend practice.

Trey shoved the back door open and then dragged his feet over to the bench by the football field. A couple of the other guys were sitting, too—ninth and tenth graders who weren't ready for first string yet. Not like Trey.

"Donnelly!" Hanford barked. "You're late!"

"I'm still serving my sentence," Trey called back to him.

He couldn't even look at the guys on the field. He knew Chad was out there, living in the glory of Trey's spotlight. Chad was, after all, their backup quarterback.

Disgusted, Trey pulled out his phone and forced himself to think of other things. Like how he was going to gather a band like he'd promised D-rock. He had tons of friends on social media, but he wasn't just going to blast them with a strange request through his own name.

"Trey." Hanford's voice was close and Trey had to force himself not to jump up off the bench.

"Yup," he said, not even looking up from his phone.

"You're the captain of this team," Hanford said in an irritable voice. "Don't you think you should be paying attention to practice?"

Trey flicked his eyes up. "Why should I if I won't even get to play our biggest rivals?"

Hanford put his fists on his hips, his eyes narrowing. "If you had kept your hands to yourself, you'd be out there right now."

Trey bit his tongue. He'd already explained to Hanford that Chad was just as much to blame as Trey was, and that he had, in fact, started the fight. But it didn't seem to matter.

"Got it," Trey said, before dropping his gaze to his phone again.

♪ ♫ ♪

Staring from beneath lowered lashes, Chloe listened to Jaden's impassioned speech about the pollution on the beach. His sallow skin was normally so pale, but when he ranted, he almost had flushed cheeks. Today he was trying to rally their group to go down to the beach to clean up, but so far the others were all too busy that weekend.

"I'll go with you," Chloe said timidly.

Her face heated up when he turned his lopsided smile on her. "Cool. See you there."

She smiled back and then dropped her gaze to her phone. Mindlessly scrolling while passively listening to her friends was how she spent most of her lunches. It wasn't that she didn't like her friends. There just wasn't always a lot of substance to their conversations.

A neon green blip on her phone caught her eye and slowly she scrolled back up to read the words on the post.

CALLING ALL CLOSET MUSICIANS.
DO YOU HAVE A SECRET LOVE FOR MUSIC?
DO YOU PLAY AN AWESOME INSTRUMENT?
ARE YOU LOOKING FOR SOMEONE TO PLAY WITH?
IF YOU ANSWERED YES TO THESE QUESTIONS, THEN WE'RE
LOOKING FOR YOU. COME JOIN US.

Chloe's mind drifted to her violin. In her head, she'd answered yes to all of the questions. She loved playing her violin, but she'd never joined a band and her friends didn't know. And if she were honest, until she could afford new strings, she wasn't sure if she wanted to let anyone listen to her.

But that didn't stop her from reading the caption on the post that had instructions for how to join. All she had to do was send them a message, which she inexplicably did. Two seconds later there was an enthusiastic response with details on their first meeting. Tuesday night at an address that was near her apartment. Perfect.

Across the cafeteria, Amber was staring at the same post, holding her phone close to her so her friends wouldn't see. They would absolutely make fun of her if they knew she still played the clarinet. They'd all taken music class in middle school but had dropped it after that. It had been three years since any of them had even seen her with a clarinet and she wanted to keep it that way.

It wasn't that she was ashamed. She *loved* playing. She just didn't think they'd understand. Her older brother, Bryan, was the only person who knew, but they ran in totally different circles. Not to mention they hardly ever talked to each other anymore.

But Bryan liked playing his guitar. Or he used to. Music was just about the only thing he and Amber had in common anymore. Not including their parents who liked to fight more than anything else.

Amber shook her head. She didn't want to think about that. If this band got her out of the house on Tuesday nights, then that was even more reason to join. And maybe she could convince Bryan to go with her.

Chapter Three

As Marty tapped out a rhythm on his twin bongos, he smiled at the group gathered around him. He liked to kill time on Mondays after school when his mom came late to pick him up. It gave him something to do and he was even starting to cultivate a little fan base.

Not that that was why he did it. He genuinely enjoyed playing the drums and these bongos were just a small part of that. He had five more at home, plus his full kit. And he loved playing for his friends after school. But he was more excited about meeting a group of mysterious musicians tomorrow night.

Warmth rushed through him, extending all the way to his tapping hands. Now that he'd found a group to play with, he might finally have people who would love him for what he was good at—instead of judging by what they saw and knew of him.

As Marty played, Bryan slowed his rushed pace. Normally, he would have hung out at the edge of the crowd, watching the younger boy play. Marty's beats were fresh, and Bryan liked listening to him. But today he had to rush home and see if the strings on his guitar were still good.

He hadn't played in almost six months. It used to soothe him when his parents' arguments got too much to handle. But he'd stopped playing one night after his mother had chided him for being too loud. She hadn't seemed to care that he was getting good—or that it was the only thing he cared about.

Well…he did care about his sister, but he would never admit it. Amber was one of the cool kids, a crowd he'd never quite seemed to relate to. And if he were totally honest, she didn't fit the persona either. But that didn't stop her from ignoring him in favour of her exclusive friends.

It didn't matter, anyway. If he could play guitar with a new group of people and have music back in his life, maybe things would get better for him. Maybe he could find a place he belonged, where he didn't feel like a loser all the time.

When he got home, he headed straight to his room, flung his backpack on the floor, and grabbed his guitar. As soon as it was in his hands, it was like no time had passed. The fingers of his left hand moved smoothly across the frets and his right hand picked a melody he'd almost forgotten. He was so into the music that when someone knocked on his door, he jumped and nearly dropped his guitar.

"What?" he shouted irritably.

He gritted his teeth as the door opened and in walked a tentative Amber. "You're playing again," she said in surprise.

He put the guitar down and crossed his arms. "What about it?"

Her brown eyes flashed, as they often did whenever she was annoyed. "I just thought it was nice to hear you play again."

Even though it was nice to hear, he rolled his eyes. "What do you want?"

"I was going to ask you if you wanted to do something with me tomorrow night," she said.

He froze. "Tomorrow night?" Why did it have to be *that* night of all nights? She hadn't asked to hang out with him in forever and now this? "Sorry, I'm busy."

"You're busy," she repeated, crossing her arms like him. "The one time I ask you to do something with me and you're...*busy?*"

He shrugged. "I don't know what to tell you."

"Okay, then," she said placidly.

The way she slammed his bedroom door as she left was anything but placid. He felt bad, he really did. But he saw Amber every day, and he didn't want to miss his chance at joining a band. Plus, maybe if it was good enough, he could ask her to come another week.

♪　♫　♪

With his arms crossed and his trumpet on his lap, Trey watched D-rock pace back and forth. He had his bow in his hand and he was twisting the knob, tightening and loosening the hairs of it. Tonight would be their first meeting with their prospective bandmates and they had chosen to gather at D-rock's house. More specifically, in his basement where they would be out of his mom's hair.

"Would you relax?" Trey said, shifting in the hard folding chair D-rock had scrounged up from somewhere. There were 12 chairs of different sizes and types sitting around the basement waiting for musicians to occupy them.

D-rock threw him a nervous look as he clutched the neck of his upright bass. "What if no one comes?"

Trey shrugged. "Then no one will know about it but us."

"Well, what if a bunch of people show up, but they just came to make fun of us?" D-rock asked.

"Then I'll handle that," Trey said calmly.

D-rock grunted, pushing the shaggy hair out of his eyes. "How? You gonna threaten them?"

Trey sighed. He and D-rock weren't exactly best friends, but the dig hurt. He knew by now the whole school had heard about the fight that had gotten Trey into so much trouble. But that wasn't what he was normally like.

"I'm not a monster, you know," Trey mumbled.

D-rock's face softened, and he murmured, "Sorry. I shouldn't have said that."

Trey shrugged uncomfortably, but he didn't get a chance to answer before the doorbell rang. They looked at each other, a moment of pure anxiety passing between them.

"Well?" D-rock finally said.

"It's your house, dude," Trey answered, even as he rose.

"Right."

D-rock headed for the stairs as Trey set his trumpet down on its stand to follow him. D-rock's mom had already answered the door and was letting in a well-dressed boy. His hazel eyes sparkled as he greeted them and then he held up a violin case as if to explain why he was there.

"Oh, here's Derek now," Ms. Allen said, gesturing to him.

"Hey," D-rock said as she walked away. "Friends call me D-rock."

"I'm Max," the violinist said, stretching out his hand.

"And I'm Trey," Trey said as Max and D-rock shook hands.

"As if you need any introduction," Max said, also offering his hand to Trey. "I'm surprised to see you here, though. This…is a real band, right?"

Trey chuckled. "It will be once the rest of our bandmates show up."

"I see," Max said. He stood there with one hand wrapped around the handle of his violin case, the other hand fiddling with his red tie.

"I'll take you downstairs," Trey offered.

"I'll wait for more up here," D-rock said, nodding at them.

And more did come, despite D-rock's fears. Amber with her clarinet. A very reserved girl named Claire, lugging a cello. Another violinist, Chloe, who was elated to find she wasn't the only one. Hacks, who had brought a small keyboard. Marty and his large conga. TK, who shared some mutual friends with D-rock, brought his sax. A younger kid named Corbie, who brought a trombone. And…

"Harmony?" D-rock said, confused when she stepped inside with her flute. "What are you doing here?"

She smiled, tossing her long caramel-coloured hair over her shoulder. "I'm here for your band. I'm…assuming it's yours, that is."

"Uh, yeah…" D-rock looked her up and down. It should have been no surprise to see her. Harmony had joined just about every other band that was available to her. "But I—"

"Is this the house for the band?" a rough voice at the door grabbed his attention.

Bryan from his English class held up a hard guitar case, nearly hitting Harmony with it. She stepped farther into the house, out of his way, and scowled at him.

"Do you want mind watching what you do with that?" she said.

Bryan looked down at her. "Sorry," he muttered.

"Yes, this is the house," D-rock said, cutting them off before an argument started. "We're all downstairs."

"Yay," Harmony squeaked.

Bryan brushed past her before she could follow D-rock and she mumbled something about him being rude, but he didn't respond. D-rock followed them down, only to find chaos in his basement.

Hacks was struggling to set up a keyboard stand that didn't seem to want to cooperate while Marty tapped a constant—and loud—rhythm next to him. Claire had already gotten her cello out and was warming up quietly. Next to her, Max and Chloe had their violins out but weren't playing.

Rather, they were very heatedly arguing, pointing their bows at each other.

Trey was ignoring them to chat with TK and Corbie while Amber sat quietly, waiting for the others to do anything but make noise. She looked up at D-rock, Harmony, and Bryan and then did a double take.

"*Bryan?*" she said, standing up and clutching her clarinet.

Bryan scowled. "What are you doing here?"

"Same thing you are, genius," she answered, holding up her clarinet.

"Oh, good, you've met," D-rock said quickly, trying to hold off another argument.

"She's my sister," Bryan spit out.

"You don't have to say it like you hate me," she muttered, slumping back down in her chair.

Bryan shrugged. He spun halfway, saw Claire and D-rock's bass near her and headed in that direction. Claire glanced up at him and then looked past him, her eyes narrowing.

"Hang on," she said. "What is *she* doing here?"

She glared at Harmony, who had made her way over to Hacks. He'd given up on his keyboard stand in favour of letting her try.

D-rock shrugged. "She's here to play."

"Harmony," Trey said, immediately gaining her attention. "Are you really here to play with us?"

She giggled nervously and glanced at the trumpet in his hand. "Why else would I be here?"

"But you're, like, already in a million bands," he said slowly.

"So?" she said, shrugging. "Isn't this band for anyone who wants to play? That's what the post said, right? Who made that, anyway?"

Trey bit his lip as everyone looked at him. "I did."

"But the post also specifically said for people who have a *secret* love for playing," TK added. "Not a very obvious one."

24

Harmony looked around her, waiting for anyone to come to her defense. When no one did, she put a hand on her hip and huffed. "So, what? I'm not allowed in unless I'm ashamed of being a musician?"

Her question caused a commotion among them as they all proclaimed to absolutely not be ashamed of their music. She raised her eyebrows at TK, who came close to her, gesturing to the sax strapped to his neck.

"Does this look like I'm ashamed?" he asked, his face turning red.

"I came here because I *love* playing," Chloe heatedly added.

"Me, too," Max said.

"I'm not trying to, like…hide," Amber told her, her face all scrunched up.

"I'm kind of hiding it…" Hacks whispered, gesturing to his keyboard.

"Do you really need another band, though, Harmony?" Bryan asked. He'd already taken out his guitar and had the strap over his shoulder. He didn't even wait for her answer to start tuning the strings.

Harmony looked around once more and threw her hands in the air. "Fine. Have your secret shameful band."

With that, she turned and stalked up the stairs. Once her footsteps had receded up the staircase, everyone turned their attention to Trey. He shrugged.

"What do you want me to say?" he said.

"I don't get it," Corbie, the younger boy with the trombone, said. "Why is she not allowed in our band?"

"She's not…not allowed," D-rock said hesitantly.

"But she already has places to play," Claire said, her eyes flashing.

"For the record," Marty piped up from behind his conga, "she's right. I mean, I play outside on Mondays. But…do you guys play for anyone else?"

The others all shook their heads and Marty smirked. D-rock looked at Trey, who set his trumpet down and jumped up from his seat.

"I'll go get her back," he said.

Trey rushed up the stairs and out of the house. Harmony was already in her van and had started it up, so he bolted for it. He caught up to her just as she started pulling away from the curb and knocked on her passenger window.

She screeched to a halt and scowled at him. After putting down the window, she shouted, "Trey Donnelly, are you trying to get yourself killed?"

He grinned at her. "No. Just trying to get you back."

"What?" she snipped.

"For the *band*, I mean." He shoved his hand through his hair. "We were wrong for making you go. Will you come back inside? Please?"

Harmony sighed and gave him a tiny smile. "Does any girl ever say no to you?"

He frowned. "Lots of times. Why?"

She rolled her eyes. "I'll come back in."

"Thank you," he said, stepping away from the car.

She parked again and together they went back down to D-rock's basement. The mix of sounds—a cross between various instruments, casual chatting, and arguments—rose to their ears.

"Some band you got here, Donnelly," Harmony murmured as they took the stairs.

"Hey, you know a lot about bands," Trey said. "Can you wrangle these guys together?"

She stopped at the bottom of the stairs, looking around with one hand on her hip. Chloe and Max were arguing, Hacks had finally figured out his keyboard stand but it was too low, TK was jamming noisily with Marty, and the others were chatting.

"If I could get them to listen for a minute," she answered.

Trey put his thumb and forefinger into his mouth and let out a shrill whistle. Within seconds, everyone had stopped and turned silently to him.

"Good," he said. "Looks like we're all here. Harmony, it's all yours."

"Okay…" she said. "Hacks and Marty, let's get you on opposite sides of the room. And we'll fix your stand, Hacks."

Harmony went over to Hacks while Marty took his conga across the room. As she readjusted the height of the keyboard stand, she said, "Bryan, Claire, and D-rock, you guys go hang out by Marty. Woodwinds—me, Amber, TK—will go in the middle with brass behind us. Violins, what's going on with you guys?"

"I was told I could play first violin," Chloe said. "And Max is having a hard time accepting that."

"But *I* was told that, too," Max said, waving his bow in the air. "And I got here first. I don't do second place."

Chloe's eyes narrowed at him. "Well, maybe you should learn to live with second best for once, rich kid."

Max bit his lip and looked away. Harmony pinned Trey with a stare.

"You told them both they could play first chair?" she asked him.

Trey shrugged. "It didn't make a difference to me."

She sighed. Having finished adjusting the stand, she got a chair and dragged it over to TK and Amber. "Good job, Trey. You know that's like having two quarterbacks on the field, right?"

"Oh," Trey said, understanding dawning on his face.

"Look, it doesn't really matter that much," D-rock spoke up, earning glares from the violinists. "There's no music anyway."

"There's no music?" Claire asked sharply.

He shrugged and looked down at her. "I was supposed to whip up music for kids I didn't even know would show up tonight?"

"Let's just play a scale," Amber said before anyone else could start arguing. "And see if we're even in tune."

"Great idea," TK said.

"Hacks, give us a Bb chord, please," Harmony said.

Hacks nodded and ran his fingers from the lowest Bb all the way up the other notes of the chord until he'd reached the top of the keyboard. Harmony smiled but didn't say anything as she put her flute to her lips. The others followed her lead and together they slowly played a scale. It was messy at first, but with Marty's help they found a tempo that suited them all.

Once they'd finished, Harmony set her flute down and looked at Trey. "There we go. Looks like we're a band now."

Chapter Four

Their meeting didn't last much longer after that. They all agreed they would meet again at the same time and place next week and passively said goodbye to each other. After the last member had left, D-rock shut the door and breathed out a sigh of relief. Trey grinned at him.

"That was fun," Trey said.

D-rock shoved a hand through his messy hair, raising his eyebrows. "It was?"

"Yeah," Trey said with a shrug. "What part wasn't fun?"

"Hmm, maybe the part where we almost kicked out one of our bandmates in the very first meeting because she likes music too much?" D-rock rubbed his scruffy chin. "Or how about the violins who didn't play because they were arguing too much? The brilliant pianist who can't even figure out a keyboard stand? The siblings who hate each other? I could go on..."

Trey chuckled and headed back to the basement. "Are you always like this?"

"Like what?" D-rock asked as he followed him down the stairs.

"You know," Trey said. "Pessimistic and...kind of like you always expect things to end badly."

D-rock shot Trey a sharp look, watching as he put his trumpet away. Maybe it was easy for a guy like Trey—good-looking, athletic, friends with everyone—to be confident about everything he did. But it wasn't so simple for D-rock.

D-rock picked up his bow and loosened the knob. "I'm used to failing," he said quietly. "It comes naturally to me."

After a beat of silence, Trey said, "That's rough."

D-rock nodded and reached for his bass. He ran his fingers up and down the strings, making a soft scritching sound.

"You know what else comes naturally to you?" Trey said. He nodded at D-rock's bass. "Playing."

"I guess."

"You guess?" Trey said incredulously. He came closer so he could look at D-rock eye-to-eye. "Dude, you're an amazing player. You should live your life the way you play your bass."

Finally, D-rock cracked a smile. "And you should become a life coach."

Trey laughed out loud. "I always thought I'd be coaching football some day. Not life coaching. But I'll take it."

"Is that what you want to do?" D-rock asked. "Coach football?"

Trey nodded, his mouth slipping into a serious smile. "Yeah. I love football. I could see me doing that."

"That's cool," D-rock said, glad to be discussing anything but himself.

Trey nodded. "Anyway, I should go home. Thanks again for doing this at your place."

D-rock shrugged. "I'm still surprised Mom let me have you over after how much trouble I got in at school."

Trey frowned. "What happened, anyway? Why'd you get so much

detention? Did you beat someone up, too?"

D-rock smiled wryly. "No... My buddies were vaping, and they ditched me with their stuff. Mrs. Stringer caught me with two vapes and didn't believe they weren't mine. I guess I don't blame her."

Trey's mouth twisted into an even deeper frown. "That's garbage. It's not like it's an unforgiveable sin. Plus, half the kids at school vape."

"I don't," D-rock whispered, as if he were embarrassed by it.

"What?"

"I don't smoke," D-rock repeated louder, shaking his head. "I don't do drugs. I don't drink. I'm just really bad at school. And Stringer hates me."

With a smile, Trey came closer and thumped him on the shoulder, nearly knocking him over. "Don't flatter yourself," he said. "Stringer hates everyone."

D-rock laughed. "Thanks so much."

♪　♫　♪

As they left, Amber timidly asked Bryan for a ride home. Begrudgingly, he said, "I guess."

"It's not like it's out of your way," Amber said. "Also, I think Marty's on the way."

Bryan threw his free hand up. "Anyone else want a ride?"

"Yeah, I wouldn't mind," Max said with a cheeky grin.

Bryan rolled his eyes but didn't say anything as the four of them attempted to shove themselves and their instruments into Bryan's sedan. Marty lived close by—close enough that he could have walked, but Bryan kept quiet about that. Max lived on the other end of town, a fact Bryan was sure Max knew already.

Once they'd dropped them both off, Amber turned to Bryan and said, "Why didn't you just tell me this was what you were doing tonight? I thought you blew me off for no reason."

"Sorry." Bryan jerked the car into Drive and took off down the street.

"Did you even consider asking me to come with you?" she asked, grabbing on to her door handle.

"I thought about it," he said, taking a sharp right turn. "But then I thought you wouldn't think it was cool enough to join."

Scrunching her face up, she asked, "Since when does that matter to me?"

"Uh, since you became one of the cool kids at school." Bryan screeched to a halt at a stop sign and barely waited before going again. "And none of the kids in that band are really your scene. Except maybe Trey."

"Bryan," she said, exasperated. "Why do you think that? You know I love playing. And I don't care who's cool or not."

Her grip tightened when he glanced at her quickly and then back to the road.

"Could have fooled me," he said.

She scowled. "You know what? Stop the car, I'm getting out."

"We're almost home," he said, accelerating just enough for her to notice.

"I said stop the car!"

Glancing at her once again, he gently rolled to a stop next to the curb. As she jerked the door open, he said, "That time of the month, eh?"

"Why are you such a jerk?" She didn't wait for an answer before slamming the door and stalking up the sidewalk.

Bryan sighed when he realized she'd left her clarinet in the car. He raced home, took out both their instruments, and then waited for her in their front hall. When she walked in, he held out her clarinet and smiled smugly.

"Didn't you say you love playing this?" he asked.

Huffing, she wordlessly grabbed her clarinet and stomped up to her room.

♩　　♫　　♩

"How was it?" Chloe's mom asked as Chloe climbed into the backseat of her car. Her little sister, June, was in the front seat as she often was.

"It was fine," Chloe answered, trying to sound like she had really liked it.

"Better than being in a stuffy orchestra?" her mom asked hopefully.

No, not at all. "Yeah," Chloe lied. "There are all kinds of instruments. It's pretty neat." At least that part was true. She had been surprised and impressed by the assortment of instruments—and the people who played them.

"I'm glad," Ms. DesCloches said. "It's good for you to have a place to play."

Chloe bit her lip and looked out the window, watching the houses pass by. She'd had her chance to play with the Bridgetown Youth Orchestra, but they weren't able to afford the membership fees. Chloe had wanted to beg her dad to help out but her mom had denied her. So now she was stuck with a ragtag group of kids from school.

Including Max Ford.

Why, *exactly*, did a kid like him need a band like that when he could have bought his way into any fancy orchestra he wanted? And why did he *have* to insist on playing first violin?

"Are there any cute boys in your band?" June asked, breaking Chloe's thoughts.

"No," Chloe immediately said. Well, okay, D-rock was kind of cute if you liked scruffy and disheveled. And Trey was obviously the hottest jock at school, but not really her type. Besides, June was nine. She didn't need to be thinking about cute boys. "How's your math homework coming along?"

June turned in her seat to scowl at her. "I *hate* math. Who cares if I fail? It's not like I'll need it later on."

"*June*," their mother chided, before launching into a discourse on why math was so important and how June shouldn't be so flippant.

Chloe smiled to herself. Now that they had stopped talking about the band, Chloe could relax a little. She could just quit. They probably wouldn't notice her absence. But…what if this was her only chance to play with a group? They hadn't asked for anything but her presence. But they also didn't have any music and she knew as soon as they started asking for money to cover the costs, she would have to bow out.

She could bide her time until then. Maybe she could even convince Max he didn't deserve the first spot just because everything else in life was handed to him.

♪   ♫   ♪

Of course, Max never felt like things were handed to him. Yes, his parents were rich, he had a huge house and nice things to wear, and never lacked for anything. He had a top-of-the-line Yamaha violin and seven different bows, a baby grand piano in the basement, and an entire bookshelf full of sheet music. The one thing he didn't have was his parents' support for his passion.

After Bryan had dropped him off, he went into his large, cold home and slammed the door shut so at least one of his parents would notice. Evidently his mom did, as she casually called out for him not to shut the door like that. Smiling, he followed the sound of her voice to her home office.

"Hey, Mom," he said from the doorway.

She turned to him, glancing quickly at his violin case. "Oh, so that's what you were doing tonight."

"Yeah, I was just playing with some friends," he said, hesitating just slightly over the loose term.

She lifted an eyebrow. "But did you finish that history essay yet?"

Max resisted the temptation to roll his eyes. "The one that's due in two months? No, I'm not finished that yet."

"How will you get it done if you're spending all your time playing?" she asked.

His heart sank. "All my time? I haven't played in weeks and I was barely out for an hour. I think I can make time for the band and my schoolwork."

He turned on his heel but before he could walk away, Mrs. Ford said, "Max, if you really want to play that badly, we should talk to a *real* band. The orchestra—"

He whirled back around. "The orchestra didn't want me, remember? Not much we can do about that now."

"I'm sure if your dad talked to the director—"

"Besides," he said, cutting her off again. No way was he going to let his dad buy Max's way into an orchestra he wasn't good enough to play with. "Any organized group of people with instruments in their hands is a real band."

Okay, so Trey and D-rock's band wasn't exactly organized, but he had a point to make. When she made a face at him, he shoved his free hand into his pocket. He immediately felt the small piece of rosin Chloe had left behind when she'd rushed out of D-rock's house before anyone could say goodbye to her. Not that he would have bothered.

Max tried not to stomp as he walked away from his mom's office. She called his name a couple of times and he knew it was rude to ignore her. But he didn't turn back. Why couldn't she understand that music was his passion? That maybe he *could* have been good enough to get into a community orchestra or band if he'd been allowed to practice more or take lessons like he'd wanted?

He stalked up to his bedroom and reminded himself to gently set down his violin. On his music shelf, he had a box full of brand-new pieces of rosin. He took a piece out and set it next to Chloe's old ratty piece on his nightstand.

As annoying as she was—and truly, he wished he could have found anyone else to play with—he recognized in her the same eagerness for music that he had. Maybe with a little time—and a gift or two—she might become easier to play with.

The next day, Max made sure to take both pieces of rosin with him. Just in case for some insane reason, Chloe would want her old piece back. He waited by Chloe's locker and when she saw him there, she rolled her eyes. Forgoing a proper greeting, she asked, "What are you doing here?"

Biting back a sigh, he held out the shiny new piece of rosin. "You left this at D-rock's house last night. Didn't think you'd want to wait a whole week just to use it again."

She looked at the piece in his hand and scoffed. She turned to her locker and pulled out a textbook. "That's not mine," she said before slamming the locker shut.

"Chloe," he said flatly as she started to walk away from him. When she turned back, he shoved a hand in his pocket and pulled out her actual piece of rosin. It was so small he had no idea how she was still using it. "Here."

Lifting an eyebrow, she glanced at his hand. With feather-soft fingers, she picked it up, brushing the inside of his palm, and pocketed it. "Thanks. But why didn't you just give me that in the first place?"

He shrugged. "It looked like your last piece, so I thought…"

"That I couldn't get a new piece on my own?" She put a hand on her hip. "For your information, I like to use things up until they're actually not useful anymore. And also, I don't need your charity."

Max bit his tongue and nodded. "Duly noted."

Chapter Five

Claire looked at her cello with disdain, as if it had wronged her for stealing her heart. Maybe if she didn't love playing so much, if she didn't long to share that love with others, then she never would have bothered with this weird band. And to find out it was being run by Trey Donnelly was a big red flag.

Still…she didn't hate the combination of instruments. And once they'd finally put their issues aside and played, they weren't half bad. She could give them another chance. Maybe she would even consider writing something for them.

With a sigh, she got out of bed so she could get ready for school. The house was quiet, as it always was when her parents were away. Wednesdays were grocery delivery days, and if she was lucky maybe the driver had already come so she could have a decent breakfast before school.

Stepping out into the enclosed porch, she breathed a sigh of relief when she saw the few bags sitting there. She picked them all up and brought them into the kitchen. As she put everything away, she thought about her band again. She knew the right thing to do would be to write some music so they could play properly together. She would ask Trey about that.

Once she'd had breakfast and was ready for school, she called out, "Bye, Mom and Dad!" There really was no need to since they'd been gone for four months and weren't expected back until Christmas. And when they were home, she rarely said goodbye to them or anything that sounded affectionate.

She was glad it was a nice September day. She hated walking to school in the cold winter months. Even better still was that Trey was outside training with his football team, so she wouldn't have to wander all over the place looking for him.

She sat on the nearby bleachers, watching him running around the field. His blond hair was dark with sweat, his mouth turned down in a determined frown. It still boggled her mind to see Trey play trumpet when she—and everyone else—had always thought of him as an athlete.

The coach blew his whistle to end practice and with a heavy breath Trey started walking away from the field. One of the other guys tried to approach him, but Trey brushed him off without a word. He began jogging but glanced at the bleachers just as he passed by.

Claire lifted a hand in greeting and Trey slowed his pace. Smiling, he came closer to her, brushing the hair off his forehead.

"Hey, Claire," he said. "What are you...doing out here?"

She chuckled. "I actually just came to ask you—"

She stopped abruptly when a couple of the other football players walked past them. She wasn't sure if Trey had kept his trumpet playing a secret from them and didn't want to put him in an awkward position. He lifted an eyebrow at her.

"I was going to ask you about the band," she said quietly.

"Oh." He looked around as if to make sure they were alone. "What is it?"

"Who's providing the music for the band?" she asked.

"Oh, umm..." He shrugged. "I hadn't really gotten that far. Maybe

I'll…buy something?"

"You might have a hard time finding music that fits all of us," she said. "But I was thinking that maybe we could write something ourselves?"

"I don't know anything about that," he said, putting his hands up in the air. Then he snapped his fingers, his eyes lighting up. "But D-rock writes stuff. You should ask him."

"D-rock," she said flatly.

"Yeah," Trey said with a little laughter in his voice. "You know, the guy whose house we were at yesterday? You sat next to him for a whole half hour."

The guy with the shaggy hair, wrinkled shirt, ripped jeans, and a gorgeous bass. "I know who he is," Claire said impatiently.

"Cool. Can't wait to see what you guys come up with." With that, Trey took off towards the school.

Claire sighed as she rose from the bleachers. She would give it one chance. If things didn't work out, she would simply drop out. Easy enough.

At lunchtime, Claire would usually sit alone at a corner table or in the library. Today she scanned the cafeteria for D-rock and found him scarfing down a sandwich. He was alone but didn't seem bothered by it. Cautiously, she made her way over to him.

When she sat across from him, he looked up with surprised eyes. "Oh, hey, Claire," he said, giving her an easy smile. "What's up?"

"Trey told me you…write music?" she said uncertainly.

His expression changed and he looked down at the table, nodding. "Yeah. Sort of. Sometimes."

"I write music, too," she said.

He looked up quickly, his green eyes sparkling with excitement. "Cool!"

"Yeah…" she said slowly. "And now we have a whole band we could practice our writing skills on. Together."

His eyebrows rose. "You want to write music with me?"

"Well, not really, but I don't have much choice," she blurted out.

"I see," he said, his eyes darkening.

"I didn't mean it like that," she said quickly. "Just...yes, I want to write music with...*someone*. You. If you want to try."

He shrugged, but there was a frown on his face now. "Well, I'm still grounded, but my mom would probably let me have you over if it was for the band. Or I can come to your place."

Her place? Her aunt wouldn't be around until the weekend and even then, she would only stop by to see how things were going. No, that wouldn't do.

"No, no, your house is fine," she said hastily. "Tomorrow night?"

"Sure," he said, before going back to his sandwich.

Not wanting to watch him eat the rest of his lunch, she left and headed to the library. She could do this. She didn't have to be such a loner all the time if it meant feeding her passion. Maybe it wouldn't be so bad.

♪　♫　♪

Meg rushed to homeroom just as the bell rang. Inside, her classmates were chatting, using up the last bit of their time before class started to socialize. It was one of the main reasons Meg liked showing up just in time—so she could avoid that.

Unfortunately, it also meant she never got her choice of seat. And today the only open one was right next to Trey. She hadn't spoken to him since the incident with Chad. In fact, he'd barely even acknowledged her existence since...well, since kindergarten, though that was a moot point.

"Miss Ritz," Mr. Garrison said, gesturing for her to enter the classroom and take her seat.

She walked over to the desk, managing not to trip over her own feet. Not until Trey turned his ice-blue eyes to her and nodded. Thankfully, she was already almost seated and he didn't seem to notice her practically falling into the chair.

Meg made it through her class with minimal distraction. She certainly didn't pay attention to the way Trey said "here" during roll call, or how he answered questions more eloquently than any of the other jocks did. Because she didn't care and was focused on her schoolwork.

She was relieved when the bell rang, but in her haste to get away, she bumped right into the very person she'd been trying to escape. How this had happened she had no idea. Trey was taller and thicker than most of the other football players—hard to miss.

Her face flushing red, she mumbled, "Sorry."

He turned and glanced down at her. "Oh, hey, Megs. Didn't even notice you there."

Story of my life, she thought to herself as she left the classroom.

At lunchtime, she sat in her customary spot, far away from the throngs of friend groups. Rach joined her soon after, her brown eyes glinting with excitement. It didn't take long for Meg to find out why.

"You've seen this, right?" Rach asked, waving her phone in Meg's face.

Meg tilted her head back, giving her a wry smile. "I've seen your phone, yes."

"Girl." Rach pulled her phone back. "The band. You must have seen it. Are you joining?"

"Rach…" Meg groaned. She loved playing, but the thought of playing in front of a bunch of other people made her nervous.

"They said they'd love to have a tuba and *another* trumpet player," Rach said hastily.

"You asked them about me?" Meg asked, her heart sinking. "Without telling me first?"

Rach gave her a sympathetic look. "I didn't tell them who we were. It's all supposed to be anonymous."

"Yeah, until you get there and realize you're playing with a bunch of people who—"

"Hate your guts?" Rach said with a teasing tone. "No one hates you, Meg. Come on."

"No one hates you, either," Meg said softly. Sure, Rach got teased a lot, but it wasn't outright hatred.

"Great," Rach said in a perky voice. "All the more reason for us to join."

Meg bit her lip and shook her head.

"Please," Rach said, her eyes serious. "I don't want to go alone. And I know you wouldn't either. And we're both too talented to not join."

Meg sighed. Rach was right. "Okay. I'll try it." Rach grinned. "But if the other trumpet player ends up being some jerk from our school, I'm dropping out."

"Deal," Rach said.

♪   ♬   ♪

Rach went to her social studies class, ignoring the guy in the back who started humming the Darth Vader theme as soon as she'd walked in. This class was the worst because a large group of her bullies had all been clumped together with her. She brushed it off and went to the seat in the back that had been unofficially reserved for her. On the first day of class, she had sat in the front row, which had proven to be a mistake. Five other students had complained they couldn't see and the teacher had been forced to ask her to switch seats.

"Hey, skyscraper," one of the other guys said.

Rach ignored him as she took out her notebook and textbook.

"Guys," a weak voice said as the teasing comments went on. "Come on..."

Rach looked over to find Amber Hart sighing. Amber sent her a sympathetic but brief look.

"Aw, Rach knows we're just joking," Stacey said in a fake sweet voice. "Right, Rach?"

Rach just rolled her eyes and looked forward, waiting for the teacher to finally start his lesson so the other kids would have to shut up. Once he did, her mind wandered.

Though Rach would never admit it out loud, she was just as terrified to join a band as Meg was. She put on a good façade at school, always downplaying the teasing she never seemed to be able to escape. But deep down, she hated it.

Usually, it was her height that drew people's attention—almost always in a negative way—but if it wasn't that, they would find something else. She had yet to find a product that could completely tame her frizzy hair. Her clothes were ill-fitting. She was "shy," so she got called out for never engaging with other students. She only really had one friend, and since Meg was graduating this year, Rach would have to suffer next year all on her own.

If the other kids could look past all that, they'd see that she wasn't shy, just tired of worrying about being bullied. That she had talents other than being tall. Like being a musician. Hopefully this band would understand that and treat her…like a normal person.

Chapter Six

Surrounded by the sounds of keys clicking and the whirr of machinery, Hacks was relaxed. The school's computer lab was where he felt most comfortable, especially when it was just him and his nerdy companions. No one else quite understood him like the rest of the computer science club.

Well...no one but a band of misfit musicians. With a guilty pit in his stomach, he looked around the room. Five other guys and one girl all with their heads bowed over their keyboards, working diligently on their coding projects. Hacks loved it.

But not as much as he loved the piano. He could never admit that out loud, not even to the band. Most of them were clearly hiding their love of music as well—why shouldn't he? Sure, it made him feel dishonest. But he couldn't give up his socially acceptable passion for music.

Right?

"Hey."

Hacks turned at the sound of the whispered voice. Julian pushed his glasses up his nose before pointing to Hacks's screen. "Your code's off."

"What?" Quickly, he scanned the lines and found the one tiny blip that would throw the whole thing off. "Oh. Thanks."

"Are you okay?" Julian asked, his eyebrows scrunched low over his glasses.

"Yeah, I'm fine," Hacks said. He saved his document and shut off his computer. "I'm gonna quit early. Got some other...stuff to do."

Julian shrugged and waved and that was that. Hacks practically breathed a sigh of relief that he didn't ask for any details. He didn't really have anything else to do at that moment. But now that he was thinking about his piano, his fingers ached for the keys.

He rushed home as fast as he could. He would have run, but running wasn't exactly in his DNA. And honestly, it wasn't apparent that music was in his blood either. None of his close relatives had been particularly musical. The old upright piano that he'd grown to love was a gift from his paternal grandparents—it had sat silently as a decoration for years in their home before Hacks had discovered an affinity for playing it.

He ran his fingers over the keys as he sat at the stool. He had several music books out on the music desk, but he ignored those and let his hands do the thinking for him. It wasn't always easy for Hacks to shut his brain off, but his piano helped.

"You warming up for Sunny Meadows already?" Mrs. Ackenstein asked as she approached the piano.

Hacks let his hands drop. He didn't mind playing in front of his mom, but she had a tendency to talk the whole time he did. "No, just clearing my head."

"Is everything okay?" she asked.

He got up from his stool. "Yeah, I'm fine. Got some homework to do before I go."

"Alright..." she said as he left.

He didn't like brushing her off, but if he stayed and played too long, she would start bugging him about other things. And he really did have homework to do. Not that it typically took him all that long, but it was a good excuse to be by himself.

Once he'd finished his homework, he left the house, taking his bike all the way downtown. Sunny Meadows Retirement Community was in the heart of Bridgetown, close to the quaint old shopping district that everyone loved so much. Hacks didn't care much for shopping, but he did have to admit his hometown was beautiful. He would be a little sad to leave it after he graduated this year.

But he couldn't think about that now. The residents would be having dinner soon and he was there to keep them happy, not fret over his future. As soon as Hacks walked into the dining hall, he was greeted with a chorus of happy voices.

"It's Joe!"

"Joe's here!"

"Hi, Joe!"

Hacks smiled. His name wasn't remotely close to Joe. But the old folks could never seem to remember it and once they'd latched on to Joe, that was what he'd become.

When he'd first started playing here, the program director had asked him to play light mood music. Something to lift the residents' spirits to encourage them to eat better. But the residents had other ideas. Every time they saw Hacks, they made special requests. Some of the songs he knew—especially well-known hymns—but if he didn't know the songs, he made a note to learn them before he returned the next week.

Usually while Hacks played, his mind wandered to math or physics or coding. But instead, today he thought about his new…friends? No, they weren't quite his friends. He wasn't sure they were quite a band yet, either. Though he supposed that was what they were trying to be with their strange assortment of instruments.

Something tapped him on the leg and he looked down to find Mr. Anderson's cane.

"Can you do 'The Old Rugged Cross'?" he asked in a deep, gruff voice like he was annoyed Hacks hadn't played it yet.

"Oh, yeah, sure," Hacks said in a pleasant voice.

Smoothly, he transitioned from the jazz piece he'd been playing to the familiar old hymn. Would anything in his repertoire fit whatever his new band chose to play? What if he wasn't good enough for them?

♪   ♫   ♪

"What are you working on, Derek?" his mom asked.

D-rock gestured to the blank sheet music in front of him. A couple of the pages had some scribbles on them, something he'd been working on before he and Trey had decided to start a band. "A friend is coming over to write music for the band with me."

His mom's eyebrows lifted momentarily in surprise. "I'm glad you're enjoying your band, but shouldn't you be doing homework?"

"What homework?" he said with a cheeky grin. She lifted an eyebrow. "Relax, Mom, I already studied for my test tomorrow and started my English essay."

She put a hand on her hip. "You know you're still grounded, though, right?"

"Well...she'll be here in, like, five minutes, so..." D-rock said, lifting his hands.

"You didn't say it was a girl..."

"Don't start," he warned. "We just want to write music."

She bobbed her eyebrows. "Uh-huh."

Feeling his face flushing for no reason, he said, "Seriously, Claire's really skittish."

"What is she, a cat?"

D-rock rolled his eyes as the doorbell rang. But he couldn't help a tiny chuckle at his mom's goofy grin. He went to the door and there was Claire with a frown and a laptop bag, and her hair up in a ponytail.

"Hey, D-rock," she said in a friendly way. Maybe it wasn't a frown on her face. Maybe that was just how she looked at rest.

"Hey. Come in," he said.

He led her to the dining table where he had all his notation stuff. He shuffled the papers to make piles while she stared wide-eyed at it. Once he'd made a space big enough, he gestured to the chair in front of the spot.

As she sat, she said, "Wow, you weren't kidding about all this."

He shrugged. "It's one of the few things I don't feel like I'm terrible at."

"What were you working on?" she asked, reaching out for one of the papers.

"Uhh…" He quickly shuffled the papers once more, pulling them just out of her reach. "Nothing."

"Well," she said, dropping her hand. "If we want to write for a whole band, we're going to need more than this."

"Okay…"

She opened her laptop and D-rock watched as she started up an expensive music-writing program.

"If I'd known you had that kind of money, I would have suggested that already," he said wryly.

She laughed, finally showing him a real smile. "It's not that. My parents are professional musicians, so it comes with some perks."

"That's cool!" he said. "What do they play?"

Claire started clicking around, adding tracks for the various instruments in their band. "My dad's a pianist and my mom's a singer. Any idea what song you want to try?"

Claire's brief smile had disappeared and her abrupt change in topic was clear. Which was fine with him. They hadn't gotten together to talk about their parents.

"I thought about something classical, but…"

She snorted. "With bongos and a sax? I don't think that'd work."

"I know," D-rock said. "Although I've been wondering if Marty has a full kit."

"Wouldn't fit in your basement anyway," she commented.

"You're right," he said, though he was starting to wonder if Claire was negative about everything.

"It's fine," she said. "Better than nothing." With a sigh, she clicked one last time on her laptop and then sat back to look at the empty score. "What now?"

"I've got the perfect playlist for this," he said, plunking his phone on the table.

"You do?"

"Yeah, it's just pop music with a lot of instrumentation." He scrolled for a couple of seconds before stopping abruptly. "*This* one. We could easily do this with Marty's bongos."

As he played the opening to "4 Minutes" by Madonna and Justin Timberlake, he watched Claire's face intensely. She looked less than impressed.

Shaking her head, she said, "No. We don't have the brass for that. Or the low end."

D-rock bit his lip. He certainly could have carried the bass line just fine but chose not to point it out. "I'm sorry, Claire. You're my guest here. What song would *you* like to do?"

She shrugged. "If you like old school, I really like OneRepublic. Maybe their song 'Secrets'?"

D-rock supressed the urge to laugh. "Could have just said you wanted something that featured the cello."

Her eyes widened. "But it's such a great song."

"Yeah, and I really love those shot notes the bass plays for half of it," he said.

"*Marcato*," she said emphatically.

He shrugged, wondering how long he could keep pulling her leg. "I prefer accented *staccato*. And actually I prefer not playing them at all."

"It has other great instrumentation, too," she insisted. "The violins and piano. When the drums kick in at the chorus, it's awesome. And we could easily convert the other lines for the woodwinds and Trey."

"Uh huh," D-rock teased one more time as he searched for the song in his phone.

"Alternatively, we could do Pachelbel's Canon and I could play the same eight notes over and over," Claire said with so much contempt that D-rock laughed out loud.

"Claire, no," he said. "I'm just kidding. Let's do 'Secrets.' I think that would work really well for us."

She crossed her arms and pinned him with a look. "Can we be serious about this?"

"I'll try, but it's not my forte," he quipped.

"Was that a music pun?" she asked incredulously.

He chuckled. "It wasn't until you said that."

She rolled her eyes. "Can we just…do this?"

For her sake, D-rock schooled his expression and nodded. For the rest of the afternoon, they worked on making the lines from the song work with what they had. They started with the original instrumentation and filled in the rest with sax, clarinet, trumpet, and flute, trying to make sure everyone had a chance to shine.

"I'm going to have to take this home and fix some of it up," Claire said.

D-rock opened his mouth to ask what she meant but didn't get the chance before his mom came over with two bowls in her hands. She set them on the table and then left again.

"Thanks, Mom!" D-rock called out, before digging into the spaghetti and meatballs.

"Oh, I don't need to eat here…" Claire said weakly, trying to ignore the delicious smell.

"You might as well," D-rock said. "She doesn't know how to portion pasta. There's probably enough for our entire band leftover."

Claire chuckled and finally picked up the fork. "Okay. Thank you. But really, I have to leave after I'm done. I've got other stuff to do."

"No one's keeping you here," D-rock murmured.

With how much time they'd already spent arranging the music and now having to eat dinner here, Claire would have disagreed with him. But she didn't. She was just glad they'd been more productive than she thought they'd be.

Chapter Seven

Running his fingers up and down his sax as the smooth tones came out the bell always worked to calm TK's mind. It was one of the few things that could help him shut out the rest of the world. Unfortunately, it was also a huge distraction from his priorities—though he would maintain playing *was* his priority.

"TK!"

The sweet, motherly voice floated up to him, but he was in the middle of a really great lick so he didn't stop. She probably just wanted to know how his homework was going—and it wasn't—so there was really no point in answering.

"Terrence!"

Okay, that voice—while still motherly—was a little less sweet. Pulling the sax away from his mouth, he shouted, "What?"

When there was no immediate answer, he put the sax back to his mouth and continued playing. But he was abruptly interrupted a moment later by a loud knock on the door. A second later TK's little brother, Nick, waltzed in like he owned the place.

"Hey, Mom's mad," Nick said as he helped himself to a seat on TK's messy bed.

TK's eyebrows scrunched up. "I'm about to be real mad if you don't get out of my room."

Nick shrugged, staying planted where he was. When it came to Nick, all of TK's threats were empty and they both knew it. They weren't biologically related, but TK loved his nine-year-old brother as much as if they were. But that didn't mean he liked being bothered while he was playing.

"I'm just the messenger," Nick said in a bored voice. "Mom sent me here to get you and also loudly wondered what you're doing with your life. I'm not sure if I was supposed to pass that part along, though."

With a sigh, TK took the strap off his neck. "It's okay, I've already heard that one many times."

Reluctantly, he put his sax down and started to leave. But then he stopped and turned towards Nick, who was still sitting on his bed. He motioned to the door and Nick rolled his eyes but complied anyway.

TK went straight to the kitchen, where his mom was preparing dinner. "Hey, Mom," he said in a perky voice.

She whirled around and pinned him with a glare. "Why am I hearing the sounds of a saxophone when I should be listening to a boy typing up his essay?"

TK grimaced. "Don't you find it really annoying when people type that loudly?"

She huffed and went back to vigorously stirring her pot of soup. "Not half as annoying as hearing a sax."

"You don't like the way I play?" he tried again, avoiding the real issue.

"Of course I do," she said in a softer voice. "But I also want you to succeed at school. It's your last year of high school. Don't go throwing that away when you're already very good at playing the sax."

"Mom…"

"I'm serious, Terrence," she said. "You need to manage your time better. Set the table, would you? After dinner, we'll look at your essay outline. And have you even touched your math yet?"

TK cringed while her back was turned. The essay was one thing. He knew he could pull that off with a decent grade in very little time. But the math… Well, he had plans to make a career out of anything that didn't involve more than basic math.

Instead of answering, he started setting the table like she'd asked. It was better than trying to come up with any excuse that didn't start with "I'm too dumb for math." Everyone knew it anyway; he just hated to admit it. It made him anxious to even think about taking another math test, but his teacher had a penchant for pop quizzes.

After dinner, once Nick had cleared away the dishes, TK and his mom sat and looked over the essay outline he'd made. Although…it was less of an outline and more of a point-form list of anything that came to his mind when he thought of Shakespeare's *King Lear*. Which wasn't very much, considering he had yet to finish reading it.

"Oh, TK," his mom sighed after reading his jumbled thoughts. "What are we going to do with you?"

He shrugged. "Send me back to the orphanage?"

She chuckled and ruffled his hair. "We didn't get you from an orphanage. We picked you out of a catalogue."

TK smiled. It had never bothered him that he'd been adopted and his parents always came up with creative origin stories for him. They'd never treated him as less than their very own, even after Nick was born. It also meant their well-intentioned lectures were inescapable.

"What is this play even about?" his mom asked, sounding just a tad irritated.

"I don't know, I haven't finished it yet," he answered. When she gave him a wary look, he waved a hand at her. "Yeah, I know. Put the sax down. Get to reading. Thanks for your help, Mom."

♪　♫　♪

As Hacks stood in the pew next to his parents, listening to the church choir sing, he couldn't help watching Corbie. He didn't seem to have any problem sharing his love of music with other people, considering how fervently he sang with his eyes closed. Hacks liked church music, but singing wasn't his thing.

Then again, could he really call playing the piano his "thing" when he didn't want anyone to find out? His gaze slid over to the forlorn piano in the corner of the platform. It seemed each week it got pushed farther and farther back, waiting for expert hands to bring it to life. A guilty pit formed in his stomach. He was no expert and didn't consider himself capable of bringing anything to life.

After church, Hacks waited patiently while his parents talked to *everyone*, as if they hadn't seen them just seven short days ago. Some of them his mom saw midweek, but she still had to have long conversations with them while his dad got caught up with all the other dads. Old or young, didn't seem to matter to them. They were natural extroverts, unlike Hacks. He was happiest when no one noticed him or asked him too directly about his extracurricular activities.

Of course, now that Corbie was part of one of those activities, he was harder to avoid. When he approached him with after-church coffee in his hand, Hacks gave him a polite smile.

Corbie asked, "Can I ask you a question?" and Hacks's smile fell.

"That depends on the question," Hacks said.

Corbie smiled. "Why does everybody in the band call you Hacks?"

For a second, Hacks was frozen. It had never occurred to him Corbie might use his *real* name in front of the other band members. When they'd both arrived at the first practice, they had given each other a casual wave of recognition. Now, Hacks wished he'd addressed this earlier.

"You didn't tell anyone my name, did you?" Hacks asked urgently.

"No, it didn't really come up," Corbie answered with a shrug. "Is that, like, a secret or something?"

"Corbin, seriously, you can't tell *anyone* in the band what my name is," Hacks said hastily, his voice cracking on the last word.

"Why not?" Corbie asked. "I like the name Fa—"

"*Don't,*" Hacks cut him off in a quiet but firm voice, holding up a hand. "Please, I'm begging you. Everyone at school knows me as Hacks, even the teachers. No one calls me..." He paused, closing his eyes momentarily. "No one calls me *that*. It's super embarrassing. I really prefer Hacks."

Corbie's eyebrows drew in as he hesitated. "Okay. Hacks. That's fine. Can I ask you another question?"

Hacks glanced over to where his mother had been pulled into yet another conversation. There was no getting out of this. "Okay, what is it?"

"Why are you not playing piano for the church?" Corbie asked. "You know they've been looking for at least six months, right?"

Hacks sighed as the guilt returned. He should have guessed that would be the next question. "No one at church knows I play. In fact, very few people know, and it's bad enough there are so many people in the band now who do. Please don't say anything."

"But...but why?" Corbie asked with wide eyes. "You're amazing at it. And they would love it!"

"Yeah, my mom has only told me a million times," Hacks said, glancing uneasily at his mother. "Look... I like to keep this life separated from my school life and my—" he leaned in and lowered his voice "—piano life separated from both of those."

"Wow, so many identities," Corbie said, a slow smile growing on his face.

Hacks cringed and bit his tongue before he accidentally told him about "Joe." "Please, Corbie."

Corbie scratched the back of his neck with a frown and shrugged. "Alright. I mean, that sounds like a lot of work just to keep people from finding out you're amazing in more than one way, but okay."

"Thank you," Hacks said, leaning back out. "And I'll take the compliment, but I really prefer if you would just…not say anything."

Corbie smiled. "Okay. I can do that for you."

"Thank you," Hacks said.

"Even though that really feels like it'd be exhausting to keep all that inside," Corbie said.

Hacks rolled his eyes. "Okay, thanks for the tip. I think my parents are finally ready to leave."

Corbie chuckled. "See you Tuesday?"

"Of course." Hacks turned and left before Corbie could find any more interesting questions to ask.

Corbie shook his head as he watched Hacks walk away. He couldn't imagine not wanting to share his music with anyone who would listen. In fact, he'd been disappointed to find that both concert bands and the jazz band at his school already had too many trombone players to make space for him.

He understood, though. He was only in grade nine, so he'd been told to wait *at least* a year before trying again for one of the bands. But that didn't satisfy his insatiable itch for making music. Stumbling upon Trey and D-rock's social media post calling for musicians was a blessing. Even if it was a fluke.

Since he'd found out all the other kids went to Bridgetown High and he was at Jules Verne, he assumed the post had been meant for their classmates. But so far, no one had questioned him on it. Maybe he had secrets of his own.

"Who's your little friend?"

Corbie turned to smile at his grandpa. He was bowed over his cane as he pointed a liver-spotted hand in Hacks's direction. Grandpa didn't always remember a lot of details, but Corbie didn't want to break the promise he had *just* made to Hacks.

"Oh, he's just a boy who goes to Bridgetown High," Corbie answered. "I don't really know him. Come on, let's go find Mom and Dad."

He took his grandpa's free elbow and guided him slowly over to where his parents were talking to another set of parents. He tapped on his dad's shoulder.

"I think Grandpa's ready to go," Corbie said when his dad turned to him.

His mom and dad said goodbye to their friends while Grandpa waited patiently. By the time they'd gotten him to the car, his eyes were droopy. When they got home, Grandpa started walking towards his bedroom. But he stopped when he caught sight of Corbie's trombone on its stand in the living room. He changed course and sat on the couch.

Pointing with his cane at the trombone, he said, "Will you play something for me, Corbin?"

"Sure, Grandpa," Corbie answered eagerly.

He picked up his trombone and after a couple of warmup notes he played the last song they'd sung in church. It was an old hymn, a difficult one to play, but Corbie did his best. He wasn't totally accustomed to playing by ear but he knew his hymns like the back of his hand. Plus, Grandpa didn't seem to mind. In fact, in just a few minutes, he had been lulled into a peaceful sleep.

Corbie stopped playing and put his trombone down. Why would anyone want to hide this part of themselves?

Chapter Eight

Tuesday night, Meg picked up Rach in her dad's truck. Was it the coolest ride? No, but Meg had never been concerned with being cool. In fact, she stayed far away from the cool kids at school. And pretty much the rest of them, too.

When Rach opened the cab door to put her tuba in the back, Meg said, "Maybe we shouldn't do this."

Rach halted, hesitating for a moment. "Meg...we talked about this. We're too talented not to join. But if we don't like who's in the band, then we can leave. Okay?"

Meg took a shaky breath and let it out slowly. "Okay..."

Rach shut the door and hastily got into the passenger seat before Meg changed her mind. "Thanks for giving me a ride."

"I mean, you're welcome," Meg answered as she pulled away from the curb. "But also, I just really didn't want to show up alone."

"Yeah, me neither," Rach said. For once, she sounded uncertain.

Meg took them all the way across town to a street lined with townhouses. There were some other cars parked along the side of the road, so she parked a few houses down from the corner house.

"I think we're looking for the one on the end?" she said as she got her trumpet out of the back.

Rach grabbed her tuba and they both nervously made their way over to the house. Rach rang the doorbell and after a minute, the door opened and there was D-rock with a bow in his hand. He looked first at Meg and her trumpet before settling on Rach's tuba case. His face broke into a wide grin.

"Oh, wow, am I glad to see you!" He stepped aside to let them in.

"Can't say I've ever heard that before," Rach muttered.

D-rock smirked. "Well, Claire will be happy, since I'm not good enough for her apparently."

"What?" Rach said, wrinkling her nose.

"Nothing. Come on." He pointed with his bow down the hall.

Rach exchanged a look with Meg, who shrugged before following D-rock. He led them to a set of stairs, where the strains of different instruments floated up to them.

Meg scanned the basement quickly, her eyes passing by the strings and woodwinds to settle on a small brass section. Frozen in place, she watched as Trey played a warm-up scale on his trumpet in unison with the trombone player.

Rach followed her line of vision. She turned to stand in front of Meg, effectively cutting off her view.

"What do we think?" Rach whispered. "Jerk or not?"

Distracting, sure, but Trey Donnelly was no jerk. Meg shook her head.

"Great," Rach said happily, turning back towards the band.

"Look, Claire," D-rock said as they passed by him. He picked up his bass and plucked a string. "More brass *and* low end."

"But—" Claire sputtered. "We don't have music for them."

Meg followed Rach towards Trey and the trombone player she didn't recognize. Rach gave her an encouraging smile before sitting at the end of the row. Meg sat at the other end next to Trey.

"Hey, Meg," he said as he turned to her in his chair. "I didn't know you played trumpet. How long have you been playing?"

Her heart sank and she looked down at the case she had yet to open. "Um…" Should she say it? "I've been playing since grade five. When we both learned."

Trey's eyes widened slightly. "Oh, right! No, of course. I just meant I didn't know you *still* played."

Feeling generous, she smiled and allowed him his clumsy save. "I didn't know you still played, either. I figured you were just—"

"A dumb jock?" he said with a grin.

"I wasn't going to say that," Meg said quietly.

Harmony turned around in her chair and looked back and forth between them. "I've never met trumpet players who talk more than they play."

Trey leaned towards her with a cocky grin. "And I've never met a flute player who can keep her opinions to herself."

"That's because they don't exist," TK threw over his shoulder.

Instead of getting in on the teasing, Meg took the hint and got her trumpet out. After gathering her courage, she did her typical warmup—mid tones first, upper tones, lower tones, and then a two-octave A scale to finish. There was nothing special about it, but by the time she'd reached the top A, everyone had turned to stare at her. Slowly, she put her trumpet down and stared at her lap.

Her face flushing, she asked timidly, "Too loud?"

"Nah, that was perfect," Trey said with awe in his voice.

Her cheeks reddening even more, she asked, "So, what are we playing?"

D-rock jumped in. "We have a secret arrangement for you."

"Yeah," Claire said with a sigh. She held up a stack of papers and gave the brass a furtive glance. "But there's none for Rachel or the other trumpet."

Meg said quietly, "My name is—"

"You guys wrote this?" Trey interrupted as he went over to them.

Claire had already started handing out the music. "Yes, but now it's incomplete. Why didn't you tell us they were coming?"

"I didn't think it was a big deal, "Trey answered with a shrug. "Why didn't you tell me you were writing music for the band?"

Claire's jaw dropped. "We had an *entire* conversation about it."

"Oh, sorry, Claire," Trey said, sounding at least a little contrite.

"Here, just—" She handed him some of the music. "Take this to your section and tell them to do their best."

"Um, Claire?" Chloe said as she held her music up. "Neither of these violin parts are labelled. Which one is the first part?"

Claire gave her a passing glance before giving TK his music. "Both of them."

"*What?*" Max and Chloe both said in indignation.

"We just didn't want you to argue over it," D-rock said gently. "Has anyone heard from Amber and Bryan?"

"We're here!" Amber's voice came from up the stairs.

Footsteps followed and soon Bryan showed his sullen face while Amber was all smiles. D-rock shoved some music at Bryan, who frowned at him. Amber happily took her music and headed towards the empty chair between Harmony and TK. She stopped when she locked eyes with Rach.

"Hey," Rach said, giving her a little wave.

"Oh, Rach," Amber said. She gestured loosely to Rach's tuba. "You still play."

Rach nodded. "You, too?"

"Yeah." Amber pulled her clarinet and music closer to herself, as if to show they were a part of her. Her eyes scanned the row of brass and landed on Meg. "Hey, Meg."

Meg smiled genuinely, grateful that Amber actually knew her name. "Hey, Amber."

"Alright, everyone," Claire's voice cut across the murmuring of the rest of the band. "We *almost* all have music. A couple of additions, but we'll work through it. You all know this song, right?"

Some of them nodded, others making sounds of assent. But Marty got up and held out the music he'd been given. Claire, confused, stared at it.

"What's wrong?" she asked.

"I don't know what to do with this," he said.

Her brows drawn together, she asked, "What do you mean?"

"I, uh—" He glanced at the rest of the band uneasily. "I can't read music, so…" He shook the pages he still held, trying to get her to take them back.

Claire sighed and closed her eyes. "Great. A tuba I wasn't expecting, an extra trumpet, and now a drummer who can't read music. Does anyone else have a problem with the music?"

"Well, actually," Trey spoke up. "I don't know this song very well and I don't really understand how my part fits into it."

Meg shifted through the three pages of music on the stand in front of him. "You're playing the melody at the chorus," she told him.

"The rest is just some random notes and stuff," Corbie added helpfully.

"Oh," Trey said, looking at the spot Meg was pointing at. "Perfect. We're all good then, Claire."

"Well, no, actually," Corbie said. "You wrote mine in…tenor clef? Is that right? I don't know how to read that. I play in bass clef."

Claire deflated with a heart-wrenching sigh and looked at D-rock. He said, "That's my bad, dude. Any other problems?"

"Yes, actually," Max said. "Chloe and I have been looking through and, uhh…I don't play the lower parts. We switched music."

"The parts were equally built," D-rock said patiently. "Because we didn't want you to argue. So please—"

"We're not arguing," Chloe said. Then she turned to Max. "But we also didn't agree to switch music. Just a few parts here and there so that *I* would be playing the high parts and you would play the lower harmonies."

"I don't remember that part of the conversation," Max said.

"Hey, you guys?" TK said, putting up his hand unnecessarily since his voice carried so well. "I'm *pretty sure* my music is in the wrong key…"

"What?" Claire shrieked, rushing over to him. She looked back and forth between TK's music and Amber's before letting out a long and disappointed sigh. "That's it. I give up. I'm going home."

"Claire," D-rock said, reaching out a hand as she brushed past him. "It was an honest mistake…"

As Claire packed up her cello, D-rock sent Trey a frantic look. Trey put his trumpet down and came to stand at the front of the group. He put a hand up to halt Claire, which miraculously worked.

"Hey, guys," he said. He took a moment to make eye contact with every person in the room—the same way he did while giving pep talks to his football team. "I really should have told you this when we first got together. D-rock and I started this band because we both *love* playing. And we just wanted to share that with other people.

"I never expected all of you to join, but I'm happy about it." He paused to smile. "I also never expected that we'd be perfect or that we'd know what to do with ourselves once we were here. I guess I didn't think this completely through…"

D-rock leaned close to him and whispered, "Where are you going with this, dude?"

"I'm getting there," Trey answered quietly. Louder, he said, "Look, if this doesn't seem like it's going to work for you, you're welcome to leave. No one's keeping you here, you're not getting any credits for this, and it's never going to contribute to your community hours. I just wanted to have fun with other…"

"Musicians?" Harmony filled in for him.

His eyebrows drew in, like it had never occurred to him to call a roomful of musicians "musicians." "Yeah. I wanted to have fun with other musicians. But if it's not fun, then go ahead and leave."

No one moved or made a sound. The room was still as Trey held his breath and searched their faces. They weren't having any fun at the moment, but they also weren't getting up to leave.

"I think I figured it out," Hacks finally broke the moment. He'd been silent since he'd come in and now as everyone turned to him, his cheeks went bright red.

"Figured what out?" Trey asked.

"The, you know—" Hacks gestured at everyone. "The mixup with the music. We can fix that. Assuming that very long and awkward silence means you're all staying?"

When no one answered, he rose from his chair and went up to the front of the room. "Great speech," he said, slapping Trey on the shoulder.

Trey let out a tiny chuckle. "Thanks?"

"Okay." Hacks looked around the room. "Meg, you can share music with Trey. Rachel, I'm assuming that's a concert pitch tuba?" When she nodded, he gave her a tight smile. "Great, you and Corbie can come and sit by D-rock and try to play off his music. Claire, Amber, Harmony, and Bryan, you guys are good. TK, can you transpose on the spot or…?"

TK shrugged. "I could try?"

Hacks nodded. "No one's grading you. Violins…" He turned to Max and Chloe who wore matching frowns. "Just play what you were given. It sounds like a lot of thought was put into your parts. And, Marty? Follow the beat as best you can. Make something up. I'm sure it'll be great."

"He's…right," Claire said slowly.

"Generally speaking, yes," Hacks said as he made his way back to the keyboard. "So, are we doing this?"

Everyone watched as Rach got up. She brought her tuba and chair over to where D-rock was set up. Then she looked around and said, "What? This is what he told me to do. Are you coming?" she asked Corbie.

"Yes," he said excitedly as he stood, too. "Let's do this!"

And so, they played the arrangement. It was messy. But at times, it was also beautiful. Put so plainly, it was clear that when no one cared about how bad or good it was, when they just relaxed and enjoyed the music, then it went smoothly.

D-rock and Claire had made sure that everyone felt featured at some point in the song. Claire hoped they would notice that she had tried to not leave anyone out, while D-rock hoped they liked it enough to want to play it again.

When they had played it through once, everyone put their instruments down. There was a beat of silence before Trey said, "That was *so* good!"

The others all jumped in with compliments for the arrangement. But they also started looking over each other's music, wondering if they could figure out what was happening when and if there were ways they could improve the rough patches. By the end of the night, everyone left much happier than when they'd arrived.

Chapter Nine

Max didn't hate playing with his band. He certainly didn't hate playing with Chloe—as she seemed to—and didn't even mind what D-rock and Claire had done with the violin parts. What he *did* hate was not being able to play without being elbowed by Chloe because they just didn't have the space in D-rock's basement.

Halfway through their meeting, she had reluctantly agreed to switch seats with him, but that just meant it was *him* elbowing *her*. And of course, that set her off even more than the music did.

While everyone else said a more or less friendly goodnight to each other, Chloe ignored him and hastily headed out of D-rock's house. Amber, at least, was kind enough to say goodbye to him.

"Thanks for the music," Max said to D-rock before he left. Claire had already gone.

"Yeah...I guess," D-rock answered with a shrug, looking disappointed.

Max felt guilty. He shouldn't have let Chloe make such a big deal out of it. "It's really not as bad as Chloe said. She just...likes picking fights with me for some reason."

"Seems like it," D-rock answered. "But you didn't hear that from me."

Max made a motion like he was zipping his lips and finally left. Outside, his mom was waiting in her bright white Mazda. He got in and gently set his violin at his feet while she looked around with disdain.

Before she could start complaining about the neighbourhood, he asked, "Mom, can I have my friends over next Tuesday night?"

"Who?" she asked distractedly as she drove away. "Silvia and Bradley?"

"Erm, no." He hadn't hung out with those two in ages. He gestured vaguely to D-rock's house behind them. "These friends. My band?"

"Oh." Mrs. Ford glanced quickly at her rearview mirror as if she could assess Max's friends from the driver's seat of her car. "Aren't there a lot of them?"

"There are fourteen of us, including me," he answered.

"I'm not sure we have the space…"

"In our basement?" he asked incredulously. Their basement had a huge, *unfurnished* living room area, two storage closets, and its own bathroom that no one ever used. "I'm pretty sure there's enough space down there."

"Well, what about your piano?" she said.

He snorted, thinking about his baby grand that probably had more dust on it than his father's pool table. "I'm sure Hacks will love playing it instead of having to lug his keyboard out every Tuesday."

"Bite your tongue," his mother chastised. "That is *your* piano."

"Yeah, and it sounds real great when I don't play it," he retorted. "Come on, please, Mom. These guys just…really love music. Like I do. And it'd be way better if we could play in our basement instead of D-rock's."

His mom hemmed and hawed over the question for the rest of the ride home. And while she did that, Max started a group chat with every single one of his new band members.

Max: new rehearsal location: my basement. 14 Rockaway Blvd. who's in?

Responses started pouring in, most of which made Max smile. Of course, half of them were likely only interested because of where his house was located. But it wasn't beneath him to use that to his advantage.

"Okay, Max," his mom said as she pulled into their long circular driveway. "If you can prove that you can keep your grades up, then maybe you can have your friends over once a month."

"Uhh…" Max's good vibes quickly deflated. "Can that once a month start next Tuesday? Because I already asked my friends and they're very excited about it."

"*Max.*" Her eyebrows furiously drawn in, she wrenched the car into Park and turned to him. "You didn't even wait for an answer."

"Mom, what's the big deal?" He clutched his violin close to him as if that would provide some protection from her wrath. "My grades are always good. No one's using that space, and my band is… We're *good*. You know? It would just be like an hour once a week. And you and Dad aren't even usually home on weeknights!"

His mom didn't answer. She simply got out of the car and made her way to the house. Clenching his jaw, Max jumped out of the car and hastily caught up to her.

"Why do you hate this part of me?" Max asked heatedly.

Mrs. Ford turned so abruptly that Max nearly ran right into her. "Max…" she said softly, lifting a hand to caress his cheek. "You're my son. I love you. But you won't get anywhere in life playing the violin."

He drew back like she'd slapped him. "Tell that to Lindsey Stirling!" he shouted, before running into the house.

He hurried to his room, slammed his door shut, and then flopped onto his bed. Still holding his violin close, he squeezed his eyes shut. If he tried hard enough, he could imagine that he was still with the band, happy to just be playing with no one judging him. Not even Chloe.

♪   ♫   ♪

Amber sat on her bed, clarinet in hand, music spread out in front of her. Oh, she knew it'd be better if she found a good chair to sit up in and pulled out her music stand. But all the good chairs were in the kitchen where her parents were fighting. And she'd learned from a very young age to not get in their way when they fought.

She put the clarinet to her mouth, took a deep breath, and…squeaked out a few notes. She glared at the mouthpiece, noticing the tiniest nick in the reed. Which meant it was totally unusable. Great. She grabbed her only other reed—it was a little warped, but there were no chips or cracks in it.

"There," she said. "Now I'm ready."

She went to play again but just as she did, a loud crash sounded from downstairs. It was followed by more shouting, the kind she wouldn't be able to drown out with her clarinet. With a frustrated sigh, she stalked over to her bedroom door to…do what, she didn't know. She never interrupted her parents when they were like this.

When she opened the door and found Bryan standing outside of his own bedroom looking miserable, her heart fell. She thought he'd at least be able to suffer through it, or put on his loud music like he always did.

"Hey, squeaks," he said in an unimpressed tone.

She cringed. "You heard that?"

"You can hear *everything* in this house," he said loosely.

"It's not my fault," she said, ignoring his meaning. "I have two old reeds and one of them just got a chip in it and… Well, I'm not gonna ask Mom and Dad for new ones right now."

Bryan looked at her for a moment, his face softening. "Come on, I'll take you to the music store."

"Thanks," she said with a sigh. "But I don't really have the money for that right now."

"I'll pitch in," he said.

Amber didn't get a chance to answer as he went inside his room to pick up his keys and wallet. She was going to tell him to not worry, that she could deal with it on her own later. But then her mom screeched some very choice words to her father and Amber changed her mind.

"Ugh, let's leave before they break something," Bryan said.

Amber's startled eyes met Bryan's. Without a word, they both went into their rooms and quickly gathered up their clarinet and guitar. The thought that something bad might happen to their precious instruments ran through both of their minds as they snuck past their parents. Not that they were even paying attention.

After securely stowing her clarinet in the back of Bryan's car next to his guitar, Amber got in with just a hint of hesitation. Bryan wasn't exactly the...*safest* driver. But right now, he seemed like he was in a chill mood.

Of course, that didn't stop him from peeling out of the driveway at what she considered a breakneck speed. To distract herself, she said, "I don't know why they don't just get a divorce. They can't really be staying together for us, right?"

"I'm gonna go out on a limb and say they just don't have the money for a divorce or living in two separate homes," he said as he ground to a halt at a stop sign.

Gripping the door handle, she said, "You think?"

He shrugged. "When was the last time you got an allowance?"

"Good point," she muttered.

"It's either that, or there's something going on in their bedroom we don't know about," he said.

"*Ew*, Bryan." With a scowl she looked out the window. That was something she didn't need to think about.

"I'm just saying."

"Well, can you, like, *never* say that again?" she sassed.

In response, Bryan turned on the radio and cranked the volume. Amber almost immediately reached out to turn it down. But she noticed with the louder music came slower, slightly more cautious driving. So, she let it go. Besides, for once he was being kind to her. She didn't want to ruin that.

When they got to the music store, Bryan headed straight to the guitar section without a single word to Amber. She rolled her eyes. Whatever, so long as she could get new reeds and not sound terrible the next time she played, she was happy.

There were so many brands that she stood there for a good long while considering them all. She probably *could* pay for the cheap ones herself. And then...suffer with something subpar. With an unhappy frown, she started reaching out for the least expensive ones on the shelf.

"Just get the fancy schmancy ones I know you want," said Bryan's voice from behind her.

She breathed out a sigh of relief and grabbed a box of the most expensive ones. She wasn't going to argue with him or make him change his mind. He held out his hand and she put the box on top of the strings he was buying, for once grateful. When was the last time she'd been grateful for Bryan?

As they left the store, she said softly, "Thank you."

His eyes narrowed and he looked around as if he'd lost something. "I need a burger."

"Okay..." she said slowly.

Back in the car, he got on the highway and started driving out of Bridgetown. The music was still loud, the driving too fast but…Amber still preferred this to listening to her parents' marriage break down.

After ten minutes, Bryan finally pulled off the highway and went straight to the nearest rest stop. There he ordered three burgers in the drive-through and then parked in the parking lot. He handed Amber a burger, and she wasn't going to say no to this, either.

As they ate, Amber asked, "So, uh…what happened with that girl you were going to ask out?"

Bryan looked at her for a moment, his eyebrows raised. "Who? Britt?" He rolled his eyes. "I have concert tickets for Painsteaks and I asked if she wanted to go with me. Then she said, and I quote, *'I don't really listen to music.'*"

Amber gasped. "No, she did *not*."

"Yes, she *did*," he said, mimicking her tone. "I asked her if what she meant was that she doesn't listen to the kind of music Painsteaks plays because if that were the case, we could go somewhere else. But no. She doesn't listen to music, period."

"What kind of person doesn't…listen to music?" Amber asked, feeling horrified at just saying the words.

"I know!" he exclaimed before taking another huge bite of his burger. He held up a greasy thumb and forefinger an inch apart. "I was *this* close to having a really hot girlfriend."

"Uh, I'd say you were that close to dodging a bullet," she answered. "And don't you think that makes her a lot less hot?"

"Yes," he said miserably.

"Come on," Amber said. "You don't need someone like that in your life. Like honestly, who doesn't listen to any music ever? That's crazy."

"I know," he said, still sounding sad.

She patted him on the shoulder. "Thanks for the burger. And the reeds."

"I only bought the reeds so I don't have to listen to you squeaking anymore," he grumbled before starting in on his second burger.

Amber looked away to hide her smile. He sounded grumpy, but she could still choose to be thankful he'd decided to be nice to her tonight. "Well, I don't want to listen to scratchy strings either, so I'm glad you got those, too."

Bryan chuckled and then scarfed down the last of his burger. Finally, they headed back home and by the time they got there, their parents had cooled off. Amber realized—belatedly—that it was never about the food. Bryan had gone out of his way to make sure they were gone long enough that they could avoid the end of their parents' argument.

If he would have let her, she would have hugged him. But he went straight to his room and she was left on her own with her beautiful new reeds.

Chapter Ten

Once again, D-rock and Claire sat at D-rock's dining table so they could go over their arrangement and fix it. Claire had the music pulled up on her laptop while D-rock was…playing with a fidget spinner.

"Must you?" she asked, pointedly looking at it while it spun around on his finger.

"It's either this or I get out my bass," he said. "Helps me think."

"Okay," she said, choosing to drop it. No point in arguing since he was always fidgeting with something. "Let's see…Corbie's music is easy, we'll just convert this to the bass clef." With a single click, his line was fixed.

"Yeah, don't know what I was thinking with that," D-rock said.

"Don't worry about it," she answered. "TK… What did we do wrong?"

"He plays an alto sax," D-rock said. "For some insane reason we were both thinking tenor. But wouldn't a tenor look good on him?"

Claire bit back a smile. "That's a moot point. Let's write some new parts for the trumpets since we have two now and add in the tuba. Is there *anyone* else joining us next week or do we think this is it?"

"This is it," D-rock promised. "Trey mentioned giving the higher part to Meg. Oh, and I was told Marty's bringing a full kit to Max's house, so we can write for that."

"What's the point?" Claire asked. "He can't read it anyway."

D-rock was quiet a moment as he watched Claire add in the extra instrumentation they needed. Then he asked, "Will you feel satisfied with an incomplete chart?"

She sighed. How did he already know her that well? "No."

He smiled but said no more about it. Instead, they worked to fix up their mistakes and add in the extra instruments. They even checked over the other lines to make sure everything was okay.

At some point, bowls of chili were placed in front of them. Claire looked up just as Ms. Allen walked away.

"That's really not necessary..." Claire said weakly.

"Seriously," D-rock said as he picked up his spoon. "She's very bad at portioning." He smiled when his mom came back in with her own bowl. "But very good at making chili."

"Thanks, kid," Ms. Allen said. She nodded at Claire. "I guess I should have asked if there's anything you can't eat."

Claire looked down at the bowl. It smelled delicious but she couldn't keep eating dinner here. "I'm allergic to shellfish."

"*Oh*," Ms. Allen said. "Well, aren't you in luck? I am banned from having shellfish in this home because Derek hates it."

He chuckled. "How can I ban you from cooking something in your own home?"

Ms. Allen looked at Claire, her eyes flashing with meaning. Claire couldn't help laughing. Finally, since it seemed rude not to, she took a bite. And then several more.

"Okay, this really is good," she said. "Thank you, Ms. Allen. You really don't have to feed me, though."

"I don't mind," she answered. "But I do mind being called Ms. Allen. Ugh… What am I? A hundred? Just call me Dawn."

"Okay," Claire replied quietly.

After they ate, Claire and D-rock finished off the last of their edits. Finally, she said she had to go. When he offered her a ride, she refused a little too fast. They'd already been too nice to her. Plus, she didn't live that far away. Walking would be just fine for her.

Although, as she left their house, she wished she'd had a second bowl of chili.

♪   ♫   ♪

Rach looked at herself in the mirror, smoothing down her ponytail. Finding clothes that fit her body wasn't impossible. But it *was* hard and often expensive. So yes, sometimes she wore men's shirts that didn't look horrible and the same two pairs of jeans every day.

It wasn't her fault she'd been built like this. She'd been assured of this all the time. But it didn't make it any easier to fit in. Girls made fun of her for her *unique* style and the boys wouldn't even approach her if they weren't at least 5'10".

At 16, Rach was already 6'1"—and growing still, according to her doctor. With a sigh, she looked down at her chest.

"At least I got you ladies for company," she said as she readjusted her bra.

With a few minutes to spare, she stuffed her lunch in her backpack and grabbed a jacket. The late-September air was finally starting to cool off and winter would start soon after. Then everyone would be dressed like dorks and Rach would feel a little less like an outcast.

"You look nice today," Rach's mom said as they went out to her car.

Rach again looked down at the plain black t-shirt she'd put on. Her mom told her that almost every day, but maybe she could switch up the compliments to fit the mood. "Thanks," she said anyway.

Her mom, at an adorable 5'2", would never understand her struggles. Her dad was taller, but even he wasn't 6'. Neither of them knew why Rach had grown so tall. There were no abnormalities; it was just in her genes. Lucky Rach.

At school, she did her best to ignore everyone else. It would have been easy if some of them didn't go out of their way to make her life miserable. Asking her how the weather was up here, or if she could grab something that they'd intentionally tossed on top of the lockers was fairly harmless. But the girls who took one look at her outfit and said "ew" were worse. There was really no reason to be so rude.

"Hey, Rach," a happy voice said.

Rach turned to find cute little petite Amber smiling at her. She waited, wondering when the teasing would start, but when she realized there would be none, she said, "Hey, Amber."

"Ew, Amber, step out of the shadows and let's go," Stacey said, pulling on Amber's arm.

Amber rolled her eyes, but then she smiled kindly at Rach. "Bye," she said with a little wave.

"Bye," Rach said barely above a whisper.

By lunchtime, Rach was less than impressed with her classmates, though this was nothing new. At least she had Meg...until she graduated.

Normally, they didn't talk much while they ate, but as soon as Rach sat down, Meg said, "Is he still staring at me?"

"Who?" Rach asked, lifting an eyebrow.

"Trey," Meg whispered.

Rach couldn't help it. A wide grin broke across her face and she stood up to look around the cafeteria for him.

"Rach," Meg whisper yelled. "Don't do that! Come on…"

Rach sat back down, her smile still in place. "Yup, he's staring at you. Or…maybe it's me he was looking at. But probably more likely you."

Meg groaned and ducked her head. Rach managed to stifle more laughter. If she were in Meg's shoes, she would relish positive attention from a guy like Trey. But she knew Meg was far too socially anxious to deal with that.

"What?" Rach teased. "Did you not enjoy playing trumpet with him the other night?"

Meg hesitated, shrugging in that way Rach knew well. "It wasn't horrible, it's just… It's nothing. I just don't want him staring at me."

Rach laughed but didn't say anymore. She could respect Meg's wishes, even if other people didn't understand it. And she was perfectly happy to keep her only friend happy.

"Did you enjoy having to share music with D-rock and Corbie?" Meg teased back.

Rach shrugged. It wasn't bad but it wasn't the best either. First of all, with D-rock standing and her and Corbie sitting, it made too many height differences for them to all even see the music clearly. So, they had all played terribly—including D-rock, who helped write the music! On top of that, the music wasn't exactly written for a tuba or trombone, so the lines were awkward to play.

"Would you be mad if I didn't want to go again?" Rach asked.

"No," Meg said sympathetically, though Rach could see disappointment in her eyes. "I understand. We don't have to."

"I didn't say *we*," Rach said. "You should still go. Enjoy the eye candy at least."

Meg laughed and shook her head. Rach laughed with her, but her smile fell when Claire approached them. What did pretentious, snooty Claire want now? And what was she smiling about? It looked fake.

"Hey, Rach," she said in a friendly way. "Hi, Meg."

"What do you want?" Rach asked.

Claire's smile fell. "I...want to give you this music?"

She held out her hands to show them the small stacks of sheet music, one labelled "Tuba" and the others "Trumpet 1" and "Trumpet 2." Rach stared at the music while Meg took the trumpet parts.

"What's wrong?" Claire asked, her eyes widening innocently.

When Rach didn't answer, Meg said timidly, "We were...just deciding if we wanted to come back again. That's all."

Claire's countenance fell as her whole being seemed to droop along with her shoulders. "But I spent hours working on this with D-rock..."

"You didn't seem too happy about it on Tuesday," Rach said, the words coming out more snarky than she'd meant.

"What are you talking about?" Claire asked, her eyebrows drawing in.

"You were all frazzled over the extra instruments," Rach answered. "*Me.* I should have figured it'd be another place where I just...don't fit."

"Rach..." Meg said softly.

With a thoughtful frown, Claire sat down, laying the music out in front of her. "Rachel, I didn't mean to make you feel unwelcome. I wasn't annoyed at *you*. I was annoyed because boys don't know how to communicate properly, and I felt unprepared, and I *hate* feeling unprepared. Not to mention all the mistakes we made in the other parts." She rolled her eyes.

"Oh," Rach said, not sure how to feel about that.

"Look—" Claire pushed the tuba music towards her. "It's a *tuba* part. It's meant to be played by you. Not D-rock or Corbie. It only fits the tuba."

"Oh," Rach repeated, this time overwhelmed with emotion. Gingerly, she took the sheets and looked at the music. Yes, it was indeed different than the bassline D-rock had played, and much more appropriate for a tuba. "Thank you. I'm sorry. I didn't know."

"It's okay," Claire said softly. "I know what it's like to be an outcast, too, you know."

"Can't imagine how," Rach said. "You're so cute and average-sized. And I bet you look good in all the clothes you try on."

Claire pursed her lips. "I can't pull off half the clothes I want to. I don't have the confidence. I wish I could hold my head up high above everyone else's like you do." She shrugged and got up to leave while Rach just stared at her.

"Wait, Claire," Meg said. When Claire turned back around, she said, "There are two trumpet parts here."

"Oh, yeah, can you give one to Trey?" Claire answered. "D-rock said Trey would take the lower part, but I didn't want to decide that for you. Plus, I really don't like the jock table. Bye!"

Meg groaned as Claire walked away. "But I don't like the jock table, either."

"So, give it to him after school," Rach suggested.

"I was hoping you'd offer to do it for me," Meg whispered.

"Nope," Rach said with a smirk. "That's all on you."

♪   ♫   ♪

At the end of the day, Meg did nervously make her way over to Trey's locker, hoping she could catch him before it got crowded. She definitely didn't belong here, standing next to a jock's locker, waiting to give him sheet music. This was ridiculous. Why couldn't D-rock give Trey the music? Weren't they friends?

Deciding to just pass it along to someone else, she turned on her heel only to bump into 190 pounds of pure muscle. Trey's muscle. Her face flushing, she took a huge step back.

"Hey, Trey." Awkwardly she stuck out her hand, clenched around his music. "This is for you."

He looked down at it, his surprise turning to confusion. "Where's the second part?"

"I took it," she said, for once sounding confident.

"But…I told D-rock I would take the lower part," he said, still ignoring the papers.

She could have let it drop and just switched the parts. But instead, she asked, "Why?"

"Because." He shrugged and looked around as other students headed to their lockers. He took a step closer and in a quiet voice said, "I can't play those high notes like you can. You're way better than me."

"And you expect to get better by…not playing them?" Gently, she pressed the pages against his chest, letting go when he finally clasped a hand to them.

With a tight smile, she left him standing there, bewildered by her gentle criticism. She put a hand up to her hot face, willing herself to calm down. She would never in a million years have said something like that to Trey about anything else. And yet, when it came down to trumpet playing, she felt like she had the upper hand. Her expertise was the thing that caused her to speak out like that.

Sure, she would go with that.

Chapter Eleven

14 Rockaway Boulevard. Never in her life had Chloe seen the inside of any of the mansions that lined Rockaway. And usually she only saw the outside at Christmastime when all the houses were decorated and everyone from Bridgetown and the surrounding towns came to see them.

But now in the late-September evening light, it looked totally different. The house was wider than it was tall, made of grey brick and red shingles covering the multiple gables. The three-car garage took up a good third of the house—or at least what was visible. And though the flowers had long ago died, the gardens were still immaculate and free of weeds.

"You sure this is the house?" Chloe's mom asked uncertainly as she pulled up at the curb.

The driveway was empty, but Chloe knew for sure Max was waiting inside. "Yup, this is it."

"Wow," her mom said. "You think they actually have three cars in that garage?"

Chloe shook her head. "Max is only sixteen, but I wouldn't be surprised if he already had his own car."

"Alright, well…I'll just wait here to make sure you make it in okay," her mom said.

Chloe resisted the urge to roll her eyes. She knew her mom just cared about her, but that was a little unnecessary. "Thanks for the ride, Mom. See you tomorrow."

Chloe got out of the car and waved but her mom didn't take the hint. It was bad enough she had to get dropped off super early so her mom could take her on her way to work. But now she was actually waiting to see her inside?

Chloe squared her shoulders, refusing to be embarrassed by her mom, and rang the doorbell. Max answered a moment later and Chloe waved again at her mom. Thankfully, she drove off.

Max moved aside to let Chloe in and looked her up and down. She was wearing all black again today and had plaited her long dark hair into two braids. It was a good look for her.

"Hey, Richie Rich. Thanks for letting me come over so early," Chloe said, shrugging like she felt uncomfortable. "Sorry."

"It's fine," Max said plainly.

He watched as she lifted her head to look around. He suddenly felt very self-conscious about his pristine house. Were the paintings straight? When had the cleaners come in last? Friday? Were the crown mouldings too gaudy?

Chloe smiled, her dark eyes sparkling. "My mom didn't believe me when I told her I have a friend who lives on Rockaway."

"Did you tell her we're not exactly friends?" he blurted out without thinking.

Thankfully, Chloe just laughed. "No, she never would have dropped me off if that were the case. This is the house that does the Dr. Seuss theme every Christmas, right?"

He could feel his face heating up as he said, "Yeah, that's us."

"I knew it! Big fans?" she asked.

He shook his head. "No, it was just the only theme that wasn't taken by anyone else on the street. And we couldn't pick someone else's theme. What would the people think?"

Chloe laughed again, a melodic sound he was starting to like. "Sooo…do we just wait in the foyer until the others show up or are you going to let me look around?"

Oh, how his mother would hate it if he showed off the house to a girl she didn't know while she wasn't home. "Welcome to the grand tour, Chloe!" he exclaimed, waving his arm in a wide gesture. "Here, you can leave your violin on the settee."

She giggled and put her violin down. "Oh, the settee. Okay."

Max just shook his head and led her farther into the house. He took her across the main floor, which held a living room, a parlor, a sunroom, the kitchen, the pantry, one of the offices, and two bathrooms. After that they climbed the huge spiral staircase to the second floor.

The whole time, Chloe made little comments about how *much* there was—how extravagant the furniture was, how many dishes in the kitchen cupboards, how soft the carpets were, how many landscape paintings were hung on the walls. Max agreed, it was a lot. But so was the number of times she'd mentioned just how wealthy his family was.

"You climb these stairs every day, rich kid?" she said, clutching the dark wooden banister and exaggerating her breathing.

He halted on the steps and turned to her. "If I may ask, what is your socioeconomic status?"

"*What?*" she said, scowling in indignation.

He forced a nonchalant shrug. "I just figure if we're doing cute nicknames based on socioeconomic status, I should know yours, right?"

For a moment, she just stared at him, her cheeks tinging the slightest shade of pink. She dropped her gaze and said, "Okay, you're right. I'm sorry...*Maximus.*"

He rolled his eyes, a gesture lost on her since she still wouldn't meet his eyes. "It's Maximilian, actually."

She looked up with a tiny smile. "Like...Maximilian dollars in the bank?"

He tried to hold it back, but a chuckle still escaped his lips. He quickly drew his lips in and looked away. "Yeah, something like that." He turned and continued up the steps. "And yes, I do these stairs all the time. Obviously."

"I take my groceries up five flights of a walk-up every week," she said in a cheeky voice.

"Ah, that must be why it hurts so much when you elbow me while you're playing," he teased.

"No, I try extra hard for that," she said. "Oh, wow!"

Now that they'd reached the second-floor landing, she went straight to the large bay window that looked over the yard. Max cringed when she put her fingers against the glass, leaning in so she was breathing on it, too.

"You know, if you squint, you can almost sort of see the neighbours," she said.

Frowning, he came closer, wondering if there was something wrong with Chloe's eyesight. He could see the house clear as day, even if it was a bit far away... Oh. She was joking.

"Very funny," he said.

She turned away with another giggle. While her back was turned, Max quickly wiped her fingerprints off the window with his sleeve. His mom would definitely have noticed that.

"Is that *your* room?" she asked in an overly interested tone.

He looked over and followed her line of vision. Down at the end of the hall was a door with brightly coloured letters that spelled out "Maximilian." She started towards it, albeit hesitantly.

"Who else's?" he said. Making a split-second decision, he opened the door and let her in but didn't follow her.

Inside, Chloe took in the whole room. Clean, with very few things out of place. The bed was made, covered by a brown and blue checkered bedspread. The carpet was a little more worn out than in the hallway. There was a desk with a very expensive laptop on it.

Choosing to not make mention of it, she turned around, only to find a wall *full* of concert ticket stubs. And by the looks of it, Max had very eclectic tastes. There were things she expected, like musicals and orchestras, but also several rock bands, pop artists, and even a couple of country singers.

"Are these *all* yours?" she asked.

"Yes, of course," he said, sounding suspiciously far away.

"Max...?" She looked over to the doorway where he was chilling just outside of the room. "What are you doing out there?"

He shrugged, his face going bright red. "Waiting?"

"Oh." She glanced once more at the wall of memories, taking a mental snapshot before leaving his bedroom. "You look like you stepped right out of the 1800s."

"In this *tie*?" he asked, holding up the navy-and-white-striped tie he had on.

She flicked his tie over his shoulder. "Yes?"

Smoothing the tie back down, he smiled at her. "They didn't wear ties until the 1920s."

She stared at him for a moment, then her gaze slid down to his shoulders, his tie, his white button-down shirt, his navy dress pants and finally to his black socks. Feeling like he'd been thoroughly assessed, Max took a step back, adjusting his tie unnecessarily.

"You *would* know that," Chloe finally said.

He shrugged again and was saved from further awkward conversation when the doorbell rang. Max and Chloe hastily made their way down to the front door where D-rock was waiting. He didn't seem to find it odd that they were there together, as excited as he was to be at Max's house.

"Thank you *so* much for having us, Max," D-rock said as he lugged his bass through the door. "My mom's pretty cool, but I don't know how many more Tuesday nights she can handle." He went farther in, then turned around with a grimace. "Don't tell her I called her cool, though."

Chloe chuckled and picked up her violin off the settee. She had yet to see the basement, so she followed the other two downstairs. Within minutes, the others had trickled in, with Bryan and Amber being the last to arrive again. They were all excited to be in Max's house, especially Hacks, who hadn't taken his hands off Max's baby grand since he'd gotten there.

As they all got out their instruments, they carried on amicable conversations. *Almost* all of them. As soon as Trey got in and saw Meg, he sat next to her and pulled his somewhat crumpled music out of his trumpet case.

"Here," he said, laying it haphazardly on top of her closed case. "Can I please have *my* music now?"

She picked it up and gently smoothed out the creases. "This *is* your music."

"I can't, Meg," he said, defeated.

"Maybe you just need to practice it a bit more," she said softly.

He opened his mouth to tell her how impossible it was for him to get practice time, but then decided against it. Instead, he took the music back and put it on his stand.

Meg felt bad and was tempted, once again, to just give him the part he felt would be easier. But she didn't get a chance before Max stood in front of everyone, calling on them to get their attention.

When they'd settled down, he said, "Just to address everyone's question—no. I can't take you through the house. I'm already in enough trouble just having you in the basement." He punctuated his statement by rolling his eyes.

"Wait, we *can't* see the rest of the house?" Chloe asked.

He looked at her for a moment and then said, "Absolutely not. To address everyone's second question—yes, I will accept the position as first violin."

Chloe scoffed while Max chuckled and retook his seat.

"Okay, we've all got new music," Claire said as she turned one of the tuning pegs on her cello. "Are we ready to try it?"

D-rock nodded and then he looked back at Trey. Trey gave him a miserable thumbs-up, to which D-rock tilted his head questioningly. But the others had already started preparing to play, so there was no time to answer the question.

Since they had no conductor, Claire dove right in with the cello part that started off the song. D-rock joined her a couple of bars later with Rach playing the same low notes. Amber and Harmony got to start off the first verse on their clarinet and flute. They were soft enough for the mood of the song, but their clear tones cut delightfully across the basement.

Everyone was added into the chorus. Hacks and Bryan played chords, while Corbie and Rach held the lower end. Trey and Meg played their two-part harmony, sharing the melody with TK on his sax, while Amber and Harmony played some higher tones above them. The trumpets played the first half of the second verse, and then TK played the faster second half of the second verse.

D-rock and Claire's arrangement had managed to capture the song in a new way while still retaining the climactic escalation of dynamics and timing of the original song. Although they didn't play it perfectly and sometimes it was hard to find Marty's downbeat, it was far better than last week. When they finished, they looked around at each other, most with happy smiles or impressed looks on their faces.

They started to pick apart what worked and where they made the most mistakes. Meg nudged Trey when she noticed he was still sitting there with a frown on his face.

"What's wrong?" she asked. "You played it perfectly."

He grunted. "I did *not* play it perfectly. Far less than perfect, actually."

"And I did what, exactly?" she asked, a little laughter in her voice. "In fact, there's an entire line I skipped because I was five bars behind. And I scratched my first note. Did you notice?"

He licked his lips and finally looked at her. "Yeah, I did, but I wasn't gonna say it."

She smiled. "I'm sure you know that you don't get good at things unless you do them a lot."

"Yeah, you're right. Alright," he said louder. "Who wants to play it again?"

Chapter Twelve

Before they ended their practice for the night, D-rock asked if there was anything else that needed to be fixed or changed before next week, or other suggestions.

"Yeah, actually, I've got a suggestion," Bryan said. "I'm thinking some, like, Black Sabbath or Iron Maiden. Or just maybe…something with a little more guitar. Just a bit." He held up his thumb and forefinger.

"Seconded!" Marty shouted.

"Oh, I meant—" D-rock started.

"Okay, that sounds terrible," Amber cut him off, scowling. "But I could go for some jazz, or modern swing, or…"

"Musicals?" Harmony suggested.

"Oh, I could go for musicals," Amber said excitedly.

At that, everyone started getting in on the song suggestions, each of them calling out the names of songs or bands that they preferred or that featured their instrument more. Claire shot D-rock a frantic look, but he couldn't seem to get them all to stop talking over each other.

Trey stood up, put two fingers in his mouth, and gave a shrill whistle.

When everyone immediately stopped talking and turned to him, he said, "Country."

"*No*," D-rock said forcefully before they could start again. "What I meant was suggestions for the 'Secrets' arrangement. Not for new songs."

"We can't keep playing the same song over and over," Hacks piped up. "That would get frightfully dull."

"You guys are welcome to write your own arrangements," Claire stated quietly.

No one answered her at first as they looked around at each other. Finally, Harmony said, "Even if I had the time, I don't think I could write something as good as this. I don't even have the software for it."

"I can't even read music," Marty reminded them.

Claire surprised everyone by laughing. "Okay, I get it. I'll..." She looked up at D-rock, who nodded at her. "*We'll* work on some more music. But write your suggestions down somewhere, I'm not remembering all that."

With that, she started putting her cello away, signaling the end of their practice. As everyone else got ready, D-rock went over to Trey.

"Still need that ride?" D-rock asked.

"Yeah, thanks," Trey said distractedly, his gaze settled on the staircase.

D-rock turned just in time to watch Meg and Rach go up the stairs together, carrying on a friendly conversation. He lifted his eyebrows but didn't say anything. Upstairs, Max was ushering people out of his house like his life depended on it.

"Hey, Max, thanks for having us," Trey said.

"Yeah, you're welcome," Max clipped. "Now...go, please. My dad's on his way home. And if we're lucky, he won't see just how many people were here."

"It's not like we had a house party..." Trey muttered.

"I'll not be explaining that to him," Max said, giving him a patient smile. "See you next Tuesday…*if* they don't find out."

"Alright, we get it," D-rock said as he lugged his bass out of the house.

While D-rock positioned his bass in the back of his mom's van, Trey got into the front seat, placing his trumpet at his feet. D-rock bit back that resentful feeling of not having chosen a smaller instrument. So, he would be a van guy for the rest of his life. No big deal. He loved his bass.

Trey was quiet when D-rock got in. Not knowing what to say, he started driving. A little farther up the road, he caught sight of Claire carrying her cello on her back. He slammed on the brakes, cringing at the sound of his bass slamming into the back door. Trey put his hands out to absorb the shock but didn't say anything.

D-rock lowered Trey's window and shouted, "Get in!"

Claire looked over with a scowl, hunched her shoulders, and kept walking. D-rock slowly trailed her.

"*Get in?*" Trey said quietly, lifting an eyebrow.

D-rock sighed and tried again. "Sorry, I meant do you want a ride?"

"No," she called back, this time not bothering to even look at him. "I live close by. It's fine."

D-rock shrugged and stepped on the gas, once again cringing at the bashing sounds coming from the trunk. Trey shifted in his seat in anticipation that D-rock might stop and start any old time.

"You don't spend a lot of time with girls, do you?" Trey asked lightly.

"What makes you think that?" D-rock casually avoided the question.

"I'm just saying I would have tried harder to give Claire a ride," Trey said.

D-rock shrugged uncomfortably. "I'm not going to force her to spend more time with me than she wants to."

"Oh."

Trey fell silent after that. D-rock glanced over a couple of times before saying, "Okay, what's wrong?"

Trey shook his head and looked away. "Nothing. It's dumb."

"I'm pretty dumb, so you're in good company," D-rock said with a smile.

Trey looked at him sharply. "*You're* dumb? How does a dumb guy write an arrangement that good?"

D-rock shrugged. "Claire did most of the work." When Trey just looked away again, D-rock pressed further. "Come on, just say it."

"I wanted to start this band because I love playing and I don't get to do that anywhere else," Trey said softly.

"You and me both," D-rock responded in the same tone.

"Yeah, well, I didn't expect everyone would be better than me." Even to Trey's ears, he knew he sounded sulky, childish. But it didn't change the way he felt.

"That's what's bothering you?" D-rock asked, not unkindly. Trey shrugged. "Why do you think that?"

Trey turned his hands up. "I can't write music. I can barely read it. I can't transpose on the spot. I can't focus on what other parts are doing while I'm playing. And I can't play the first trumpet part well at all, but Meg refuses to do it. Even though she's *clearly* a better choice."

For a moment, D-rock was quiet as he turned onto Trey's street. "Ohh, I get what's happening here. You're used to being the best at everything."

"What?" Trey said, waving a dismissive hand at him. "That's not..."

"How many sports do you play?" D-rock asked.

"I'm only on the football and basketball teams at school," Trey said.

D-rock pulled up to the curb in front of Trey's house, a smile playing on his lips. "Captain of both, though, right?"

"Yes…"

"Trey…" D-rock put the van into Park and turned towards him. "You can't always be the best at everything. But I guarantee no one in the band is thinking about how Trey, captain of the football and basketball teams, can't play high notes like a…shy wallflower."

Trey groaned. "When you say it like that, it sounds even worse."

D-rock pulled his lips in like he was trying not to laugh. "I'm sorry. Meg's amazing. Who knew? But it's okay to let someone else have the spotlight."

"I can't, though!" Trey threw his hands up. "She literally will not take the higher part. She thinks it'll help me play better if I, like, play it terribly or something."

D-rock's eyes widened. "She's not wrong…" Trey just glared at him. "Okay, new suggestion. Just ask her for help."

Trey frowned but not in an unhappy way. He still didn't look impressed though.

"Pretend it's like you're…asking her on a date," D-rock said, his eyes sparkling with humour. "But the date is her teaching you how to play better. Not that you play bad."

Finally, Trey's face broke into a grin as he laughed. "That's…terrible advice, actually. And again, I'm wondering how much time you spend with girls."

"I know girls well enough to know they would never say no to you," D-rock said with a cheeky grin.

"Sure," Trey said disbelievingly as he opened the door. "Thanks for the ride."

♪   ♫   ♪

Harmony had never been the type to procrastinate or put things off, no matter how unpleasant a task it was. And truly, practising her flute was the highlight of her day, every day. She had her choice of music—either from the school concert band, the flute choir, the Bridgetown Youth Orchestra, the jazz band, or the solo pieces she rehearsed for her private instructor's sake.

But all of those paled in comparison to the arrangement that Claire and D-rock had whipped up. Even though she didn't belong with the misfits, even though Claire didn't seem to want her there and the others kind of acted like she didn't need to be there, she still got her very own, personalized piece of music. And now it was the only thing she wanted to play.

She hadn't been lying when she'd said there was no way she could write something like this for a band like *that*. For two people who liked to hide their talent away, Claire and D-rock seemed to know what they were doing.

Ignoring the residual resentment from almost being booted from the band, she took out the "Secrets" piece again. She'd never played pop music before. The closest she'd gotten was the showtunes book she'd enjoyed when she'd first started on the flute. But she absolutely adored OneRepublic. And in fact, she liked listening to any pop music better than classical.

But she could never tell any of her music friends that, especially not the orchestra kids. No, better to keep that—and her new band—a secret.

So maybe she *was* ashamed in a way. It made her feel guilty for judging the others for hiding their music. While she still felt that they were all very talented—and clearly loved playing—she should never have been pushy about how and if they chose to share that with the world.

She shook her head of those thoughts and pushed her new music aside. She had to practice for the youth orchestra. She'd recently been given the piccolo part in the Overture from "The Magic Flute." It was a highly sought-after and esteemed part and she wasn't going to mess it up.

However, every time she went to practice, she kept coming back to "Secrets." Yes, it was easier by far and maybe that was a part of why she enjoyed it so much. But it also spoke to her so much more than "The Magic Flute" did. Mozart, as amazing as he was, now felt...empty. Or she did.

Or she was just overthinking her life and needed to get herself in gear.

By the time her orchestra rehearsal rolled around on Saturday, she regretted not having practised her piccolo more that week. She made more mistakes than she had last week, a clear sign to everyone that she hadn't spent enough time with the piece.

"Harmony," Maryanne, the conductor, finally said. "What is going on?"

"I'm sorry," she said, her face flushing. "It's...been a rough week. I promise I'll do better next week."

Maryanne shook her head. "If it's too much for you, we could give the piccolo part to someone else."

"No!" Harmony nearly shouted. "No, I can do it. Please. I'll try harder."

One slow blink later, and Maryanne was turning back to the rest of the orchestra, her baton raised. Harmony was relieved, but also embarrassed that she'd been called out like that in front of everyone.

She managed to get through the rest of rehearsal without totally breaking down. But in the back of her mind, she couldn't help thinking everyone was judging her. Hard. This felt especially true when her friends reluctantly said goodbye to her before carrying on with their own conversations.

She could feel tears press at the backs of her eyes and she quickly went to the bathroom of the community centre where they rehearsed. "No, Harmony, we're not doing this," she mumbled to herself. Splashing cold water on her face just made her look more flustered and didn't take the red from her eyes. But at least it was refreshing.

With a heavy sigh, she left the bathroom and almost walked straight into someone.

"Hey."

She looked up into the hazel eyes of Bryan Hart. His hair was disheveled, his clothes mussed, and he was leaning against a janitorial cart.

"You all finished?" he asked, jutting a thumb towards the bathroom.

"Um, yes…" she said slowly. "What are you doing here?"

"Working?" he said, gesturing down at his clothes. There was a mirthful twinkle in his eye as he took a "wet floor" sign off the cart.

"Oh, I didn't know you work here," she said.

"Yup. Every weekend. It's a *blast*," he added sarcastically.

She couldn't help a tiny giggle. She wiped the last of her mini-meltdown from her eyes and turned to go.

"Are you okay?" he asked from behind her.

"Yeah, I'm fine," she lied.

"Alright," he said. "See you Tuesday."

Tuesday. He almost sounded happy when he said it. She smiled.

"See you."

Chapter Thirteen

It took Trey until the end of the week to gather the willpower to actually…ask for help. It wasn't something he was used to doing. Normally other people asked *him* for advice. But he wasn't above it. He could do this.

At the end of the day on Friday, he rushed to Meg's locker, hoping to catch her before she left. He might be late for football practice, but he could afford a couple of minutes. He made it to her locker just as she was shutting it and skidded to a stop in front of her. She jumped, putting a hand on her chest.

"Oh, Trey," she said, her eyes flashing faintly with a hint of irritation. "You scared me."

"Sorry," he said, giving her a nice smile. The kind he might use if he were taking D-rock's advice. Which he wasn't.

"Okay, well…bye," she said as she tried to step past.

"Wait, Meg," he said urgently. When she turned back around, he said quietly, "I need help."

"With what?" she asked in a confused voice.

He looked around uncomfortably while she waited. Instead of saying it out loud, he lifted his right hand up to his face and made a motion like he was pressing the three valves of a trumpet.

Meg smiled. "You don't need help with that. You just need to practice more."

Feeling irritation rise inside him as she turned once more, he said, "Easier said than done. Do you have any idea what it's like to live with three younger siblings, two dogs, three cats, and five birds and still be told that *you're* the loud one in the house when you play?"

She turned back to him with sympathy in her eyes. "Is that all true?"

"Yes," he said, feeling frustrated just thinking about it. "Even when I have the time between sports and school, I get shut down pretty quickly."

She tilted her head and frowned thoughtfully. After a moment of quiet contemplation, she said, "Look, I can't magically make you a better player. You're already pretty good to begin with. But...if you want a place to practice, you can come over sometime."

His breath caught in his throat. "Really?"

"Yeah," she said lightly. "It's just me and my dad. And our cat. He's only loud when he wants cuddles, which he gets all the time anyway since he's spoiled rotten."

Trey laughed. "Really? Okay. That would be awesome! Thank you. Tomorrow?"

She hesitated a second before saying, "Yeah. Tomorrow. That sounds great."

"Thank you," he repeated. "Okay, now I really have to go. I'm super late for practice."

With that, he turned around, feeling happy. Meg, on the other hand, felt anything but settled. What had she done? How could she have just invited him over like that? She pulled out her phone and sent a frantic text to Rach.

Meg: i just invited trey over and he said yes HELP

Rach's only response was a series of laughing emojis, which wasn't particularly helpful. Not that it mattered. The damage was already done. She couldn't tell him not to come over now that she'd already offered.

Well, okay, she could. But she wasn't going to. For once, she could share her practice space with another trumpet player. Which was all he was to her, anyway.

The next day, as Meg and her dad shared a lazy lunch together, she regretted not having changed her mind. She couldn't have Trey in her house. Why? Because she already didn't know what to do around him in a neutral setting like school. And now this.

"Who did you say is coming over today?" Meg's dad asked.

Her face flushing for no reason, she said, "I didn't. But it's Trey. You know…from school?"

He lifted a greying eyebrow. "That big dumb jock? I thought you would have gone for someone…softer."

"He's not a big dumb jock," she said, trying to keep the exasperation from her voice. "Well, he's not dumb. And he's just coming over to play trumpet with me."

Pursing his lips, he nodded slowly. "Is that something the kids say these days?"

"Dad, no." She couldn't help a little chuckle. "We really are just *playing the trumpet* together. For our band that we're in?"

"How come you didn't tell me he was in that?" her dad asked.

She shrugged. "You didn't ask."

"I didn't ask," he said flatly as he collected their lunch dishes. "I'm sorry I didn't ask if Trey Donnelly, the boy you've known forever who lives down the street, the big meathead you definitely don't have a crush on is in the random band you just joined."

"He's not a meathead," she said patiently. "I *don't* have a crush on him.

And our band is…well, it *is* kind of random, but I still like it."

"I'm glad you do," he said, getting up from the table. "Even if it is with Trey and his big…meaty head."

"Dad…" She laughed and wiped a dirty spot on the table with a paper towel. "He's going to be here soon. Please don't be weird."

As he brought their plates into the kitchen, he said, "Oh, I'm going to vacate before he gets here."

"Wait, no," she said, following him. "You really don't have to do that."

"Eh, I already told your grandma I'd do yard work for her," he said, waving a dismissive hand. "Two weeks ago… Now's a perfect time!" He gave her a cheeky grin.

Resisting the urge to roll her eyes, she said weakly, "Okay, but that's really not necessary."

"Margaret." He put his hand on her shoulder and squeezed. "I just want you to enjoy having…friends. But you can always text me if you want me to come home."

Since there was no changing his mind, Meg let it drop. A few minutes later, when her dad opened the door to leave, there was Trey, reaching out his hand to ring the doorbell.

"Excellent timing," Meg's dad said. "Perfect for a musician. Or a football player!"

"Dad," Meg breathed.

"Thank you," Trey said with a polite smile. "I think?"

"It's a compliment." Her dad stepped through the door and looked back at them. "You kids have fun. But not *too* much fun." He pointed at Trey before turning and going to his car.

"*Dad.*"

"Yes, sir," Trey said.

"I'm so sorry," Meg said as she led him inside. "My dad's just being…"

"A dad?" Trey filled in for her. "Yeah, I could tell by the socks and sandals."

Meg groaned and then laughed. "Come in, I'll show you my practice room."

She led him through the house, past the kitchen and into the sunroom. It wasn't strictly a practice room, but they didn't use it for anything else. And at this time of day, the lighting was perfect. Her trumpet was already waiting next to her music stand, which had the "Secrets" arrangement on it.

A grey tabby lay next to her trumpet. He meowed loudly when they walked in and showed them his belly.

Trey leaned down to scratch the cat's belly. "You get this whole room to yourself?" He asked in awe, looking around.

There was a shelf full of Meg's music and a table that had some mutes and cleaning supplies for her trumpet. It was very much her room.

"Yeah," she said softly. "I can shut the door whenever Dad's working from home, so it doesn't disturb him. And sometimes to keep Mercutio out because I'm always tripping over him. The reverb is amazing. Try it!"

"Okay," he said eagerly.

He put his trumpet case on the table and opened it. After popping the mouthpiece in, he lifted it up and played some high notes and then some low notes, followed by some in-between notes. Meg watched with a smile as he played more to listen to the echo in the room.

"That *is* amazing!" he exclaimed.

She chuckled and glanced into his case. "Is that your music all scrunched up in your case?"

"Well, it's *your* music," he said as he pulled it out. "But yeah, that's it."

Biting back a retort, she took it and smoothed it out on the table. Some parts of it were in the upper range, above the treble C that any trumpet player should be able to play. She could easily have taken this part off his hands. But she wasn't going to back down now.

"This isn't so bad," she said. "Not counting that one B flat, but I heard you play that on Tuesday."

"It...sounded gross," he said bitterly. "Look."

He lifted his trumpet and attempted the high note. It took him a couple of tries, but when he finally got it, it came out weak and thin.

"Trey." She picked up her own trumpet. "You can't just play that cold. Although I have noticed you don't really warm up before you play."

"So?" he said.

"*So?*" She laughed. "Would you ever run onto the field right as a game is starting without stretching first?"

For a moment, he was quiet and then he said, "No, of course not."

"How is this any different?" she asked, chuckling.

"Okay, that's fair," he said.

Feeling generous, she said, "When I warm up, I play some mid notes first, since those are the easiest to hit. Then I do low notes, back up to mid and then I keep going higher and higher until I'm uncomfortable."

"And what note is uncomfortable for you?" he asked.

She flicked a hand. "That's not important." He bobbed his eyebrows at her, and she finally said, "A D. But that's not important."

"A *D?* Why can't you just take the first part, Meg?" he asked plaintively.

"Because I like playing the harmonies," she stated. It was partially true anyway. "Now do the warmup with me.

He shook his head but lifted his trumpet to his mouth anyway. Following her lead, he watched her fingers to try to figure out what notes she was playing and played along. When they started going into their upper range, he took her advice and stopped as soon as it became uncomfortable. She stopped when he did.

"Okay, *now* play that B flat," she said. When he hesitated, she said, "Either that or drop and give me twenty."

Lifting an eyebrow, he put his trumpet down and started crouching to the floor. As much as she would have loved watching that, she laughed and said, "No, *Trey*, come on."

"*Alright*," he said with laughter in his voice. He shook his head and took the first option, peeling off the note on the first try in a strong, clear tone. "Okay… I get it now."

"There you go," she said quietly with a hint of pride in her voice. "Here, let's play your part together."

That seemed to make him happy and he quickly placed his creased-up music on her stand. For the next little while, they played the piece together, going slowly over the tough parts. Meg backed off a bit when it came to the higher parts to let Trey try them on his own. When they'd played it a few times through, Trey finally stopped and put his horn down so he could have a break.

"Well, look at that," Meg said. "You *can* play it."

"You don't have to be so smug about it," he said, though there was laughter in his voice.

"Me, smug?" she said as she sat at the table. "Never."

"Sure." Trey sat, too, and watched as Meg started wiping down her trumpet. Mercutio immediately jumped into his lap and Trey stroked his head. After a quiet moment, he asked, "So…have you talked to Chad lately?"

Meg's hands stilled and she shook her head. "Not since the day you guys got into that fight."

Trey grunted. "Good. He's pushy."

She let out a humourless chuckle. "You don't have to tell me."

"What do you mean?" he asked.

Meg chewed on her lip, debating whether to tell him the whole story. But Trey won her over simply by waiting patiently.

"Last year," she said, "Chad started talking to me. Like *talking* talking to me. It was kind of weird, but I wasn't super bothered by it. Then one day, he asked me out and I…" She looked down at her trumpet, swallowing her embarrassment. "I kind of laughed. I was nervous and honestly, I thought it was a joke, you know? Like if I said yes, all his friends would pop out of the lockers and point and laugh at me."

"Oof." He gave her a sympathetic frown.

"I didn't think he was serious," she continued. "Until he asked me a second time. I'm sure lots of other girls would have said yes—"

Trey scowled and she couldn't help a tiny giggle.

"Well, they would have," she insisted. "But I wasn't interested. We barely know each other and have nothing in common. So, I said no, as nicely as I could."

"And I bet that hurt his fragile ego," he muttered with disdain.

She shrugged. "I don't know. I guess so. We didn't see each other at all over the summer since, you know, we literally have zero in common and don't run in the same circles. I don't even have a circle. I figured he forgot about it."

"But he didn't," he said plainly.

"No." She paused, remembering the events of that day. "He said hi to me. I said hi back, and apparently that was enough invitation to ask me for more."

"*Ask* you?" he said flippantly. "I didn't see any asking happening."

"You know what I mean," she said quietly.

"Yeah, I do."

She shrugged off the unpleasant memory and smiled at him. "I'm grateful for what you did. But you didn't have to get into a fight over it."

Trey looked away, shifting uncomfortably, and she wished she hadn't brought up the fight. But then he turned back to her with fire in his eyes.

"That wasn't why we started fighting," he admitted quietly. "Well, not the only reason. He was being a total jerk to you."

"What was it, then?" she asked. By now, she'd ditched the cloth she'd been using to wipe her trumpet and had turned her full attention to him.

He told her the whole story, including everything Chad had said about Trey getting all the girls, the thing with Lacy, how Chad had thrown the first punch, and the two-week detention. Meg looked invested in the story, but not particularly surprised.

"On top of that," he said, "Coach Hanford wouldn't let me play the game that weekend. That was our rival game. I was supposed to lead us to victory and instead…they won *without* me!"

"Aw, Trey," she said sympathetically. "That whole thing sucks."

He crossed his arms and leaned back. "Yeah, it does. It sucks knowing my girlfriend went after my best friend and that my team doesn't even need me."

"Well, first of all," Meg said gently, "the fact that your team won just means they're a good team. Not that they're better without you. And second…sometimes you're better off when people show you their true colours. You could spend years with someone and never really know who they truly are. Maybe you're lucky you found out sooner rather than later."

He looked up at her, showing her the unguarded hurt in his blue eyes. Caught in the moment, she held her breath as Trey took his time thinking about what she'd said.

Finally, mercifully, he looked away. "Maybe you're right. It's better this way. Besides—" He smiled at her. "If I hadn't gotten detention at the same time as D-rock, we wouldn't have our cool band."

She smiled back at him. "There you go! Silver lining."

"Thanks for having me over." He got up and took the mouthpiece out of his trumpet, indicating it was time for him to go. "That's real cool of you."

Meg's heart fluttered. That was possibly the highest compliment she'd ever had from any guy at school…not counting Chad's creepy comments.

"It's nice to have someone else to play with," she said. "You can come back anytime."

"Thanks."

She walked him to the door and down the porch steps. Then she watched him walk down the street to his own house. When he turned before going up his front steps and winked at her, her heart double tapped. Great, she'd been caught staring. Well, that was perfect.

Chapter Fourteen

Claire sat on her bed, scrolling through all the song suggestions that had flooded their group chat since Tuesday. 14 different people with vastly different tastes meant there was a *wide* range of songs. They even spanned different eras of music, which shouldn't have surprised Claire, though it did. And of course, for every suggestion, there was an onslaught of negative or positive opinions to go with it.

How would she ever sift through these and decide which ones she should try to arrange for them? She had initially started making a list of songs that already had heavy instrumentation. But then she realized she could easily convert most of the others for the band. With help, of course.

Biting her lip, she considered what D-rock would say. He'd already seen all the suggestions himself. But he hadn't said anything about them. And she wanted to ask him, but also…hadn't she spent enough time with him already? Surely he wasn't prepared to spend more with her just for *her* passion.

Maybe a few well-placed hints Harmony's way would get her a new writing partner. Yeah, she would try that.

Claire: hey girl what's your range?

Harmony: my range?

Claire: yeah there's a song that would be fun to try but it needs some pretty high notes

Harmony: i play piccolo if that helps

Claire: GREAT!! wanna help me write it?

Claire cringed as soon as she hit Send. Not only did that sound *so* desperate but it was too sudden. Claire herself would have immediately balked at an out-of-the-blue proposition like that. What had she been thinking?

Harmony didn't respond for a few minutes, which just made Claire feel even worse.

Harmony: ok so now not only do you suddenly want me in the band but you also want me to write music with you even though i said i couldn't do that?

Claire frowned at her phone in confusion.

Claire: what do you mean i "suddenly want you in the band"? Of course i want you in the band

Harmony: that isn't what you said when i joined??

Claire sighed and fell back against her pillows. Harmony was right. She had been unkind when she'd first seen Harmony show up in D-rock's basement. *And* she hadn't exactly rushed to defend her, either, when others had voiced their objections to her being there. Not that Harmony knew that, but it didn't make Claire feel any better.

Claire: i'm sorry i was mean to you

Harmony: ok

Claire's heart sank. This was a disaster. What was she supposed to do now?

She went back to the group chat, this time searching specifically for Harmony's suggestions. Maybe if she chose something Harmony liked, that would soften her up. It looked like Harmony had an eclectic taste, but one song stood out among the rest: "Holding Out for a Hero."

"Can't believe I'm going to do this…"

Shaking her head, she found the song and played it. It was long, dramatic, and extravagant. Sure, it was cheesy, but there was actually a lot more instrumentation in it than Claire expected to find. It was clear Harmony had tried to think of songs that would fit their band, and this one was no exception.

"Alright…" Claire bobbed her head to the music. "This could work. I might need a hero myself to pull it off, but…" Looking down at her phone, she chose D-rock's name. "Close enough."

There was a knock on her bedroom door and Claire nearly jumped out of her skin. She took a deep breath to calm her racing heart before getting up to answer. Thankfully, it was just her aunt.

"Hey, Aunt Pam," she said, opening the door wider.

"Hey, girl, how's it going?" Pam asked, looking around the spotless room.

"There are no boys here," Claire said with laughter.

"Why not, though?" Pam said, throwing up her hands. "Man, at your age, if my parents left me alone so often for so long…" She grimaced.

Claire laughed some more. "Well, let me know next time you're coming over and I'll hide one in the closet for you. *If* I can get my boy bait to work and trap one, that is."

Pam's eyes widened as she looked Claire up and down. "*You're* supposed to be the bait."

Claire looked down at her leggings and sweatshirt—the one with the grease stain that she would definitely never wear in front of anyone but

Pam. "And *you're* supposed to be a good role model…"

"That's fair." Pam sat on the bed and Claire joined her. "Anyway, I just wanted to know that you're okay. You're okay, right? Not too lonely? You can always come over if you are."

"I'm fine," Claire answered, shrugging loosely. "Actually, I joined a band with some other kids from my school. I'm even writing music."

"Oh!" Pam's eyes lit up. "That's awesome. Did you tell your parents?"

Claire's shoulders drooped and she looked down at her phone clasped tightly in her hands. "No. I don't think they'd really care that much."

"Right…" Pam drawled. "World-class musicians would definitely *not* want to know about their talented daughter playing in a band and writing music."

"Sounds about right," Claire said, trying to force a light tone into her voice but failing.

"Oh, Claire." Pam put her arm around Claire's shoulders and squeezed before getting back up. "Your parents do care." Claire just shrugged. "Well, *I* do."

"Thanks," Claire said. "That means a lot to me."

"Of course, baby!" Pam said. "Okay, I'll leave you alone now. But first…do you mind if I borrow a dress?"

Claire chuckled and went over to open the closet door. "There are no boys in my closet."

Pam shook her head. "Such a weird kid. Love you! See you next week. Call me if you need me."

Claire closed the door behind her, shaking her head. What kind of boy was she supposed to be keeping in her house? Her phone buzzed in her hand and she looked down. A message from D-rock asking her if she'd looked at the "million" song suggestions yet.

Claire: yeah i think i know which one i want to do

D-rock: so you coming over or what

She rolled her eyes.

Claire: or what

♪   ♫   ♪

Max had graciously agreed to let Marty practice his drums at his house during the week, with the provision that if Max had to kick him out quickly because his parents were unexpectedly coming home, then he had to leave. They also had to cover the kit with a sheet just in case Max's parents actually went down to the basement at any point.

Marty thought it was a little overkill, but he wasn't going to complain. Having the space to practice away from his little brothers and sister was wonderful. He would take what he could get.

Much to his surprise, Max chose to do his homework in the basement while Marty drummed. He didn't seem bothered by the noise and, in fact, was bobbing his head in time to the beat. It made Marty smile. He loved when people enjoyed his music.

He was never really sure if people "got" drumming the way he did. Sure, most people could figure out how each drum fit into any given rhythm, how the symbols enhanced the low, hollow sounds. But most of them didn't understand how drumming was an extension of the drummer's body.

Every movement was tied to a sound and every sound tied to a beat. When Marty drummed, his body, mind, and soul felt connected to the drums. Or maybe he was overthinking it and it was just drumming.

He took a chance and looked over at Max. Max had stopped doing homework to watch him, his mouth slightly agape. Not that Marty minded the attention, but when it was so focused on him, it was a bit distracting. He hit the snare wrong, and his stick went flying across the room.

Max laughed, his hazel eyes twinkling. "And here I was thinking how amazing your drumming is."

Marty got up from his stool and laughed, too. "Yeah, that…happens sometimes." The stick had rolled near the piano, so he went over and picked it up. "I'll try not to hit your piano, but I got no guarantees."

Max shrugged. "I never play the thing. In fact, I wish I could just give it to Hacks. It's, like, alive when he plays it. The best I've got on piano is 'Fur Elise.'"

Marty's mouth twisted up. "Ick, please don't ever suggest that to Claire and D-rock. Talk about overdone."

"Totally," Max said. He watched Marty sit back at his set and asked, "Have you thought about maybe…learning to read music?"

Marty shrugged uncomfortably. "I feel like I'm getting by just fine."

"Oh, by yourself?" Max said, his eyes widening. "Absolutely. You're amazing!"

His face brightening, Marty said, "Thanks!"

"But you know," Max said gently, "in a band setting it's a bit different. You could follow along or try to do your best to figure things out. But not knowing what the composer wants you to do next is a drawback."

"Oh." Marty looked at the sticks in his hands. They'd never failed him before. He didn't expect them to now.

"I'm not saying that to make you feel bad," Max said quickly. "Really, I think you're the best drummer I've ever seen. It's just that when you know where the piece is going with the music, then you'll be better able to anticipate. And really, you shouldn't be following the band. You should be leading them, driving the beat. And that's hard to do if you don't know what the beat is supposed to be."

Marty thought about his words, trying not to take them personally. He knew they came from a place of kindness. "I get that," Marty finally said. "But I…I just don't know how. No one's ever taught me, and I've never thought to ask."

"Yeah?" Max said eagerly. "Why didn't you just say so? I'll help you!"

Marty licked his lips, looking into Max's earnest eyes. "You know how to read drum music?" he asked skeptically.

"Sort of?" Max said. "I can read regular music and that's half the battle. The rest is just learning which symbol matches which part of the drum set."

Marty shook his head, but he had to admit that it *would* be nice to do what everyone else in the band could do. Maybe Max was right; maybe it would make his playing better if he could read music. Plus, Max's energy right now was so cute Marty couldn't possibly say no.

"Alright, let's do it," Marty said reluctantly.

"Great!" Max jumped up. Then he looked down at his expensive watch. "Oh, but not right now. My dad's going to be home soon."

"Ah, well, another day, then," Marty said as he grabbed the bedsheet for the drum kit.

Max took the other end of it and together they covered the set. Marty put his drumsticks in his back pocket and followed Max to the front door.

"Thanks again," Marty said.

"Mmhmm, bye," Max said quickly, practically shoving him out the door.

Marty couldn't help laughing as he stepped down the wide stone staircase. Max was generous, but he guessed Max's parents weren't.

At least it was still nice enough out that Marty didn't mind walking all the way home. It would be a good 40 minutes, but Marty was used to walking everywhere he went.

Back in Guadeloupe, where he was born, they hadn't even owned a car. Marty had learned from a young age to love walking—but also to make good use of each trip he took. This one was worth it.

Of course, when they'd moved to Canada, things had changed. Not only was it far colder—and for far longer—than they were used to, but they'd learned they couldn't get by on walking or even biking for at least half the year. Marty had been eight at the time and it had taken him at least three winters to get used to the change. At 15, he now loved winter.

Marty was still lost in his thoughts by the time he got home. The smell of a good homemade meal greeted him—along with his two younger brothers and sister. And then his mother, waving a wooden spoon around.

"*Tu étais où là?*" she asked, wondering where he'd gone.

Biting back a sigh, he answered, "*Avec un ami.*"

At that, his mom started bombarding him with all kinds of comments and questions from "What friend?" to "We need your help at home, but you chose to be out *avec un ami.*" He smiled patiently. His mom got like this every time his dad went home to Guadeloupe for whatever reason. He was usually never gone for more than a week, but it had been a week and a half already.

"*Maman,*" he said, putting his hands on her shoulders. "It's Sunday. You don't have to work so hard to be the perfect mom today, okay?"

She relaxed her shoulders and gave him a small smile. "Okay, but can you help Pierre? *Il a besoin…*"

Marty started nodding before she even told him what his eldest brother needed. It was always something. Usually help with his homework. As he went to find Petey, he felt his drumsticks slip out of his back pocket. He knew it was Marine, his eight-year-old sister. She always took his drumsticks just to annoy him.

"Don't lose those," he cautioned as she snuck away from him, giggling. No wonder his mom was always exhausted.

Chapter Fifteen

Monday morning, Amber woke up late. Which was *perfect* since she had a presentation to do for social studies and she had wanted to take the time to straighten her hair, do makeup, and actually look good for once.

She rushed around, trying to get dressed and print her assignment at the same time. Yes, she should have printed it last night, but she was normally an early riser and figured she could do it in the morning. But now, of course, the printer was giving her attitude and her hair was only half straightened and if she didn't leave in the next two minutes, she would be late.

Her dad was still out working the graveyard shift and her mom had left for work already. Which only left one option.

"Bryan!" she called, knocking frantically on his door. She heard a thudding sound in his room and she cringed.

He opened the door, his eyes still half closed, his hair sticking out in every direction. "What…what is it?" he mumbled.

"I need a ride to school," she said urgently.

His eyes narrowed more as he took in her appearance. "What's wrong with your hair?"

"Have you looked in a mirror?" she snipped before hastening back to the bathroom.

As she continued to straighten her hair, Bryan joined her. He splashed water on his face, put some gel in his hair, and then...looked perfect. Because that was all it took when you were a boy.

"Ugh, boys have it so easy," she huffed.

"Sure," he said. "I'm gonna pee, are you staying?"

Rolling her eyes, she left the bathroom, telling him to be quick. Maybe by now the printer had sorted its issues out. She went downstairs and saw that her assignment had indeed printed. But it was low on ink, so the words were faint. Oh well, she would just have to do her best with it.

After finishing her hair and stuffing her assignment into her backpack, she was finally ready to go. But Bryan? He was...already leaning against his car and waiting for her. Hastily she got in and breathed a sigh of relief. They had plenty of time to get to school.

"Thank you," she said.

"You're welcome," he answered, sounding much more alert.

"Whoa, when did you get so polite?" she teased.

"Um, this morning when you banged on my door while I was having a good dream and I fell on the floor?" he answered in a cranky voice.

Biting back her laughter, she said, "Sorry. I really do appreciate the ride."

Bryan just grunted, which was much more like him, and turned on the radio. It didn't matter to Amber though. As long as she made it to school on time, she'd be fine. She didn't love giving presentations, but it wasn't the worst. When she was prepared. Which, with the exception of having almost no ink in her printer, she was.

She made it to social studies just as her friends were arriving. She greeted them happily, but her mood soured when Yuri pointed to the back of the room and giggled. Through her laughter, Amber could barely make out the words she was saying to Stacey. She glanced over to where Rach was waiting with a passive expression on her face.

"It's just a ponytail," Amber said, once she'd finally decoded what her friend was trying to say.

"You're not getting it," Stacey said, still laughing. "Don't worry, I'll explain it later."

Amber shook her head and took her spot. She heard a few more whisperings among her friends but she ignored them. She had other things to focus on.

Mr. Duncan called on her name, and her stomach fluttered nervously. She could do this. It was just a silly little presentation. It was well researched and she had edited it five times. All her friends were here. She was fine.

"My presentation is on the economic impact of colonization on the Indigenous Peoples of Canada," Amber stated confidently.

Stacey turned and whispered something to Yuri, to which Yuri snickered. Licking her lips, Amber ignored them and squinted at the paper in her hand. She took a deep breath and continued on, trying her best to sound like she knew what she was talking about. Which she did, since she'd worked hard on the assignment.

But the words on her paper were so faint and the fluorescent lighting really didn't help. She looked up in time to see Garrett flick something directly at Rach. With a frustrated sigh, she lowered her paper.

"Excuse me, I'm trying to do my presentation," she snipped. "Do you mind?"

She looked straight at Stacey, who narrowed her eyes. Then she turned around and loudly said something derogatory about Rach that Amber would certainly never repeat. Her face going red, blood boiling, she opened her mouth but was cut off.

"Yes, please continue with your presentation," Mr. Duncan said impatiently, waving his hand.

"How can I?" Amber sputtered. "They won't stop talking, and teasing Rach, and throwing things at her."

Mr. Duncan looked over at Rach and asked, "Is that true?"

Rach shrugged uncomfortably, staring down at her desk. "It's…it's fine. Amber, just finish your thing."

"But, *Rach*," Amber said, confusion in her voice.

"She says she's fine," Mr. Duncan said. "We don't have all day."

He might not have had all day, but she certainly did. "You do realize this happens every single day, right?" she asked him. "They're always bugging her. It's very distracting."

"That isn't your concern," Mr. Duncan said, waving his hand again at her.

"You're right," she said. "It's *yours*. *You're* the teacher, so do something about the bullying in your classroom!"

A hushed gasp ran through the class. Amber didn't dare look at any of her friends and instead forced herself to hold Mr. Duncan's gaze. His face growing red, he stood up and came closer to her.

"As I said," he said in a low voice, "that is none of your concern. So unless you want detention and an F on your presentation, I suggest you finish."

"*Fine*," she said heatedly. "I'll take the F." With that, she stalked over to her desk and slumped down into it, crossing her arms.

"Amber, no," Rach whispered to her.

"Wow," Mr. Duncan said, as he began filling out a detention slip. "Just like your brother. I had higher hopes for you."

A chair scraped across the floor and everyone turned towards the sound. It was Rach, rising to her full height. "Mr. Duncan, that's extremely unprofessional."

"Rachel? What—"

"Comparing one student to another just because you didn't like what she had to say?" Rach continued with a scowl on her face. "Also, what's wrong with her brother? Did he say something you didn't like, too?"

"Rachel, sit down," he said, not too kindly.

"No." Rach lifted her chin. "Amber's right. Every day I suffer through this class and you don't do anything about it."

Mr. Duncan shrugged. "You said you were fine."

"Well, I'm *not.*"

He sighed. "Please…sit down or I'll have to give you detention, too."

Rach looked at Amber, who smiled at her. Crossing her arms, she looked back at the teacher. "Fine. I'll take detention, too."

"Really, girls…"

Rach picked up her backpack and started heading for the door as whispers followed her from her classmates.

"Where are you going?" Mr. Duncan asked in a defeated voice.

"To the office to report your behaviour," Rach said as she swung the door open. "Have fun chatting with my parents about that one."

"I'm going, too," Amber said.

"*Amber,*" Stacey hissed through gritted teeth.

Ignoring her, Amber calmly got her own backpack and stood back up. She laid her presentation, faint writing and all, on Mr. Duncan's desk and took both hers and Rach's detention slips from him. Then without another word, she left the classroom.

Rach was already halfway down the hall, so Amber scurried to catch up. "Rach!" she called out.

Rach turned to her with a worried look on her face. "You shouldn't have failed your presentation for me, Amber."

For a moment, Amber was stunned. How could Rach say that after everything she'd just gone through? "Well, you shouldn't have told Mr. Duncan you're fine when you're clearly not."

"Look…" Rach sighed. "It was nice of you to speak out, but you didn't have to go that far with it. I can deal with this on my own."

"You don't have to be on your own," Amber said softly. "It's okay to let someone else fight your battles with you, you know?"

Rach looked down at her for a moment and then the smallest smile touched her lips. "Thank you," she said.

Amber smiled back. "Oh, by the way, this is for you. A parting gift from Mr. Duncan." She held out Rach's detention slip.

Rach laughed and took it. "Aw, he didn't have to get me anything."

Amber giggled and they continued walking, holding their detention slips like badges of honour.

♪　　♫　　♪

Meg kept her head down as she made her way through the busy halls between first and second period. It was always so crowded and noisy, and she inevitably always got bumped by someone since she was unnoticeable like she always wanted to be. It wasn't exactly the best perk about being a wallflower.

Without meaning to, she slowed her gait as she passed by Trey's locker. One of his friends threw a football right over his head and he didn't even notice. Or maybe he did, but he didn't care. He laughed at something another friend said, and Meg unconsciously slowed down even more.

He shut his locker, turning just in time to catch a glimpse of Meg. Smiling, he said in a sweet voice, "Hey, Meg."

A sweet voice? No, he had a jock's voice, the kind that carried across the hall so that it felt like everyone could hear him saying hello to her. Willing her face to not heat up to a million degrees, she picked up her pace.

"Hey," she breathed before scurrying along.

Her locker was around the corner and she let out a sigh of relief as she approached it. It was quieter here, but her relief was short-lived.

"What do you think you're doing?" an icy voice asked.

Tilting her head past her locker door, Meg came face-to-face with none other than Lacy Donovan. Her long chestnut hair fell in perfect waves past her shoulders and her makeup was camera ready. Meg felt frumpy just being this close to her. Normally, she didn't give much thought to Lacy, let alone disliked her. But after hearing Trey's story, Meg's opinion of her had changed.

"I'm getting ready for class," Meg said timidly.

Lacy crossed her arms, her eyes narrowing to slits. "I *meant* with Trey. What are you doing with *Trey?*"

Meg's eyebrows drew in. "Um, nothing?"

"That's right, you're doing nothing with him," Lacy snipped. "And I'll tell you why. Because he's *mine*. You can't have him. Got it?"

Meg frowned. Wasn't this the girl who had ditched Trey for Chad? What did she care if any other girl was doing something with Trey or simply saying "hey" to him in the hallway *after* he'd already initiated the greeting?

"Okay," Meg said lightly.

Lacy made a high-pitched huffing sound and turned to go. Meg should have just kept her mouth shut but couldn't resist one last thought.

"But he's not a toy," Meg said firmly. "He's a human being and you can't own him."

Lacy wheeled around on her heel, fire burning in her dark brown eyes. She came so close to Meg that they may as well have been kissing. Meg was overwhelmed with the urge to back up, but she held her ground, refusing to be intimidated.

"I'll decide which boys at this school are my toys. And you?" Lacy looked down Meg's entire body and then back up to her face. "Stay. Away.

From. Trey. Donnelly."

"Okay," Meg said with a careless shrug.

With one last sneer, Lacy stomped away. Meg let out a long breath. This was why she preferred to never be noticed. Oh, why did Trey have to go and ruin that for her?

Chapter Sixteen

At the end of another disappointing Monday, Chloe went over to her locker to retrieve her math textbook. Her brow furrowed, she noted something quite out of the ordinary: a black envelope with her name written in swirly pink letters. She looked around quickly, but the other students were all doing their own things.

She opened the envelope and pulled out a thick linen card, again with her name written on the front. Inside, it read,

Chloe,
Your smile shines as bright as the Northern Lights in winter.

Her heart skipping beats erratically, she looked around again. No one seemed all that interested in watching her read this dorky and beautiful love note. This was…unexpected. Not terrible, but very strange.

She was still holding the card in her hand when Amber and Rach walked by. Chloe did a double take. Yes, they were definitely talking and laughing together. Amber caught her eye and smiled. Then her gaze slipped to the note.

"Oh, whatcha got there, Chloe?" Amber asked.

Not wanting to disclose *all* the details, Chloe closed the card and showed her the outside. "Someone left this on my locker. But…it's gotta be a mistake, right? Why would anyone leave this for me?"

"Pretty sure you're the only Chloe in the school," Rach said. "Now, if it said *Rachel* and was left on *my* locker, I'd know that was a mistake since there are seven Rachels and I'm not the first pick."

"Oh, Rach," Amber chided affectionately. "Well, who's it from, Chloe?"

"It doesn't say," Chloe answered with a shrug.

"Ooooh," Amber squeaked. "A secret love note!"

"Amber, shh," Chloe said through laughter. "Everybody doesn't need to know."

"Sorry," Amber whispered. "Oh, I would love to solve this mystery for you, but Rach and I have detention."

Chloe looked up at Rach and then at Amber, amusement twinkling in her eyes. "You two have detention together?"

"Yup," Rach said proudly.

Chloe chuckled. "Wait a sec and I'll walk over with you guys."

Quickly, she grabbed her chemistry textbook and put it in her backpack along with the note. Just because it was anonymous and weird didn't mean she had to get rid of it. As they walked, Chloe asked what had happened to land them in detention.

"Well, my friends were being idiots," Amber said, rolling her eyes.

"Uh, speaking of your friends…" Rach grabbed her elbow and stopped her from walking.

Stacey, Yuri, and their posse were standing in front of them, blocking the hallway. Chloe lifted an eyebrow, Amber swallowed down hard, and

Rach crossed her arms, imitating their stances but doing a way better job of it.

"Excuse us," Amber said. "We have to get to detention."

"Oh, do you?" Yuri said. "Guess what? We don't care."

"Come on, guys," Amber pleaded. "Why are you being like this? You didn't even get in trouble."

"Yes, we did," Stacey said, scowling at her. "Mr. Duncan yelled at us for five minutes after you left. Because apparently we were being uncool. And now we have to have a seating chart. So thanks a lot."

"Oh, no, not a seating chart!" Chloe said sarcastically, putting a hand over her heart.

The whole crew turned their attention to her. Fiona scoffed and flicked her wrist. "Get out of here, you witch. You're not even a part of this."

Rach took a step forward. "Don't talk to her like that."

"Don't talk to *anyone* like that," Amber added.

"Um, what's happening here?" came a pretty voice from behind them. They half turned to see that it was Harmony, her flute case clutched close to her. "Are we...on strike?"

"No, these losers just won't move out of our way," Chloe said.

"And Rach and I are late for detention," Amber added.

"Detention?" came another voice. Meg sidled up to the group, assessing the situation with her eyes. "How'd you guys get detention?"

Amber glared hard at Stacey. "As I was explaining before, my friends were being idiots and somehow *I* got in trouble for that."

"*You're* the idiot," Stacey said. "Taking the giant freak's side while we all sat there waiting for you to finish your horrible presentation!"

"*Excuse me?*" Amber squealed. She stomped up to Stacey. "You were *not* waiting patiently, that was a *good* presentation, and *you're* the freak!"

"Guys," Meg said gently as she came up next to Amber. "This is a little bit silly. Just let us pass."

Stacey didn't even respond to Meg. Instead, she lashed out and grabbed Amber's wrist, pulling hard. Chloe, Rach, and Harmony rushed forward, grabbing on to Amber's arms to keep her upright. Several of Stacey's friends surrounded her and started shouting insults.

"Stacey, let go!" Amber cried. "What are you doing?"

Stacey's fingernails dug into her wrists. "Trying to get my friendship bracelet back since it obviously doesn't mean anything to you."

She slid her fingers under the bracelets and hair elastics on Amber's wrist, tugging hard.

"This isn't a movie," Amber said, trying to pull her arm back. "It's not just gonna snap off."

"*Stop*," Harmony said, reaching out to pull Stacey's hand away.

Yuri stepped forward to stand between Harmony and Stacey. As the girls played tug-of-war back and forth with Amber's body, Harmony nearly lost her grip on her flute. It fell and she caught it just as it hit Yuri in the chest.

Yuri clutched her breasts and gasped hard. "How *dare* you, you basic musical reject?"

Harmony stepped back, but Yuri reached out and grabbed her flute case. Before Yuri could pull it away, someone slapped her hand soundly.

"Hands off!" came a sassy voice.

Harmony turned wide eyes to Claire as she firmly held her flute against herself. "Where'd you come from?"

Claire gestured loosely down the hallway as she stepped in front of Harmony. "Don't touch her stuff," she said to Yuri.

"She *hit* me with it!" Yuri shouted back.

Claire's face scrunched up. "No, she didn't. You walked into it. Also, it's a *flute*? You'll survive."

Instead of responding, Yuri grabbed Claire's shoulders and pushed for all her worth. Claire's arms flailed, but Harmony caught her before she could fall.

Amber and Stacey were still in a battle over a stupid bracelet that was definitely not ever coming off Amber's wrist without a pair of scissors. The multicoloured nylon bracelet had been weaved specifically for Amber four years ago at camp and tied on tightly. It hadn't left her wrist since then.

"Stacey, seriously, you're hurting me," Amber said as the bracelet cut into her skin.

"Just let her go," Meg said, wishing her voice could sound strong and confident for once in her life.

By now Rach had a firm grasp on Amber's shoulders but she knew if she pulled, it would just hurt Amber more. Suddenly, a shrill whistle cut through the noise of their altercation. Everyone stilled and looked for the source of the noise, fear striking their hearts when they realized it was Coach Trifano.

"What's going on here?" Trifano asked in her harsh, bloodcurdling voice that scared the living daylights out of anyone but the women's lacrosse team.

The girls all looked around, daring each other to break the silence using only their eyes. When no one spoke, Trifano put her whistle in her mouth and blew once more, causing all of them to jump.

"Who's responsible here?" she asked.

Amber took a deep breath, squared her chin, and said, "I am. I'm already in trouble for defending a classmate in class. So...fine. Do your worst, Coach."

"Two days' detention," Coach Trifano said, surprising Amber. She'd been expecting worse. "Anyone else?"

"Yeah, me," Rach said, lifting her chin.

"And me," Chloe said. "I mean, if we're punishing people for trying to help, then—"

"Okay, two days for you two as well," Trifano said, cutting her off ruthlessly.

Harmony came to stand next to them, clutching her flute as if someone might try to steal it again. "I'm with them."

"Me, too," Meg said, finally finding her confident voice.

Claire glared at Stacey and her rotten friends. "Yeah, I'd rather be on this side, too," she said, coming to stand with her brand-new friends.

"Great," Trifano said sarcastically. "Anyone else? Last call."

"No," Amber said. She gestured loosely in Stacey's direction. "They're so innocent and blameless, I'd hate for them to get detention, too."

"Are you looking to add days, missy?" Coach Trifano asked, staring her down with a menacing scowl.

Rach gave her a warning look. Amber knew when it was time to quit. "No, ma'am."

"Right, then," Trifano said. "March."

Heads held high, they walked right past Stacey's crew, who parted like the Red Sea, their heads bowed to avoid incurring Trifano's wrath.

As they went, Harmony tapped Claire's arm. "Thank you," she said softly. "I thought I was going to lose my flute."

"Ugh." Claire waved her hands dramatically. "If someone had touched my cello like that, I would have slapped them right across the face."

Harmony smiled before Coach Trifano barked out an order to be quiet. By the time they'd gotten to detention hall, their adrenaline had worn off and Amber was regretting having dragged her friends into this mess.

Coach opened the door only to find the detention hall empty. "Who...who's on duty today? Ugh, I am *not* here for this today, ladies. Not today. Stay in here and don't talk while I find out who's supervising you."

The girls obediently filed into the classroom and chose seats near each other.

"And don't even think about leaving," Trifano added. "Otherwise, there will be worse consequences."

She shut the door soundly and Amber half expected to hear it lock. But all she heard were Trifano's heavy steps heading away.

After a moment, Amber said quietly, "You guys didn't have to get detention for me."

"I was already on my way, remember?" Rach said.

"What…was that all about?" Meg asked.

Amber told them what had happened in social studies. Rach added in her part, too, after which the other girls just stared at them.

"Ugh, Mr. Duncan," Harmony said with disdain. "I had him last year, too, and…he's not a good teacher."

"Yeah, remember that time he told us that a thing that was definitely racist wasn't *as bad as it seems?*" Meg said, making air quotes around the words.

Harmony's eyes widened. "I forgot about that!"

"Gross," Chloe said.

The girls were quiet after that, each of them lost in their own thoughts. Meg, though she wished to be anywhere else, felt less lonely than she had in a long time. Chloe was fired up over having fought an injustice, even if it didn't have anything to do with her. Harmony looked over at the other girls like they were her personal responsibility, including Claire. Claire looked back at her, grateful she'd been able to keep Harmony's flute safe from yucky Yuri's hands. Amber was overwhelmed by the support she felt from people she'd only barely become friends with, while feeling a sense of grief at having lost one her longest friendships. And Rach couldn't believe all these girls had fought for something that had started with her.

"You guys want to start a band?" Claire asked, her eyes crinkling at the corners.

Chloe snorted and Amber giggled. The others joined in until they were all laughing a little too hard, working off the excess energy from their snafu.

"That's a great idea," Amber said. "I wish I'd thought of it."

Meg laughed. "Well, you know…with our instrumentation, it could really work."

"I'm in," Harmony said, still laughing.

"Can't wait to tell the guys," Rach said. "I'm sure they'll be so happy for us."

"Oh, definitely," Chloe said.

"Speaking of guys…" Amber said, turning to Chloe. "Let's see that note so we can figure out whose handwriting it is!"

Chloe laughed, even as her cheeks went pink.

"Ooh, what note?" Harmony asked.

Chloe shook her head and decided to just cave and get it out of her backpack. She showed it to the others, and they leaned their heads over it, analysing the handwriting as if they were a special forensics task force.

A teacher finally did come to supervise the last twenty minutes of their detention. By then, they hadn't settled on the note's author, but they had formed a stronger, deeper bond.

Chapter Seventeen

On Tuesday night, the girls were more chatty than they'd ever been, which perplexed the boys in the band. And they didn't seem in any rush to actually warm their instruments up and play. Chloe had yet to tune her violin, Amber still hadn't even put one of her new reeds on her clarinet, and Meg and Rach hadn't even taken their horns out because they were too busy talking to Harmony, who had at least blown into her flute. Once.

Max, feeling anxious that they were going to waste their practice time before he had to kick them out, finally asked what was up.

"We all spent the afternoon in detention together," Amber said with more than a hint of pride in her voice.

"And yesterday," Rach said.

"You did?" TK asked in surprise. Though he wasn't playing his sax, he hadn't stopped pressing the keys, making a hollow sound pop out whenever he did.

"Yup," Harmony answered.

"Yeah, and we decided to start a band together," Claire added in a saucy voice, lifting her bow as if to illustrate. "Just us girls. So, you know…"

"Oh, did you now?" D-rock said, half in disbelief, half in amusement.

"Wait, can we go back to the detention thing?" Trey said, his brow furrowed seriously. He glanced at Meg. "What was that like?"

"You've been on the inside," Harmony said in a teasing voice.

"Yeah," Trey said, rolling his eyes. "But I've never been in *all-girls detention*."

"Oh, we had several pillow fights in our underwear," Chloe said, bobbing her head in a sassy way.

Some of the boys stared wide-eyed at her while Trey just laughed.

"I figured," he said.

"And your new all-girls band?" Hacks said, quite seriously. "You mean...you're ditching us."

"Yeah, we're branching out," Rach said. "We figured we've got all the parts covered."

"That's *eight* parts you don't have covered," Corbie said. He lifted his trombone. "Including the most important part."

"Plus, aren't you forgetting something?" D-rock asked, pointing at his bass with his bow.

"Oh, yeah..." Chloe drawled. She looked at Max with a cheeky grin. "We still need a place to rehearse. So...I guess...you can stay."

"I can stay," Max said flatly. "In my own home. How generous."

"And I kind of do need D-rock." Claire's eyes widened when she realized how that sounded. "I mean, I need him to write music with me. So...you know, you can stay, too."

D-rock pulled his lips in like he was trying to hold back laughter. Hacks slumped back, having not quite figured out that they were only joking.

"Oh, and, Marty, you can stay, too," Meg said, waving a hand at him. "For the rhythm."

"What?" Bryan said an octave higher than he normally spoke. "What exactly do I look like to you?"

While Meg looked him up and down, guitar and all, Amber stage whispered, "I'll sneak you in later."

"Um…" Corbie put up his hand. "Petition to be snuck in later, too."

"Okay, yes, because you're cute," Amber said hastily.

TK looked back at Trey and said, "They're joking, right?"

"They better be," he muttered. "Since I'm the one that recruited them. That's right! *I'm* the face behind all those anonymous social media posts you all responded to. *Me.*"

"Yeah, Trey," Meg said softly, putting a hand on his arm. "We already knew that."

"Oh, right," he said.

"You guys," Harmony said, laughing. She gave TK a kind smile. "We're kidding. Obviously, we don't want a band without you."

"Wait, so you're being serious now?" Hacks said from the piano. "Or…what is going on?"

"We're all still a band, little dude," TK said in a slightly annoyed voice. "Relax."

"Wait, actually, though," D-rock said. "*Can* we go back to the detention thing? How did you *all* end up in detention?"

Rach immediately got up and told everyone the story from social studies and how that had carried over to the end of the day. Each of the other girls added how they ended up in the fray, though Chloe left out the part about finding an anonymous note on her locker. She could share that with her girl friends, but she didn't want all the boys in the band to know.

"And then…Claire showed up?" Harmony said. "I'm not sure when that happened, but I'm still really glad she was there."

Claire shrugged. "I was just down the hall and heard a *lot* of angry voices. I was going to ignore it and go around, but then I heard Amber saying she was hurt. So I went and... Well, there was a lot happening."

"And she saved my flute's life!" Harmony exclaimed, cradling her flute close to herself like it was her baby.

Claire chuckled and ducked her head self-consciously. "Well, I think Amber's our MVP this week. You should have seen her stand her ground against Coach Trifano."

The boys all cringed, except for Corbie, who asked, "Who's Coach Trifano?"

"You don't...you don't know?" Trey asked incredulously. "She's the scariest teacher at school!"

Corbie looked from Trey to the others, who had turned towards him, his face going bright red. Hacks laughed out loud and then said, "You guys know Corbie doesn't go to BHS, right?"

"Oohhhh, that explains a lot," Marty said. "Coach Trifano is terrifying. You should be glad you won't randomly run into her while you're doing some *horrible* crime."

"Like chewing gum with your mouth open," Bryan said, totally serious.

"Or tapping your foot while listening to music, by yourself, in an empty hallway," D-rock added, shaking his head.

"Or having a huge fight and blockading the entire hallway," Amber said.

"When you say it like that, it sounds like a legit reason for her to be mad for once," Chloe said with a little giggle.

"I think I get it now," Corbie said, nodding.

"In any case," Meg said, giving Amber a soft smile. "Since Amber is our superstar, I think she should get to decide what the band does next."

Amber tilted her head, her heart warming at how...loving everyone was being towards her. Tapping her lips, she said, "Oh, I know what we're gonna do." She paused dramatically. "We're gonna name the band."

"Little Hackers!" Hacks called from the piano.

"Anything but that," Amber said without even thinking about it.

The others started calling out suggestions, most of them involving a band member's name. Amber laughed good-naturedly at those, recognizing that most of them wouldn't encompass what their band was all about. No, not even Rach and Her Little Beanstalks, the Winning Losers, or D-rock's Rockers. When the suggestions started bordering on ridiculous, Amber laughed and held up her hand, trying to get them to quiet down.

Finally, when there was a lull, Meg said softly, "How about Less than Perfect?"

It was the first one Amber didn't think was horrible. And judging by how the others seemed to be considering it, they maybe liked it, too.

But Trey's brow furrowed as he said, "What?"

"You said it yourself, Trey," Meg said. "We're a little less than perfect."

"No," he said in a low voice, recalling their conversation. "I said *I'm* less than perfect."

"And the rest of us are what, exactly?" Meg asked. She looked around at the others. "I mean, no offense. You guys are all amazing, but no one's perfect."

"I like it!" Amber exclaimed. "Who else does? Let's vote."

One by one, they put their hands up, starting with Meg and ending, reluctantly, with Trey. He smiled at them.

"Alright, Less than Perfect it is," he said.

"Now that that's settled, let's play something quickly before I have to kick you out," Max said, his voice tinged with impatience.

While the girls finally got their instruments ready, Chloe asked him, "Why don't you just tell your parents about us?"

He watched her pluck her strings and carefully turn the tuning pegs to the right positions, wondering how she could do that effectively with the noise of the others playing. "I tried that already. They weren't exactly thrilled. So, if you want to keep practising here—and keep me in the band—then please just follow my rules."

She leaned in and said in a quiet voice, "And I guess I shouldn't tell anyone that you let me wander your house before our practices?"

"Absolutely not," he answered in the same tone.

She gave him a smug smile but didn't answer as they got ready to play.

While the others warmed up, Trey asked Meg if she could show him that warmup she'd done with him before. She gladly obliged, happy that Trey remembered it better than she expected.

"You know," she said, "I have a whole sheet full of warmup exercises. I pretty much have them memorized if you want my copy of it?"

His whole face lit up, making the butterflies in her stomach come alive. "Really? Thank you, that'd be awesome."

"Yeah, it's no problem," she said.

Marty, having waited long enough for his band members, tapped a beat on his drum set, starting off with something strong before melding into a beat that more or less matched "Secrets." Once he had their attention, he stopped and pointed at D-rock and Claire with his sticks.

They played the piece only once through before Max jumped up, glaring at his watch. "Okay, seriously, everyone pack up quickly. Let's go!"

Everyone dove into action, putting their instruments away as quickly as possible and rushing up the stairs. Whether it was the urgency in his voice that made them do it, he didn't know. But he was grateful when the drum set was covered and the last member had left. Less than Perfect. That they were.

♪　♫　♪

As soon as Amber and Bryan got home, Amber went in search of a pair of scissors. Bryan followed her to the kitchen where she found some old scissors in the junk drawer. She slipped them under the bracelet that Stacey had so desperately tried to take from her. Closing her eyes, she snipped. Or at least she tried to, but the scissors were too dull.

"Bryan, do this," she said in a sad voice.

"Do what?" he asked, looking over at her. His eyes widened. "Are you sure?"

She nodded, blinking back her tears.

"But…you've been friends with Stacey forever," Bryan said slowly, even as he took the scissors.

"And I've been ignoring how horrible she is for a long time," Amber said. "Cut it."

"You're sure?" he asked one more time.

"Yes."

"Okay…"

It took a lot of sawing and several snips, but he managed to break through the woven strings, and with one final cut she was free. The bracelet broke away from her red skin, feeling like a shackle falling off her. She wiped away the one tear that had dared to break through her barrier.

"Thanks," she whispered.

Not knowing what to do, he patted her on the back, giving her a sympathetic frown. She sniffled, put the bracelet in her pocket, and moved on. She didn't need Stacey. She had new friends.

♪ ♫ ♪

Meg woke the next morning feeling pretty proud of herself. The other girls didn't know, but she'd gotten an extra day of detention by talking to Coach Trifano to try to convince her that Amber had done nothing wrong, and that Stacey was the one who should be punished. Trifano told her she should have said something in the first place and that it was too late to change her mind. And then she'd added a day of punishment because Meg was too "worked up" over it.

But Meg didn't mind. She knew she'd done the right thing and she would gladly take one for the team if it meant she had finally spoken up for once in her life.

Just before she left the house, she picked up her sheet of trumpet warmups, carefully slipping it into her backpack. Maybe Trey didn't care about the condition of his music, but she did. Hopefully he would keep this one safe. She also hoped he'd be able to use it at home. Though she wouldn't mind if he had to come over again just to practice.

She headed straight to his locker as soon as she got to school. Smiling, she rounded the corner and then stopped abruptly. There at the end of the hall was Trey…with Lacy. He was leaning back against the lockers. She had her hands threaded through his hair and her lips tightly locked on his.

Meg only watched for a second before whirling back around, her heart breaking. Why had he gone through the trouble of telling her that whole story only to take back his cheating girlfriend? And how foolish had Meg been to think he was different, that he cared about more than a pretty face?

Walking woodenly down the hall, she broke her own rule and crumpled up the music in her hand. Then she shoved it into her backpack and went to class. She might not have needed the music anymore, but she wasn't going to give it away to Trey, either.

In fact, she was tired of giving anything to Trey. Her time, her attention, her affection. And certainly not these tears falling down her face. She wiped them away before walking into the classroom. No one needed to know that she was crying over Trey, of all people. There were probably many other girls who had done the same and she wouldn't be joining their ranks.

Even if he was kind of sweet, and a good listener, and a great trumpet player.

Sighing, she looked inside her backpack at the sad crumpled-up music. How was she supposed to play next to him now? And would Less than Perfect miss her if she just…didn't show up next week?

She blinked back more tears. They wouldn't miss her as much as she would miss them.

Less than Perfect Friendships

Book 2

Chapter One

They were only one month into the school year and TK was ready to throw his math workbook across his bedroom. Or rip it to shreds and then feed those shreds to the ducks that lived by the river.

"Mom has a shredder," he muttered to himself. "That'll do it."

He went down to the kitchen, where she kept her paper shredder. The kitchen table was her unofficial home office space, and he usually steered clear so he wouldn't be in her way. He had just located the shredder under the table and was seriously considering tossing the workbook into it when he heard footsteps behind him.

"What are you doing, Terrence?" his mom asked.

He froze. Sighing, he turned and gave her one of his specially reserved mom smiles. "Nothing. Just looking for...*you*. Because I love you."

He went to give her a hug, but she stepped back, lifting an eyebrow and staring at the workbook. "So, you...weren't going to put your homework in the shredder?"

"Mom." He forced a laugh that went on a little too long. "This? Why would I shred my math homework? I love math!"

"Mmhmm. Let me see that." She held her hand out and waited.

Reluctantly, he passed her the book. She flipped through the first few pages, each of which had a failing grade written on it. He scratched the back of his neck as she kept flipping back and forth, looking over his work.

Finally, she closed the book and said, "Go get your sax."

"Mom, no, please," he said, putting his hands together in prayer. "Please, *anything* but that. Take my phone or my Switch. Just not—"

"I'm not going to do anything to it," she said calmly. "It was expensive. I'm just going to hold on to it until you bring these grades up."

"Mom…" he said weakly, giving her sad eyes.

"No, TK." She shook her head. "Go and get it."

He sighed and walked away, trying not to stomp and give her the satisfaction of knowing how much it bothered him. How could she take away the one thing he loved more than anything in the world, the thing he was best at? All because math wasn't his strongest subject? It was so unfair.

As he took the mouthpiece and neck off the sax, he thought about how he was supposed to tell his new band he wouldn't be coming back—ever. Less than Perfect, as they'd named themselves, was his haven and now he couldn't even have that. Though it was doubtful they'd miss him as much as he would miss them, he dreaded telling them they were out their only sax player.

Claire and D-rock, who had taken it upon themselves to write arrangements for Less than Perfect, would be the most disappointed, he was sure. But not more disappointed than he was. Harmony, their flute player, would probably not miss him, since he seemed to be too energetic for her. Some of the guys might miss him. Like Trey and Bryan. Maybe even Marty. None of the girls would miss him, but that was *just* fine. He didn't have time for girls anyway right now. He was busy trying to pass his classes and pick universities.

Once his sax was safely tucked into its case, he brought it downstairs and had to force himself not to throw it at his mom's feet. No matter how mad he was, he wasn't going to damage his sax.

"Thank you," his mom said. He almost turned but then she put a hand on his wrist. "Now let's look at your math."

He bit back a sigh and sat at the table with her. She opened up the next page in his workbook and asked him what he thought. Personally, he thought algebra was the worst and whoever had invented math that involved numbers and letters must have been a monster. But that wouldn't help him get his sax back.

"I don't know," he said plaintively.

"Just try," she said gently.

Frustration welled up inside him. His mom was a real estate agent, and his dad was an accountant. Might have been nice to inherit the intelligence it took to do either job, but since that was a virtual impossibility, he was stuck sucking at math.

"Maybe if I'd gotten smart genes from you," he said sadly. "Then I wouldn't be so bad at everything."

"Stop that," she chided, running her hands through her greying hair. "You know I won't allow you to talk about anyone in this house like that, including yourself."

He mumbled something unintelligible after which she put a gentle hand on his cheek. He frowned but leaned into her hand anyway. Being adopted as a baby had never bothered him and his parents loved him as much as they loved their biological son. In fact...maybe they loved him too much because sometimes he felt like he couldn't escape his mother's hovering.

"You're not bad at everything. In fact, you know you're good at a lot of things. And you're not bad at math," she added before he could say it.

"You're just having a mental block."

"Some mental block," he muttered. This was nothing new. He had always struggled with math.

"We'll figure this out," she said.

He peeked up at her and asked timidly, "And when do I get my sax back?"

"When you get a better grade on your next test," she said.

"But, Mom, our next test is over a week away," he said, his heart sinking.

"Lots of time to study, then!" she said cheerfully.

"Yeah, but what about Less than Perfect?" he asked. She furrowed her eyebrows in response. "My band? What about our meeting on Tuesday? What, am I supposed to go without my instrument?"

"Um, you won't be going at all," she said, her eyes wide like she couldn't believe he would even suggest that. "Not unless someone in the band is going to help you with your math."

"So, wait, if I can get someone in the band to help me, you'll let me go back?" he asked, his heart lifting with hope.

"Sure," she said, shrugging lightly. "As long as your grades stay high enough for you to graduate and get into university, you can do whatever you want with your sax and that band."

He stuck his hand out. "Deal?"

She half rolled her eyes but smiled and put her hand in his. "Deal. But get on it, please. By the way, the shredder's broken and has been for weeks."

"Well, I don't need it anymore anyway," TK said cheekily, taking his workbook back from her.

He gave his sax one last longing glance, silently promising they would be reunited soon.

♪　　♫　　♪

Chloe should have been happy to hang out with her friends today. They were, after all, her best friends. Best friends who had gone to a concert over the weekend and hadn't even invited her, but best friends, nonetheless.

"Chloe, remember the drummer dropped his stick?" Dylan said.

"Yeah, and he kept drumming with one hand for a while?" Ashley added. "That was so funny! But he was awesome."

Chloe nodded, trying not to snap at them. "I actually don't remember that. Since I wasn't there. Remember?"

"Oh, sorry," Sydney said, at least having the decency to look like she felt bad. "I forgot you didn't come."

"I didn't not come," Chloe said quietly, staring at her lunch. "You guys didn't invite me."

"Sorry," Sydney repeated.

"Like your mom would have let you come," Dylan added derisively. "When was the last time she let you do anything?"

Chloe huffed but didn't answer. The last time she'd asked her mom for something was a ride to Max's house so she could play with her band. She'd never really asked about the band, but her mom didn't mind. Then again, since it was free—unlike membership with the Bridgetown Youth Orchestra—it was no problem.

"We'll remember to ask you next time, Chloe," Jaden said in his soft, low voice. He pushed the dark hair out of his face and smiled at her. She smiled back because it was Jaden, after all. "Anyway, guys, who's coming to the beach cleanup next weekend? You get hours."

While the others mumbled answers that definitely didn't sound like they liked that idea, Chloe said, "You know I'll be there."

"Thank you," he said with another smile.

Her heart warmed up. So, she didn't get to see the concert with them, but at least Jaden was still the nicest and most beautiful boy she'd ever met. She watched him out of the corner of her eye. They'd gone back to talking about the concert and he was animatedly reliving some part of it. It was a nice look on him, but she was still too salty to enjoy it.

After school, Chloe headed to the library to do research for her history essay. She probably could have checked out the books she needed and brought them home. But cramped into a two-bedroom apartment with her mom and June, it was hard to concentrate sometimes. Especially when June was constantly asking questions.

She loved her little sister, but June's inquisitiveness had no bounds. Chloe was never like that when she was nine. Maybe she had *some* questions, but June's inquiries always had follow-up questions. It was exhausting.

After referencing several books, taking notes, and starting an outline, Chloe realized she'd spent an hour at the library—and that was long enough for her. She took two of the books she knew she would need and finally left.

Just as she reached the front doors of the school, she saw Meg. "Hey, you're still here, too," Chloe said, opening the door for both of them. "Are you also researching for a boring essay?"

"No," Meg said quietly. "I was in detention."

"What?" Chloe said, confused. "But we did our time."

"Yeah." Meg sighed. "I got an extra day for overexplaining the situation."

Chloe rolled her eyes. The girls in the band had gotten into a fight with Amber's friends—former friends?—and when they'd been caught by a scary coach, they had all taken the blame. But honestly, Amber's friends were being terrible and it had started to get physical. It was a good thing Coach Trifano had found them when she did, but she'd also given them two days of detention while Amber's friends got off scot-free.

"Oh, Trifano," Chloe said. She pulled her jacket closer around herself. It was early October and the air had already started cooling off. "I appreciate that you tried, though."

"Yeah," Meg said quietly.

"Are you okay?" Chloe asked.

Meg nodded and said quickly, "Everything's fine. See you later, Chloe."

Chloe watched her walk away. Meg had always been reserved around other people, but this was strange. Yesterday, she'd been as happy as the rest of the girls to brag to the guys in the band about getting detention. Now she looked sad. But Chloe knew if she pressed, Meg would retreat further into her shell.

By the time Chloe got home, the sun was starting to set. She loved autumn but having such short daylight hours wasn't the best part of it. *And* one of the lights was out in the stairwell of her apartment building, making it extra spooky in there. Now she had to walk up all five flights in semi-darkness.

But at least she had her violin. It was always waiting for her on its stand when she got home. And it always greeted her happily whenever she set her bow to it. She burst into the bedroom she shared with June and went straight to her violin. Except…where was the bow?

She looked around, wondering if maybe she'd accidentally left it on her bed this morning after she'd practiced. But it wasn't there and it wasn't on June's bed, and it didn't seem to be anywhere in their room.

She went out to the living room, where June and her mom were sitting together. "June…" she said nicely. "Have you seen my bow?"

"No," June answered quickly.

"Okay, well, I always leave it on the stand with the violin," Chloe answered patiently. "And it's not there now. Did you touch it?"

"No." This time, June shook her head adamantly.

"I won't be mad if you did," Chloe said. "I just want it back so I can play."

"I didn't touch it!" June exclaimed.

"June—"

"Chloe," their mother finally cut in. Her eyes held a warning in them. "She says she didn't touch it."

"Okay, then," Chloe said. "So, where did *you* put it, Mom?"

Her mom looked up with startled eyes. "Me?"

"Yeah, if June didn't touch it, as she's claimed several times, and I was at school studying, then it must have been you," Chloe said. She tried to tamp down her attitude, but this was her bow they were talking about. She couldn't play without it!

"Chloe, be reasonable," her mom said with a hint of irritation. "You must have misplaced it. Just look again for it."

"I'll help you look in our room if you want," June said sweetly, standing up.

"Or you could just tell me where it is, June, and then we don't have to waste time," Chloe said.

"I don't *know* where it is," June said, stomping her foot.

"Chloe!" her mom shouted. "Stop bothering your sister."

Chloe turned to her mom. "How am I supposed to practice without a bow? What am I supposed to do next Tuesday night?"

Her mom scoffed. "You won't be going. You're grounded."

"For what?" Chloe yelped.

"For accusing your sister without any evidence," her mom said.

June huffed and crossed her arms, looking vaguely smug. So, that was it. Chloe was outnumbered and she still didn't have a bow.

"Fine," Chloe gritted through her teeth.

She went back to her room and thoroughly tore it apart, her side and

June's. She was already in trouble; would making a huge mess really make that much of a difference? It didn't matter anyway—the bow was nowhere to be found. She slumped onto her bed and stared longingly at her violin.

Chapter Two

Trey slid into his seat in homeroom and immediately put his backpack on the chair next to him. A few people longingly glanced at the chair as they came in, but he refused to move it. Not until he saw Meg.

When she walked in, he moved the backpack and nodded at the seat for her. For some reason, though, she looked around the classroom. However, the bell was about to ring, and all the other seats had already been taken. Sighing, she sat, but didn't greet him.

"Hey," he said quietly, leaning towards her.

She looked up briefly and then got her books out of her backpack.

Ignoring her avoidance of him, he asked, "Can I come over again this weekend?"

"It's not a good time," she whispered.

Furrowing his brow, he leaned even closer so he could hear her above the noise their classmates were making. "Sometime next week, then?"

"I'll see."

His shoulders slumping, he wondered what the sudden change in her attitude was all about. Last week, he had come over to her house and she'd shown him a great warmup for his trumpet and played through his part in "Secrets" with him. Not only that, but he'd felt comfortable enough to tell her everything about Chad and Lacy.

"I really like playing with you," he said after a moment.

Finally, she looked at him, sadness in her eyes. "Me, too," she admitted quietly.

The bell rang, and she went back to arranging her books unnecessarily while he wondered what, if anything, he'd done wrong.

After class, Meg rushed out like her life depended on it. So he guessed she was done talking to him. Confused, he went to his locker to get his gym bag. When he felt a hand on his arm, he turned, hoping it might be Meg, and then jumped back a foot. Lacy. Hopefully she wasn't going to try to kiss him again, because... He shuddered just thinking about it.

"Trey," she said, laughing off his reaction. "What's the big deal? I barely touched you."

"Can we keep it to no touching?" he said.

She put one hand on her hip. "You're *still* being like this? Come on. I'm your girlfriend."

Trey bit his lip, resisting the temptation to yell at her like he wanted to. "You're *not* my girlfriend. We broke up. Actually, *you* broke up with *me*. For Chad."

Finally, because he needed things from his locker, he went back over to it, gently nudging her out of the way with his body. She didn't take the hint and sidled up closer to him.

"You're really going to take Chad's word over mine?" she asked, running a hand up and down his arm.

He pulled his arm away under the guise of needing to use it to get his gym bag. "Chad's a lot of things, but he's not a liar." He looked down at her. "And you've lied to me before."

"About what?" she said lightly.

So many things. The time she said she couldn't do something with him because of period pain, but later he saw pictures of her partying with her friends. All the excuses she gave for games that she'd missed and he'd accepted them all, but the one time he couldn't go to her family's BBQ, she got mad at him. The time he saw her with Duncan, and it felt very suspicious, but she said nothing happened.

Looking back, he couldn't believe he'd ever found her attractive. Yeah, she had flawless makeup, and her hair was dark and shiny and always perfectly wavy. And she always knew how to shut him up one lovely kiss at a time. But now that he thought about it, she seemed to do that a lot and never really wanted to hear what he had to say.

"Lacy, please stop doing this," he said in his nice voice. "It's over between me and you and I don't want to get back together. I thought you were cool with that."

"I was," she said, pouting at him. "At first. But...seeing you again at school...with all these girls that are in love with you, I realized I gave up too much."

Trey frowned and tried to think of a single girl who had declared her love for him since school had started. He didn't think anyone had come remotely close to that. He pulled his gym bag out of his locker and put his backpack in.

"I'm really not sure what you're talking about," he said, closing his locker soundly. "But we're over, okay? Please don't ambush me anymore."

She scowled just before he turned around. What was wrong with the girls in this school? Why couldn't any of them act normal?

♪　♫　♪

After carrying around the specially woven rainbow-coloured camp friendship bracelet that Stacey had made her four years ago for days, Amber was finally ready to give it back. Stacey had tried to rip it off Amber's wrist, nearly taking her skin with it, and landing Amber and the rest of the girls from Less than Perfect in detention. The least Amber could do was return the oh-so-precious heirloom.

It was bad enough Amber had received an F for interrupting her own social studies presentation to call Stacey out on her bullying towards Rach. But now she had to see her old crew every day in class and they had turned their bullying towards her.

By Friday, she'd gathered enough courage to confront Stacey at lunchtime. But her bravado drained away the closer she got to their lunch table. One by one, each of her old friends turned to glare at her. Swallowing hard, she forced her feet to move.

"What do *you* want?" Yuri spit out.

Amber ignored her and locked eyes with Stacey. "I just came over here to give this back."

As she held out the bracelet, Stacey's eyes widened and her jaw went slack. Hurt crossed her eyes momentarily before she gritted her teeth and glared up at Amber.

"Seriously?" Stacey said in a low, raw voice. "You're going to choose that freak—*all* those freaks—over *me?*"

"I wish I didn't have to," Amber said, trying to keep her voice level. "But you left me no choice. All you had to do was just…stop being mean to someone who's never said a bad word about any of you."

"Oh, please," Stacey said, rolling her eyes spectacularly. "Like Rachel is oppressed or something. Give me a break."

"Oh, yeah," Fiona said, her mouth twisting up sarcastically. "Look at me! I'm so tall, and I have thick hair, and all the boys are looking at me and my booty. *Poor Rach.*"

"You guys are…*jealous* of her?" Amber asked incredulously. "Are you serious right now? You're mean to her because of *that?*"

Stacey huffed. "You're not hearing us. We're not mean to her."

"You call her skyscraper," Amber reminded them.

"Well, compared to the rest of us bungalows…" Yuri sniggered.

Amber shook her head, pursing her lips at the audacity. "Yeah, okay, try telling *her* that the way you guys bully her isn't mean." She tossed the bracelet on the table in front of Stacey and turned on her heel.

Across the cafeteria, she found Rach and Meg watching her openly. Rach waved and Amber didn't have to think twice before joining them. She plopped down in the empty chair. Meg seemed as down as she felt, but she didn't make mention of it.

"So, you got rid of it?" Rach said, gesturing to Amber's wrist.

Amber rubbed her bare wrist. "Yeah… I feel naked now."

"Here," Rach said, flicking a lightly used napkin at her. "You can wrap this around your wrist and think of me every time you wipe your mouth with it. Function and beauty!"

Amber laughed and flicked the napkin back at her. "You're hilarious, Rach. I'm sorry I spent so long ignoring you just because my friends didn't like you."

"Not gonna lie," Rach said, "being ignored is better than being made fun of."

Meg grunted and Amber turned towards her.

"You okay, Meg?" she asked nicely.

"Yeah, I'm fine," Meg answered tersely.

"Meg…" Rach said in a calm, somewhat motherly voice. "Tell her the truth."

"I can keep a secret," Amber said eagerly.

Meg sighed excessively. "On Saturday, Trey came over to practice with me."

"Ooh," Amber said, her eyes lighting up. Rach elbowed her and she clamped her mouth shut.

"While he was there, he told me that Lacy cheated on him with Chad over the summer," Meg continued, ignoring Amber's ribbing. "That's why he got into that huge fight with Chad a few weeks ago. And also…because Chad wouldn't stop throwing himself at me."

Amber's face scrunched up. "*Ew.*"

"Yeah," Meg said, her eyes flashing with disdain. "Anyway…I saw Trey and Lacy making out on Wednesday. So I guess everything he told me was just…" She shrugged and looked away.

"Oh, Meg," Amber said in a sweet way.

"Please, don't 'oh, Meg' me," Meg said, her hazel eyes flashing with irritation. "It's not the way it sounds."

Rach and Amber exchanged a look and Rach asked, "It's not?"

"I don't like him," Meg said, though her voice came out uncertain. "I just thought he was better than that. And now it feels kind of like he lied to me."

Rach and Amber were silent for a moment. Rach chewed on her lip, not knowing what to say. She elbowed Amber, and then nodded to Meg.

"That does seem pretty terrible," Amber said softly. "I can understand why that would bother you. Even if you don't…like him."

"Which I don't," Meg said quickly.

"Right!" Amber said. "Exactly."

"You don't believe me," Meg said flatly.

"Of course I do." Amber smiled. "And I believe you when you say that doesn't seem like the type of thing Trey would do."

"But if it is, you're totally better off without him," Rach said.

Meg couldn't help chuckling. "Stop. I'm not into him."

Amber and Rach shared one more secretive glance while Meg looked around the cafeteria, almost certainly not looking for Trey. Amber's heart warmed. It felt good to be part of a group of girls who were nice and who got her.

♪   ♫   ♪

Corbie leaned on his hand while his French teacher went on about the book they were reading in class. He knew if he paid a little more attention, he would be better able to understand her. But truthfully, it was all Greek to him. Or French. Or any other language.

He wondered what the others from Less than Perfect were doing right now. Sure, they'd be in class. But they probably got to share classes together, and then eat lunch together. And then they would all walk home together, and it just sounded so nice.

Most of his friends had gone to BHS after graduating from grade eight. Now he was left with acquaintances, ones who were nice enough but weren't close to him. And certainly no one who understood his love of music.

It was bad enough he couldn't make it into the school band because there were already enough trombones, and they were all upper years. Joining Less than Perfect had been a godsend. And at least he knew Hacks from church, but there were so many rules surrounding his friendship that it almost didn't feel like it was worth it. Almost.

The longer he sat in French class, the cloudier his brain got. In fact, his throat was starting to hurt, too. Now that he thought about it, he didn't feel so good. But the school day was almost over and it was Friday.

By Saturday morning, Corbie had developed a full-blown fever. As he lay in bed, practically dying, his foggy thoughts were focused on his one true love: his trombone. He would have loved to play it one last time...

"Corbie, stop being so dramatic," his mom said. "You have a sinus infection and you're taking antibiotics."

157

"Did I say all that out loud?" he mumbled, feeling like there was cotton in his mouth.

"Yes," she said, laughing a little. She ruffled his hair and then checked his sweating forehead. "Don't worry, the doctor says you'll live to play your horn another day."

"Oh."

"Get some sleep, kiddo," she said as she stood up from his bed, where he lay...practically dying. "You're not dying. You're just staying home for a few days. Relax, it'll help you heal."

"Okay," he said.

As she left his room, she turned off the light and shut his door. Corbie's last thought before he slipped back into sleep was to let his precious band know that regrettably he would not be joining them anytime soon.

Chapter Three

TK didn't have any classes with Hacks, since Hacks had chosen the highest-level stream there was. In fact, TK was pretty sure Hacks had already been enrolled in a university course while TK was…failing basic math. This was so embarrassing.

During his free period, TK messaged Hacks, asking where he was. The answer: the computer lab. He should have guessed. Hacks was, after all, half computer. TK headed up to the second floor, where the library extended into the computer lab.

He burst the door open and said, "Hey, nerds!" Half of the students turned to him with glares. The others had headphones and likely hadn't even heard him. "Sorry," he whispered. "I meant that in a nice way."

They went back to their work, some of them still giving him lingering, uncharitable glances. Hacks rose from his station and came over with a confused look on his face.

"TK, what are you…doing here?" he asked quietly.

"I need a math tutor," TK said under his breath.

"Oh!" Hacks turned and looked at his companions. "Well, I could recommend…Sara? She would definitely say yes to you."

TK looked straight into Hacks's eyes. "I was hoping you'd do it."

"Oh…no," Hacks said. He reached up to readjust his glasses, a little frown appearing between his eyebrows. "I can't. You know how they say 'those who can't do, teach?' Yeah, I'm the opposite. I'm a terrible tutor."

"Please, buddy," TK said, lifting his hands in a praying gesture.

"Why me?" Hacks asked. "I could just get someone else—"

"No," TK said, glancing quickly at the others in their own little worlds. "They wouldn't understand. I don't need to be amazing at it, I just need a passing grade or my mom won't give me my sax back."

Hacks tilted his head, giving him a sympathetic look. "She took your sax away?"

"Yes," TK said emphatically. "I know you'll never know what it's like to have your piano taken away for poor grades, but you could imagine, right?"

Hacks shrugged. "Well, it is awfully difficult to remove a piano on a whim." TK sighed at him. "But you're right. Yes, that would be terrible. I…I'll do it. Or I'll try."

"Yeah?" TK said, his face breaking into a wide grin.

"Yeah, but don't say I didn't warn you," Hacks said, putting his hands up. "I really am a terrible tutor."

TK clapped him on the shoulder. "I have faith in you."

"Show me your homework," Hacks said. "We'll start right now."

"Um…" TK didn't even have his backpack. He patted his empty pockets. "I don't just carry math around with me."

Hacks gave him half an eye roll, like this wasn't even worth a full one. "Who doesn't— Never mind. We'll start after school."

"That feels too soon," TK said, already stressing out just thinking about it.

"Do you want your sax back or not?" Hacks asked firmly.

"Yes, I do," TK said hastily. "Okay, after school. Thank you so much."

Hacks just shook his head and went back to his computer station. But nothing could take away the hope in TK's heart.

Nothing except actually sitting down with Hacks and trying to do the homework. True to his word, Hacks was short and impatient with TK. And TK felt even dumber when each of Hacks's explanations went over his head.

They sat in the school library together, trying their hardest not to make too much noise as they argued back and forth over whether TK was the dumbest student at the school. Of course, Hacks said he wasn't, but that didn't stop TK from feeling like it.

"Okay…" Hacks shoved the textbook and workbook aside, grabbed a blank piece of paper, and wrote on it. "Solve for x."

TK stared at it. $4x + 7 = 2x + 1$. He shook his head. There was no way. "I don't even know where to start."

Hacks passed him a pencil, folded his hands on the table, and said, "It's very simple."

"Then, can you explain it like I'm a five-year-old?" TK asked.

Hacks put his hands up and scoffed. "A five-year-old wouldn't be able to grasp this concept because they don't have the necessary mathematical foundations to—" He cut himself off and looked at the equation he thought was so easy to solve. "Oh, I see what's happening here. You don't have the mathematical foundations to solve this equation."

"I guess not," TK said in frustration.

Hacks took the pencil again and said, "I'm gonna give you the answer—"

"How is *that* supposed to help?"

Hacks held up a hand. "I'll tell you what it is, then show you how to reduce the equation on both sides. You'll get it, trust me."

Hacks rewrote the equation, replacing the x with a -3. Then he had TK solve each side of the equation so that he had $-5 = -5$. That was the easy part.

"So now, when we put the x back in..." Hacks went through the equation again, *slowly*, while TK watched in silence. "Does this make more sense to you?"

"Sort of?" TK said, feeling slightly less overwhelmed.

Suppressing a sigh, Hacks wrote a new but similar equation. "Here, try this one."

While TK worked through the problem, Hacks had to force himself not to jump in every time he thought TK might make a mistake. There was a reason he said he was terrible at teaching and it was because he had little patience for watching people fail over and over. But for TK, he could try.

And when TK managed to do the whole thing by himself *and* get the right answer, Hacks was almost surprised. He shouldn't have been though, since he'd just shown him how to do it.

"That's great!" Hacks said. "Let's move on to another one."

They spent another half hour together, Hacks pulling apart every explanation and TK painstakingly and slowly solving the equations. He didn't always get them right but he did try, at least.

When it was time for them to go, Hacks said, "I'm sorry I won't see you tomorrow night. But we'll get there soon."

TK nodded, looking sad. "Please don't tell anyone in the band."

Hacks smiled. He knew a thing or two about having secrets and keeping them. Nodding, he said goodbye and left.

♪　　♫　　♪

Why did Amber and Bryan always have to be so late for Less than Perfect? Admittedly, one time was her fault because she'd needed to regrease the cork on her clarinet. But she hadn't expected it to take so long.

Tonight, Bryan had decided to restring his guitar. While she waited impatiently by his open bedroom door, tapping her foot at him.

"Standing there isn't going to make me go faster," Bryan said.

"Well, are you almost done?" she asked.

"I'm on the fourth one," he said.

She grunted but didn't move from her spot until he was finally done with his restringing. When he started tuning them, she let out a long groan.

"Bryan, let's *go*," she said. "Tune at Max's."

"Alright, alright," he said, finally getting up.

Quickly he packed up his guitar and they went out to his car. He drove a little too fast for Amber's liking, but that was just what it was like when they were always dragging their feet about stuff.

At Max's house, they didn't even bother with the doorbell, opting instead to just let themselves in. Amber rushed downstairs followed closely by Bryan. She was happy to be back again with friends that cared about her and the things she liked. But she stopped abruptly when she noticed several empty seats.

"Hey, we're not the last ones today," Bryan said sarcastically.

"Um, where's the band?" Amber asked as she headed to her seat.

Max shrugged and gestured to Chloe's seat with his violin bow as if he didn't know what to do without her. TK's chair was empty but at least Harmony was there with her flute. Corbie had so thoughtfully messaged the group chat earlier to let everyone know that he was "so sick he couldn't even bone," to which TK had promptly told him to never say that again. So, that explained where Corbie was though TK had never given an explanation for himself.

Meg's seat was empty. Amber looked back at Rach, who shrugged and then glanced very quickly at Trey. Amber wouldn't go there. It was unlikely he knew how Meg was feeling or that he was probably the reason she'd ditched tonight.

"Well, what are we supposed to do without Marty?" Amber asked, waving her hand loosely in the direction of the drum set that was still covered with a sheet. "He's our rhythm."

"What do I look like to you?" Bryan complained as he tuned his guitar.

"Sorry," she whispered.

"Regardless, I think this is going to be it for tonight, so can we please hurry it along?" Max said in his anxious my-parents-will-be-home-soon voice.

Though the others didn't know why Max couldn't just tell his parents they'd been using the basement of his mansion for their meetings, they respected Max's wish to stick to his time constraints. None of them wanted to risk losing the space or getting him in trouble with his parents.

"Well, Claire and I were going to ask you guys if you wanted to go over some of the *many* songs you suggested," D-rock said. He had his double bass out already, standing next to him, though he had yet to set his bow to it. "Maybe help us figure out what you envisioned for them."

"Although with half the band missing…" Claire said. She ran her hand up and down the neck of her cello.

"It's less than half," Hacks spoke up from the piano. She gave him the side eye and he shrunk a bit into himself. "Semantics… Got it."

"*Anyway,*" she continued. "With *just over half* of us here, it'll be awkward. But if you guys want…"

"Yeah, I want to see," Amber said excitedly, ditching her half-put-together clarinet.

"Me, too," Harmony said.

They both went over to Claire, who had some notes written out. Max made a little impatient sound and set his violin down, figuring they weren't going to get any actual playing time tonight. But he went over with the others and soon enough, everyone was crowded around Claire and D-rock.

"This is too much," Hacks said as he looked through the songs in vastly different genres.

"I know," D-rock said. "It's a lot. I love all of these. I wish I could do them all with you guys."

"When would we even have time to learn them all?" Max asked. "There are at least...fifty? Is that right?"

"That's why we need your help," D-rock said.

"Yeah, it would take us way too long to figure out arrangements for all of these *and* transcribe the music," Claire said. "We were thinking maybe we could focus on the songs that are already heavy on the instrumentation and then..."

"Some mashups?" D-rock said, bobbing his eyebrows at her.

She rolled her eyes. "I really prefer medley. We'll make some medleys."

"What kind of mashups?" Trey asked. "Like, similar songs or...how would that work?"

"The *medley*," Claire said, "could be anything. Whatever we think would work."

"Wait," Harmony said, letting out a giggle. "Did you actually write down 'Holding Out for a Hero'?"

Claire chuckled. "I laughed at your suggestion at first, but after listening to it about fifteen times in a row, I realized it has so much potential. Especially for our band."

D-rock cringed. "Yeah, we're still discussing that. As in, I'm still trying to change her mind."

"And you won't," Claire said confidently.

"I think it'd be so much fun," Harmony said.

"We have about fifteen minutes," Max said urgently. He went back to his seat and picked up his violin. "If you want to play something, we're doing it now."

He seemed crankier than normal which D-rock took in stride. "That's fine. We'll put these away and we can talk about them again next week and hope everyone will be here."

They went back to their instruments. Even with some of their friends missing, they played through the one arrangement they had—"Secrets" by OneRepublic. It still sounded good, even if it was lacking some parts. But for Claire, it was disappointing. It hadn't occurred to her what it would be like if they weren't always together. She hoped the others would be back next week.

Max managed to kick everyone out of his house mere minutes before his dad came home. His mom came soon after. Neither of them seemed to notice anything amiss. And of course, why would they? Max didn't let any of the band members wander his house, and always made sure they left without delay. His parents never went into the basement, so they wouldn't notice the chairs set up specifically for a band of 14 kids, or the extra drum set Max didn't own that he covered with a sheet whenever Marty wasn't around.

He hated keeping all that from his parents. He had tried desperately to share his music with them. But since they didn't consider being a musician a valid means of making a living, they always brushed him off. Now he had to sneak around just to enjoy playing with other people. It was awful.

Chapter Four

With his headphones on, music blaring in his ears, sitting in an empty school hallway, it was easy for D-rock to tune out the rest of the world. It was also way easier to hear all the melodic lines in "Kings & Queens," the song he'd actually wanted to do before Claire suggested "Holding Out for a Hero." Then when she'd suggested a *medley*, he had almost immediately shot her down.

Discovering that both songs were in the same key and roughly the same beat hadn't helped his case. But the more he thought about it, the more he liked the idea of the songs together. Closing his eyes, he leaned his head back against his locker and let the music rush over him.

He could totally imagine Less than Perfect doing this song. There was so much he could do with the bass, plus the melodic lines had such a range it'd be easy to feature any of the woodwinds or brass. Even Bryan could have a more interesting line than they'd given him for "Secrets." Hacks might have to take a backseat, but if they mashed it together with "Holding Out for a Hero," then—

D-rock was pulled out of his thoughts when someone kicked his leg. He looked up into the glaring eyes of Ted and G. He hadn't said a single word to either of them since they'd ditched him with their vapes and let him take the fall for them a few short weeks ago.

D-rock jumped up and whipped around, not in mood to be tangled up with them again. One of them grabbed his arm while the other pulled the cordless headphones off his head. He had no choice but to stand and face them.

Snapping his headphones back from Ted's hand, he asked, "What do you guys want?"

"We want our vapes back," G said irritably.

"So, ask Stringer for them, Guy," D-rock said as he placed his headphones calmly and gently around his neck. "I'm sure she's got a million of them in her office."

G's dark eyes narrowed. "Don't *Guy* me, *Derek.*"

Ted put his hand out in front of G as if to hold him back. "Obviously, we want you to pay us back."

D-rock let out a short, humourless laugh. "Yeah, that's not gonna happen."

"You *owe* us," G said, taking a step closer to him.

D-rock refused to be intimidated. Could he hold his own in a fight like Trey? Definitely not, but he knew neither could Ted or G. He wasn't scared of them.

"I already paid the time for your crime," he said. "Two weeks of detention, remember? *And* I didn't even rat you guys out." He glanced quickly at Ted, who had always been slightly nicer to him than G. "So, get off my back now, alright?"

"No way," Ted said, though his voice came out feeble instead of tough. "Those were hard to get and it's been almost a month. We expected you to cover us."

D-rock raised his eyebrows. "Little tip, Ted. Don't leave your stuff with someone who doesn't care about your stuff."

G balled up his fist and reached out. But instead of hitting D-rock's flinching face, he knocked the expensive headphones off his neck. Then he stomped past D-rock, making sure to get one good shot at his headphones. D-rock cringed at the crunching sound.

Ted walked past, too, giving D-rock a lingering glance. He looked down at the ruined headphones but didn't walk on them as G had. Instead, he rushed to keep up with G, leaving D-rock alone and heartbroken.

The bell rang and with a heavy heart, D-rock crouched down towards his headphones. How did this always happen to him? First he'd gotten in trouble for his friends, not just at school, but major trouble with his mom. And he hadn't even touched their vapes. Then he'd lost his two best friends over it and now they were punishing him even more. Could he not just have something nice that didn't get ruined?

A pair of hands reached out and took the broken pieces of the headphones before he had the chance. He gave up. What did it matter if someone stole them now? They were useless.

"I could probably fix these."

D-rock looked up into Hacks's kind, bespectacled eyes. He scrunched up his face into a disbelieving frown and Hacks laughed.

"No, really," Hacks said, straightening. "I've seen way worse. Just leave them with me for a couple days."

"Okay," D-rock said like he still didn't believe him. "But if you're just going to slap some duct tape on them, then don't bother."

"*Please*," Hacks said, waving his hand dismissively. Carefully, he put the headphones into the front pocket of his backpack. "Trust me."

"Okay," D-rock repeated. He watched Hacks walk away, feeling, for once, like maybe everything wasn't terrible.

♪   ♫   ♪

After spending an entire week trying to figure Meg out and get her attention, Trey was nearly ready to give up. He'd always been told to let girls come to him—easy enough—and to not be pushy, and to give them time to cool off. So he tried to be friendly to her, but she just turned a cold shoulder to him. Either Meg didn't subscribe to those rules or he'd really messed up.

Finally when he couldn't handle it anymore, he threw the rules out the window and approached her directly. It was Friday afternoon, and he only had five minutes before he had to get to the field. But here he was, halfway across the school from the locker rooms at Meg's locker.

As soon as she saw him, she ducked her head.

"Hi," he said. She nodded. "Okay, what did I do wrong?"

"Fumble a pass?" she said quietly.

"*When?*" he nearly shouted. A tiny smile appeared on her lips. "Oh, you're joking. You haven't talked to me in over a week and now you're joking with me. You know what? Forget this. I've been trying so hard to be nice to you."

"Trey," she said just as he turned. "I'm not not talking to you."

He looked down, confused, and said, "So…you are talking to me?"

"Yeah, you want to talk?" she said, facing her locker again. "Let's talk. How are you? How's football? How's your…"

The last word was so mumbled and quiet that Trey couldn't even hear it. "My what?"

"Your girlfriend," she said in a stronger voice, still not looking at him.

He put up his hands, a gesture lost on her since her perfectly organized locker was so interesting to her. "Who?"

"Lacy," she said, a hint of frustration in her voice. She reached into her locker and moved a stack of textbooks from the right side to the left. "I saw

170

you guys kissing the other day."

"Oh." He grimaced just remembering it. "*Oh.* No. That wasn't... We weren't kissing."

"You weren't?" she asked nonchalantly.

"No, *she* was kissing *me*," he said. "And it was gross. She had her tongue shoved so far down—"

"*Trey.*" Finally, Meg looked at him, giving him a warning look before he gave her all the details.

"Sorry, you're right. TMI." He sighed and shoved a hand through his blond hair. "Is that why you're mad at me? Because you saw that?"

She shrugged but he could tell it was a forced gesture of indifference.

"Meg," he said softly. "Nothing's going on between us. Also, why should that make any difference to you?"

She swallowed hard and looked down at her shoes. "After what you told me...it felt like you had lied about it. I just thought you were better than that."

"Am I?" he asked.

She held his gaze for a moment, and he felt like she was staring into his soul.

"Yeah, you are." She shook her head. "And now that I know the truth, I feel kind of stupid for acting that way."

"It's okay," he said, though he was still confused over why she'd been so bothered by it as to stop talking to him. "But I meant what I said about her. And Chad. I don't want to be friends with either of them. Let alone..." He frowned. He had no desire for Lacy to force herself on him again.

"I'm sorry," she said. "I should have thought a little harder about it before getting so worked up."

He looked her up and down, a smile growing on his lips. "Is this you worked up? Because I could handle that." She laughed and he felt better knowing she didn't suddenly hate him. "But also, I really did mean it when I said I liked playing with you."

She nodded, chewing her lip.

"I gotta go," he said, as he started slowly walking backwards. "I'm late again. But I'll see you around."

"Come over tomorrow," she said quickly, her hazel eyes lighting up. "We'll practice some more."

He grinned, waved, and then jogged down the hall.

♪   ♫   ♪

Spending a Saturday morning cleaning a beach wasn't Max's ideal aesthetic. On the other hand, seeing the beach covered in garbage was even less his aesthetic. He'd been in a good mood when he signed up for the clean-up and it looked like there were several other people expected to come today, too. However, when he got to the beach, he only saw Jaden, who had organized the whole thing.

"Hey, dude," Jaden said cheerfully. Or as cheerful as Jaden could get with his sullen disposition.

"Hi…" Max looked around again. A breezy October morning meant there weren't a lot of people out. "Weren't there like fifteen people who signed up today?"

"Yeah," Jaden said. He ripped open a box of gloves and held it out for Max. "This is how it usually goes."

"I see." Max took some of the gloves and tried not to sigh. He'd been hoping for light work, but considering the condition of the beach and surrounding grassy area and the lack of volunteers, that would not be the case.

"Sorry," Jaden said with a shrug. He handed Max a black garbage bag. "Just do as much as you feel like."

"It's fine," Max said. He looked down the beach where the water crashed up against the retaining rock wall. "I'll start down there."

He worked for a few minutes, grabbing as many tiny little pieces of garbage he could find. Why it didn't occur to people to just use the provided garbage cans, Max would never know. He could see at least three from where he was standing. He also saw a very familiar figure.

Chloe.

She got out of her mom's car, waved goodbye, and then looked around. Her gaze lingered on Jaden, who had begun near the children's playground. Then she looked over to the beach, where she found Max. Staring at her. Lifting her hand in a greeting, she headed over to him.

"Hey, Chloe," Max said as soon as she was close enough.

"Max," she said with surprise. "What are you doing here?"

He held the bag up and then gestured to the beach.

"I just thought—" She cut herself off and pulled in her lips.

"That rich people don't clean beaches?" he said, his eyes dancing.

She smiled. "I figured they don't clean anything, let alone beaches. What if you break a nail?"

"Oh, then I'd have to cancel my modeling contract," he quipped.

Chloe stared at him for a moment, taking in the nice pants, the leather fall boots, the jacket that likely cost her entire year's allowance. His bright hazel eyes, reddening cheeks, stylish blond hair, and finally his lips, which...looked just like regular lips.

"That's a joke," he said, leaning down to pick up a straw wrapper. "I'm not that pretty."

"Hmm" was her only response.

"I need the hours just like you do," he said, ignoring whatever that sound was supposed to mean. "And I care about the beach."

"Me, too," she said, sounding genuine.

"Oh, so you're not just here for..." He nodded towards Jaden. "Edward Cullen?"

Chloe gave him an amused smile. Jaden had pale skin and dark hair and was, admittedly, wearing a sweatshirt with sequins on it that sparkled in the sunlight. "I'm here for my hours," she said diplomatically. "But the view isn't bad."

He leaned towards her and followed her line of sight. "You're staring at a garbage can."

She nudged him away with her elbow. "He was there a second ago."

She moved away a few feet to start cleaning. He watched her pick things up with her bare hands and then went over, shoving a pair of disposable gloves at her.

"Thanks," she mumbled.

"Mmhmm." He went back to his spot and then asked, "So, where were you on Tuesday? We missed you. Actually, a bunch of people didn't show up."

"Did they all lose their bows, too?" she asked miserably, even though it felt nice to be told someone missed her.

Max looked over at her, his face scrunched up. "How does one lose a bow?"

Chloe huffed. "One has a little sister that can't keep her hands to herself and a mother who believes her lies."

"You should have told me," Max said. "I have seven bows. You could have borrowed one of mine."

She shrugged, her face flushing. "It doesn't matter. My mom grounded me anyway for being mean to June."

"Well...if you're ungrounded by Tuesday, you can still have one of mine. *Borrow*," he corrected when he saw her opening her mouth to protest. "Until you find yours."

"I can't..." she said weakly.

"Yeah, you're right," he said, waving her off. "It'll be really awkward for me to play with only six bows. Forget I said anything."

She bit her lip and looked over at Jaden, who had moved on to the grassy knoll near the parking lot. Then she looked back at Max who was patiently waiting for her to come to her good senses. "Thank you," she said. "I appreciate that. Though I think my bow is probably gone forever."

Max shrugged. "I'll never be able to play as well as you with only six bows, but I'll do my best."

Chloe turned away as heat from his compliment warmed her cheeks. He was probably just saying it to be nice. There was no way he *actually* thought she was better than him, right?

She glanced back at him. It was hard to tell with the way he was scowling at a napkin that kept blowing in the wind just out of his reach every time he tried to pick it up.

Finally, he snagged the napkin and lifted an eyebrow at her. "Are you gonna go clean with him or are you really not tired of my company?"

She smiled. "Thanks for the gloves," she said, before skipping away towards Jaden.

Chapter Five

"Okay, TK, let's do it one more time," Hacks said.

He watched TK sort through the latest problem quietly. As in, without complaint this time. He had met with TK every day for almost a week now. It was Monday afternoon, which meant Hacks had to leave soon to go to Sunny Meadows. But he didn't want to rush TK—or tell him where he was going.

"Am I doing this right?" TK asked when he was halfway through.

"Just keep going," Hacks said, trying not to sound impatient.

He checked the time again. He would have to leave in five minutes at the latest if he wanted to make it on time. Maybe it didn't matter much to the residents of Sunny Meadows, but Hacks wouldn't mar Joe's good name by being late. The residents *loved* Joe and his piano playing.

"I don't mean to rush you, but I have somewhere to be soon," Hacks said as gently as he could.

TK gave him a miserable look. "I'm almost done."

"You are," Hacks agreed. "But you're about to get the answer wrong."

TK glared at him, flipped his pencil over, and erased everything he'd done.

"No, no, no," Hacks said urgently. "It wasn't all wrong. I'm sorry, I gotta go."

"Two more minutes," TK said as he started rewriting. "And then I'll drive you anywhere you want to go."

Hacks huffed and set a timer on his phone. "You have *exactly* two minutes."

TK didn't spare another moment. He worked through the problem while Hacks watched anxiously. He never felt on edge doing math himself but watching someone else do it—especially TK—made him nervous. But he didn't say anything as TK made mistakes, erased them quickly, then filled in the correct answer.

TK stopped before the timer even went off. Hacks nodded with a tight smile. "Good job. Now let's go. I don't want to be late."

They shoved their work, pencils, and books into their backpacks, heedless of the mess they would have to deal with later. Hacks practically sprinted out to the student parking lot next to TK until they got to his car. TK asked where they were going as he started driving.

"Sunny Meadows," Hacks answered.

"The old folks home?" TK asked, his face wrinkling up. "Or the pet cremation place?"

"It's a *retirement community*," Hacks corrected. "The pet cremation place is called Endless Meadows."

"Oh, right," TK said as he headed into town. "What are you doing there? Visiting grandparents?"

"I have no living grandparents," Hacks said quietly. "I'm..." He hesitated. He supposed it wouldn't hurt to tell TK, since he already knew Hacks played the piano. "I play piano for the residents. It keeps morale high and encourages them to eat at dinnertime. Or so I've been told."

"Wait, wait," TK said as he turned onto the street that led to Sunny Meadows. "You've got a gig? How do I get in on that?"

Hacks clutched the door handle as TK halted to a stop. "I don't know. My mom recommended me a while ago."

"Come on," TK said. "I want to play with you. That sounds fun!"

Hacks opened his door and gave TK a placid smile. "Why not? Bring your sax inside."

TK smiled and then remembered... His mom still had his sax. He scowled. "That's cold, man."

Hacks got out of the car. "Study hard for your test. I'll see you tomorrow night." Then he shut the door a little too hard and rushed up to the building.

TK shook his head. But Hacks was right. He spent the rest of his evening studying, barely taking a break for dinner. He filled out exercise after exercise in his workbook, hoping he was doing them right. He didn't want to check the back of the book for the answers because he knew he'd be tempted to cheat that way.

The next day, he went into his math class more or less confident. Without Hacks there to coach him, he felt like he'd be totally lost. But when he looked down at the questions, they looked...less like a foreign language than they had a week ago. And in fact, they looked way easier than the ones he'd worked on with Hacks.

Carefully, he worked through each question. Some of them were word problems that he had no problem extracting information from so he could make the equation. From there it was even easier to solve. Once he'd filled in every question, he looked up at the clock. He had plenty of time to spare, so he checked over his work. He couldn't see anything he would change.

He walked up to Mrs. Lassiter and laid the test on her desk. Her eyebrows rose momentarily and then she said, "Thanks. You can go."

"Actually, can you grade it now?" he asked.

"What?" she asked, surprised.

Bracing his hands on her desk, he leaned forward and quietly said, "My mom is holding my sax hostage unless I get better grades in math and I want to go to my band practice tonight. So…would you mind? Please?"

Mrs. Lassiter considered him with kind eyes. "Okay. Go and sit and I'll grade it right now."

TK sat and nervously waited, watching her while she went over his test. He couldn't tell whether she was writing checkmarks or Xs and it was killing him. After a couple minutes, she called him back up.

Before handing it back, she said, "You didn't cheat, did you?"

"No," he said. "Why would you ask?"

She showed him the front, where she'd written 100% next to his name. He could hardly believe it.

"I didn't cheat," he said quickly, his eyes wide. "I promise. I just got a tutor and studied really hard."

"You must really like playing the saxophone," she said with a smile as she handed him the test.

"I do," he said enthusiastically. He took the test and clutched it to himself. "Thank you."

He went out into the hallway and took a picture of his test to send to Hacks. Hacks sent back a text that simply said, "See you tonight."

♪　♫　♪

And while TK was receiving the highest score he'd ever gotten in math, Corbie was dismayed when his French teacher handed back his most recent test. It wasn't a passing grade. Not even close. There was no way he could show this to his mom.

"Please have your guardian sign that and send it back," Mr. Gagnon said. Corbie cringed and the teacher gave him a sympathetic look. "I would suggest you look into tutoring or attend my virtual sessions on Tuesday nights."

"Tuesday nights?" Corbie squeaked, cursing his changing voice. "I'll find a tutor…"

He didn't show his parents the test that night. He couldn't bear the thought that they might not let him hang out with his band. Besides, maybe one of his bandmates could help him out.

♪   ♫   ♪

Chloe was quiet while her mom drove her to Max's house. She was still mad that her mom had taken June's side, that she still hadn't found her bow, and that she'd missed last week's meeting.

"Did you ever find your bow?" her mom had the nerve to ask just as they turned down Rockaway Boulevard.

Chloe suppressed a frustrated sigh as they passed the swanky houses that made up Max's neighbourhood. "No."

"How are you going to play, then?" her mom asked.

Chloe bit her tongue. If it weren't for Max's generosity, she would have just ditched Less than Perfect entirely. But she didn't feel like telling her mom that. "I'll play it like a guitar, I guess."

Her mom pulled up in front of Max's house. "Be gentle with your violin. You know how old it is."

Chloe opened the door and couldn't help saying, "Maybe you should tell June to be careful with my stuff."

"*Chloe.*"

Chloe slammed the door shut before her mom could lecture her again. Her mom lingered for another moment until Chloe threw a wave over her shoulder. She shouldn't have talked to her mom like that. She knew it was wrong. But what was done was done.

The door opened and Max stood there with a neutral look on his face as Chloe stared at her mom driving away. "Are you coming in?"

"Yes," she said as she dragged her feet inside.

He peered at her curiously. "Still need that bow?"

"Yes, please," she whispered.

"I left them upstairs."

He gestured for her to follow him. He took her all the way to his room and this time went inside with her. In his closet, he pulled out a box that literally had seven bows in it. He set it on his bed and then stepped back.

As soon as she looked through them, she could tell Max had organized them by cheapest to most expensive. She picked up the least expensive one and tightened the hairs on it.

"Thanks," she said.

"Oh, but—" He ran his hands over the other ones. "That's the cheapest one."

"I know," she said.

"You're...you're really going to play a one-hundred-year-old German Strad with that one?" he asked incredulously.

"Yes," she said as she headed out of his room. "Also, don't be creeping around and checking the serial numbers on people's instruments."

He quickly grabbed the nicest bow of the set and left with her. "I couldn't help it. It's a gorgeous instrument. You should take *this* bow."

She waved him off and headed down the spiral staircase. "No. I don't trust my sister or my mom now. I'm not losing that to them, too. Besides, that's the bow you play with."

Max sighed. "Now who's being a creep?" She just shrugged. "At least take a new piece of rosin if you're going to play with my bow."

"Fine."

"Chloe, what's wrong?" Max asked.

She swallowed hard and turned to him. "Look at you. Seven bows, all the space in the world to practice, a three-thousand-dollar Yamaha, and I bet you've had the best music teachers to teach you everything you know.

And what do I get? An old instrument I was lucky to find at an auction that I can't even play because I don't have a back-up bow for when my sister loses the only one I have."

Max gave her a soft smile. "And yet despite all that you still play better than me."

"I don't think that's true," she admitted.

He lifted an eyebrow but didn't acknowledge the loose compliment. "Are you almost done wallowing? Everyone else is going to be here soon."

Finally, she smiled. "Yes, I'm done wallowing. Thank you for the bow."

"Keep it as long as you need," he said.

Chloe went downstairs and started playing. Max was right; she was doing her violin a huge disservice with the bow she'd chosen. But she'd made her choice and he wasn't going to change her mind.

Soon, more members of Less than Perfect began arriving. As soon as Corbie got there, he went straight to Rach and pulled out his French test.

"Oh, hey, little buddy," Rach said, giving him a wide grin. "You feeling well enough to bone today?"

He took in a big breath and let it out slowly, closing his eyes. "I was deliriously ill when I wrote that. Thanks for your concern, though. I need a tutor."

Rach jutted her thumb in the piano's direction. "Hacks is the smartest kid in the room."

Corbie took his test over to Hacks, who'd been warming up at the piano with some scales, and held it out. "Can you help me with this?"

Hacks glanced at the test and dropped his hands heavily on the keys, causing a cacophonous sound. He stood up, never once taking his eyes off the paper. "I...I don't have the time to unpack *any* of that." He put his hands on Corbie's shoulders and turned him around. "Go show that to Marty."

Corbie slowly went over to the drums and waited patiently while Marty played. Marty's eyes were closed and he was lost in his own rhythms. Corbie had no idea how he could play the drums without even looking, but he was impressed, to say the least. After a minute, Marty opened his eyes, found Corbie standing there, and immediately stopped playing.

"Um…I was told to show this to you," Corbie said, holding out his test.

Marty took it and his dark eyes widened as he read Corbie's answers. "Oh… Oh, you sweet summer child. Who hurt you?"

"I've just never been good at French," Corbie said weakly.

"What part of this is French?" Marty muttered, peeking at the second page of the test.

Corbie sighed and snatched it back. "Never mind."

Marty reached out and put his hand on Corbie's forearm before he could turn away. "Wait, I'm sorry. I'll help you, okay?"

"Really?" Corbie asked hopefully.

"Yeah, I can't let you walk around like that." He shrugged. "Sorry. But I mean it."

Corbie smiled. "Thank you!"

Chapter Six

"New music!" Claire called out. She laughed as everyone flocked to her. "Whoops. Guess I should have done that a different way."

She took half the music and handed it to D-rock. The parts weren't labelled with their instruments but rather with names, so everyone took what was theirs. When Marty came to get his, D-rock gave him a surprised look.

"Come on, give me the music," Marty said, making an impatient gesture with his hand. "I've been learning with Max. I'll do my best."

"Aw, that's great," D-rock said as he handed the music over. "Is Max also learning to drum?"

"Ha," Max said. His answer was to set his bow to his violin and start playing his music.

"Is this for real?" Harmony asked as she looked over her music.

"You're reading it right," D-rock said. "'Kings & Queens' and 'Holding Out for a Hero.' It was Claire's idea…"

"I love it," Amber said excitedly.

Once everyone had their music and had gone back to their seats, Claire said, "Okay, first four bars belong to the girls. Plus the pickup."

"Wait, why just the girls?" TK asked, his brow furrowed.

"Because they wanted their very own band," D-rock said sarcastically. "Remember?"

"So you gave us four bars?" Amber said, lifting an eyebrow. "Wow… Wonder what you're like on a date."

D-rock winked at her. "We can talk later."

"Anyway," Claire said, her eyes flashing. "Boys except Marty come in on the fifth bar. Marty, make sure you wait a full eight bars… You do see those rests, right?"

"Yes, Claire," Marty said with exaggerated patience. "I see the rests."

"Good, let's try it," Claire said.

"Am I…the only one doing this pickup?" Amber asked, looking around.

"No, I'm with you," Meg said confidently.

"I'll count us in slowly," Claire said. All the girls raised their instruments and she called out, "One and two and three and four—"

Amber and Meg played the pickup and the other girls joined them more or less confidently. A few bars later, when the boys came in, it was far too loud, but Claire would just point out the dynamic markings later. For now, she enjoyed listening to the arrangement she and D-rock had written come to life.

The first verse was shared between Amber's clarinet, Harmony's flute, and TK's sax. The strings took a back seat, supporting the music with their lower and higher harmonies. There was a musical bridge where Bryan should have played the melody. He was clearly unprepared for it, but did his best to muddle through. He was followed by Harmony's flute and Meg's trumpet, playing the rest of the bridge an octave apart with Hacks playing some echoes on the piano.

Claire cringed when they transitioned to "Holding Out for a Hero."

Either the music was wrong or her band was, but she would look at it later. Marty did okay with the beat, though he missed some of the notation. Hacks stopped playing at some point. But at least when Rach played the melody for the first verse on her tuba, it sounded good.

Until she stopped abruptly. Without the melody, the others slowed to a stop, too, until it was just Marty jamming to himself. He finally ended his impromptu solo with a *badum-ching*!

With a grin, he said, "I have no idea how this song goes. Did we do it right?"

D-rock laughed out loud and said, "Not really, no. But that's okay."

"You didn't write it right," Rach said irritably as she placed her tuba down. "I don't do melody."

"You do now," Claire said firmly, a challenge in her eyes.

"Change it," Rach said.

Claire crossed her arms as everyone else watched their showdown. "Make me."

Rach stood up, but Corbie put his hand on her arm, laughing a little. "Rach, stop. It sounded great until you realized you were playing alone."

"Yeah, I liked it," Trey said. "If you want, we can switch instruments and you can play this really awesome part at the bridge on my trumpet!"

Rach turned to him sharply, her eyes narrowed. "Touch my tuba and I'll break your throwing arm."

Trey pulled his lips in, curling his arms protectively around his trumpet. "Never mind, then."

"Suggestion," Max said, standing up. "You all go home now and practice your little hearts out and we'll play it better next week."

"I guess that's our cue," Harmony said diplomatically.

As everyone put their instruments away, Rach went over to Claire with her music. "Change this," she repeated.

Claire huffed as she loosened the hairs on her bow. "I didn't even write that line. D-rock did."

Rach turned to D-rock, who smiled sheepishly. "It sounded really good," he said. Rach just stared at him harder. "Look, what's the big deal? We're trying to make sure everyone has a chance to stand out."

"I already stand out enough, thanks," Rach said. She shoved her music at him and went back to her tuba.

Meg sighed and put her hand on Rach's shoulder but didn't say anything. Instead, she went over to D-rock, who looked terribly disappointed, and gently took the music from him.

"I'll take care of this," she said softly.

"Thanks," he said heavily.

"Okay, thanks for coming, everyone," Max said as he waved his hands at them. "Bye. See you at school. Oh, except you, Corbie. Sorry."

Corbie shrugged, his lips pursed, and followed the others as they filtered out of his house almost as quickly as they'd come. It was tiring for Max to make sure they left no evidence of their rehearsals behind so his parents wouldn't find out. And for the last few weeks, he'd done just fine.

Maybe if his parents cared more about his love for the violin, or if they hadn't frowned upon his non-conventional band, then he'd be more willing to tell them about it. But Less than Perfect were the only ones who truly understood him.

♪ ♫ ♪

The next day, D-rock sat at his locker during his free period like he did every day. Normally he would spend the time arranging music in his head while listening to music. But without his headphones, it was pointless.

He sighed into his phone. He had their new score displayed so he could scroll through Rach's part. How was he supposed to take out these beautiful lines he'd written specifically for her? He could swap them with his own, but they wouldn't have the same effect or work as well. What was he supposed to do with this?

"Hey."

He looked up and there was Hacks.

"Sorry these took so long," Hacks said, holding out D-rock's headphones.

"Oh!" D-rock said, hopping up. He hadn't expected Hacks to actually bring them back.

"Try them," Hacks said, his eyes alight with expectation.

D-rock put them on, connected them to his phone, and started his playlist. His eyes grew wide as the sound came out clear and strong. "These sound like five-hundred-dollar headphones!"

Hacks smiled like he wanted to laugh out loud. "You don't have to shout about it, though."

D-rock pulled the headphones down. "Oh, sorry. But seriously! These are amazing. What did you do?"

Hacks shrugged and shook his head. "I just tinkered."

"Wow," D-rock said. "You should come tinker on my mom's laptop so she'll stop bugging me about it."

Hacks smiled. "Sure. I'll let you know when I have time."

♪ ♫ ♪

Bryan got ready for work, putting on his typical uniform—his worst jeans and an old shirt with holes in it. The rec centre didn't really care what he wore to clean for them on weekends, and he didn't care what he had to clean to make money. The money went right back into his car for the insurance, gas, and maintenance.

Well…not all the money. He had just changed the strings on his guitar and bought himself a new strap. And new picks. And music.

As he worked, he ignored the other kids his age who had come for their various activities. Even the gaggle of dancers couldn't entice him today. They all giggled as they went past him to get to the change rooms. He just turned his music up louder.

He waited outside the change room so he could go in there once they'd all finished. With his eyes closed and his music filling his head, it was easy to forget where he was, what he was doing, and sometimes even who he was.

A tap on his shoulder brought him back to reality. He opened his eyes and found Stacey, Amber's former best friend, smiling up at him.

"Oh. Hi," he said.

Her smile widened. "Hi! Come on, don't pretend you don't know me just because Amber doesn't want to talk to me right now."

Bryan suppressed an eye roll. He was pretty sure Amber wouldn't want to talk to her ever again, but he chose not to mention it. "Hi, Stacey, how are you?" he asked in his most polite, detached voice.

"Better now," she said. She stretched down and touched her toes while Bryan tried not to cringe. "I've been dancing."

"That's nice," he said. "Is the change room empty?"

She straightened up and looked right into his eyes. "Why? Are you looking for a place to be alone?"

"No?" He lifted an eyebrow and motioned to the janitor cart. "I have to clean it before my shift is over."

"Oh." She looked at the cart and back at him. "If you're almost done work, do you want to hang out after?"

"What?" he said dumbly.

"Do you want to hang out with me?" she asked, her eyes widening innocently. "We could grab a late lunch or something."

Bryan stared at her for a moment while she twisted up her hair around her fingers. "Are you...asking me out?"

"Yeah," she said breathlessly.

He frowned. "To…get back at Amber?"

"What? No." She waved a hand at him and then patted him on the shoulder. "I just kind of forgot how hot you are until now."

"No," he said, turning away from her.

"No?" she asked incredulously. "No, what?"

"No, I'm not hot," he said. "And I don't want to go out with you."

Her mouth slacked open. "Because of Amber?"

He shrugged. "No, because of you. But if you want to blame Amber to feel better about yourself, I'm sure she won't mind."

Stacey scoffed and turned on her heel, not even deigning to answer. She stomped away while he tried not to laugh out loud. He hadn't meant to be mean to her, but he also wasn't going to spare her feelings when she wouldn't do the same for Amber.

"I am *so* glad I got to witness that," came another voice.

Bryan turned around and there was Harmony with her flute, smiling in a smugly amused way. He shook his head and pulled one of his earbuds out. "Please don't tell Amber about that. That's so cringy."

"I won't," Harmony said. "You're a good brother."

He drew his eyebrows in. "To be honest, I wouldn't have said yes even if she had nothing to do with Amber. Stacey is the fakest girl I know."

"Oh," she said in surprise.

He knocked on the door of the change room and cracked it open. "Hello?"

"There's no one in there," Harmony said. "I'll see you around."

"Cold out there," he commented as she zipped up her thin coat.

"It's not a long walk," she answered.

After a moment's hesitation, he said, "I could drive you home if you want to wait a few minutes." He gestured to the change room he still had to clean.

"Sure," she said. "That would be great. Thank you."

Harmony waited on a bench by the front doors for about ten minutes while Bryan did his thing. It wasn't really that cold. She could have walked. But by the time she'd decided that maybe she'd leave him alone, he was already heading towards her, pushing his arms through his coat sleeves.

He waved his hand and nodded towards the door, her cue to follow him. So, he wasn't exactly a talker like his sister, but that was just fine with Harmony. She could fill the silence with— Oh! His music came through super loud as soon as he turned the car on. She clasped her hands together, wringing them in her lap.

As he drove, Bryan glanced over at Harmony several times. Finally, he turned his music down and said, "Don't take this the wrong way, but you seem really tense."

"I'm...kind of stressed out," she said. "I feel like I spend all my time trying so hard and I still am not as good as I want to be."

"Good at what?" he asked as he made a right turn.

"Playing," she said, holding up her flute even though he wasn't looking at her. "I want to be a performance major next year at a good school and I'm starting auditions soon. So on top of all the practising for that, I've got the concert band, the jazz band, the orchestra, the flute choir, Less than Perfect. It's...a lot."

He glanced at her very quickly. "That's not just a lot, that's too much. Why don't you just drop one of your bands?"

"Drop—" She gripped her flute case harder. "*Drop* one of my bands? I can't just do that."

He shrugged. "Why not?"

"Because I—I—" She knew she had an answer for that. But the answer escaped her as Bryan pulled into her driveway. "I...don't know."

He put the car in Park and looked at her. "You don't really need all those bands, you know. You're already good enough. I doubt being in a million places at once is going to help you with your auditions."

"But I love all my ensembles," she said. "I don't even know how I would choose."

"Umm…" He looked away, running his hands over the steering wheel for a distraction. "I think we both know which one you should pick. In any case, that's really a lot."

Placing her hand on the door handle, she paused. "Maybe you're right," she said. "But I'm more inclined to think you're wrong."

She got out of the car as he chuckled softly. "Let me know how that goes when you strain your embouchure."

She put a hand up to her lips. Her eyes widened as he laughed some more. She rolled her eyes. He was teasing, but she knew his advice was sincere.

Chapter Seven

Corbie's parents weren't too happy to see his disastrous grade on his French test. But they were relieved to know that he'd already found himself a tutor. Not that Marty had any experience tutoring, but at least he was bilingual and willing to help. Those were good enough qualifications for them.

Corbie's mom drove him to Marty's house, which turned out to be a cozy-looking bungalow on the lakefront. The breeze off the lake was cool as he got out of the car. He slung his backpack onto his shoulders and went up to the house's quaint red door.

Before he could press the doorbell, the door opened, and a younger boy peeked out. Corbie waved shyly at him and the boy just stared back. He shared a lot of Marty's features—wide nose, full lips, high cheekbones—but maybe Corbie had gotten the house wrong.

Then Marty appeared, putting his hands on the younger boy's shoulders. "Thanks for getting the door, Seb. Come in, Corbie."

Corbie followed Marty inside. They walked through the house, past the living room and kitchen to the back door. Marty's other brother and sister came and stared curiously. There was a delicious odour in the air that

Corbie couldn't identify, but his stomach rumbled at the mere thought of what it could be.

When they reached the patio door, Corbie could see the lakefront. He smiled. "Wow, this is such a great house."

"Don't be fooled," Marty said. "We're poor as dirt."

"*Marthel!*" came his mom's chastising voice from the kitchen.

"Sorry, *Maman!*" he called back. He lifted his hands palms up. "I meant poor as church mice. She prefers that term."

"I can still hear you, Marty," she said in her island accent.

He winked at Corbie. "Let's go outside. It's still nice enough to sit on the patio."

He led Corbie out to the glass-top table on the deck. After brushing some fallen leaves off two of the chairs, he sat and motioned to the other. Corbie sat down and looked out at the calmly rippling lake.

"I can't believe you get this view every day," Corbie said slowly.

Marty smiled. "When my parents moved here from Guadeloupe, they didn't have very much. But they were adamant they wanted a house by the water like they had back home. Honestly?" He leaned forward and whispered, "This one is wayyy nicer than that old rickety thing they had."

"You remember it?" he asked.

"Yes," Marty said. "Now stop stalling and show me your homework."

Corbie sighed and dug into his backpack. He tossed his notebook onto the table and Marty picked it up. Crossing an ankle over his knee, he leaned back and opened the book. After leisurely reading it for a few minutes, he put it back down.

"Dude."

"I *know*," Corbie groaned.

"It's not horrible," Marty said. "It's not as bad as your test. But it's still..."

"I know," Corbie repeated. "Wait'll you hear me speak French."

Marty waggled his fingers at him and Corbie sighed again. Awkwardly, Corbie said a few sentences in French, ones he should have known well. But with Marty staring intently at him with a defined frown on his face, Corbie botched most of the words and even forgot a few.

"*O, mon gars,*" Marty said. "We've gotta work on that. And this." He gestured to the notebook. Then he smiled. "But it's fine. You'll be fluent in no time."

"You'd think after five years I'd be better than this," Corbie groused.

Marty shrugged. "It took me a long time to get good at English. And I know I still have an accent and there are still people who think I'm weird."

Corbie's eyebrows drew in. "Why do you think people think you're weird?"

"When I first moved to Canada, I was that foreign kid who couldn't speak any English," Marty said. "I was eight and everyone already had their special friend groups. I learned to understand English sooner than I could speak it and trust me—I knew they thought I was weird."

"I'm sure they don't anymore," Corbie said softly.

"Yeah, well…by the time I was more or less fluent and integrated, I realized I like boys. And most of them don't like me back." Marty chuckled self-consciously.

"That's rough," Corbie said.

"It's okay," Marty said. "I discovered drumming around the same time. And I like drumming more than anything else in the whole world. I feel like the only time people see the real Marty is when I'm drumming. You know?"

Corbie shook his head. "I think the real you is all of that. The kid who likes drumming, and likes other boys, and speaks…two languages?"

"Technically four, but who's keeping count?" Marty shrugged.

Corbie smiled. "That's amazing! Everything about you is what makes you you. So what if some people think parts of you are weird? I can't think of anyone I know who doesn't have that one weird thing." He frowned in thought. "Except maybe Harmony."

"She's in a flute choir," Marty said.

"Okay, yeah, that's weird," Corbie agreed. "See? We're all a little weird."

Marty smiled and leaned back in his chair. "So, what's your thing?"

"Other than my terrible French accent?" Corbie quipped.

Marty laughed out loud. "No, seriously."

"I have twenty-one cousins," Corbie said. "The oldest is twenty-seven and the youngest is four months old."

Marty nodded, his eyes wide. "That is a *lot* of cousins."

"Tell me about it," Corbie said. "Some of them are really into boxing, too. Our family reunions are interesting."

"I'll bet," Marty said. "Okay, no more chit-chat. Unless it's in French."

"You're right," Corbie said.

They spent a good hour outside, speaking back and forth in French. Marty had to prompt Corbie so many times he lost count. But Corbie was determined to get better and he tried his hardest. Of course, by the time Marty's mom called them in for dinner, Corbie was sick of French.

"You really don't have to feed me," Corbie whispered to Marty as he followed him inside.

"Dude." Marty turned to him his eyes wide. "She made her porc columbo and there's always lots. Trust me."

"Oh, good," Corbie said eagerly. "Because it smells delicious."

"That ain't even half of it," Marty said with a smile.

Inside, Marty's younger siblings were already at the table conversing rather rapidly in French. Corbie tried to follow their conversation, but there was no way. Maybe one day.

Marty's mom handed him a plate of food and he said *"Merci!"* with such fervor that she laughed out loud. Maybe being tutored at Marty's house wouldn't be so bad after all.

♪   ♫   ♪

Instead of working on his essay like he should have been doing, Max twisted the knob on his bow, ready to get lost in a world of music. He had already tuned his strings and was about to set the bow to his violin when his mother called him. Sighing heavily, he put it down and went upstairs.

Max walked into his mom's office only to find both his parents waiting for him with disappointed frowns. His dad gestured to the seat by the desk and Max sat.

"Max," his mom said. "We've been looking at the security footage."

"Did we get robbed?" Max blurted out without thinking.

"We better not have with all the kids coming in and out of our house all the time," his dad barked.

He turned the monitor so Max could watch the front door footage. It was from the last Tuesday night, sped up so Max could watch his bandmates, his *friends* arrive at his house for practice. Most of them waited for him to answer, but some of them let themselves in, which had never bothered him. He glanced at his parents. They were definitely beyond bothered.

He opened and closed his mouth a few times, wondering how to explain without getting into so much trouble they would take away his violin and all seven bows. Oops—make that six, since he'd given one to Chloe.

"We checked back a few weeks," his mom said. "Every Tuesday night? Really, Max? What is this?"

"That's my band," he squeaked out. "Remember, the band I joined? See? They're all coming in with instruments."

"What about this kid?" his dad paused the footage on a boy with glasses and messy hair.

"Hacks has been playing the piano," Max whispered.

"Max!" his mom shouted.

"And this boy?" his dad asked, pausing once again on a boy with dark curly hair and a huge smile.

Max looked down at his tightly clasped hands in his lap. "Marty…brought his drum set here."

"So." His mom paused dramatically, long enough that he finally timidly glanced up at her. "Even after we discussed it and I said I would think about letting you have them over once a month, you went behind my back and have been doing it anyway?"

If there was any defense he could have given, anything he could have said to prove her wrong, he would have said it. Instead, he decided on full honesty and simply said, "Yes."

"And these kids have been coming over thinking that we're just okay with that?" his dad asked.

Max hesitated and shook his head. "No," he said quietly. "They know you're not. They come and go when I tell them to and they never go into any other part of the house. They're very respectful. They don't—"

"Not even this girl?" his mom cut him off.

There on the screen was a girl with long dark hair, brown eyes, and a brilliant smile that didn't match her black clothes. Max's face went aflame when he realized they had probably checked out the indoor security camera footage, too.

"That was just one time," he said weakly.

"*Twice*," his mom corrected.

"Yes, okay," Max said. "I gave her a bow on Tuesday and they were up in my room."

"So now you're giving away your stuff to random people, too?" his dad said, like he couldn't fathom why Max had done any of this. "Well, it's going to stop now. No more Tuesday-night parties."

"And we'll see if we even let you play with them again," his mom snipped.

Max's heart dropped and his mouth gaped open. "*No*," he said firmly. "You can't. Please! We don't party on Tuesday nights. We just play music together. And they're not random people, they're my friends. They're musicians and they're all very talented."

"That may be the case, Max, but—"

"I refuse to stop playing with them," Max said, cutting off his mom. "I belong with them and I won't stop. Also, this is my house, too. I should have a right to invite my friends over."

His dad crossed his arms while his eyebrows inched up his forehead. "When was the last time you paid the mortgage on this house?"

Max clenched his jaw. "Fine. Kick us out. But I will *not* stop playing with them. I'll just cram myself into someone else's tiny basement."

With that, he stood up to go, but when his mom said his name softly, he waited.

"If you really wanted to play—"

"I don't want to be in the orchestra," he said to her. "Okay? I want to play with this band. I want one night a week where I can forget about everything else and just relax with a bunch of other kids who are doing the same thing."

His mom looked at his dad, whose face surprisingly softened. Maybe Max's words were finally getting through to them.

"Look, can you at least listen to us once before you decide they're not worth my time?" he pleaded. "Listen to us. We're good."

Max would have given anything to know what was passing telepathically between his parents as they stared at each other. His dad sighed and lifted a hand and his mom turned back to him.

"Okay, Max," she said, though she wasn't happy about it. "We'll come home early on Tuesday night to hear your band."

"Really?" he said.

"Or you can drop out and tell them to play somewhere else," his dad said. His arms were still crossed and he wasn't amused. But Max could handle that.

"Okay!" he said. "That's fine. That's great! You're gonna love it."

His mom made a face like she wasn't so sure about that while his dad just grunted, but Max didn't care. He rushed out of the office, grabbing his phone from his pocket. Hastily, he opened the group chat and started a heartfelt message.

Max: bad news. my parents found out. BUT they agreed to listen to us on tuesday night and if they like what they hear we get to keep playing in my basement and i get to stay in the band. i totally understand if you don't want to have to try to prove yourselves just to have a place to practice so no hard feelings if no one shows up.

With hope in his heart, Max hit Send. Within minutes, there was an influx of messages from everyone pledging to play their best so they wouldn't lose the basement *or* Max. Tears pricked at his eyes, but he rubbed them away. He would never admit to the band how much their willingness meant to him.

Chapter Eight

Meg swept the floor for the fifth time, even though it was already free of dirt. Trey had called an "emergency brass meeting" and Corbie and Rach had both agreed. So, she'd offered to have them come over Sunday afternoon. Which meant the house had to be pristine. Admittedly, it always was, but that didn't stop her from triple checking everything.

Rach showed up first, followed by Corbie. Trey, who lived down the street, was late for his own meeting. When he showed up, his hair wet and eyes fired up, Meg forgave him easily.

"Sorry I'm late," he said as they headed to Meg's sunroom turned practice room. "I had football and then I had to shower and…well, we're all here, so let's do this."

"Do *what*, exactly?" Corbie asked as he looked around the room.

Trey's eyes widened as he helped himself to a space on the table to put his trumpet case down. "*Practice*. So we can be perfect on Tuesday night and save our band."

"We're not going to lose our band if we're not perfect," Rach said, even as she got her tuba out. "At worst, we'd just have to practice somewhere else."

"No, at worst we'd lose Max," Trey said. He took his mouthpiece and popped it into his trumpet. "And then we wouldn't have our full band."

"Aw, and I didn't even know you felt that way about Max," Corbie said, giving him a teasing smile.

Rach snorted but Trey just rolled his eyes. "Come on," he said. "It was really nice of Max to let us all come in when he didn't even know us. And he lets people sneak in to play sometimes, too. Wouldn't you feel bad if we didn't try our hardest for him, or...or anyone else in the band?"

"Of course we would," Meg said softly. "Right, guys?"

"Yeah, yeah," Rach said. "Look, I'm here and I'm ready, let's play."

"Great," Trey said excitedly. "I was thinking we'd do 'Holding Out for a Hero' since we didn't get far with it on Tuesday. And I'll bet if we can play it perfectly—or even slightly less than perfectly—we could pretty much carry the rest of the band."

Rach groaned. "Is this what your team pep talks are like?"

"Yup," he answered seriously.

"Trey...I don't want to play this song at all," Rach said. "Look at this..."

She showed him her music and Corbie and Meg leaned in to get a good look, too. Rach was supposed to play a lot of the melody throughout the first verse, the very part she'd refused to play on Tuesday.

"D-rock wrote that especially for you," Corbie said. "I think that's really nice!"

Rach just frowned and looked down at her tuba. "I don't want to do it."

"Can I play it?" Trey asked seriously. Her frown deepened. "Please. Just once? I want to know how hard it supposedly is to play tuba."

Rach lifted an eyebrow. "Fine. Wash this."

Trey's eyes lit up as she handed him her oversized mouthpiece. He ran to the kitchen and they could hear water running.

"Is this going to be as bad as I think it will be?" Corbie asked.

Rach shook her head. "Probably."

Meg shrugged with a little smile. Trey returned and very carefully picked up Rach's tuba, putting the mouthpiece in it.

Before he even put his mouth on it, he said, "I have no idea how to play this."

Rach crossed her arms. "Just press the buttons. It's not that *hard*. You'll figure it out."

He shrugged and took a deep breath before plunging in. He blurted out a few low notes, pressing the valves at random. He took a moment to read Rach's music and then attempted to play it. All that came out were more flat, non-sequential notes. He didn't even get the rhythm right.

"Trey," Rach said.

He played some more gross notes as Corbie hid a chuckle behind his hand and Meg lifted her eyebrows, pulling her lips inward.

"Trey," Rach repeated. "Seriously. Okay, just stop! I'll play the piece, okay?"

He stopped playing and she reached out and took the tuba back. With a smug smile, he held his hands out for Corbie and Meg to high five, which they did.

"Very clever," Rach said as she pulled the mouthpiece off to clean it. "Okay, I'll play it as written if you promise never to touch a tuba again."

Trey put a hand over his heart with a smile. "That's not a promise I can honorably keep, but okay."

Rach just rolled her eyes. After she'd washed her mouthpiece, they were finally all ready to play together. While it was somewhat difficult to tell how the whole piece should sound without the rest of Less than Perfect, they did their best to figure out their own parts. And while Meg felt certain the whole thing could fall apart if even one of their bandmates got lost, Trey seemed more confident than ever. Then again, that was just the way he was.

They played until they felt comfortable with their parts. Not perfect— they knew they never would be without hearing the rest of the band come together. But at least they would be more prepared this time.

After a while, Rach and Corbie left, but Trey lingered. Once they were gone, he said, "I could totally play more if you're up for it."

Meg smiled. "Sure." But she didn't move to pick up her trumpet, and instead watched Trey shuffle his music around. "That was really nice of you to help Rach. I don't know how you knew your silly trick would work."

He bobbed his eyebrows. "I figured every brass player is as competitive as I am."

"I'm not," she said simply.

"Oh, really, little miss I'm-gonna-make-you-play-the-first-part-so-you-can-get-better?" he sassed, his eyebrows rising to his hairline.

She laughed at his description. "Okay, that's fair. But it worked, didn't it?"

"Exactly."

Laughing more, she picked up her trumpet. Trey got his and suggested they try the hard parts of the medley—the ones Meg had quickly realized Trey loved the most. It didn't matter what he wanted to play. She would always have a hard time saying no to him.

♪　♫　♪

TK balled up his fists and refrained from shouting the slew of curses running through his mind. Maybe if he'd been alone in his own room, he'd let them out. But he was sitting in Hacks's living room and TK didn't think his parents would appreciate hearing that when they were supposed to be working on math together.

"Now there's *shapes* and numbers and letters," TK said. "I'm *never* going to need this in real life. Do the teachers know that?"

"Never say never," Hacks said calmly. "You aced the last test. I'm sure you can do that again."

TK shook his head and turned away. He'd brought his sax with him for fear of ever leaving it out of his sight again. But Hacks hadn't let him take it out yet, and TK yearned for it.

"Nope," Hacks said, not even looking up from the textbook. "Ten minutes of math, five minutes of playing."

TK let out a long groan and forced himself to focus on the task at hand. It was hard when all he wanted to do was practice Less than Perfect's arrangements so they could impress Max's parents. TK didn't need math for that, yet here he was.

"This is the worst thing ever," TK said as the word problems danced before his eyes.

"Agreed," Hacks murmured.

TK's eyebrows lowered in surprise. "What?"

Hacks finally looked up at him. "I agree. I dislike trigonometry. It has very little bearing on *any* of my interests and I suffer through it every single time I come across it."

"Then why—"

"Because sometimes you have to do things you hate to enjoy the things you love," Hacks said. "Math as a whole, I love. And you love playing your sax. So let's just get through this. Once you pass this class, next semester will be a breeze and you won't have to bother with most of this ever again."

Hacks nodded encouragingly and after a moment, TK nodded back. He could do this. He would get through it so that he'd never have to do it again.

"Okay, set the timer," TK said.

"That's the spirit," Hacks said pleasantly as he started the timer on his phone.

They worked straight through problem after problem. When Hacks slowed everything down and pulled apart the word problems, they weren't as overwhelming as TK first thought. And true to his word, Hacks stopped as soon as the timer went off.

"Oof," he said, heading straight for his piano. "Let's wash that down with some music."

TK smiled as he got his sax ready. Maybe Hacks really did hate trigonometry. It made TK extra grateful that Hacks would go through the trouble of doing all his homework with him.

"Here's my problem," Hacks said, breaking into TK's thoughts. He had the "Kings & Queens/Holding Out for a Hero" medley in front of him and he was pointing to a section near the end. "I am going to break Max's piano if I play this the way they wrote it. But if I tone it down, Claire and D-rock are definitely going to notice."

TK looked at the music and snickered. Not only were there a lot of chords in fast succession, but the *fff* was a fun addition, too. "Yeah, but when else are you ever going to legitimately get to play fortississimo on a fancy baby grand?"

"True," Hacks said.

But as he placed his hands on the well-worn keys, TK could tell this piano meant a lot to him. And if possible, Hacks was even more in his element here than in the computer lab at school.

"Let's play that part," TK said. "Guaranteed if you do it well enough, Max's parents won't even notice if the rest of the band is falling apart."

Hacks's eyes flashed. "Maybe," he said doubtfully.

Regardless, they played the section in question, and while TK played the supporting harmonies that he knew fit somewhere with the other upper end instruments, Hacks went to town playing his little fortississimo heart out. Since they were already near the end, they played until the piece was finished.

TK lowered his sax and said, "It's really unfair that you're so smart *and* so good at music."

Hacks chuckled self-consciously. "Well, at least I'm not handsome, too."

"You could be!" TK exclaimed. "You just dress really badly."

"I—" Hacks looked down at himself. His black t-shirt had a picture of a piece of pie with a speech bubble with that said "Mmm, pi." He had regular jeans and black socks on. Confused, he looked back up at TK.

"I can't be the first person to tell you that," TK said. "Right?"

"Well...no," Hacks mumbled. "But normally people only say it to be mean."

TK gave him a sympathetic smile. "I'm not trying to be mean. But like, dude. That shirt is at least a large and you're tiny. And those jeans are..." He sighed and gestured vaguely. "Also, no offense, but rectangular glasses aren't really in right now."

"I feel like the rectangular ones offer me better peripheral vision," Hacks said as he pulled his shirt out to see just how large it looked on him.

"That's fair," TK offered.

"And what about all this?" Hacks asked as he made a circular motion around his face.

TK lifted an eyebrow. "There's nothing wrong with that. It's all in here, bro." Gently he tapped the centre of Hacks's chest.

Hacks looked down. "My heart is here, if that's what you meant," he said, pointing to the correct spot.

TK rolled his eyes. "Yes, that's what I meant."

"Hmm."

"Are you done...being like this?" TK asked. "Can we play again?"

The timer went off. Silently, Hacks turned it off and glanced surreptitiously at the math homework on the table. "Yeah, we can play again."

Chapter Nine

Max adjusted his black-and-blue tie. Not that his parents would care for his presentation. It was his playing that he was worried about. What if he wasn't as good as he thought he was? What if he had overhyped Less than Perfect or his parents just flat-out hated their music?

The doorbell rang and Max knew, without even looking at the time, that it was Chloe. With a nervous smile, he opened the door to let her in.

"I'm sorry I'm always so early," Chloe said, even as she made her way comfortably through his house to the basement.

"It's okay," he said as he followed her down the stairs. "I mean, my parents definitely noticed, and I tried to explain, but…"

"Oh, man," Chloe groaned. "I'm sorry. You shouldn't have to prove yourself to your parents like this. Don't they already know you're a great musician?"

Max blurted out, "If I were such a great musician, I would have joined the youth orchestra a long time ago."

"What?" she said, turning to him sharply.

He shook his head as he got his violin out of its case. "Nothing. It doesn't matter."

She opened her case, but couldn't let the matter drop. "Is there a reason you're not in the orchestra?" she asked, trying not to let irritation creep into her voice.

He shrugged and looked away. "I didn't pass the audition. And I wasn't going to let my parents pay my way in."

She stared at him for a good solid moment, her mouth pressed into a thin line. "You—you could have been in the orchestra?"

He looked her straight in the eyes, a frown on his face. "No, not really. Not like that. I'd rather earn it."

She glared down at the violin in her case, chewing on her lip. Was she more angry at herself for not being able to afford it or at Max for not taking every advantage offered to him?

"Chloe?" he said softly.

She flicked her gaze at him and roughly took out her violin. Without speaking, she ignored him and tuned the strings.

"Did I say something wrong?" he asked in a confused voice.

"I got into the orchestra," she admitted quietly as tears pressed at the backs of her eyes.

"That's awesome," Max said in awe.

"No." She looked up at him. "I auditioned on a whim because I didn't think anything would come of it. And then I got in, but we can't afford it. So now my seat is just left open for—for—" She waved her hand at him. "A guy who doesn't want to pay for something he could rightfully have."

Max's shoulders slumped. "No, Chloe," he said quietly, dejectedly. "Not when there are people more deserving."

She shook her head, but their conversation was cut short by the doorbell.

"I should get that," Max said as he practically ran away from her.

She sighed into her violin. She didn't want to let her thoughts linger on the youth orchestra. If this was all she and Max had now, then she had to pull herself together and play as best as she could. Hopefully, the rest of the band felt the same way.

Soon, the basement was filled with all their bandmates. Even Amber and Bryan came on time for once. As they warmed up, Max looked around nervously, gratitude in his heart. If it was the last time he got to play with them, then he should say something meaningful.

"Thanks for coming, guys," he said. "This is so ridiculous. I'm sorry."

"No, it's not," D-rock said. He leaned close to his bass so he could tune his strings while the others warmed up. "We have to play in front of other people eventually, right?"

"We do?" Max asked.

D-rock shrugged and Bryan, sitting close by, nodded. "I assumed we'd be doing that eventually, too," Bryan said.

"Well, I wouldn't have chosen my parents as a tester audience," Max said. "But okay. Oh! I think I hear them."

Max went upstairs to greet his parents. His mom was still putting away her coat and purse, while his dad was frowning at the extra cars outside their house.

"I suppose your band is here?" his dad asked.

Max nodded. "You…said they could be here tonight. Are you still coming to listen?"

"Yes," his mom said on a sigh.

Feeling like he'd already been defeated, Max led them downstairs. Someone had thoughtfully put out two extra seats facing the band, so Max gestured to them.

"Here they are," Max said, trying and failing to sound enthusiastic. "Mom, Dad, this is Less than Perfect. Band, here are my parents."

They all timidly but politely said hello to Max's parents, who sat in the chairs offered to them. Max took his place next to Chloe and waved his hand at Claire and D-rock.

"'Secrets'?" D-rock said, nodding at everyone else.

Since it was the only arrangement they really knew well, it was what they would have to play. Claire positioned her left hand on the neck of her cello and got her bow ready. Then she started the song, as written.

Max nervously played his part, every once in a while glancing up at his parents. They were distracting enough that he missed several notes. But at least everyone else played it perfectly. They finished the piece strongly, letting the last chord ring out before lowering their instruments.

"Interesting," Mrs. Ford said. Her expression gave away so little Max couldn't tell how she felt. "What song was that?"

"It's called 'Secrets,'" Claire said. "By OneRepublic."

"This is an odd mix of instruments," Mr. Ford said with a pronounced frown.

Trey chuckled. "We know. We…like it that way."

"Plus, D-rock and Claire write our arrangements just for us," Max said, motioning to them.

"Your arrangements?" Mr. Ford said, his eyebrows raised slightly in surprise. "Are there more?"

Max shifted uncomfortably. "Well, there is another one we tried last week…"

"And others in the works," D-rock said. "But—"

"We've been practising," Trey said confidently. Others around the room said the same thing. "We can try it."

Max bit back a sigh. He'd been practising it, too, but if it fell apart… Never mind. He had no choice. The others were already preparing to play it and he had to trust them. And himself.

The first half of the song, which featured "Kings & Queens," wasn't bad. In fact, it was better than last week, and Max could tell his bandmates had indeed practised it. But his parents still didn't look particularly impressed.

There was a sticky part in the middle of the music where they had to transition to "Holding Out for a Hero." D-rock, Marty, and Bryan should have driven the beat, but they weren't in sync with each other. But then Hacks came in, forcefully beating on the keys, which…surprisingly helped the others get it together.

Now that they knew what was happening with the beat, it was easy for the rest of them to come in. Rach, who had refused last week to play her part, now confidently came in, carrying the melody in her warm low tone.

Max glanced up at his parents and nearly dropped his bow. His mom had a huge smile on her face and was gripping his dad's hand. Even his dad had lightened up and was smiling, too.

Max focused back on his music as the others played. They'd done a shortened version of the song, with only one verse before the bridge. Marty, Hacks, and the brass were clearly enjoying playing as loudly and obnoxiously as they could. But to be fair, that was how the piece was written, after all.

It wasn't perfect. And in fact, when they ended there were a couple of stray notes and Marty wasn't quite sure when to stop. But once everyone had fallen silent, they looked up at Max's parents, whose smiles had grown even more.

Mrs. Ford's voice had a whimsical quality when she said, "I can't believe you kids know that song."

"It was Harmony's suggestion," Claire whispered.

"Thanks, Claire," Harmony muttered.

Mrs. Ford smiled again at her husband. "That was…*our* song once upon a time."

"When we were young like you," Mr. Ford said.

"*Oh*," Max said, now understanding their reaction.

"I am *so* sorry," D-rock said, his eyes wide. "I definitely didn't do it justice."

"Me, neither," Marty piped up.

Mrs. Ford shook her head, looking at each of them. "It was beautiful."

"Yeah, I liked it," Mr. Ford said.

"You...did?" Max asked in surprise. When they nodded at him, he asked, "Can I keep the band, then?"

Mrs. Ford looked at Mr. Ford, who nodded and waved his hand loosely. "Of course," Mrs. Ford said.

Mr. Ford stood. "Also, your mother made me bring home enough snacks for fourteen teenagers, so..."

"Snacks!" TK shouted excitedly.

He quickly unhooked his sax from the neck strap and put it down and the others followed suit. Max's parents led them upstairs while Max calmly put his violin down. Why had his parents made him go through all the trouble when it seemed they had already been prepared to let everyone stay?

"Uh, are you coming?" Chloe asked, standing at the base of the stairs. "Or are you really going to risk your parents telling embarrassing stories about you while you're not there?"

Max hadn't even realized she was still there, but he smiled at her. "Yeah, I'm coming." But even as he said it, he looked across the room at the abandoned instruments. "Who needs an orchestra when we've got all this?"

Her smile lit up the entire basement. "You're right. This is better."

They went upstairs, where everyone was crowded around the kitchen island. An assortment of healthy food had been laid out, but none of Max's friends seemed to mind that they weren't the kind of snacks to get excited over.

Max's parents were trying to get to know everyone. No doubt they were trying their hardest just to remember everyone's names. When he and Chloe entered the kitchen, Mrs. Ford turned to them.

"Oh, and you must be Chloe," she said. "The girl who's been up in our son's bedroom."

Chloe choked on air while Max's face went bright red. The others turned to stare curiously, some of them looking like they were holding back laughter.

"*Mom...*" Max said under his breath.

"Yeah, that's me," Chloe said, clasping her hands together. "I'm sorry. I asked him for a tour because—" She gestured around. "I've just never seen the inside of a mansion before."

"Max told us we *couldn't* see the rest of the house," Amber said, sounding the slightest bit jealous.

"He was right, dear," Mrs. Ford said.

Amber frowned but didn't argue.

"Please do stick to the basement and the kitchen from now on," Mr. Ford said, eyeing Chloe but including the rest of them.

"You mean, we can still come back here for snacks?" Trey asked hopefully.

"Well, we don't expect a bunch of kids to starve in our house," Mr. Ford said.

Max shook his head but didn't complain. Sometimes it was hard to tell whether his parents were being genuine or if they just did things to impress people. Like putting on a big spread for people they claimed to never have wanted in their house in the first place.

But as Max watched them interact with his friends, he realized they seemed like they were honestly interested in each one of them. They asked everything from their ages to what they liked outside of music. Maybe Max hadn't given them enough credit.

Still, after everyone had left, Max couldn't help saying to his parents, "I can't believe you made me go through all of that when you were just going to say yes to us anyway."

"Hey, now," Mr. Ford said, holding up a finger. "We were serious about determining whether or not we thought you were any good."

"*And* you punished my friends for *my* mistake," Max added, ignoring what he was sure was a half-lie.

"You said yourself they were complicit," Mrs. Ford said, pinning him with a look. "If you had just listened to me in the first place, we could have found a better compromise."

"You didn't seem very willing to compromise," Max said without thinking. "You're always talking about how I shouldn't play so much, how my friends aren't worth my time. And I'm sorry but…you're wrong about that."

She tilted her head with a thoughtful frown. "Maybe I am. But that doesn't excuse you from sneaking around and lying to us."

"I know," Max said quietly. He looked at both his mom and then his dad. They still looked disappointed. "I'm sorry."

Her face softened into a smile. "You were also right when you called them all talented. Yourself included."

"Thanks," Max said begrudgingly.

"I can see your friends mean a lot to you," she said softly. "You can have them over to play on Tuesday nights. But I expect you to still get your homework done and for the house to stay in one piece."

"Of course," Max said. "Can Marty still come over to practise? It's kind of not practical for him to bring a full drum set every week."

"Yeah, that's fine," his dad said. "But no more girls in your bedroom."

Max suppressed an eye roll and nodded. "Yeah, I got it the first five times you mentioned it."

"*Max…*"

"Sorry," Max said quickly.

"We're serious," Mrs. Ford said. "Stick to the rules this time. Also, tidy up these leftovers, okay?"

"Alright." Just before they left, Max said, "'Holding Out for a Hero'? Really?"

"That was an absolute banger back then," his dad said, holding up a finger. "As it clearly still is now."

Max chuckled. "Okay. Goodnight."

"Goodnight, Maxy." His mom ruffled his hair and then left him in the very messy kitchen. But that was fine. He could handle that if he got to keep Less than Perfect.

Chapter Ten

Now that the days were getting cooler with the mid-October air, Chloe was already starting to resent having to walk to school. Soon there would be snow on the ground, and wind gales to keep her company.

She and June put on their fall jackets before heading out the door. Chloe was still annoyed at June for lying about losing her bow—she assumed—but that didn't mean she was going to let her walk to school alone. Especially when the elementary school was down the street from the high school.

"They better not make us play outside today," June muttered as she pulled her jacket tightly around herself using just her hands in her pockets.

Chloe bit back a chuckle. "Maybe if you zipped up your jacket?"

"Can't," June said, showing her the bottom of the zipper. "It's broken."

Suppressing a sigh, Chloe reached out and took it gently to look at it. "Why didn't you tell me? I could have fixed that this morning." June just shrugged. "Never mind, I'll do it after school."

"Okay," June said quietly.

What June really needed was a new jacket, but Chloe knew she wouldn't ask their mom. They didn't ask for new things unless they really needed to. Until the fabric was disintegrating and they had totally outgrown their clothes, they didn't need new ones. Chloe could take care of June's jacket.

When Chloe got to school, she was greeted with another happy little envelope. Well, okay, it was black, but it had her name on it in pretty, loopy pink writing. She shook her head at the coward who couldn't just talk to her face-to-face but smiled anyway. The writing inside was decidedly more masculine than the way her name was written on the front.

Chloe,
Your hair looks nice today. How do I know? It looks nice every day.

She ran her hands down her long, dark hair. She had washed it this morning but done nothing else to it. It had a bit of a wave to it and fell halfway down her back but was otherwise unremarkable. At least she had thought so, before she'd been given this note.

Gently she placed the note in her backpack alongside her textbooks. She had other things to think about. Like the costume she was working on for Halloween. This year, she'd been planning on going to the school dance and dressing as a female medieval knight and she wanted it to be good for…the two people who would actually notice her.

Sighing, she shut her locker and headed to her English class. Claire was already there, since she was almost always the first one in class, and Chloe slid into the desk next to hers.

"I got another one," Chloe whispered frantically to Claire.

Claire's green eyes widened. "Got another what?" she asked full-voiced.

"Another random note," Chloe said.

"Can I see it?" Claire asked, leaning in closer.

Chloe hesitated, not really wanting to pull it out of her bag in class. "Can I show you at lunch?"

"Sure," Claire said before focusing her attention on getting prepared for class.

At lunchtime, Chloe only felt a little bad for ditching her friends in favour of once again overanalysing a mysterious letter. Claire met her at the cafeteria doors and as soon as they walked in, Amber raced to catch up to them.

"Hey, you two sitting together?" Amber asked eagerly. "You can hang out with me and Rach and Meg."

"Oh, good," Claire said, a light teasing in her voice. "You can help us dissect Chloe's new note."

"Another one?" Amber squeaked.

Chloe's cheeks tinged pink as she chuckled. "Yes."

They plopped down at the table where Rach and Meg had already started eating. Rach lifted her eyebrows briefly in surprise, but Meg smiled pleasantly at them.

"Okay, let's see it now," Claire said excitedly.

Chloe pulled the note out of her backpack along with her lunch. Since it was just her and the girls, she let them open the note, feeling her face flush harder as they read it together.

"Oh, my gosh!" Amber said, turning to Chloe. "Your hair *is* really pretty today."

"Thanks," Chloe said softly as she ran her fingers through its length. "Did you write this?"

"No," Amber said, chuckling. "But I'm confident we can figure out who did."

As they ate, they left the note in the middle of the table, trying to find any clues that would lead to its author.

"That is by far the nicest stationery I've ever seen," Claire said, touching the thick linen card stock.

"Nice handwriting, too," Meg said as she stuck a fork in her salad. "Are we sure a boy wrote that?"

"It *is* exceptionally neat and…proper," Chloe said. That was the only word she could think to describe it. "But it doesn't look girly? Hard to say."

"There's no way a girl would do her Ys that way," Amber said, completely seriously.

Rach laughed. "Are you an expert on that?"

Amber just laughed with her and shook her head. They fell back to eating silently for a few minutes before she asked, "So, who are you all asking to the Halloween dance?"

Silence met her question as the girls looked around at each other. Chloe quietly admitted, "I would have asked Jaden but apparently all my friends are going as a group. So, like a group date thing. Yup."

Amber smiled and then looked at the note. "You don't think that's his writing, do you?"

"No, his is crazy," Chloe answered a little too quickly. Amber raised an amused eyebrow at her. "Okay, so I know what his chicken scratch looks like. And unless he was *really* trying to hide it, then I know this isn't his note."

"Okay," said Amber. She looked around the table. "Who are you guys going with?"

"I'm not going at all," Meg said, twisting up her blond hair. "So…" She shrugged.

"Seconded," Rach said as she put her lunch containers away.

"Third," Claire said. "Although if I was going to go, I don't think I'd be asking anyone."

Amber's eyes widened. "You're really all not going? But...it's a school dance!"

"Mmhmm," Rach said in an unimpressed tone. "And which cream of the crop are you taking?"

"Oh, I haven't asked him yet," Amber said. She looked around the cafeteria and pointed to the far corner near the emergency exit. "I was going to ask Tyler."

"Tyler *Hasting*?" Rach asked incredulously. She looked over at the dark-haired boy, sitting by himself with his hood over his head and looking sullen.

"Yes," Amber said confidently.

"There's no way he'll say yes," Rach stated. "Are you kidding?"

"No, I'm gonna ask him," Amber said.

Rach shook her head and then reached into her pocket. She threw a five-dollar bill on the table. "Five bucks says he'll say no."

"I'll take that bet." Amber stood with a perky smile.

The girls tried not to be obvious as they watched Amber go over to Tyler. It was a short interaction and Amber's proposition was clearly a surprise to Tyler, whose eyebrows rose to his hairline. But they couldn't tell what the outcome was as Amber walked back to their table.

She sat down and smiled at all of them, her gaze lingering on Rach. "He said no."

Rach laughed out loud and took her money back, then held out her hand.

Amber threw her hands up as her smile fell. "I don't have five dollars on me! I didn't think he'd say no."

"Figures," Rach said, rolling her eyes.

"So I guess you're not going to the dance, then?" Claire said.

"Oh, no, I'm going," Amber said. "I'll just ask...Hacks."

"What is this?" Rach asked, pinning her with a look. "What are you doing? Is this a charity where you ask out boys you think can't get dates?"

"Oh, that's a really good question, actually," Chloe said, leaning in with interest. "What *are* you doing?"

Amber's face flushed. "I'm not doing anything wrong. I'm not asking for dates from boys who can't get dates. I'm just..." She looked down at her clasped hands and cleared her throat. "Look, I'm not trying to lead anyone on. I just think it's nice sometimes to be asked to do things when you don't typically get picked. That's all."

"That is nice, actually," Meg said, patting her on the arm.

"So, who are you asking?" Amber asked, looking up at her.

Meg chuckled. "I don't think anyone needs my charity."

"And I'm not dressing up for a dance," Rach said.

"Why not?" Chloe asked.

"Oh, here we go," Meg murmured.

Rach gave her side eye before answering, "Because I can't...wear skirts. There."

"What?" Claire said, her eyebrows scrunching up.

"I...I can't," Rach said quietly. "Regular skirts look like mini-skirts on me."

Amber's mouth gaped open. "I'm not gonna lie. That sounds *amazing.*"

Rach just rolled her eyes.

"In any case," Meg said, cutting off a potential argument. "You have fun at the dance. I'm *sure* someone will say yes to you, if not Hacks."

"Oh," Amber said. "I was really hoping we'd all be there together."

"Well..." Claire said. "We could just do something fun together on our own. Like without half the school around, and house music pumping out of gigantic, crappy speakers."

"So, I guess you won't be writing house music for the band?" Chloe teased.

Claire snorted. "Not unless D-rock wants to."

Amber bobbed her eyebrows. "Would you go to the dance if he wanted to?"

"No," Claire said firmly.

"Okay, so what kind of fun thing do you want to do, Claire?" Chloe asked.

"I don't know…" Claire said. "I don't really…hang out with a lot of people."

Amber snapped her fingers and her eyes lit up. "Oh, how about a girls' night?"

"Uhh…" Claire hesitated.

"That sounds fun!" Chloe said.

"Less terrible than a school dance," Meg said, with a thoughtful frown.

Rach pursed her lips. "Like…like a sleepover where we play truth or dare but it's really just Amber trying to figure out who everyone has a crush on?"

Amber scoffed, waving a dismissive hand. "As if I don't already know that. No, I meant we could like get dressed up really nicely, go out somewhere fancy, no boys whatsoever. Just us."

"And by someplace fancy, I assume you mean a place we can pretend is fancy but is really inexpensive," Chloe said hopefully.

"One hundred per cent," Amber said as she took out her phone.

"I dunno…" Rach said.

"I already texted Harmony and she loves the idea," Amber said. "Who's free Saturday night?"

"I am," Chloe said.

"Me, too," Meg surprised them by saying. "It sounds fun. But *no* boys, right?"

Amber put her hand over her heart. "I promise. Rach? Claire?"

"Okay, I'll go," Claire said reluctantly. "You're right, that is better than a school dance. Just…hanging out with you girls."

They all turned towards Rach, who knew she couldn't deny them their request. To be fair, Amber was right—it *was* nice to be asked to do things when you never got asked.

"Okay," she finally relented, smiling at the others when they let out tiny cheers. "But I won't wear a skirt."

"I'll see what's in your closet," Amber said, winking.

The lunch bell rang, and the girls quickly gathered their things. Chloe carefully folded her card back into the envelope and put it in her backpack. She said goodbye to her new friends, her spirits lifted from this morning's cold walk.

By the time school ended, the sun had warmed the earth and nothing could ruin Chloe's mood. She let June talk her ear off. She even almost forgave her for the bow incident.

And speaking of her bow… The first thing she did when they got home was pick up her violin. After a quick tune, she put the bow to it. She still had the "Holding Out for a Hero" arrangement on her music stand.

She didn't need a hero, but she couldn't help loving the arrangement Claire and D-rock had written. And while she played, she remembered the huge, sweet smile on Max's mom's face. Maybe he thought they were strict, but he was lucky to have two parents who still clearly loved each other—and loved him enough to take good care of him. She wondered if he even realized.

Chapter Eleven

Bright lights shone onto the glistening field as Coach Hanford gave some tough instructions for their fourth quarter. Trey adjusted his helmet, his breath coming out in puffs. After Coach was done, they got back into position on the field.

They were only 20 yards from the endzone. Trey was confident if he could get the ball to their fullback, they could score a touchdown. Unfortunately, their fullback was Chad, but although their friendship had soured, he was still one of the best players Trey had ever seen.

The play started and Trey caught the ball from their centre, Owen, and quickly backed up to give himself some space from the opposing team's linemen. Chad had already started booking it for the endzone, prepping his arms to catch the football.

Trey didn't hesitate. He threw the football with a perfect trajectory just before he got knocked over. When the lineman who'd gotten him realized Trey was no longer holding the ball, he got up quickly and they turned their attention the endzone.

Despite the light rain, Chad dodged three guys in quick succession and jumped straight into the endzone. But just as he landed over the goal line, one of their huge halfbacks charged at him, pulling him down. Chad was already in the endzone and they got the points, but both boys were still down.

The halfback got up when the whistle blew, but Chad lay there, his arm still wrapped tightly around the football. Something was wrong.

Trey raced forward, spitting his mouthguard out as he went. "Chad!" he shouted, pulling off his helmet.

A couple of the others had crowded around, but Trey pushed past them to get to Chad. He glared at the halfback who'd taken him down.

"What'd you do that for?" Trey said heatedly. "He was already in the endzone!"

The other guy shrugged but at least he looked like he felt bad. "I'm just trying to play the game…"

Trey shook his head and looked down at Chad. "What's wrong?" he asked.

Chad looked up at him with pain in his eyes. "Landed on my shoulder. It doesn't…feel right."

Trey looked over to the sidelines where Coach Hanford had finally decided to leave his post to investigate. Glancing back at Chad, he said, "Let go of the ball and let's get you up."

"It hurts real bad," Chad said weakly.

"I know," Trey said gently.

He leaned down and forced the ball out of the crook of Chad's left arm. Chad winced and groaned. Trey took his other arm and hefted him up. Chad leaned on him for half a second before regaining his balance. By then, Coach Hanford and their team physician had finally arrived to take over.

Trey walked alongside them as they went back to the sidelines. "Are you okay?" he asked.

"I'm fine," Chad said woodenly, avoiding his gaze.

"Okay," Trey said quietly.

He knew things had been rocky between them but that didn't mean he didn't care if Chad got hurt. Except maybe if Trey was doing the hurting. Trey swallowed hard. He never should have gotten physical with Chad, no matter how poor his behaviour. But it wasn't the right time to bring it up.

Once Chad was situated on the sidelines with the physician looking after him, Trey went back to his team. Play continued and they finished off the game, winning 20-17. But it felt almost as bad to win this game without Chad as it had felt to watch the team win without Trey's help.

As the team showered and got changed after the game, Chad sat dejectedly in the locker room, his arm now hanging in a sling. Trey hesitated for a moment before deciding to stop in front of him.

"Are you okay?" Trey asked kindly.

Chad shrugged and then winced. "I can't play the end of the season, so no."

"I'm sorry," Trey said, meaning it entirely.

"I guess this is what I deserve," Chad said, flicking a glance at Trey. "For being a jerk and all."

"I'm not saying that," Trey said.

"You were thinking it," Chad said bitterly.

Trey huffed indignantly. "No, I wasn't." He sat down next to Chad and said, "What's going on with you?"

Chad glared at him. "You haven't talked to me in weeks and now you want to know what's going on?"

One of the other guys on the team who was walking by glanced briefly at them with eyebrows raised and then turned heel. Trey waited until he'd left before speaking again.

"Yeah, actually," Trey said in a low voice. "We're still…friends. I still care about you."

Chad clenched his jaw. "Really? Do you?"

"Yes," Trey insisted. "But honestly? I don't want to be friends with someone who treats girls the way you do."

Chad looked at him sharply. "Think maybe you tightened your chastity belt a little too much this morning."

Trey's eyes narrowed and he got up from the bench. "I'm trying to be nice, but I just feel like hitting you again."

He started to walk away but then Chad bolted off the bench and grabbed his arm. Trey turned and stared into Chad's intense eyes for a moment.

"Look, I'm sorry, okay?" Chad said, sounding genuine enough. "I didn't mean to…be one of *those* guys."

"You don't owe *me* an apology," Trey said, before shaking off Chad's hand. "Sorry about your shoulder."

With that, he left, still not sure he wanted to get his friendship with Chad back. Chad clearly didn't understand that it wasn't about looking good in front of his friends or not becoming something bad. It was deeper than that, and Trey wasn't here for it.

♪   ♫   ♪

While all of Chloe's friends were talking about their weekend plans, she kept silent. Sure, they wouldn't mind if she had other plans with other friends. But they hadn't yet included her in what they were doing. She knew it wasn't because they didn't care about her, but rather because they'd given up on inviting her places, figuring the answer would automatically be no.

The topic of the Halloween dance came up and they confirmed once again that everyone was going together. As a group. No dates. Chloe peeked at Jaden from under her eyelashes. There was really no sense in asking him now.

"You're still coming, right, Chloe?" Sydney asked in her sweet voice.

Chloe smiled. "Yeah, I've been working on my costume for weeks."

Dylan turned to her with his eyebrows scrunched up. "We're not really doing costumes."

Chloe sighed. "Well…Chloe likes Halloween, so she's wearing a costume. You guys can do whatever you want."

She packed up her lunch box just before the bell rang. As they left, Jaden caught up with her and tapped her gently on the shoulder.

When she turned to him, he asked, "So what are you dressing up as?"

"A knight," she said plainly.

"Cool," he said with a smile. He flipped his hair off his face and his smile grew cheeky. "Maybe I'll go as a princess."

She laughed. "You really don't have to do that."

"Oh, good," he said, putting a hand over his heart. "I don't think I can pull off a sexy princess costume."

She looked him up and down. There wasn't much to Jaden aside from his beautiful smile and dyed black hair. Imagining him in a revealing princess dress costume just made her laugh harder.

"You'd need to shave your legs, but it wouldn't be so bad," she finally said.

"Hmm, yeah, I think I'll pass," he said, cringing. "See you around."

Chloe smiled and watched him turn down another hall. She would have gladly accompanied him dressed as a princess to the dance, but she clearly still didn't have the guts to actually tell him.

Speaking of guts… When she got to her locker, there was yet another little black envelope. She shook her head. Why couldn't this guy just be upfront with her? Probably for the same reason she could barely talk to Jaden, she guessed. Reluctantly, she opened the envelope.

Chloe,

When you smile, it lights up my life like the first rays of a sunrise. And when you laugh, it's like a thousand tiny butterflies have taken off in my stomach. Your beauty is like the first lily in spring.

This was such a beautiful but quite frankly strange way to reach out to her. The handwriting gave her no clues that she hadn't already gathered from the last letter. The words themselves were far too poetic to belong to anyone she knew personally. Or so she thought, anyway. Clearly this guy felt close enough to her to leave her these notes. What was she supposed to do with this?

What she did do with the letter was, once she got home, leave it in a stack with the other three. She had one drawer that had a lock on it and exactly one key for that lock that she kept on a bracelet at all times. So the letters went in there, away from June's curious fingers and her mom's prying eyes.

Once they were safely stowed away, she turned to her closet to pick out an outfit for girls' night. She still had no idea where they were going—though Amber had assured her it wouldn't be costly. And since she wasn't going on any dates any time soon, she might as well look good for her girls.

She pulled out a beautiful pleated black and green plaid skirt. She'd bought it a while ago, but she'd never worn it after she discovered it didn't even fit her. It was also longer than she would have gone for a pleated skirt. But she knew the perfect model for it.

Taking out her phone, she sent a message to Rach.

Chloe: i have the perfect skirt for you

Rach: no thanks. i don't do skirts.

Chloe: hear me out. i don't like how long it is on me, and

honestly it's too big anyway but it would fit you perfectly!!

For good measure, she sent a picture of it. Rach didn't answer for a long time and finally, Chloe just called her.

"Hi, Chloe," Rach answered with a sigh.

"Just please come and try it," Chloe said without preamble. "I'm never going to wear it and I'd rather it go to someone it would look good on."

Rach hesitated. "Okay, I'll try it on. But if it looks terrible, I'm never wearing it again."

"Terrible is in the eye of the beholder," Chloe teased. When Rach didn't answer, she laughed. "Come *on*. It'll be great! Come over after dinner."

A long sigh came over the line. "Fine. I'll see you after dinner."

"Yay!"

Chloe knew the skirt would look amazing. As for convincing Rach...well, that was a nearly impossible task, it turned out. She'd come over like she said, but so far hadn't even touched the skirt, let alone put it on.

Rach took one look at it and said, "I'm not wearing that."

"Then why'd you come over?" Chloe asked, her eyebrows scrunched up.

Rach shrugged. "You asked me to."

Chloe smiled and handed her the skirt. "I appreciate that you came over when I asked. But now that you're here, I really think you should try this. It's just me and you."

"And me!" came a perky voice from the doorway.

"And June," Chloe said, flicking her wrist in the younger girl's direction. "But she's contractually obligated to say nice things about my friends."

Rach gave June a wary glance before finally accepting the skirt. They respectfully turned around while she took her pants off to put the skirt on.

She couldn't believe it! The skirt fit her waist perfectly. How had Chloe just had this sitting around?

"Chloe." When Chloe turned around, Rach asked, "Where did you really get this skirt from?"

Chloe's eyes widened and her jaw dropped open. "Rach, your *legs*!"

"I know…"

"They're amazing!"

"Amazingly long, I know." Rach self-consciously tugged at the hem of the skirt, which fell a few inches short of her knees.

"And just plain *wow*," Chloe said, coming forward. "Stop pulling on it. It's sitting exactly as it should. You *have* to wear this on Saturday. It's fate!"

"It does look very nice," June said, sounding like she really meant it.

Rach chewed on her bottom lip and looked down at herself. She felt totally naked in this skirt even though admittedly it was still long enough to be appropriate.

"Just us girls?" Rach said aloud.

"Nobody else will see you," Chloe said.

"Okay," Rach finally relented. "I'll wear it."

"Eee!" Chloe squealed. "They're gonna love it."

Finally, Rach smiled. "Okay, what are you wearing?"

Excitedly, Chloe pulled out a navy dress from her closet. It had an asymmetrical hemline and straps that crisscrossed at the back.

"It was a thrift store find," Chloe said. "Most of my clothes are, to be honest. It was a lot longer, so I chopped off like half the length. I also put these straps on because it had these ugly cap sleeves I *so* was not into."

"Wow, Chloe," Rach said as she touched the straps. "I didn't know you were into sewing."

"Well…" Chloe shrugged uncomfortably. "It used to be out of necessity because we don't buy new clothes very often. But I've grown to love it."

"That's so cool," Rach said.

Chloe smiled. "I could probably teach you how to tailor clothes so you can wear stuff that fits better. No offense. I can just imagine it's hard for you to shop."

Rach snorted. "You can say that again. I would like that, actually."

"Great," Chloe said. "And keep this skirt."

"Are you sure?" Rach said, running her hands along the pleats.

Chloe waved her hand. "I was never going to wear it. But you better wear it on Saturday."

"Okay, I get it," Rach said, laughing. "Thank you for this."

"Anytime," Chloe answered.

Chapter Twelve

Bryan went about his work at the community centre while also half paying attention to the people who came in for their regular activities. By now he knew where to go to avoid Stacey—and also when Harmony would be done her orchestra rehearsal. Not that he had any particular reason for searching for her in the throng of young musicians.

When she came out of the rehearsal hall looking calm and content, he smiled. But he quickly schooled his expression when she turned towards him.

"Oh, hey, Bryan," she said in a cheery voice.

He nodded. A few others followed Harmony out of the room as Bryan needlessly fiddled with his cleaning cart.

"I think that's all of them," she said when there was a lull.

"Thanks," he said. He raised an eyebrow at her when she didn't leave. "Are you waiting for a ride?"

She smiled, her bright brown eyes lighting up. "No, but I'll take it if you're offering."

He pointed into the rehearsal hall. "I have to clean this out first."

"I can wait," she said.

He shook his head but when he turned away from her, he couldn't help smiling again. The rehearsal room quickly took care of his good attitude. Not only did he have to disinfect all the chairs and put them away, but the floor was... Oh, he didn't even want to think about how much spit had dripped out of the instruments onto the floor.

As quickly as humanly possible, he washed the floor, the lemon detergent flooding his senses. It wasn't the worst scent. And this wasn't the worst job. He just had to keep reminding himself of that.

He was disappointed to find the hallway empty when he left. Obviously he'd taken too long to clean for Harmony to stick around. And that was fine with him. He didn't need her talking over his music in his car again anyway.

He put his cart away and then headed to the front doors, jiggling his keys as he went. He started whistling, his head entirely in his music. When someone fell in line with him and started whistling in harmony, he stopped abruptly, nearly tripping over his own feet.

Harmony grinned at him. "Did you...forget about me?"

"No," he said. "I didn't see you, so I figured you didn't wait for me."

"I mean..." She paused to giggle. "You were *so* focused on hitting the right notes you didn't even look for me."

Bryan could feel his face heat up. "Well, you know, you don't have to harmonize with me just because your name is Harmony."

Harmony put her hand on the push bar of the outer doors and gave him an exasperated look. "I really wish that were the first time anyone's ever made that joke."

"Then maybe you shouldn't harmonize with people out of the blue when they're just trying to get their whistle on." Bryan immediately cringed at how lame that sounded but Harmony just laughed.

"I'll keep it in mind next time, but no promises," she said as she followed him to the parking lot. "I just can't help myself from making music."

"Clearly," he answered. He hit the button on his fob to unlock his car and got in.

Harmony jumped into the car quickly as if she thought he'd take off without her. As she buckled in, she said, "Yeah, I know you think I do way too much. But I did take your advice."

"What advice?" he asked as he pulled out of the parking space.

She reached out and turned the volume on his radio down. "I dropped one of my ensembles."

"Oh," he said, trying not to sound too disappointed. "I'll miss seeing you on Tuesday nights then, I guess."

"No, you won't," she said plainly.

"But you said—"

"I dropped one of my ensembles," she filled in for him. "Yeah, I chose the flute choir. I have enough flute in my life."

"Harmony." He stopped at a light and turned to her quickly to give her a confused look. "When I said you should drop one, I meant Less than Perfect. Not one of your serious groups."

"Oh, I know," she said. "But I didn't want to. Like I said, I don't really need *more* flute right now. Less than Perfect is fun and I'm still playing. It's a win win."

"You're sure about that?" he asked. "I mean, you're really way too far advanced for the rest of us."

"You know," she said as she cracked her window open. "I thought maybe when you first said it, it was because the band was trying to get rid of me—again—and they asked you to do it. But you actually care, don't you?"

"No," he lied. "I just think if I were in your position, I would have dropped out of the thing that was least valuable to me."

She shook her head even though he wasn't looking at her. "I guess that's where we have a difference of opinion. Because Less than Perfect isn't the least valuable to me."

Bryan took a hard left onto Harmony's street. "You really mean that, don't you?"

"Yes, I do," she said.

He was quiet as he pulled up to the curb outside her house. Then he turned to her with a half smile and said, "I guess I'll see you Tuesday night, then."

Her smile outshone his. "See you on Tuesday."

Bryan went home, still whistling the same song he'd had in his head all day. His parents' cars were gone—even better. As soon as he went inside, Amber called his name. He found her in the bathroom with her hair in a bun and half her makeup done.

"Oh, Bryan," she said, giving him a nice friendly smile. "Can you give me a ride tonight?"

He scrunched up his face. "Are you going on a date? Ew, no, I'm not driving you."

She rolled her eyes. "I'm not going on a date," she said in an exasperated voice.

"Then what?" he asked.

"Just...a thing." She turned back to the counter and picked up her eyeshadow.

Crossing his arms, he leaned against the door jamb. "I'm definitely not taking you somewhere if I don't even know what you're doing."

"Okay," she said as she swished her brush into a light pink. "Just, you can't say anything, okay? I'm doing a girls' night. That's all."

"Girls' night?" he said, straightening up. "With who? Not Stacey and Yuri…"

Amber scoffed so hard she almost choked. "The girls from the band."

He paused a moment. "I want to come."

"It's a *girls'* night, Bry," she said. "You're a boy."

"Yeah, but I like girls. Let me come," he said.

"No way." She turned to him and lifted one carefully groomed eyebrow. "There are absolutely no boys allowed. So don't be telling anyone, either."

"Do you want that ride or…?" he pressed.

"Look," she said, turning back to the mirror. "Take me downtown and I'll…I don't know, put in a good word for whoever you're into right now."

He thought about it briefly, but then shook his head. "No. At least let me get out of the car and say hi."

"Okay, fine. If you drive me there and back then you can say hi," she agreed.

"Oh, no," he said. "You want a drop-off *and* pick-up? I get to say hello *and* goodnight."

"*Fine*," she said, her eyes flashing in irritation. "As long as I don't have to walk in my heels or pay for a ride."

"Great," he said cheerfully. "I'll go change."

"For what purpose?" she called to him as he rushed to his bedroom.

He ignored her as he opened his closet. If they were all getting dressed up, so was he.

♪   ♫   ♪

Rach pulled down the hem of her skirt for the fifteenth time. If she rushed upstairs now, she would probably have time to change before Meg came to pick her up. Or maybe she could ditch altogether. She didn't need a girls' night anyway.

Just as she turned to go to her room, she nearly ran right into her mom.

"Wow, Rachel, you look adorable," her mom said, taking in her entire outfit.

"Thanks," Rach said. "But you're obligated to say that."

Her mom laughed. "No, really. Where'd you get that skirt? It's so cute!"

Rach's heart warmed. Her mom was always trying to make her feel good, but she could tell this time she really meant it.

"A friend gave it to me," Rach said. "So we could all look pretty tonight or something. I don't know. I'm just going along with it."

"Oh, yeah, I can tell by your makeup and hair that you're just going with the flow," her mom said, her eyes dancing.

Rach laughed and smoothed down her freshly straightened hair. She didn't usually bother because it took forever. But the effort was worth it for her friends.

"Thanks, Mom," she said. "I think Meg's here. I'll see you later."

Rach grabbed her purse and hurried out to Meg's truck before her mom could make any more comments or ask any more questions. When she got inside, her jaw dropped. Meg looked totally different with her smoky eyes and bright red lipstick.

"Wow," Rach said, her eyes wide.

"No, *you*," Meg said, taking in her full outfit.

Rach looked down at Meg's black dress that hugged her body. "How long have you owned that dress? And that lipstick?"

Meg laughed as she put the truck in gear. "Forever and no, I haven't worn either one yet."

"Wow," Rach repeated.

"And you?" Meg said. "When was the last time you straightened your hair?"

"Who knows?" Rach said. "It just takes so long. Even longer than it takes to shave my legs. I don't even know why I went through the trouble."

"Because…" Meg shook her head as she came to a stoplight. "Amber asked us to, and it is *so* hard to say no to her."

"No kidding," Rach said. "I can't believe Tyler turned down a date with her."

"Maybe she's not his type?" Meg suggested.

"Then who is?" Rach muttered.

Meg just chuckled and continued driving quietly. The restaurant they'd chosen, La Fourchette D'or, was in a crowded downtown location. The nearest parking lot was a block away, but Meg and Rach didn't mind. Though it was nearly the end of October, it was a mild night and neither of them minded the short walk.

Rach did, however, mind the amount of leg she was showing and as they walked, she tried pulling her skirt down over and over. Meg finally admonished her to which Rach scoffed. Their pre-argument was cut off by the sight of Chloe, Claire, and Harmony waiting outside the restaurant's front doors.

They were all dressed pretty and as soon as they were clumped together, the compliments started flying. Meg's lipstick, Harmony's long hair in perfect waves, Chloe's wing-tipped eyeliner, Rach's legs, Claire's cute floral top—everything was fair game.

"I know Amber likes to make a dramatic entrance," Chloe said once they'd finished gushing over each other, "but I still can't believe she's late for her own thing."

Rach chuckled. "Maybe it was all just a big plot to get us out of our comfort zones."

"Nope, there she is," Harmony said pointing to the nearby intersection. "*Oh.*" Her face went red as she pulled her denim jacket closer around herself.

Chloe followed her line of vision, her eyes narrowing. "What is *he* doing here?"

Amber threw her hands into the air as she approached them ahead of Bryan. "He's just dropping me off, saying hello, and then leaving."

"You said no boys," Rach said, a warning flashing in her eyes.

"Ew, he's not a boy," Amber said, her lip curled up in disgust. "He's my brother."

"Yo, Amber, move," Bryan said as he pushed Amber to the side. "You're blocking my view. Ah, that's better."

He smiled at them, but his smile fell when all the girls crossed their arms, turning menacing frowns at him. At least they *would* be menacing if they didn't all look so adorable. Which brought Bryan back to his smile.

"Okay, you can go now," Amber said. She put her hands on his chest and pushed but he didn't move at all. "Bryan, come on."

"You never said I had to leave after I dropped you off," he said, finally acknowledging Amber.

"But can you?" Amber said.

"Yeah, can you?" Rach repeated.

Bryan turned his attention to Rach and his gaze travelled all the way down her long legs to her flats. Amber snapped her fingers in his face.

"Bye, Bryan," she said.

"Okay, bye," he said. "I'm just gonna…stand over there and wait for a couple friends. No big deal."

"*What* friends?" Amber said, her eyes narrowed.

"A couple guys," he said. "What? I wanna hang out on a Saturday night, too."

"Are your friends closet musicians, by any chance?" Claire asked, her eyes narrowed so far they were almost closed.

Bryan looked away and coughed into his hand. "Maybe..." he mumbled.

"I'm out!" Claire said, stomping past them.

"Wait for me," Meg said, with Rach following on her heels.

"Why'd you have to ruin our night like that?" Harmony snipped at Bryan as she walked past him.

"Wait, hang on," he said. "I'm not trying to ruin anyone's night. Come on. Can't we hang out, too?"

"*No!*" all six girls shouted at once.

As the other five started walking away, Amber turned to Bryan with her hands on her hips.

"It's just a couple guys," Bryan said. "We won't bug you, okay?"

Amber tilted her head and then smiled. "Just a couple guys?"

Bryan shrugged.

"Okay," she said sweetly. "I'll go talk to the girls. You go inside and ask if they can add a *couple* seats to our reservation."

"Really?" he asked in genuine surprise.

"Yeah," she said. "I'm sure I can convince them to come back."

"Sweet!" he said. "Thanks. See you inside."

She watched him walk inside with a smug smile on her face. "Oh, no, you won't," she whispered to herself.

Once he was inside, she raced off to find the girls. They were all heading to the parking lot and when she caught up with them, they didn't acknowledge her at first.

Finally, she said, "Are you mad at me?"

"We're not mad," Meg threw over her shoulder. "But why did you tell Bryan about tonight?"

"I needed a ride," Amber said softly. "I didn't think he'd care that I was just meeting up with some girlfriends."

"Have you *met* your brother?" Harmony snipped.

Amber stopped walking. "Okay, well...I told him that we'd go back into the restaurant to hang out with him and I was thinking that we could just like...leave him hanging?"

Chloe turned and at first just looked at her. Then she burst out laughing. "Okay, that is pretty funny."

"So you're not mad at me?" Amber asked, clasping her hands together.

"No," Chloe said. "But we should get out of here before his *friends* show up."

"Yeah, but where are we gonna go now?" Claire asked.

"You can come over if you want," Meg said. "My dad won't mind. My cat might, though..."

Rach smiled. "To Meg's house!"

They laughed and continued to the parking lot. Rach got back into Meg's truck while Claire, Chloe, and Amber went with Harmony in her mom's van. So they wouldn't have their fancy night out, but they could at least still enjoy each other's company with a nice night in. *And* without the guys.

Chapter Thirteen

"Amber, why did you tell Bryan about our girls' night?" Claire asked as Harmony drove them towards Meg's house.

"Sibling politics, Claire," Amber said. "I wanted the ride and I had to promise he could say hi to you guys, but I also told him he couldn't tell anyone else about it. It's not my fault he didn't uphold his end of the bargain."

"Next time ask *me* for a ride," Harmony said as she glanced at Amber in the rear-view mirror.

"I didn't think of it…" Amber mumbled.

"It's okay," Chloe said. "It was only one boy who saw us. And with some quick thinking, I think we've got them off our trail, right?"

"Oh, yeah," Amber said looking down at her phone. She giggled. "He's going to think I'm hanging out by the river allll night long."

"Won't he get worried?" Harmony asked.

Amber snorted. "Are we both talking about the guy who was worried he didn't have a good view of you because I was standing in his way?"

"Good point," Harmony said.

She turned onto Meg's street and pulled into her driveway behind the truck. As soon as they got out of the van, the front door opened, and Meg and Rach greeted them cheerfully.

"I already ordered takeout," Meg said as the others took off their beautiful but uncomfortable shoes. "My dad's treating. He felt bad that our party got crashed."

"Hey, girls," Meg's dad said from behind her. "Come on in."

"Thank you so much," Chloe said as she followed them past the front hall.

"Mr. Ritz," Amber said as she walked past him. "If our male...*acquaintances* show up—"

"Don't worry," he said nonchalantly, holding up a hand. "I got you covered. No boys will get past me tonight."

"You're a good man," Amber said, giving him a cheeky smile.

"Amber!" Rach called. "Come on or you'll miss the tour."

"Coming!" Amber called back.

She followed the sound of Rach's voice to the kitchen, which was as adorable and tidy as Meg was. It was clear she'd had a hand in the decorating, if the bright orange walls, hanging mug rack, and frilly yellow curtains in the window were any indication. A grey tabby cat pawed at Meg's legs, yowling like he hadn't been fed in weeks.

"And this is Mercutio," Meg said as she picked up the cat. "He loves cuddles."

Chloe held her hands out and Meg passed her the cat, who promptly curled up in Chloe's arms.

"Meg, show them your practice room," Rach said with a hint of impatience.

Meg chuckled and waved a hand at her. "Okay, come on."

She led them to the double doors off the kitchen that went into the

245

sunroom turned practise room. She turned up the dimmer switch halfway and gestured for them to help themselves to the room, which they did.

"What is *that*?" Chloe asked in a sassy voice, pointing to the two trumpets sitting neatly side-by-side on their stands.

Meg chuckled self-consciously. "Surely you recognize trumpets when you see them."

Harmony lifted an eyebrow. "Do you own more than one trumpet?"

"That's *Trey's* trumpet," Rach said before Meg could answer, her eyes twinkling mischievously. Mercutio, traitor that he was, jumped down from Chloe's arms and swished his tail across the extra trumpet.

"Oooh. Why is it *here*?" Chloe asked.

"He practises here sometimes," Meg answered, shrugging uncomfortably. "He says his house is too crowded and noisy."

"What do you mean he practises here *sometimes*?" Amber asked. She gestured to the two stands with music still sitting on them. "How often is *sometimes*?"

"Well, he just lives up the street," Meg said, gesturing vaguely in the direction of his house. "So, when he has time or whenever…"

"Okay, so he comes over sometimes." Harmony bent down to scratch Mercutio's back. "And he leaves his trumpet out on its stand for…easy access?"

"Yeah," Meg said lightly. The other five girls stared at her and her cheeks flushed under their attention. "Okay, what's your point?"

"Girl, he likes you!" Amber exclaimed, throwing her hands in the air.

Meg shook her head while the others all nodded. "There's no way."

"Um, yeah, if he's leaving his stuff at your house…" Chloe said. Her high ponytail bounced perfectly when she tilted her head.

"And it's easily accessible to him," Harmony added with a teasing lilt.

"And I'm guessing he has a standing invitation to come whenever he wants?" Claire said.

"Better believe it," Rach sassed.

Meg opened her mouth, but the doorbell chimed before she could defend herself. "Sounds like our dinner is here."

Her face still feeling like it was a million degrees, she met her dad in the dining room where he was just placing their takeout bags. Taking a deep breath, she started handing out the food they'd gotten from the very restaurant where they'd ditched Bryan.

"Thanks so much, Dad," Meg said softly.

When the others thanked him as well, he saluted them and then left the room. Once he was gone, Chloe excitedly said, "Okay, so we've confirmed that Trey definitely has the hots for Meg."

The girls giggled while Meg's face flushed again.

"Oh, okay," Meg said calmly. "Are we all still pretending Chloe doesn't hang out in Max's bedroom before rehearsals?"

"Ohhhh!" the girls squealed together while Chloe bit her lip and shook her head.

"That is *not*—" Chloe was cut off by more giggling. "That was *one* time! And I was in there for like thirty seconds. I do *not* hang out in his bedroom."

"So, what do you do, then?" Claire asked, looking like she was holding back more laughter.

Chloe rolled her eyes. "Usually just argue," she said, though it wasn't at all believable.

"Oh, come on, Chloe," Harmony said in a sweet voice. "He's super cute."

"And rich!" Amber added.

Chloe tilted her head. "Tell me about it. I mean there's this—" She cut herself off, wondering if they would just tease her again. But she couldn't hold it back. "Okay, he has one wall in his room that's just, like, *covered* in concert ticket stubs. And he has really eclectic taste."

"Aw, man," Amber said. "Of course he does. I miss all my favourite artists and he's just out there living *my* life."

Chloe stabbed a fork into her chicken salad. "The grass is always greener."

Amber raised her eyebrows. "Tell me exactly how you think my grass is greener than his professionally groomed lawn."

Chloe smiled at the silly comparison. "You have a million friends, for starters. And it's not because of your money."

"Nope, definitely not that." Amber's eyes flashed.

Chloe chuckled. "I'm just saying, I think he's kind of lonely up in his castle tower. Why do you think he fought so hard to get his parents to let us keep playing at his house?"

"Maybe you're right," Rach said. "Although he kind of does hide behind his money. He could just say he likes being friends with us."

"I'm not saying I'm like *friends* friends with him," Chloe said.

While Chloe's head was bowed over her food, the other girls all gave each other looks of disbelief.

"Well, you sound like you know him pretty well for someone who's not *friends* friends with him," Claire said, bobbing her eyebrows.

"Yeah, almost as well as you probably know D-rock after spending all that time with him," Chloe shot back. "*Writing music*, or so you say."

Claire looked away, biting her lip as the other girls giggled over Chloe's comment. Maybe she deserved it, but it wasn't what they thought. When there was finally a lull, Claire cleared her throat and said quietly, "I live alone."

"What?" Meg asked in a concerned voice.

"I mean, my parents still live at home," Claire said quickly. "But they're rarely ever actually there. I like going to D-rock's house. His mom always feeds me. And even though I don't like him like that, and he can't sit still for longer than five minutes, he's still pretty good company."

"Claire," Chloe said softly. "I didn't know. I never would have teased you if I'd known."

Claire shrugged uncomfortably. "It's okay…"

"But what do you mean that you live alone?" Amber asked, her eyebrows scrunched up.

Claire shook her head, wishing she hadn't brought it up. But these girls were kind to her. They were her friends. This was a safe place.

"My parents are musicians," she finally said. "Have you ever heard of Julia and Frederick Fortunato?"

Harmony's eyes widened. "*Those* are your parents?"

Claire nodded. They were huge names in the classical music world, so she could understand Harmony's reaction.

"But that's not your last name," Rach said needlessly.

Claire snorted. "It's not theirs, either. We're not even Italian. It just sounds better than Marcs. They've been playing together since before I was born. I guess I didn't exactly fit in with the plan. They've always traveled. When I was little, they would leave me with my aunt or my grandparents. But now that I'm older…I just kick it at home by myself."

None of them spoke for several moments as they let what Claire told them sink in. Then Meg said softly, "Claire, that sounds…"

"Yeah," Claire said, nodding sadly. "It's exactly how it sounds."

"I didn't realize. I just thought you liked being alone," Chloe said gently.

Claire smiled sadly at her. "Does anybody *really* like being alone all the time?"

The girls all shook their heads, murmuring no. Amber looked close to tears. "You know you can always come over, right?" she said. "You don't have to be alone all the time."

"You're always welcome at my place, too," Chloe said. "I'll show you what *real* sibling politics are like."

"And my dad makes tacos every single Tuesday," Meg said, half rolling her eyes. "If you like tacos. There are always too many."

"And you can always come over and play with me," Harmony said. "My parents would love that."

"Or me," Rach said. "And I'll show you what a real tuba melody should look like."

Claire smiled, this time looking happier. "Thank you. I appreciate that. You guys can come over, too. There are some perks. I don't have to pay the bills. Groceries get delivered straight to me. I don't even do yard work. I just have to keep up after myself."

"And you never have to listen to your parents fight," Amber mumbled.

Claire gave her a sympathetic look. "I almost wish I had even *that*. But I can understand how that would be awful for you."

"I want to say at least I have Bryan," Amber said. She frowned. "But on the other hand, I have to put up with him, too."

"I know he crashed our party," Harmony said. "But he's not the worst person in the world. Right?"

"Ew," Amber said.

"He is *kinda* cute." Rach shrugged. "On a good hair day."

Amber put a hand to her mouth and made a fake vomiting motion. "Please stop."

"Nice smile when you can get him to smile," Chloe added.

"*Seriously*," Amber whined, holding up a hand. "Meg, please, make them stop."

"I'm in love with Trey," Meg burst out, her face flaming up. Amber looked at her sharply. "I have been for years. I just don't think he'll ever see me that way."

The girls stared at her, their mouths hanging open at Meg's proclamation. Turning her gaze to her hands clasped tightly in her lap, she sighed. She'd never told anyone that, not even Rach. Now they would think she was ridiculous for even bothering.

"But has he ever seen you like *this*?" Amber asked genuinely.

"Huh?" Meg glanced up at her.

Amber pointed up and down Meg's body and face with a sassy smirk. Meg groaned.

"No, obviously he hasn't." Meg touched the collar of her dress that was cut lower than she realized. The girls wouldn't care, but Trey? "No."

"Okay, what are we going to do about this?" Rach asked.

"What?" Meg said. "That's not neces—"

"Oh, I know!" Amber snapped her fingers. "Text him *U up?* at one in the morning. If he answers, then you know he likes you."

Meg scrunched her face up. "I'm…not texting him that. Ever. Or staying up that late just to text a boy."

"Besides," Harmony said, giving Amber an incredulous look. "What if he doesn't answer? Then they'll have a weird text between them."

"You saw the trumpet out on its stand," Claire said, pinning Harmony with a look. "And you said it yourself, Harmony. He wants a reason to come back."

"Because he likes playing with me," Meg said. "It's quiet here. He gets uninterrupted time to just be himself and not worry about what other people think and he feels—" She cut herself off, her eyebrows drawing together.

"He feels what?" Chloe asked.

Meg hesitated. "I was going to say he feels safe with me," she said in a quiet voice.

Harmony smiled while Amber squealed into Meg's ear.

"And you feel safe with him, too, right?" Rach said, a goofy grin growing on her face, too.

Meg smiled as she ducked her head. "Yeah, I guess I do."

"Tell him," Chloe urged.

"Yes, please," Amber said, clasping her hands together in front of her. "Our group mom needs a good strong group dad to be with."

"That's—" Meg burst out laughing. "Stop. That's weird. But...maybe I'll tell him."

"Tonight?" Rach asked.

Meg bit her lip and shook her head. "I don't even know...how. I've never really told a boy I liked him before."

"Makes sense, since you've only ever been in love with Trey," Rach said.

Meg groaned. Amber patted her shoulder and gave her a kind smile.

"With a boy like Trey, you just have to be really direct," Amber said. "You know? You can't just...drop hints or...stalk him for years and assume he'll get the hint."

"I haven't been stalking him," Meg said, her shoulders drooping.

"Okay, sorry." Amber chuckled. "You're not a creeper. But still...pining from a distance hasn't been working out for you. Just go right up to him and be like, *Trey, let's do this thing.*"

"Maybe not those exact words," Harmony said. "That's still kind of unclear."

"Yeah, actually," Chloe said. "Just straight up say, *Trey, I like you. Do you want to go out with me?*"

"You could even ask him to the dance," Rach said.

Meg's eyebrows pressed together, and her heart raced just thinking about it. "What if he turns me down?"

Claire laughed. "Then it's gonna be really awkward when he comes to take his trumpet back and realizes what a huge mistake he's made."

Meg gave her a tiny smile. She wanted to believe them, to be able to do what they were suggesting. But the whole situation felt impossible.

"Meg," Amber said. "I'm not going to say there's like a rush or something, but you should do it while you're still feeling as confident as you do now."

"I don't feel confident at all," Meg said.

"You should, though," Rach said. "Look at you. You're hot! And Trey already likes you. You can totally do this."

Meg made eye contact with each one of them as they gave her their most encouraging and eager looks. "Maybe," she finally said.

The others squealed while she just laughed. What had she gotten herself into?

Chapter Fourteen

"Why are we doing this?" Marty complained. "This is dumb."

One by one, the boys had all joined Bryan at La Fourchette D'or, having been assured that the girls were waiting for them. Bryan had yet to tell them that the girls had likely already gone far, far away and weren't coming back. Instead, he assured them that there were so many girls who wanted to spend their evening with them.

"To be honest, Marty," D-rock said, "we kind of thought you'd hate it, but we figured you'd hate being left out even more."

"Wow." Marty put a hand over his heart. "You guys really know me."

"And besides, I already ordered a million sliders," Bryan said.

Max looked up quickly. "Tell me you weren't going to ditch me with the bill."

"Of course not." Bryan smirked. "Although I wish I'd thought of that."

TK laughed and high-fived Bryan while Max rolled his eyes.

"But where are the girls?" TK asked. "You said there'd be girls."

"Yeah, they're around somewhere," Bryan said. "But before they get here, I just want to say one thing." He paused for dramatic effect while the others waited. "If any of you look at Amber, touch Amber, or think about Amber, I'll break your nose."

"So, we can talk to her, then?" Marty asked in a bored voice.

Bryan turned narrowed eyes on him. "I will break. Your. Nose."

Marty put his hands up. "I'm not even into... Never mind."

"Dude, relax," Trey said, putting his hand on Bryan's shoulder and giving him a little push. "It's fine. I won't let anyone hurt Amber."

"Oh, yeah, that's real comforting coming from the guy who's got half the school in love with him." Bryan shook off Trey's hand.

Trey rolled his eyes. "Why does everyone always say that to me?"

When no one spoke, Marty cleared his throat. "Do I have to do this?" he muttered.

"Nah, I got this," TK said. "Technically, there are more girls than boys at our school. Now some of the girls are gay, but some of the boys are also gay, so it evens out. So statistically speaking, I'd say it's more than half the school."

Some of them snickered while Trey just shook his head. Hacks grinned and said, "Wow, we haven't even gotten to statistics yet. Good job, TK."

TK and Hacks high-fived and Trey sighed noisily. Thankfully, their food arrived and if there was one thing Trey could count on, it was that boys couldn't talk and eat at the same time.

TK did take a break to say, "They're never coming, are they, Bryan?"

Bryan shrugged and pulled out his phone. "Amber said they would, but...looks like now she's hanging out by the river."

"And that doesn't concern you?" Hacks asked.

Bryan snorted. "No. That means she ditched and doesn't want me to know where she went." The others groaned and complained at him. "Well, at least we have sliders."

"Nice of you to treat us," D-rock said meaningfully.

"Well, uh… I was thinking you guys might pitch in," Bryan said as he stared straight at Max.

Max shook his head and pulled on his tie. "You mean me. You were thinking *I* would pitch in. Or you really were going to leave me with the whole thing."

"Nah, man," Bryan said with a cocky smile. "I was gonna ditch you with the bill *and* the girls. I figured you'd be less mad that way. You know? I don't mind helping you out with girls."

Max clenched his jaw. Rising, he pulled his wallet out of his back pocket. He took out five twenties and tossed them on the table. "There's a hundred bucks. Have a nice night."

"Wait, Max!" Bryan said as Max brushed past him.

Sighing, Max stopped and waited.

"The bill's only like fifty bucks," Bryan said. "I don't need all that."

Max leaned in close to him, his mouth set in a thin, firm line. "Then what will you use to feed your ego?"

"Ooohhhhh," the other boys jeered. Trey elbowed Bryan so hard he was sure he'd have a bruise on his side later.

Bryan's face hardened. "You really think I'm more egotistical than a guy who throws money around to buy his friends?"

Max pursed his lips and nodded. "Yeah. Now, if you'll excuse me." He paused to smile politely at Bryan. "I'm going to go home and think about Amber. I bet she's wearing a really tight dress that would get her kicked out of school."

Bryan bolted out of his seat, holding his hands out in a threatening way. "Come at me, bro."

Max unbuttoned the cuffs of his shirt and rolled up the sleeves. "Gladly," he spat out.

D-rock tapped Trey's shoulder. "That's not gonna end well," he mumbled.

Trey stood up and got between Max and Bryan. "Nah, come on. Settle this like men. Hot wings competition. Ten wings each. Whoever finishes first gets the last word."

There was a tense, silent moment after which Marty said, "I could go for some hot wings."

"Me, too," TK said.

"I want in on that," Corbie added.

Another beat of silence passed while Max and Bryan stared each other down. Finally, Max retook his seat just as their water came back. When he asked how everything was going, Max smiled politely at him.

"Can we get eighty ghost pepper wings?" Max asked.

The waiter's eyebrows rose to a startled height. "Ei-eighty?"

"Yeah, we need ten each," Bryan said, sounding resigned.

The waiter nodded slowly. "Okay... Eighty ghost pepper wings, coming right up."

"Oh, I actually—" Hacks started to say but then the waiter left. "I really don't eat spicy things."

"You do now, buddy," TK said, slapping him on the back.

"While we're waiting for wings," D-rock said to cut off yet more arguing, "let's talk about the music."

"The music?" Corbie said.

"Yes?" D-rock lifted his hands. "You guys know you all play in a band with me, right?"

"Yeah, but you and Claire have the music covered," Corbie said. "And I like it."

"I concur," Hacks said. "I'd be willing to try, but I don't think I have the time. Besides, don't you like working with Claire?"

"Yeah," D-rock said. "She does all the hard work. But I don't think she likes me that much and it's awkward, so…"

"Yeah, but does Claire like anybody?" Bryan asked.

D-rock turned to Bryan and gave him a dead stare. "Do you ever have anything nice to say?"

Bryan hesitated, like he really had to think about the answer. Then he pointed past D-rock and said, "Wings are here."

"Yesss," Marty said, rubbing his hands together.

They split the wings up between themselves, though Hacks still looked like he'd prefer to be anywhere but there.

"Alright, rules are simple," Trey said, looking amused. "Clean bones, no water. You want to count us in, Marty?"

"Absolutely!" Marty grinned. "A one, two, three, four!"

They immediately dove into their wings like their lives depended on it. Even Hacks gave a valiant effort, though he only made it through a wing and a half before giving up and downing his entire glass of water. Max glared at Bryan the whole time he ate. Meanwhile, Bryan got an uneasy feeling as he watched just how *fast* Max could clean a wing.

"He's only got one left!" D-rock exclaimed, staring at Max's nearly empty plate.

Bryan still had two. He chowed down while Marty did a drumroll on the table. Max finished off the last wing while Bryan was still on his second-to-last. The whole table cheered except Bryan, who simply hung his head. Max grinned smugly.

Their waiter came by with a stern look on his face. "I'm sorry, *gentlemen*, but your table is being too rowdy."

"Here's fifty bucks," Max said, holding out the bill. The waiter's eyes grew large. "Give my compliments to the chef."

"Okay…" The waiter pocketed the bill and walked away.

"Hacks, you gonna finish those?" Max asked, pointing to his plate. Hacks shoved it over and the other boys watched in utter fascination as Max ate even more of the spiciest wings they'd ever had.

"Alright, Max," Trey said, laughter in his voice. "You get the last word."

Max wiped his mouth off and finally took a long drink of his water. Then he looked straight into Bryan's eyes. "Just, like, stop being a jerk to people?"

Bryan shook his head, licked his lips, and cringed. "Fine."

TK clapped him on the back and they went back to finishing off their wings. When they'd had enough of each others' company, Max did indeed pay the entire bill. As they broke apart to go home, Bryan asked if Max wanted a ride.

Max, recognizing the olive branch it was, nodded. They said goodnight to the others and headed to Bryan's car.

"Okay, tell me your secret," Bryan said as he peeled out of the parking lot.

His secret? Max had so many he had no idea which one Bryan would be referring to. "What do you mean?"

"How'd you down those wings like that?" Bryan sounded so annoyed when he asked that Max couldn't help bursting out laughing.

Max shook his head, another chuckle escaping. "We traveled to South Korea one time when I was little and ever since then I've been really into spicy food."

"Ah, the old 'traveled the world with my rich family and now I'm a superhero' back story." Bryan took a left turn that made his tires squeal. "That makes so much sense."

Max sighed. "I don't know if you know this, but I have qualities other than being rich."

"You do tie a mean tie."

"And I'd like to live until my seventeenth birthday," Max said, ignoring his comment. "So maybe you can slow down?"

"I could try, man, but this car was built for speed."

Max just shook his head and clutched the sidebar. Bryan did slow down a tad as he headed onto Rockaway and then even more as they passed the giant houses.

"You know," Bryan said, and Max cringed just thinking about what would come next. "If I had your kind of money, I would absolutely buy my way into the heart of any girl that would even look at me."

Max opened his mouth as Bryan pulled into the circular driveway of Max's home. But Bryan was apparently not finished.

"But you're not shallow like me," he said. "And I respect that."

"And I respect that you know that about yourself." Max opened his door.

"Hey, you weren't really serious about… You're not really going to be thinking about Amber all night, are you?"

Max stopped, halfway out the car and glanced at Bryan. "It's really none of your business if I do. What's the deal anyway? Why do you have to be so overprotective?"

Bryan clenched his jaw as he stared out the front window. "Our parents don't care," he said bitterly. "It's not like my dad's gonna bust down the door of any guy who breaks her heart. Someone's gotta do it."

Max's heart softened. Bryan may have been arrogant, but there was a caring person somewhere under all that. "I'm not going to break Amber's heart. Thanks for the ride home."

He slammed the door shut before Bryan could answer. Max had barely stepped away from the car before Bryan took off again.

♪　♫　♪

Trey made his way home to his quiet, lazy street. As he passed Meg's house, he noticed the lights still on inside but didn't think much of it. It was only 11, not that late by his standards. Though now that he thought about it, he was mentally exhausted from heading off too many arguments tonight.

He went inside and down to his basement bedroom, ready to fall into bed. He was just getting undressed when he heard his phone ping. He picked it up and found the most curious message from Meg.

Meg: are you up?

Trey stared at the text for a full three seconds, wondering if Meg meant that honestly or if she understood the implications of asking. Deciding to take it at face value, he said yes.

Meg: come outside?

Again, Trey had no idea where this was going. But curiosity got the better of him.

Trey: okay…

He put his shirt back on, went upstairs, and quietly opened the front door. His breath caught in his throat when he saw her under the porch light in her heels and black dress, and makeup that made her hazel eyes pop. Her full red lips curled into a demure smile.

"I didn't want to ring the doorbell," she whispered.

"Meg…" he said under his breath as he closed the door behind him. "What can I, uh…do for you?"

His heart raced when she took a step forward, close enough to put her hands on his chest. After a tentative moment, she slid her hands up to the back of his neck and pulled gently. Her lips met his so briefly he barely had time to feel it.

"Whoa," he breathed.

He slipped his arms around her waist, drawing her closer to him. Despite how surprised and confused he was, he kissed her for as long as she would let him. Which was way longer than he'd anticipated. She did eventually pull back, but not before gently caressing his lower lip with her tongue.

He stared at her for a moment before murmuring, "I had no idea."

"That's okay," she answered mildly. "You've been focused on other things for the last ten...years."

"Ten *years?*"

"On and off," she said, chuckling self-consciously. "I mean, who harbours a crush for ten whole years on someone who will never notice her?"

"I'm really starting to regret not noticing you earlier," he said.

She shrugged, taking a tiny step back to put some distance between them. "It's not your fault. I like to be unnoticeable."

He glanced down at the rest of her, a slow smile growing on his face. "You sure about that?"

She ducked her head and laughed. "I didn't come here tonight for this."

He lifted an eyebrow, wondering how he was supposed to take that. "Then what did you come for?"

"I was...going to ask if you wanted to go to the dance with me." Finally, she looked back up at him with a smile. "But then *that* happened. And also, it just occurred to me you've probably already been asked, so—"

"Yes."

"Yes?"

He nodded. "Yes, I'll go to the dance with you."

"You...aren't going with someone else?" she asked in a surprised tone.

He shrugged. "I was asked but...not by anyone I wanted to go with. Until now."

"Okay." She smiled. "I'll see you at the dance then."

He licked his lips, looking like he wanted to laugh but didn't. "We have class together on Monday."

"Right." She took a step back. "Of course. I'll see you on Monday."

He stepped forward with her. "Well, I was hoping I could come over tomorrow and practice. If you want, that is."

She nodded. "I want that. I'll see you tomorrow."

"Want me to walk you home?" Trey asked.

"That's okay, I'm a big girl." She started down the porch steps then turned to him with a sassy smile. "But you can watch me and make sure I make it home okay."

"Yeah, I can do that."

She tilted her head at him with her eyebrows drawn in. "That was a really spicy kiss."

"It's a long story," he said, chuckling. "I'll tell you about it tomorrow."

"Okay…" She threw him a little wave.

He waved, too. Then he watched her walk home, wondering the whole time what he was supposed to do with all this new information he'd been handed. How had he never known that Meg had liked him for years? And how would he ever get to sleep now with his heart thumping against his ribs and the memory of her kiss on his mind?

Chapter Fifteen

As everyone gathered at Max's house that Tuesday night, Bryan's lies started to unravel. And since he and Amber were late—again—he wasn't even there to defend himself. When TK asked why the girls hadn't joined them on Saturday night, Harmony's eyebrows drew in furiously.

"What do you mean *join* you?" she said, gripping her flute a little too tightly. "You weren't supposed to be there."

"What?" TK said, his face scrunched up.

"We were having a *girl's* night," Harmony said. "As in *no boys.*"

"You guys were not invited, and Bryan wasn't supposed to say anything," Claire said as she turned the tuning pegs on her cello. Leaning in, she plucked the C string lightly.

Marty tapped on his snare and bass drum. "For the record, I didn't really want to be there." He hit a cymbal, then held his hand on it to still it.

"Was it the company or the food you didn't like, Marty?" Max asked cheekily.

Marty laughed. "That's fair. But I'm still mad you can eat hot wings better than anyone else I know, including me."

Chloe and Claire exchanged a curious look and then glanced back at Harmony, Meg, and Rach. Rach just shrugged and Meg glanced at Trey with a smile.

"In any case," Trey said, stretching his arm across the back of Meg's chair. "We didn't know you wanted to be alone."

"I probably still would have come anyway," TK said, earning himself another of Harmony's scowls.

"I was just there for the food," Corbie said.

"Sure you were, little buddy," Rach said.

Corbie rolled his eyes and Rach laughed. Hacks had been sitting quietly playing the piano subtly while everyone else talked. They had all gone back to warming up when Amber and Bryan arrived. While she took her regular seat, everyone else stopped playing to glower at him. He paused and glared back at them.

"Why is everyone looking at me like that?" he asked.

"Did you forget about Saturday night?" Amber said as she calmly took her clarinet out to put it together.

"Nope." He slung his guitar case off his back but didn't move to open it. "Us guys had a lot of fun. Right?"

"We would have had more fun if we'd actually been invited like you told us we were," D-rock said, pointing an accusing bow at Bryan.

"Or if there'd been any girls there," TK added.

"And if you hadn't been so rude and tried to ditch me with the bill." Max smiled tightly.

"*Bry*-an!" Amber exclaimed, shooting him a dirty look.

"Hey, I had fun," Corbie said.

Bryan gestured to Corbie with a smug smile. Trey put his hand on Corbie's shoulder and said, "He didn't want to invite you. I had to convince him."

"Dude…" Bryan muttered.

Corbie's mouth turned down in an adorable frown. "What? Why?"

"Because you're like twelve," Bryan said, as if that were a good enough reason.

"I'm *fourteen*!" Corbie cringed when his voice cracked.

Bryan scowled and looked around at his traitorous friends. "Any other complaints?"

He immediately regretted asking the moment they all started chiming in with his supposedly unforgivable sins. From the way he'd looked at Rach's legs, to not following Amber's instructions, to not even being able to eat hot wings quickly, everything was left on the table.

"Okay." He held up a hand to silence them. "What is it, Bryan's turn to get kicked out of the band?"

When no one spoke, he rolled his eyes and slowly started backing towards the stairs. "Okay. Bye, then. Good luck doing the rhythm and the strings without me. You know I'm doing two jobs here, right?"

Not a single person moved.

"Seriously? No one's gonna speak up for me?" This time he actually sounded worried. He looked at Amber, but she was too busy putting the reed on her clarinet to acknowledge him.

"Bryan." Max stepped forward with his hand held out while Bryan gave him a hopeful look. "You left your pick here last week."

Bryan's face fell. "Oh, that's where that went," he mumbled as he took it from Max. "Alright. See you guys never."

With that he turned and strode towards the stairs. Just as he put his foot on the first step, Harmony said, "Bryan, wait."

Bryan whirled around while the others grumbled at her.

"Don't go," she said, ignoring them. "Why are you so obsessed with people leaving the band?"

He gave her one of his rare smiles as he finally went over to his spot next to D-rock and Claire. "Just like to keep things interesting, I guess."

"You couldn't let him suffer for one more minute?" Amber said to Harmony.

Harmony smiled as she watched him take his guitar out. "No. I wanna get playing and we can't do that without Bryan playing strings *and* rhythm."

"*Thank you*," Bryan said as he tuned his guitar.

"Ha." D-rock shook his head. "And to think I was working on a Metallica song for you."

Bryan looked up sharply. "Wait, really?" D-rock nodded. "Oh, please say it's 'Enter Sandman.'"

D-rock shook his head. "'Nothing Else Matters.'"

"Typical," Bryan said.

"You can still leave if you want to," Claire said hotly.

There was a noisy sigh from the piano before Hacks started playing loudly. Marty took no time to join him and the others scrambled to find a spot to join in, too. Once they realized Hacks was playing "Holding Out for a Hero," everyone else started playing, too, Bryan included. And while he certainly didn't need his ego stroked, they knew their band wouldn't be complete without him.

♪　　♫　　♪

"Why are there *so* many numbers?" TK grumbled as he stared at the worksheets in front of him.

He was sitting on Hacks's bed trying not to throw up on his homework while Hacks flipped the clothes in his closet back and forth. He glared even harder at the question at hand. No one should have to do this kind of thinking on Halloween. Or a Thursday. Or any day, really.

"It's math," Hacks said needlessly. "What were you expecting?"

"But there's numbers, and letters, and shapes, and—" TK let out a heavy grunt and flipped his workbook off the bed. "I *hate* this. Hate it, hate it, hate it."

Hacks went over and retrieved the workbook that now had several bent pages. He opened it to the page TK had been working on and placed it in front of him again. "I know you do. But let's just get through it. Do you like this shirt?"

TK looked up at the long-sleeved red and white checkered button down. He shrugged with a thoughtful frown. "Yeah, actually."

"Oh, good." Hacks pulled off his pi-eating-pie t-shirt and replaced it with the red and white one. "Why are you not working on your math?"

TK's frown deepened. "Why are you putting on such a nice shirt?"

"I'm going out tonight," Hacks answered. He pointed to the next problem on the sheet. "This one should be easy for you. The numbers aren't that big."

TK didn't even look at it. "Going out where?" he asked.

Hacks finished buttoning up his shirt. "To the school dance."

"Alone?"

"No."

TK's eyes widened. "Then with who?"

"SOHCAHTOA."

TK clenched his jaw. "If you say SOHCAHTOA one more time I'm going to slap those glasses off your face."

Hacks grinned cheekily and pulled his glasses off. "I was going to wear my contacts anyway. Here you go."

TK ignored the glasses Hacks was holding out and said, "Come on, tell me who you're going with!"

Hacks sighed. "It's Amber, okay? She asked and I said yes."

"Hacks." TK's lips split into a wide grin. "I mean…that's great. But also, aren't you worried about Bryan? He might actually have been serious about that."

"No." Hacks shrugged and turned to his dresser, where there was a small dual circular case. "I'm just her pity date. He won't care about that."

"I'm sure that's not true," TK said, even though he didn't quite sound convinced himself.

Hacks popped one of his contacts in while TK watched in fascination. When he'd put the second one in, he turned to TK. "She was pretty clear that she was only asking me because she didn't want me to feel left out."

"And you're okay with that?" TK asked.

Hacks nodded. "Yeah."

"Really?"

Hacks sighed again and sat on the bed across from TK. "Yes, really. I'm graduating this year. And by the time I do, I still won't be old enough to have a driver's license. There are a lot of normal high school experiences I haven't gotten. I've never had a girlfriend and I've never been to a school dance. I'm not the same age as my peers, so I'm awkward to be around and so are they. For one night, I'd like to feel normal."

TK stared at him for a moment, his frown once again turning pensive. "Man, you didn't have to get so deep with it. Could have just said you wanted the pity date with a hot girl."

"I'll be sure to tell Bryan you feel that way about Amber," Hacks said. "SOHCAHTOA."

TK groaned and went back to his math problem. Hacks rubbed his eyes. He wasn't entirely used to wearing his contacts, but he had to admit they gave him better range of vision. He looked down at TK's work.

"Good!" Hacks said in a soothing, encouraging voice. "You're doing great."

"Why are you making me do this when you had plans tonight?" TK asked as he moved on to the next question.

"I wanted to make sure you got it done in case you're going out," Hacks said.

"How very kind of you," TK muttered.

"You've only got three problems left," Hacks said. "How do I look?"

At some point while TK was working, Hacks had styled his hair into a carefully tousled look and with his glasses gone, it was easier to see his blue eyes.

TK gave him a thumbs up. "Decent."

Hacks smiled. It was good enough for him. "Great. SOH—"

"*Don't* say it!"

♪   ♫   ♪

Amber looked at herself in the mirror one last time. Her auburn hair fell in perfect beach waves, her wing-tipped eyeliner was more or less symmetrical, and her cat ears were cute. Bryan barged into the bathroom, gave her one cursory glance, and then frowned.

"You going out?" he asked.

"Yes. And can you please knock next time?" She adjusted the headband of the cat ears.

"The door wasn't even closed," he said. "Where are you going?"

Her eyebrows furrowed up. "To the dance," she said, as if that should be obvious.

"Oh. Why haven't you asked me for a ride?"

She waved a hand at him. "Don't need one. Hacks's mom is picking me up."

Bryan's face scrunched up. "Why would Hacks's mom take you to the school dance?"

She rolled her eyes spectacularly and headed out of the bathroom. "Because I'm going to the dance with him? We talked about this last week."

"No, we didn't!"

"Yeah, we did," she said, putting her hand on her hip. "But you had your headphones on, so all you did was smile and give me a thumbs up. Besides, why do you care?"

"I don't." He slammed the bathroom door shut.

"Whatever," she muttered to herself.

She went downstairs to get her shoes and her jacket just as the doorbell rang. She was just reaching for the door when she heard Bryan thunder down the stairs. He was beside her in only a few seconds, his arms crossed and eyes narrowed as she opened the door for Hacks.

"Oh, you look so cute!" Amber said when she saw Hacks.

He smiled, his cheeks going a little pink. "I was just about to say the same thing."

Bryan glared even harder. "Hi, Hacks."

"Goodnight, Bryan," Hacks said, his eyes never leaving Amber.

"I'm watching you."

"Don't be weird, Bryan," Amber said as she stepped outside.

She and Hacks went to his mom's car while Bryan stood in the doorway, his arms still crossed and frowning at them. Hacks let out a relieved sigh and opened the car door for her.

"Hi, Mrs. Ackenstein," Amber said.

Hacks's mom smiled as Hacks got in. "Hello, dear."

At the school, they thanked his mom and got out, but then Hacks just stood in the courtyard while his mom drove off. Amber gave him a funny look.

"Are we still going in?" she asked.

"Yes." He squared his shoulders and nodded. "I've just never done this before and I feel weird."

She laughed and took his elbow to force him to go with her. "I know. Come on, you'll be just fine. I won't leave you tonight, but I will find you as many dance partners as you want."

"Thank you, I appreciate that," Hacks said. Though if he were honest, he would have told her he only needed one dance partner. He pulled on the sleeves of his shirt and then patted his hair.

"Stop, you look hot," Amber said.

Hacks laughed out loud. "Now, you're trying too hard."

Amber shook her head and led him inside. True to her word, she never left him, save for the few times he danced with other people. But she was always nearby to rescue him when he felt awkward and out of place. Why she was being so nice to him, he would never know. But he would take her kindness over his schoolmates' indifference any day.

Chapter Sixteen

The door opened before Trey had a chance to ring the doorbell. Meg's dad—who was slightly shorter than Trey and generally wasn't very threatening—crossed his arms and pursed his lips as he gave Trey a once-over. Trey had met his fair share of scary dads—Meg's dad wasn't one of them. And he'd never had a problem with Trey coming over to practise with Meg.

"Hi, Mr. Ritz." Trey gave him a friendly smile. "I'm here to pick up Meg."

"About time," Mr. Ritz muttered.

Trey's eyebrows furrowed. "Am I…late?"

"Yeah, only by a few years, kid." Mr. Ritz opened the door farther and stepped back to let Trey in.

"Oh," Trey said, stepping in after him.

"You going dressed like that?" Mr. Ritz gestured at Trey's clothes.

Trey looked down at himself. He'd put on black slacks and his best blue button-down shirt. He'd even taken the time to make sure his black dress shoes were clean and shiny. "These are kind of my best clothes, and since I'm already late, I think I'll stick with this."

Mr. Ritz's lips twitched but he managed to keep his face neutral. "And she'll be back home by midnight."

"The dance only goes until eleven," Trey said.

Mr. Ritz nodded. "Then I'll see you at eleven-oh-five."

"Yes, sir."

Thankfully, Meg came down then and again Trey asked himself how he'd never really seen her before. She wore a light blue dress with spaghetti straps and a flowery pattern near the hem that fell to her knees. Her eye makeup was more natural than it had been last Saturday, and her lips were a softer pink.

"You look nice," she said. She smiled at him and he lost all ability to speak.

Her dad raised his eyebrows at Trey and nodded his head in Meg's direction.

"Oh, thanks!" Trey finally said. "You, too. You look amazing."

"Thanks!" She reached into the front hall closet for a jacket and then turned to her dad. "See you later, Dad."

"Yup," he said as he put his arm around her. "Eleven-oh-five."

She frowned. "But my curfew is one."

"Not when you're out with Trey," he said. "Have a nice time."

"Okay, Dad," she said, biting back laughter. "I'll see you later."

She took Trey's hand and led him out of the house before her dad could say anything else. "Sorry." She shrugged. "He's just being weird because he…doesn't have a lot of practise with this."

Trey smiled down at her and squeezed her hand. "That's okay."

They walked back to Trey's house, where he opened the passenger door of his dad's car. Meg got in and tucked her skirt around her legs. Trey was quiet on the short drive to the school and Meg, who had never been a big talker, wondered what she should do to fill the silence.

Finally, she said, "Thank you for driving. I love these heels, but they were not meant for driving."

Trey smiled, keeping his eyes on the road. "You're cute."

"You…have looked in a mirror before, right?" she said.

He laughed out loud, his cheeks turning a shade pinker. "I meant personality-wise. But yeah, you do look really cute, too."

He pulled into the school's parking lot and easily found a spot. After shutting off the car, he turned to her instead of getting out.

"Can we talk?" he asked.

She hesitated for the briefest moment before saying, "Of course."

He smiled and put his arm across the back of her seat. "I like you."

"That's a relief," she said, smiling back at him. "I like you, too."

"Yeah, you mentioned that." He moved his hand so it was resting on her shoulder and brushed his fingers against her cheek. "Do you want to…make this official?"

Her eyebrows rose in surprise. "Before we've even had our first date?"

He nodded eagerly.

"Trey, I really thought you just said yes to going to the dance because of…" She paused, her cheeks flushing. "How I looked when I asked you."

His smile widened and he shook his head. "No, it wasn't that. Although you did look really hot. But it was…" His gaze fell to her lips as her blush deepened adorably. "I've never had a girl kiss me first and I think that kind of confidence is sexy. So I said yes. And the more I thought about it, the more I realized how much I like you. And now that we're here I already know I'm going to ask you for a second date."

His words warmed her heart, but she still asked coyly, "How do you know I'll say yes?"

He edged closer. "You gonna waste ten years on just one date?"

"Definitely not," she said, leaning into his hand.

"So…" He drew even closer. "I can call you my girlfriend?"

She closed her eyes and murmured, "You can call me whatever you want."

He chuckled softly and then closed the gap between them. She put her hand up to his face and kissed him while butterflies took off in her stomach.

Trey pulled back and said, "We should go in. They check the parking lots."

She followed his lead without asking how he knew. They got out and he offered her his hand. Her stomach churned nervously as they went towards the school. Never in her life did she think she'd be walking into a school dance with Trey. As his girlfriend! Was this a dream?

She inhaled a deep, calming breath. Definitely not a dream. He smelled too good to be fake.

♪   ♫   ♪

Chloe smiled at her reflection. She didn't care if her friends weren't going in costume to the dance tonight. She had spent hours working on her knight outfit and she wanted to show it off. The "armour" that covered her chest, forearms, and shins was made of cardboard, which she'd easily disguised with silver spray paint. The breastplate was attached to a red skirt that matched the short cape on her back—leftover fabric from her costume last year. She'd found some old combat-style boots at a thrift store and also painted them silver. Black tights and a black long-sleeved t-shirt would keep her from getting too cold outside. She finished the look by braiding her hair and pinning it up.

"Perfect," she told herself.

At least, it would have been perfect if she'd been allowed to take a fake sword or bow and arrow to the dance. But anything even resembling a weapon was banned at school for obvious reasons. Still, she liked her outfit and if the others were too cool for costumes, then that was their loss.

Besides, once Chloe got to the dance, she discovered she wasn't the only one who'd chosen to go in costume. There were plenty of fairies and witches and zombies. Her friends weren't in costume, but they all loved hers. Jaden's eyes lit up when he saw her but he didn't say much beyond "cool costume."

She danced with her friends for a while but when they started pairing off, she ended up off to the side all by herself. As she watched Jaden and Alyssa dance together, she let the music wash over her. Sure, it was bass-heavy dance music, but for as long as Chloe could remember, any type of music had been soothing to her. And right now soothing was what she needed.

They had all come as a group of friends, but that hadn't stopped Alyssa from monopolizing Jaden's entire evening. Chloe considered choosing someone else to dance with, but what was even the point now?

Someone stuck their gloved hand in her face and she nearly jumped back in surprise. There in front of her was a knight in dark armour that in the dim lighting almost looked like it could have been real. The breastplate even had a coat of arms with a depiction of a deer crossing a low bridge over a river. The wearer's helmet completely enclosed their head so she couldn't tell who was under it. After she'd stared at the knight for a good solid moment, they nodded their head towards the dance floor.

"Okay…"

She put her hand in theirs and they led her over. Once they were standing face-to-face the knight interlocked their fingers with hers.

With a sassy smile, she said, "That's a bit much."

They immediately untangled their fingers and nodded. The music slowed down, as if the DJ knew that Chloe had suddenly found herself a worthy dance partner. Her knight put their other hand on her waist and pulled her closer, still keeping her at a respectful distance.

Chloe put her free hand on their shoulder and let them guide her in the dance, totally caught up in the moment. It helped that there was a lot of violin in the music that was playing and that the knight was admittedly a good dancer. Way better than her, considering how many times she'd nearly tripped over her own feet.

The knight didn't seem to mind as they took their time to sweep Chloe across the dance floor. But as much as she was enjoying herself, she couldn't take the mystery much longer. She reached out and touched the knight's visor. They immediately stilled and grasped her hand to stop her.

"Really?" Chloe said. "I don't get to know who's under there?"

The knight shook their head and Chloe sighed. She pulled her hands back.

"Then go dance with someone else," she said in a disappointed, flat voice.

They hesitated a moment before nodding once and turning away. Chloe almost called out to them, but she didn't. If they wanted to come back, they could choose to reveal themself to her. She crossed her arms and looked away.

Her eyes caught Trey and Meg, standing close together away from the dance floor, talking and smiling. Though she was disappointed for herself, Chloe was thrilled for Meg. And proud of her for finding the courage to do what Chloe couldn't. Her smile slipped when she saw Lacy making a beeline for them, pushing other people out of the way as she went.

Oh, no, Chloe thought to herself as she rushed forward.

Lacy injected herself between Meg and Trey and started screeching at Meg over the music. Trey held up his hands and tried to get Lacy to calm down. Chloe couldn't move quickly through the throngs of dancers, but she did get close enough to catch some of the argument.

"I told you he's *mine*!" Lacy shouted as she grabbed Meg's shoulder.

"And I told you you can't own a person," Meg said far more calmly. She tried to shake off Lacy's hand but her grip was too firm.

Trey's face was twisted into a look of consternation. "What's going on here?"

Just as Chloe reached them, her nameless knight showed up. They crowded between Lacy and Meg, wordlessly offering a hand to Lacy.

Lacy's eyebrows scrunched up in confusion, and she let her hand drop from Meg's shoulder. "What?" The knight nodded towards the dance floor. "Ew," Lacy said. She glared at Meg one more time. "I'm not done with you."

Lacy stomped away while the knight stood there with their hand still outstretched.

"Thank you," Meg said. "Who's this?"

The knight looked back at her then turned to Chloe. They opened a secret compartment on the left side of their breastplate, reached inside, and pulled out a black envelope.

"*You!*" Chloe snatched the envelope away.

As soon as it was in her hands, the knight turned and weaved quickly across the dance floor. Chloe tried to follow, but it was as if the other dancers had swallowed the knight whole.

"Wait!" Chloe called out. Disappointed, she turned to Meg and Trey. "Trey, you're big and fast. Can you follow that person and find out who they are?"

Trey hesitated, but Meg patted him on the shoulder. "Please?" she said.

Trey nodded and hastened away. Chloe looked down at the envelope. Frustration overwhelmed her and she crumpled it up without even opening it.

"Chloe." Meg reached out and gently opened Chloe's hand. She took the envelope and tried to flatten it. "You could at least read it first."

"What's the point?" Chloe threw her hands in the air. "How dare he show up and dance with me like that and act like it's cool to not tell me who he is?"

"Maybe he's afraid," Meg said as she held the envelope out to Chloe.

Chloe gave it a furtive glance and shook her head. "What's up with Lacy?"

"She's upset because she's Trey's ex," Meg said. "And I'm his…girlfriend. Now. We decided. Tonight."

Chloe smiled, despite how twisted up she felt inside. "Meg, you did it! At least someone around here has some guts."

Meg smiled back at her and then pressed the envelope gently into her hand. "It took me ten years. When he's ready, I'm sure he'll tell you."

"Well, I hope it doesn't take *him* ten years."

Trey came back and immediately slipped his arm around Meg's waist. He gave Chloe a sympathetic look. "Sorry, Chloe. I guess I wasn't big or fast enough."

"It's fine…" Chloe glanced back out through the crowd but sure enough, the knight was gone. "You have a good night. I'm going home."

"Chloe." Meg stepped forward and put her hand on top of the creased envelope. "Read this, okay?"

Chloe nodded but her heart wasn't in it. She headed for the doors, her eyes scanning the crowd again. The knight, her mystery admirer was gone. And she wasn't going to wait ten years for them.

Outside, she stomped down the sidewalk. It was unseasonably warm but still cool enough to take some of the edge off Chloe's irritation. As she passed by ghosts, goblins, jack-o-lanterns, and fake tombstones, her ire drained away from her. How could she be mad at someone for expressing themself the only way they knew how when she couldn't even muster up the courage to ask Jaden for one dance tonight?

She stopped under a streetlight and carefully opened the envelope so as not to destroy the card further. The message inside was different from the others she'd received, since it merely contained a quote. One that left her head scratching.

If music be the food of love, play on.
—Shakespeare, Twelfth Night

Now what was she supposed to do with that?

Less than Perfect Christmas
Book 3

Chapter One

Meg's breath wafted into the air as she sat huddled on the bleachers. Amber and Bryan sat to her left and Rach and Marty were on her right. The cold air and light snow didn't bother her as much as the fact that she had a hard time following number 52—or the rest of the football game. It was the last game of the season and of course Trey had invited Meg to watch.

"Does anybody know what's happening right now or if Trey's at least doing well enough for me to compliment him later?" Meg asked.

Bryan leaned over Amber, nearly crushing her, and gave Meg an incredulous look. "We're up three points and he's the *captain* of the team. So yeah, I'm sure it's safe to compliment him. Although he's probably had enough compliments to last him a lifetime."

Amber rolled her eyes and shoved her brother away, then went back to shivering inside her fall jacket. It wasn't the best clothing choice she'd made that morning, but the forest green corduroy coat was just too cute to pass up.

"But what would I say?" Meg asked.

"Just tell him that one pass was really amazing," Bryan said, flicking a dismissive hand. "He'll pick his favourite one and assume you meant that."

"Why is it *so* cold?" Rach complained before Meg had a chance to press Bryan further. "It was, like, fifteen degrees two days ago!"

Indeed, the beginning of November had brought with it gusty winds, frost, and even the first snowfall of the season. As the football players grappled for yards on the slushy field, the snowfall began to thicken.

"I can't believe they still play in weather like this." Meg chewed her bottom lip nervously as the guys on both teams lost their footing several times.

"Meg, you're just supposed to enjoy watching your hot boyfriend play a manly sport," Marty said.

Meg smiled as a warmth filled her that had nothing to do with the frigid air outside. For years she'd liked Trey and had finally decided to do something about it. It had taken all her courage to stand on his front porch and tell him she liked him, but it was worth it to find out he liked her, too.

When the game ended, Meg's friends went home. But she stayed behind to wait for Trey because she'd been invited to dinner with his family. It was a tradition, they'd said. She'd known his family for years, of course, but that didn't mean she wasn't extra shy when she saw them.

"Meg." Mrs. Donnelly smiled kindly. She had Trey's wide smile and bright blue eyes. "I'm glad you could join us today."

Meg smiled back at her and then acknowledged Mr. Donnelly, the twins, and Trey's little sister with her eyes. "Thank you so much for inviting me. That's very kind of you."

"Well, you're his only girlfriend who will actually have dinner with us," May said, tossing a hand in the air.

Meg's eyebrows rose briefly. "Is that right?"

Mr. Donnelly tugged lightly on May's ponytail. "Behave."

"I'm just *saying*," May said in a way only a 13-year-old girl could. "Like, what's wrong with our family that none of his girlfriends ever want to see us?"

Mrs. Donnelly shushed her, and May rolled her eyes. The twins started goofing off, gaining their parents' attention.

While they were busy, Meg leaned towards May and whispered, "It's not your family. It's the girls."

"Yeah, Trey knows how to pick 'em." May's eyes widened and she looked up at Meg. "Oh, but not you. You're so nice!"

Meg chuckled. "I'm not offended."

"Please don't tell Trey I said that," May whispered anxiously.

Meg made a motion like she was zipping her lips shut and May smiled. Trey came out a few minutes later, his blond hair wet and dark, his eyes shining as he smiled right at Meg. He greeted his dad, hugged his mom quickly, and ruffled Hayden's and Clay's hair before slapping May's ponytail affectionately. Then he wrapped his arm around Meg's waist and kissed her temple.

"Alright, now I'm ready to go," Trey said. "And I'm starving. We'll meet you guys there."

While his family walked towards the east parking lot, Trey took Meg's hand and led her to the south lot. It was closest to the gym and locker rooms and some of the other guys had parked out there as well. Meg looked around, scanning the lot for anyone she wouldn't want to come across.

"Who're you looking for?" Trey asked.

Meg shrugged but chose not to lie to him. "I didn't see Chad tonight, but I thought maybe I just missed him because everyone looks the same in football gear."

Trey grunted. His former best friend hadn't been particularly kind to Meg, and he could understand why she'd be nervous about seeing him. Though Trey did feel a little bad about the reason Chad wasn't there tonight.

"Nah, he dislocated his shoulder a few games ago," Trey said as he approached his dad's car. "He hasn't bothered to show up since he couldn't finish the season."

"That's too bad," she said softly.

He glanced down at her but there wasn't an ounce of ill will in her voice or face. "You don't have to be nice about him, Meg."

She smiled at him. "But I don't have to be mean about him, either."

Instead of getting inside of the car, Trey leaned back against it and pulled her close to him. The snow was still falling in large lazy flakes, but Trey's body radiated heat and Meg wasn't going to complain about *that*.

"That one pass you did was really great," she said. Even to her own ears the compliment sounded lame.

He lifted one eyebrow. "Which one?"

She bit her lip and then chuckled. "I don't know. Bryan told me to say that."

He laughed. "And we haven't learned not to trust Bryan?"

Meg laughed with him. After Bryan had tried to ruin the girls' special night out by inviting *all* the boys without telling the boys the truth, their band had lost a little faith in him. But Bryan wasn't a bad guy and he had been trying to help Meg, after all.

"He was trying to be nice," she said. "Since I had no idea what was happening throughout the whole game."

He tilted his head. "You didn't have to come if you don't like football."

She reached up and put a hand to the side of his face. "I like you enough to enjoy watching you do anything."

His cheeks turned a deeper shade of red. "Meg..." He leaned forward and kissed her gently.

When he pulled back, she said, "How long until your parents call you?"

"Yeah, we should probably..." Finally, he unlocked the car and then held the door open for her.

♪ ♫ ♪

Marty stood in front of the large red brick detached house. So, it wasn't on the lake, but it was nicely kept, and the lawn and gardens were immaculate. Even this late into the year, there were some late-blooming mums weathering the light dusting of snow.

Marty rang the doorbell and then tapped his foot as he waited. He wasn't impatient; he just couldn't help it. There was always a drum beat in his head.

Corbie opened the door and motioned Marty inside. Snow and wind breezed in behind them. Marty shook his coat off before hanging it on an available hook next to the door.

"Did you walk here?" Corbie asked as Marty took his boots off.

Marty shrugged, running a hand over his wet, dark curly hair. "Yeah, but I don't mind. I like walking and it's not that cold out."

In truth, if Corbie's house had been any farther, he might not have walked it. But he hadn't wanted to drag his mom and three younger siblings out with him just so he could tutor Corbie.

"Well, I'll get Dad to drive you home after," Corbie said.

As he led Marty into the house, an older gentleman lumbered towards them. He had a stooped back and Corbie's kind brown eyes.

"Hey, Grandpa," Corbie said in a soft voice. He gestured to his friend. "This is Marty. He's the boy who's tutoring me in French."

"Oh." The man's bushy grey eyebrows inched up his forehead as he turned to Marty. "*Bonjour. Comment ça va?*"

Marty smiled as warmth filled him at the older man's sweet attempt. "*Ça va bien, monsieur. Et vous?*"

"*Très bien*," the older man answered.

He patted Corbie on the shoulder and then did the same to Marty before continuing on his path to the staircase. Corbie and Marty went to the kitchen table, where Corbie had left his French binder and textbook.

"You didn't tell me your *grandpère* speaks French," Marty said wryly. "Was this just a trick to get me to hang out with you?"

Corbie gave a short bark of laughter. "No. I'm pretty sure that's all he can say. But I don't mind the hanging out."

Marty smiled. He knew it was true, based on the man's poor accent, but he couldn't resist the jab. "Okay, what are we working on today?"

Corbie sat at the table and pulled out a thin book from underneath the binder. "I have to read this book and then there's a test."

Marty nodded. "That's a book for children. I think you'll be fine."

Corbie sighed and put the book back down. "Alright... Well, I also have an oral test coming up that I'm pretty sure I'm gonna fail." He opened the binder and took a page out of it. "I'm supposed to answer these questions."

Marty scoured the list and frowned. "These are so boring."

"Marty, please, I just want to pass," Corbie said, putting his head in his hands. "If you're not going to help me with the book or the questions, what *will* you help me with?"

Biting back a sigh, Marty relented. "Sorry. You're right. We'll just do these. *Où es-tu né?*"

"*Je suis né à Bridgetown,*" Corbie answered.

"Shocker," Marty muttered, his eyes flashing.

"*Marty.*"

"Sorry. *Quel âge as-tu?*" Marty huffed. "This is dumb. Your teacher already knows how old you are."

Corbie sighed and took the binder back from Marty. Closing it soundly, he said, "I'm beginning to think *you* just came over for the hanging out and not to actually help me."

Marty raised his eyebrows in surprise. "I do want to help you. But this isn't the way. Sorry. I'm sure you'll do just fine knowing the answers but...really, your accent is terrible."

"I'm *trying*," Corbie said.

"I know you are," Marty said softly. "But let's just chat and work on that instead. Then maybe you can read me the book."

Corbie crossed his arms and turned to face Marty. "Fine."

"*C'est ça!*" Marty said with enthusiasm. His smile dropped when Corbie stared at him blankly. "That's the spirit…"

"Oh, I know what it means," Corbie said. "I just assumed you were being sarcastic."

"I was, yes," Marty answered, bobbing his eyebrows. "*Bon. Pourquoi as-tu choissis de jouer du trombone?*"

"Oh." Corbie let his arms drop and relaxed into his chair. "No one's ever asked me that."

Marty made a "go on" gesture. "*En français.*"

"*Au début, c'était parce que mon grandpère joue du trombone aussi.*" He stopped to smile. "*Et j'ai continué parce que ça lui plait. Et moi aussi.* Did I say all that right?"

Marty's eyes lit up as he nodded. "Yeah, you play 'cause your grandpa does and it makes you both happy. That is *so* sweet. Aww."

Corbie looked down at his lap and nodded. Marty's smile widened when Corbie asked him, in French and without missing a beat, why he'd chosen to play the drums.

"*Parce que je le sens dans mon coeur,*" Marty replied.

Corbie looked deep into his eyes for a moment before saying, "That's really cheesy."

"I know," Marty said, laughing at himself. "But it's still true. Drumming is deep down in my heart and I don't care who thinks that's ridiculous."

"I said cheesy, not ridiculous," Corbie said. "Your drumming is anything but ridiculous."

"Aw, thanks." Marty reached for the small book on the table. "Speaking of ridiculous, let's read this dumb thing together."

Corbie grumbled but took the book anyway. It wouldn't have taken that long to read if Marty hadn't had to stop him every few words to correct him. But Marty had, after all, come all the way out to his house for this purpose. And it was worth it when Corbie finished the book and accurately related what had happened in the story.

"You're gonna do just fine on your tests," Marty promised.

Chapter Two

Amber had come up with the perfect plan to help Chloe find her secret admirer. *And* she would do it in style. She'd needed a project for her social studies class anyway, and a petition was the best way to go. Of course, she would try to get as many of the boys from her year as possible to sign— since they were pretty sure the letters had been written by a boy—but just to be safe she would try to gather a lot of the girls' signatures, too. Besides, this was a cause she cared about, so the more signatures, the better.

There was no way she could get everyone in school to sign. But she could at least start with the people in her grade. She even asked her group of former friends if they wanted to sign, hoping against hope that Chloe's letters hadn't come from one of them.

Stacey sneered. "Ew. What's the petition for? Getting Rach friends that she doesn't have to steal from someone else?"

Amber let out a heavy sigh. There were obvious reasons Amber had ditched Stacey and co. for Rach's companionship, the least of which was that Stacey was a huge brat.

"Never mind," Amber said, trying to control her temper. "I don't need your signature. I'll ask someone else."

Amber turned to go but then Henry called her name. "What's the petition for?" he asked, sounding genuinely interested.

After a moment's hesitation, Amber said, "To get the municipality to hire full-time maintenance workers for the beach so it's not always gross. And unsafe. And unpleasant."

"Okay, I'll sign that," Henry said.

"Thank you," she said, handing him the paper.

He held it up against a locker and Amber curiously watched him sign it. But without Chloe's letters in front of her, it was hard to tell if they were a match. After he'd signed it, he passed it around to the others, telling them to sign it, too.

He smiled at Amber. "The beach *is* kind of gross sometimes."

"So is your acne," Stacey muttered even as she signed the paper.

Amber rolled her eyes while Henry's face went red. The comment was uncalled for, but she didn't want to start a fight. Again. Instead, she smiled at Henry as he gave the paper back to her.

"Thank you!"

She left them in the hallway to do whatever stupid stuff they normally did. Okay, she knew what they would really be doing was totally ignoring the fact that Stacey had a huge crush on Henry and absolutely had no idea what to do about it, so she overcompensated and said mean things to him. But Amber didn't care about that anymore because she wasn't a part of it. Even if she *had* been working on the perfect plan to help Stacey out and it could totally work.

She sighed as she headed towards the cafeteria. She had to stop trying to help people.

She paused along the way to ask for more signatures, which everyone happily agreed to give her. When she stopped next to Tyler Hasting at his locker, he nearly jumped at the sight of her.

"Hey, Tyler," she said nicely.

"You're not gonna ask me out again, are you?" he asked abruptly, his dark eyes narrowing.

She lifted her eyebrows in surprise and tried not to be offended. She'd only asked him to the Halloween dance, not proposed, so she had no idea why he was being so weird about it. "No… I'm collecting signatures for my petition."

She showed him the sheet and he nodded slowly, then read the information on it. "Oh. Yeah, I can get down with that."

As he signed it, she tried not to admire his black nail polish. Maybe if he were in a better mood she would have complimented it. But he clearly wanted nothing to do with her, so all she said was a quick thank you.

She had almost reached the cafeteria when she found Max. He had stopped in the hallway and was crouched down and rooting through his backpack.

"Hi, Max," she said in her happy voice.

He looked up at her, startled, and nearly crushed his bag trying to close it. "Yes. What? I mean, hi, Amber."

"Do you want to sign my petition?" she asked.

"Oh, I'm actually in a huge rush," he said, standing up quickly. "Catch me in class, okay?"

"Alright…" she said as he hastened away, his backpack still half open. She wasn't too worried about getting his signature anyway.

♪　　♫　　♪

His heart still racing, Max waited around the corner until he was sure Amber was gone. Quickly, he finished his task before heading to the library. He'd only been there for a few minutes, quietly working on his homework, when Trey plunked down next to him. Max raised his eyebrows in greeting.

"Hey, dude," Trey said.

He and Trey rarely interacted outside of band practice. Not at school in the cafeteria, or at the library…or at a school dance. But since it didn't look like Trey was settling in to get any work done, Max smiled politely anyway. "Hey."

Trey just nodded.

"Is there something I can do for you?" Max asked.

Trey shook his head. "It's not what you can do for me, but what I can do for you."

"Meaning?" Max said, lifting an eyebrow.

"Do you want my help with Chloe or not?"

Max's heart plummeted to his stomach. He couldn't answer. He didn't know what to say, even though he knew he'd been found out almost two weeks ago.

"Look." Trey leaned in closer so he could speak quieter. "I know you know I saw you at the dance."

Since no one had mentioned it yet, Max had assumed and hoped that Trey had either forgotten or just not seen him clearly. No one was supposed to have seen him as the knight at the Halloween dance, but a surprise asthma attack had forced him to take his helmet off. If he hadn't been so nervous, he probably could have avoided it.

Instead of fully acknowledging Trey's statement, Max asked, "Did you tell her?"

"No." Trey paused. "I didn't tell anyone."

"Not even Meg?" Max asked.

Trey chuckled. "No. I don't really get what your game plan is, but I do know girls talk. I didn't think Chloe should find out from anyone but you."

"Thank you," Max said, letting out a relieved sigh. Trey stared at him expectantly. "What do you want me to say?"

"What's going on? Meg said someone's been leaving Chloe anonymous letters on her locker." Trey laughed when Max rolled his eyes. "I told you girls talk."

"I didn't know how to tell her, okay?" Max admitted, his cheeks flushing. He couldn't believe he was telling this to *Trey*, of all people. "So, I went with that."

With his face scrunched up, Trey asked, "Why don't you just sign the letters?"

His eyes wide and heart thundering in his chest, Max nearly choked on the question. "I—I can't. She'll never accept me like this."

Trey looked up and down Max's whole body. Today Max had chosen to wear dark jeans, a green button down, and a green and white paisley tie. He'd recently gotten a haircut, but he doubted Trey was the type to appreciate how much effort Max put into his appearance.

"What's wrong with you?" Trey asked, not unkindly.

"Well, I'm not exactly six feet tall and athletic and radiating confidence," Max said dryly.

Trey laughed so hard that Mr. Pfizer, the librarian, shushed him. Max didn't think it was *that* funny that almost no one could compete with Trey's level of attractiveness. And in truth, it wasn't even his appearance that Max was self-conscious about. Chloe had made it clear that Max's wealth was off-putting to her. And that was something he couldn't change.

Max rolled his eyes again and finally Trey calmed down.

"I don't think Chloe's into that type," Trey said, some laughter lingering in his voice.

Max, who was not amused, said, "She's not into me, either."

"You don't know that," Trey said. "And she seems like she's getting really frustrated trying to figure out who you are."

"So, I should just tell her?"

"Yes."

Max stared at Trey.

"Look, the longer you keep this up, the more you risk other people finding out, too," Trey said, finally sounding serious. "And she'll be pissed if she's the last one to know."

Max knew he was right, even though the idea scared him. "I just don't know how."

"I know it's corny and cliché," Trey said, "but just be yourself. She's either gonna go for it and that's great! Or she won't and you can move on."

Max nodded, expelling a deep breath. "Okay. I'll try."

Trey smiled and lightly punched Max, nearly knocking him over. "Good luck."

♪   ♫   ♪

Bryan went to the back of the school, hoping he'd find Marty there. Marty usually played his bongos after school on Mondays and Bryan liked listening. But today he'd brought his guitar in hopes that Marty would let him play with him.

As soon as Marty saw him, his eyes lit up and he waved him over. Bryan tuned his guitar while Marty warned him that he usually just played whatever and that it might be hard for Bryan to keep up.

"Don't worry," Bryan said with a smile. "I'm used to your beats."

Marty smiled back and barely waited for Bryan to be ready before he started drumming. Bryan didn't mind. He liked getting to play and not having to talk much. And he *loved* Marty's drumming, though he was reluctant to admit it out loud. He was sure Marty knew that everyone felt that way about it. It didn't need to be said again.

As they jammed, Marty's regulars and then some came to watch. Even though it was cold out, no one seemed to mind as long as they had something to occupy them. They talked amongst themselves and Bryan wondered if it ever bothered Marty that they only half paid attention to him. But when he glanced at Marty, he realized that Marty didn't play for them. He played for himself.

Bryan tried to stay as long as Marty did. But when his fingers got too cold to move deftly anymore, he slowed down.

"Thanks for playing with me," Marty said, never once slowing his pace.

Bryan waved and packed up his guitar. The impromptu jam session had put Bryan in such a good mood that it was still running through his mind by the time he got home. All his good feelings disappeared when he went inside, however.

His dad was bent over the messy and cluttered kitchen table. The table was always like that. They all just seemed to dump their stuff there, never to return for it. Amidst the disarray was Bryan's entire set of brand-new sockets. Every last piece had been dumped out of the box and his dad was rooting through them.

Bryan took a deep, calming breath while inside he was screaming. There was a reason he kept his best stuff in his bedroom. Clearly his dad didn't care for that, though.

"Dad...what are you doing?" he said as calmly as he could.

His dad barely looked at him. "Grabbing a socket. I need it for work."

Bryan bit the inside of his cheek to keep from lashing out. "Those are my sockets."

His dad shrugged. "They're in my house."

"But I bought them with *my* money," Bryan said, his voice rising a notch. "You could have asked."

Finally, his dad looked at him directly. Bryan resented how much those narrowed eyes and scowl resembled his own. "How was I supposed to ask you when you were in detention?"

"I wasn't in detention," Bryan said, irritation seeping into his words. "I was playing guitar with a friend. And I have a phone, you know? You should have asked."

"Son—" His dad turned back to the sockets and picked two of them up. "These are in my house. And I don't have the time to wait for you to decide to share."

When he started walking away, anger bubbled up inside of Bryan. Flustered, he followed his dad to the door.

"You're not even gonna put the rest away?" Bryan didn't bother hiding the disgust from his voice.

"They're *your* sockets." With that, his dad left, slamming the front door behind him.

Gritting his teeth, Bryan went back to the table. He barely had the heart to put it all back. He knew he'd never see the ones his dad had taken again. What was the point of an incomplete set now?

"I tried to tell him," a soft voice said from behind him.

"You shouldn't fight with him," Bryan said flatly.

Amber sighed and came forward, picking up the box. "I didn't fight with him. I told him you wouldn't like it if he touched your stuff. He just scoffed at me. Sorry."

She started putting away the sockets since Bryan was still standing there doing nothing.

"Thank you," he said. "But please just stay out of his way. I'm not worth fighting over."

"Can you stop brooding and help me put this away?" she said lightly. "I have no idea where anything goes."

Bryan smiled behind her back. She didn't need to do this, but he appreciated her help anyway.

Chapter Three

Claire got out of the Uber, lugging her cello behind her. She wasn't exactly inclined to walk all the way to D-rock's house with her cello now that it had gotten this cold. She rang the doorbell but when there was no answer after a minute, she let herself in.

It was no wonder D-rock hadn't heard her. He was playing his bass loudly but not...noisily. In fact, whatever he'd chosen to play had a beautiful melody, so unlike the supportive lines he normally played for Less than Perfect's arrangements.

Torn between wanting to listen to him play and wanting to interrupt so they could write together, she crept forward quietly. She found him in his living room, bowing so passionately he didn't even notice her at first. When he did finally see her, he lowered his bow and clasped his hand on the strings to quiet them.

"Sorry, I lost track of time," D-rock said hastily. "Again."

Claire smiled. It wasn't the first time, and it wouldn't be the last. "That's okay. What are you playing?"

"Ah, nothing," he said.

"That was *not* nothing," she tried again. She glanced at the music stand next to him and saw a sheet of handwritten music. "Come on, show me."

He hesitated a moment before taking the music and handing it to her. "It's just…something I had in my head. That's all."

"You mean it's an original piece?" she said.

He nodded and she looked down at the music. The melody played in her head, soft and sweet. She wondered if that was what it was like for D-rock or if he had to play it to really hear it.

"Is there more?" she asked when the notes ended without a double bar line.

He scratched the back of his neck. "Well, I've been trying to figure out how to add everyone else's instruments into it, but that's hard to do when there are fourteen of us."

Claire's eyebrows rose. "You're writing this for…*us*?"

"If I ever finish it, sure," he said.

"What does the rest sound like?" she asked.

His cheeks went pink under all her questioning. He pointed to her cello and said, "Can I?"

Claire nodded enthusiastically. If anyone else had asked, she would have said no. But curiosity got the better of her, so she let D-rock take out her cello and tighten the hairs on her bow. After fiddling with the strings for a minute, he began playing a delightful, rich melody.

"So, you'd be doing something like this," he said as he kept playing. He moved his fingers down the neck. "And then the violins would be up here somewhere. And then I'll probably stick Bryan with some boring chords for being a jerk all the time."

Claire laughed. "Wow, I…" She loved it but obviously couldn't say *those* words out loud. "I had no idea you could play the cello."

D-rock stopped and grinned, his green eyes dancing. "I didn't know either until just now."

"Could have fooled me," she said.

"Thanks." He held the bow and cello out to her. "What do you want to work on today?"

"Christmas music, obviously," Claire said, taking her cello back. "I know it's a bit early, but—"

"No."

"No?"

"No, thanks?"

She stared into his unsmiling eyes, wondering why his mood had shifted so drastically. "Are you serious right now? What's wrong with Christmas music?"

He forced a shrug. "It's not just the music. I don't like Christmas at all."

"Because...you're Jewish?" she said, trying for levity.

He shook his head and gripped the neck of his bass so hard his knuckles went white. Claire frowned thoughtfully at him.

"What is it?" she asked softly.

"My dad left at Christmas, okay?" He looked down at his feet, swallowing hard. "Four years ago. He put this bass by the tree and just...left to be with his other family. So, it kind of ruined the whole thing for me."

Claire's breath caught in her throat. For a moment, she let his words hang in the air. If she'd known, she wouldn't have pushed so hard, and now she didn't know what to say. "D-rock, I—"

"It's fine," he cut her off again. "I don't want to talk about it. Or do Christmas music. But that stuff is easy. You can handle that on your own, right?"

She nodded slowly, silently. She could, but truthfully, she preferred working with him instead of alone. But for his sake, she said, "Yeah, that's fine. We don't have to do Christmas music."

He visibly relaxed, the tension releasing from his face and shoulders as he breathed out heavily. Finally, he rested his bass on its stand and turned to the table where there was more handwritten music.

"We could always work on that Shawmila medley," Claire said in a teasing voice.

"Uh, that's only marginally better," D-rock said, though now he was smiling. "Plus, I kind of half promised Bryan Metallica."

Claire sat across the table from him and pulled out her laptop. "After you *just* said you were going to give him boring chords for being a jerk?"

D-rock smirked. "I didn't say I was going to give him a *good* part."

"Okay..." She chuckled. "Metallica, then. Oh, but I'm sure we could mix some Shawmila in there."

Lifting an eyebrow, he said, "Can you stop saying Shawmila?"

"No, it's cute," she said. "They're cute."

"I had no idea you were a hopeless romantic," he mumbled.

She pursed her lips and tilted her head at him. "I'm sorry, I think you have me confused with Amber."

That got a laugh out of him. "Okay, alright. If you *really* think we can mix those things together without it sounding horrible, then you're welcome to try."

"I'll try anything with you. *Musically* speaking," she corrected herself.

"Don't worry, I'm not gonna take you sky diving anytime soon," he said dryly. "Or grave robbing. Or to a rave. Or—"

"I get it," she said, laughing. "You're as boring as I am. Let's just write."

♪   ♫   ♪

Meg sat in her beautiful sunroom/practice room, working on her English essay. She would have rather done anything else—taken a walk on this sunny but cool day, played her trumpet, visited Trey... In fact, she would have liked to do all three. But she wasn't one to procrastinate. Not even when Trey texted, asking if he could come over to practice.

Meg: we're supposed to be working on our essays

Trey: well can i come over and do that?

Meg smiled. He would be a huge distraction and probably even convince her to play with him instead of doing homework. But she said yes anyway. As soon as she sent the text, the doorbell rang.

Laughing to herself, she went to the front door and opened it. "What if I didn't say yes?" she asked Trey.

He shrugged. His lopsided smile gave her butterflies. "I guess I would have just gone home."

She led him to the sunroom and gestured to the spot across the table from her. He hesitated, glancing longingly at their trumpets sitting side by side. Meg chuckled.

"*After* we do some homework," she said.

"You're so responsible," he complained. But there was a smile on his face as he got his laptop out to work.

They worked in a companionable silence for a while, though admittedly there was a lot more typing happening on Meg's laptop than on his. He'd reread the opening of his essay three times now. Shoving a hand through his hair, he sighed. He glanced at Meg several times until she finally asked him what was wrong.

"My whole essay," he said, slumping back. "Can you look at this for me?"

"Sure, send it over."

Perking up, he clicked a couple of times. His document landed in her inbox and she stared at it for a moment.

"Did you want me to make comments?" she asked.

"Yes, please," he said, sounding relieved.

"Alright, give me a few."

He stood up and said, "I'll go for a run, then."

"Okay…" she said slowly, her eyebrows drawn in.

He left and she focused on his essay. It wasn't bad, but there was a lot of room for improvement. His tone needed to be more formal and some of the sentences were unclear. But the thesis and direction were workable. By the time Trey had returned, his cheeks flushed pleasantly, she had made several edits and corrections.

"I sent it back," she said cheerfully.

He sat down and opened it up. His smile slowly drooped as he looked over her edits. "Was there any part of it you liked?"

"I—" Her eyes widened innocently. "I liked all of it. The thesis is solid."

"You made five corrections on it," he said.

"It's a first draft." Meg shrugged. "And you asked me for help. What were you expecting?"

He dropped his gaze and Meg felt bad. She got up and went around the table to put her hands on his shoulders.

"First of all," she said, "don't confuse me correcting your grammar with me not liking what you wrote. Don't take it personally. It's just an essay."

"I know." He reached up and put his hands on top of hers. "It's not that. I'm trying my hardest to get good grades so I can get into the program I want."

"What are you applying for?" she asked.

"Teacher's college," he said definitively.

"Oh, wow, I had no idea." She squeezed his shoulders.

"Yeah, well, what I really wanted to do was coach sports," he said, looking up at her. "But I was told it'd be easier to do that if I go into teaching. And to teach high school I have to have two teachable subjects. So I was going to pick gym, obviously, but the second one? I guess English is out if I can't even write an essay."

"Aw, Trey." She sat next to him and took his hand. "I think it's really great you want to be a teacher so you can coach. The world needs more good male role models like you."

His face split into a wide, beautiful smile. "That's the nicest thing you've ever said to me."

She blushed and looked down at their joined hands. "Including that time I told you you made a great pass?"

He laughed, the corners of his eyes crinkling delightfully. "You're right. They're tied for first."

She chuckled self-consciously. "So, okay, you won't be an English teacher. What about math or science? Could you do something like that?"

He cringed. "Maybe? But I would hate that more than the kids would."

"French?" she suggested. "You're good at French, right? And they're always looking for more teachers."

He nodded. "I could do it. But I was also advised that if I get into teaching French, I'll never get back out of it."

"Would that be so bad?" she asked softly.

He shrugged. "It's not what I want. And I don't know if you've noticed, but I kind of…" He looked over at his trumpet. "Always get what I want."

She smiled pertly at him. "We can play after we work on our essays a bit longer."

He laughed. "Okay, alright."

She patted him on the shoulder and went back to her laptop. In truth, she would have rather been playing, too. And she knew if he started playing, then she would want to, and they would spend their whole afternoon doing that.

After they'd worked for a few minutes, he looked up at her and said, "What about you? What are you applying for?"

"Pre-law," she answered without even looking up.

"Okay, I *love* that," he said.

She looked up at him, her hazel eyes sparkling. "Really?"

"Yes. You're so quiet and soft-spoken, but then when you do say something it's so profound." He put his hands up to his head. "It blows my mind. I can just imagine some idiot trying to fight you in court and you taking them down because you've already thought of everything."

She smiled. "I mean... I don't think I'll be doing anything complicated, like criminal law. But, yeah, wouldn't that be totally cool?"

"Absolutely," he said enthusiastically. "I hope I get to see it some day."

"Just make sure you're not standing next to the idiot on the other side of the courtroom."

He bobbed his eyebrows and looked once more at his trumpet.

"Okay, fine." She shut her laptop. "Let's play."

"Yay!"

He stood up, but instead of going to his trumpet, he went over to her. He put his arm around her waist and pulled her closer. She put her hands on his chest as he leaned down to kiss her.

"Just warming up my lips," he teased.

"Mmhmm." Yup, having Trey over was definitely a distraction.

Chapter Four

Not wanting to bother D-rock about Christmas music, Claire decided to once again turn to her second option: Harmony. Maybe now that Harmony didn't quite hate her and Claire had made it clear she liked having her in the band, Harmony might be more willing to help out.

Claire waited by the doors of the cafeteria at lunchtime on Thursday, her eyes scanning all the students until Harmony walked by.

"Hey, Harmony," Claire said quickly.

Harmony looked up with a pleasant smile. That was a good sign. "Hey, girl. What's up?"

"I know you said you weren't really interested in writing music," Claire said. "But do you think you can help me do some simple Christmas arrangements?"

Harmony smirked. "What, are you and D-rock in a fight?"

Claire shook her head and gave her a half smile. "He just...really doesn't like Christmas."

Harmony's smile fell. "Oh. Not even Christmas *music*? I kind of thought he liked all music."

Claire hesitated and then leaned in. "He told me his dad left at Christmas a few years ago, so he actually kind of hates everything about it."

Harmony frowned sadly. "Oh, I didn't realize… Poor guy."

Claire nodded.

"Okay, I'll help you write something," Harmony said. "It should be easy enough, right?"

"Sure," Claire said uncertainly, thinking about how complicated she and D-rock sometimes made things just to make sure everyone felt like they were equally included.

Harmony smiled. "Don't worry, we'll come up with something good. I'm free tomorrow night. Did you want me to come over?"

"Yeah, that'd be great," Claire said happily. She never had friends over. She'd hardly had friends before this year.

"Oh, good," Harmony said. "Because you're, like, really pretty and if you come to my house, my little brother would be all over you. Now that he's 14 he thinks he's totally suave. But he's just…"

"Awkward?" Claire guessed, ignoring Harmony's compliment.

"I was going to say drenched in body spray." Harmony laughed. "But yeah, that, too."

Claire chuckled along with her. "Well, it's nice and scent-free at my house so you're welcome to come anytime. Plus I don't have to share my snacks with anyone."

Harmony smiled but in the back of her mind she wondered if Claire was really as happy as she projected. Sure, Harmony's brothers sometimes got on her nerves and they almost always ribbed her over her flute playing. But she felt like it would be terribly lonely to live alone like Claire did while her parents were traveling the world.

"So, tomorrow night?" Claire said. "Let me send you the address."

"Great," Harmony said, reining her thoughts in.

The next night, Harmony drove to the address Claire had given her. It was a nice, small grey brick detached house in one of the older parts of town. None of the houses on the street matched and Harmony had always loved these neighbourhoods.

After Claire let her inside, Harmony took a look around. The bare walls were all a neutral grey, the carpets beige, and the plain crown mouldings white. There was one single family photo on the wall that led up the stairs, but judging by how young Claire looked in it, it was at least four or five years old.

"Not much to look at, I know," Claire said.

"I was trying not to be obvious," Harmony said. "Sorry."

Claire shrugged. "It's not a big deal. Sometimes I think about decorating, but to be honest I spend most of my time in my bedroom, so I put all my favourite stuff in there."

But Claire didn't take her upstairs, instead leading her to the kitchen table. There she had her laptop out, a small keyboard set up, and a set of speakers.

"Oh, wow, what are we working with?" Harmony asked.

"Duly Noted is a program that lets you manually enter the notes you want to appear in your music," Claire explained as she sat down, "or you can assign the notes to different keys on your computer keyboard. But the easiest way to do it is to use an actual keyboard so you don't have to memorize what key means what note."

"Oooh." Harmony sat, too, and ran her fingers over the silent keys. "That makes sense."

"Yeah. I mean, I've gotten pretty good using my laptop keyboard for it when I'm writing with D-rock," Claire said. "But it really is easier with real notes. I usually have to fix a lot of stuff when I get home."

"In that case, why don't you just have D-rock over so you can do it all here at the same time?" Harmony asked.

Claire shifted in her seat. "I just don't really want to have him here when I'm alone. You know? I mean, he's nice and all, but..."

"Oh!" Harmony's eyes widened. "Of course. Yeah. That makes sense."

Claire shrugged and then she started a new file in her program. "So, what do you think? I love pretty much every Christmas song ever, so I was counting on everyone else to pick their favourites to do."

"You know what would be funny? If we did 'The Little Drummer Boy' but it was just all drum music." Harmony laughed and Claire just raised her eyebrow. "What?"

"That is *so* something D-rock would say," Claire said, finally chuckling.

"Sounds like he has a good sense of humour, then," Harmony said, her eyes flashing jovially.

Claire shook her head, but there was a smile on her lips. She started adding all their instruments to her new file and when she got to the bass, Harmony lifted an eyebrow.

"Why are you adding a bass if he's not even going to want to play?" she asked.

Claire shrugged. "I don't want an incomplete chart. And besides...maybe he'll change his mind. I don't want him to feel left out if there's no music for him."

"Aw," Harmony murmured.

"No." Claire rolled her eyes. "I'm hoping he *does* change his mind because the band wouldn't sound as full without him."

"*Aw.*"

"Stop that," Claire said.

"What?" Harmony said in a nice voice. "You care about him. It's sweet."

"I care about nothing but the music," she lied. "If we do 'The Little Drummer Boy' we could totally have lots of layering to it *and* feature Marty.

That being said, he still kind of does whatever he wants even though he's been learning to read the music."

"I guess you could say he marches to the beat of his own drum."

Claire pulled her lips in and turned to Harmony, who was snickering at her own joke.

"Let me guess," Harmony said. "Another D-rock joke?"

"Mmhmm."

Finally, Harmony laughed aloud. "Aren't you glad you asked me to fill in for him?"

"Yes, actually," Claire said in a serious voice. "You're a lot of fun. And…I'm sorry for the things I thought about you when you first joined Less than Perfect."

"I'm…not even going to ask. I'll just accept the apology."

"That's probably for the best. Thank you."

♪　♫　♪

Amber was *really* starting to hate social studies now that pretty much all her friends had turned on her. Even Mr. Duncan now mostly ignored her when she'd been his star student previously.

Oh, well. At least she had Rach, who patted the seat next to her as soon as Amber walked in. She knew she'd done the right thing by sticking up for Rach in front of the whole class and the teacher. And she had noticed that since the incident, her classmates had gotten quieter…at least in class. The hallways and cafeteria were a different story, but nothing Amber couldn't handle.

After lunch, she headed to her English class and quickly took the seat next to Max. She knew Miss O'Shae would give them a pop quiz today. She always did the day after their required reading was due, and thankfully Amber had managed to sneak that in during a rare quiet night at home.

"Hey, you haven't signed my petition yet," Amber reminded Max.

He shrugged. "I guess I'll do it now."

Amber was just about to pull it out of her backpack when Miss O'Shae shushed them. "Time for a pop quiz," she said, gleefully rubbing her hands together. "I hope you all did the reading."

The whole class groaned. At least the quizzes usually weren't long.

"When you're finished, just hold on to your test," Miss O'Shae said. "We'll take it up together as a class."

Amber suppressed another groan. That was even worse than just handing it in and letting her do her job.

After about fifteen minutes, Miss O'Shae told them to pass their tests to the person on their right. Max, who was sitting on Amber's left, gave her his test. As soon as she saw it, her eyes widened, and she sucked in a deep breath.

"This is yours?" she whispered to him.

"It has my name on it, doesn't it?" he said, lifting an eyebrow at her.

She looked down. Yup, there was "Max Ford" in the nicest, most proper handwriting she'd ever seen. But she'd seen it before—in Chloe's letters.

Without another word, she graded his test—he got a nearly perfect score—the whole time wondering what she was supposed to do with this information. She *could* just tell Chloe, but... She glanced at Max. No, that would be totally unfair to him. And Chloe would hate not finding out from him herself.

The rest of the class was a write-off for her. She could not stop thinking about Max and why he'd gone through the trouble to express himself like that.

After class, she followed Max out on his heels and once they were in the hallway, she said, "You have very nice handwriting."

"Thanks," he said. "Nice to know those penmanship classes my parents insisted on paid off."

"I'd say!" Amber laughed thinking about how long they'd deliberated over whether the writing even was a boy's because it was so nice.

"What?" he said, his face all scrunched up.

"I know about the letters," she said quietly.

"What letters?" Though he sounded nonchalant, red had started creeping into the tips of his ears. She knew she'd caught him.

She smiled. "The letters you've been giving Chloe, you dork."

His face growing even more red, he took her elbow and guided her off to the side of the hallway so she would stop shouting about his letters. He looked around uncomfortably, but it didn't seem like anyone was paying them any attention.

"Okay, what do you want?" he asked in a low voice.

She raised her eyebrows. "What do you mean?"

"I mean, what do you want me to give you so you won't tell her?" he asked.

"Are you...bribing me?" She laughed again. "That's such a rich person thing to do. Are you kidding?"

"No, I'm not kidding," he said, his voice hitching up a notch. "Since you girls can't keep anything to yourselves—"

"Excuse me." She held up a finger. "If she knew those letters were from you, she probably wouldn't have shown them to us and would have gone straight to you. You know that, right?"

He let go of her elbow and crossed his arms. "Agree to disagree. Now what do you want?"

She looked into his angry hazel eyes. He really didn't trust her. Well, if he wanted to buy his way out of this, then that was fine with her.

"Two things," she said, holding up two fingers. "I need a copy of *Zombies Versus Yetis 2*, a quarter-inch socket, and a three-eighths-inch one."

"That's three things," he said flatly.

"No, that's the *first* thing," she said.

His eyes narrowed. "What do you need all that for, anyway? Those are the most common sockets available, and that doesn't seem like your type of video game."

The bell rang but they didn't move, even though neither of them ever liked to be late for class.

"They're for Bryan," she said. "Not *me*."

He rolled his eyes. "And the second thing?"

"You have to tell her," she said.

"Geez, why didn't I think of that?" He threw a hand in the air.

She crossed her arms. "I could help you out and just tell her for you."

"*No*." He let his arms drop and let out a long breath. "Look, I've already been told once, alright? I'll stop messing around and find…some way…"

Amber smiled demurely. "For someone with such a way with words, it shouldn't be that hard."

The red returned to Max's face. "You were never supposed to see those letters. Why can't girls just keep things to themselves?"

She shrugged. "You chose a special but secret way to share your feelings. What did you expect her to do? Toss them in the garbage without a second thought?"

"Yeah, kind of."

Beneath his indifferent words, Amber could hear the uncertainty. Max had every reason to be overly confident and yet he wasn't. "Well, she kept them all. And she only showed us a couple of them. Would you relax?"

"I'd be more relaxed if I weren't super late for class now." He started walking away. "Just…*please* don't say anything."

"I won't," she promised. "But *you* will."

He waved her off and turned to take off down the hall. She shook her head. Now that she thought about it, it was *so* obvious. Every detail, from the nice handwriting to the expensive stationary to how awkward he was around her. It made her smile.

Chapter Five

"Can you say it one more time but, like, more nasal?" Marty said.

Corbie sighed. "I *am* saying it nasally. *Matin. Patin. Moulin.* What am I doing wrong?"

"It's just not...*in* enough," Marty said, overemphasizing the pronunciation.

"Not *in* enough?" Corbie said flatly.

"Oh, that sounded better!"

Corbie huffed.

Marty bit his lip, wondering how far he should push Corbie. "Did you not come to Marty and tell Marty that even though you did *okay* on your oral test, your teacher still said you needed to work on your pronunciation, and you were like, 'Marty, help me, I don't know what to do?' So now Marty's trying to help you, but you're too resistant."

"Why is Marty talking about himself like that?" Corbie asked, his eyes narrowed.

"Marty thought it would help. But obviously it's not."

Corbie put his hands up. "Nothing is going to help. Can we just go now?"

"Trust me, I would love nothing more than to go to Max's house so I can play my drums, but—" He sighed. "Not like this. I can't let you walk around speaking French like that."

"I don't walk around speaking French," Corbie said, shaking his head.

"Well, maybe you should," Marty said. "And then you'd be better at it."

Corbie ran a hand over his hair. "I just want to pass my class, Marty."

Marty sighed and dropped his gaze. "You know, French isn't just a school subject," he said softly. "It's a living, breathing language that people speak around the world. *C'est une partie de moi.*"

"I get that," Corbie said, matching his tone. "And I respect that. But I don't think it's ever going to be a part of *me* like that."

"Because you're so resistant," Marty said, pushing Corbie playfully. "Come on, go get your trombone and let's get out of here. I need my drums."

Corbie immediately stood up. He didn't need to be told twice. "Thanks for trying to help me," he said as he got his trombone off the stand.

"I'm not *trying* to help you," Marty said. He watched Corbie carefully put his trombone in its case. "You're getting better so I *am* helping you."

"Well, thank you either way." Corbie shut the case and started doing the clasps. "I'm sorry I keep butchering your language."

Marty shrugged. "It's not the worst thing anyone's done to me."

Corbie looked at him sharply. "What's that supposed to mean?"

Marty looked away, wishing he hadn't said anything. "Nothing. Don't worry about it."

"Is someone bothering you?" Corbie asked.

He had crossed his arms and had a little frown on his face. Marty thought it was adorable and not the least bit as fierce as Corbie probably wanted to be. It made him smile.

"No, I'm fine, man," Marty said. "Just sometimes people get weird because, you know…"

"Because you're gay?" Corbie guessed.

Marty shrugged and nodded. "Sometimes, yeah."

"That's dumb," Corbie said, his frown deepening.

"Really, it's not that bad. I promise," Marty said.

Corbie's eyes widened. "You're making it worse."

"It's not—" Marty stopped and sighed. "I'm not getting bullied or anything. But you know, you're kind of on the outside if you're a guy who's not crazy about girls. It's hard to fit in when all my guy friends just want to do stuff that revolves around girls."

"All of them?" Corbie asked, his eyebrows raised high.

"I want to say no." Marty chuckled. "But did I not get dragged out to a restaurant a few weeks ago just for the chance of seeing our female bandmates looking fine and pretty? And not a single one of you dressed to impress. Except Max, but he's always dressed like that, so it kind of doesn't count."

Corbie opened and closed his mouth a couple of times. "Okay, that's...that's fair. I'm sorry I didn't say anything."

"It's fine," Marty said. "Because D-rock was right. I like to be included in things and I like hanging out, too. I just don't want to chase girls with other guys. And honestly, it's somewhat creepy behaviour and you shouldn't let people like Bryan convince you to do that kind of thing."

Corbie suppressed a smile. *Trey* was the one who had invited him, and it hadn't been clear that's what they were going for. But he nodded anyway.

"You're right," Corbie said. "I promise I won't do creepy things around girls."

"Good."

Corbie finished putting his trombone in its case and once they were ready, his mom drove them out to Max's house. It wasn't a long drive, but it had started getting progressively colder the closer they got to Christmas, so they were grateful for the ride.

317

Max let them into the house and downstairs. Now that Max's parents had reluctantly agreed to let the band practice in the basement, there was no need to cover up the drum set anymore. Marty headed straight for it, grabbing the sticks off the snare where he'd left them. He tapped on the drums, listening for anything that might need adjusting, before starting a beat he liked.

Corbie got out his trombone and warmed it up. Max had his violin out but wasn't playing it. And in fact, he'd barely said a word to them since they'd come in.

Marty stopped playing and said, "Max, what's wrong, man? You haven't made me clap out rhythms yet."

Max shrugged but gave him a sad smile anyway. "Just not feeling it today. You should be clapping out those rhythms, though. You can't keep faking it. Claire and D-rock will definitely know."

"Wait a minute," Corbie said. "You get to be lazy about reading your music after you badgered me for an hour about my French pronunciations?"

"The difference is that yours is for marks and mine is just because everyone wants me to conform." Marty kicked the bass drum to punctuate his statement.

"That's not true," Max said with a sigh. "We talked about that."

"Yeah, yeah." Marty tapped his symbols. "Can't lead a band if you don't know where the music's going. But the stuff they write is so complicated sometimes."

Corbie nodded. "Yeah, they definitely don't realize not everyone in the band is as good as they are."

"You guys play just fine," Max said quietly. He plucked a string on his violin and then turned the tuning peg.

"Man, you're *killing* me," Marty said. "Stop tuning your violin already and tell us what's wrong."

Max slowly lowered his violin to his lap. "It's dumb."

"Good. Tell us anyway," Marty said.

Max looked down at his feet and mumbled, "I'm trying to figure out how to tell someone I like them…in a different way than I already did."

"That's so vague," Corbie said, his eyes wide. "But not dumb."

"What's the problem?" Marty asked. "You're smart, and cute, and talented, and rich."

Max cringed. "Honestly, I'm not sure any of that matters to her."

"Then maybe she's not worth your time," Marty said seriously.

Max put his hands up and sighed. "What would you do?"

"Hope he doesn't like boobs?" Marty said with a cheeky smile.

"Hope *she* doesn't like boobs," Corbie added, bobbing his eyebrows.

That coaxed a genuine smile out of Max. "Thanks, guys…" He frowned thoughtfully. "I'm pretty sure she doesn't. Ugh, I should have just called off today, but I didn't want to leave everyone hanging."

"Aw," Corbie said. "There's still time if you want us to go."

"No," Max said, looking at his Rolex. "Chloe's gonna—"

The doorbell rang and he cut himself off. He gestured upstairs and listened to the sound of her letting herself in. Retreating further into himself, he regretted not having called off tonight's meeting earlier. He could have made something up. He didn't have to tell everyone he was heartsick and worried that they would find out before her.

Chloe bounded down the steps, her twin braids bouncing against her shoulders. She smiled when she saw Marty and Corbie with Max. "Hey, friends. And Max."

Max lifted his eyebrows and tried to say in a normal voice, "Nice to see you, too, Chloe."

Her smile fell. "Hey, I was just teasing. You're my friend, too. Why the long face?"

Max shook his head, avoiding her gaze.

"Oh, he's just—"

Marty cut Corbie off with a loud and disjointed beat on his drums that drowned out all other sounds. "Sorry, what?" he called out over his own drumming.

"Never mind," Corbie said loudly, his eyes flashing.

Chloe didn't seem bothered as she bobbed her head to the beat of Marty's drums. Max sat patiently while she got her violin out. Soon the rest of them would show up and unless he wanted *everyone* asking what was wrong, he'd have to change his attitude.

Finally, he lifted his violin and played, letting the feel of the strings, the movement of the bow, and the soft notes soothe him. He closed his eyes and listened to his violin over the sounds of Marty's drums and Corbie's trombone. When he realized he didn't hear a second violin, he opened his eyes and peeked at Chloe. She was watching him with a smile.

"They must have been on crack the day you did your audition for the Youth Orchestra," she said.

He laughed so hard he had to put his violin down. "Thanks?"

"It's a compliment." She lifted her violin to her chin. "Here, play this part with me," she said, pointing with her bow at a section of the "Secrets" arrangement on her music stand.

"Did we do it wrong last time?" he asked as he got out his own music.

"No. I just like the way it sounds," she said wistfully.

"Oh."

He tucked his violin under his chin and waited for her lead. The part she'd chosen was the last chorus and Max could understand why. It was the most full-voiced part, what he would consider the most emotional part. And it was genuinely the most interesting part for the violins, though the whole piece had been very thoughtfully written so they never felt bored.

As they played, Marty pulled back to a more respectable volume and played his part of the song. Corbie joined them, too, after hastily getting his music out on his stand.

When they'd finished, Chloe smiled and said, "Hey, we sound pretty good! What do we need the others for?" The doorbell rang at that moment, and she chuckled. "Oh, look, it's the others. Never mind."

Soon, everyone else had filled their seats in the basement and Max felt more at ease. As they warmed up and got ready to play together, TK came up to Max with excitement in his eyes.

"Hey, Max, when do your lights go up?" TK asked.

Max smiled. "Normally, next weekend would be when I'd put them up. But I'm considering a redesign, so I might have to put it off for another weekend."

A hushed gasp rang across the basement, and everyone stopped to turn and stare at him.

"What?" he asked after a moment.

"If you don't do Seuss, who's going to, then?" Chloe asked.

He shrugged. "There doesn't have to be a Seuss house. That's just—"

"Pardon me?" Amber cut him off. "You're joking, right?"

"No…"

"Do you have any idea how seriously this town takes the lights on this street?" TK said, his eyebrows drawn in. "You can't just…*switch* your theme."

"Well, my parents have been making me do it basically on my own for the last three years," Max said, matching his tone of voice. "And I haven't been into Dr. Seuss since I was, like, seven. So, yeah. I *can* switch the theme."

"But, Max…" Bryan said dryly. "What would the HOA say?"

"People will think you moved," Rach added quite seriously.

Max rolled his eyes.

"It's just *lights*, you guys," D-rock said in the most annoyed tone they'd ever heard him use.

"Right," Max said. "What he said. It's just lights. And this year, I wanted to do something music-themed, and I was going to ask if any of you feel like helping. But if you're so offended it's not going to be Seuss, then—"

"No, wait, that sounds fun!" Harmony said. "I want to do that."

"Me, too," Trey said. "My mom only does those dark blue lights on our house and it's...awful."

"It is kind of terrible," Meg said. "But please don't tell your mom I said that."

He smiled at her and squeezed her shoulder.

"I am definitely here for that," Amber said. She glanced back at Rach.

"Yeah, yeah," Rach said. "Like, I'll help, but the thing is that I'm actually...ironically...afraid of heights. So, I don't do ladders."

Max pursed his lips to hold his laughter in. "That's fine. I'd be grateful for any help."

"Are we *playing*?" D-rock said in that same tone of voice. "Or are we talking about *lights*?"

"We can play now, D-rock," Claire said gently.

"New music?" Corbie asked hopefully.

"Not this week, sorry," Claire said. "Maybe next week."

Corbie smiled. "That's alright. I like the stuff we already have."

Chapter Six

After spending the majority of her weekend doing homework, Claire was looking forward to working on music with D-rock Sunday evening. Even though they'd been at it for two months, she still never quite knew what to expect from him. She was sure in his head, his ideas were clearly defined, but when he expressed them, they were all over the place. Somehow, though, when the music was written, it sounded amazing and was even better when Less than Perfect played it.

Sure enough, when she got to his house, she found him at his kitchen table, surrounded by papers full of his stream of consciousness. She tried not to cringe, but he could tell what she was thinking.

"I know, I'm a disaster," he said, gesturing helplessly at the table.

"That's okay," she said as he cleared a space for her. "You're...a talented disaster. I can work with that. Where's your mom?"

"She's on a date," he said, waving his hand loosely in the direction of the street outside. "She wouldn't say with who, which is super sus, but I'm not supposed to ask more than five times, so..." He shrugged.

"I'm sure it's fine," Claire said quietly, not wanting to rock the boat if

D-rock wasn't okay with his mom dating.

"Sure." He showed her some sheets of hand-written music. "Here are some extra lines I wrote for 'Nothing Else Matters.' I could put them in myself if you want."

"I'll try," she said, taking the papers.

Of course, as she worked, D-rock looked over her shoulder the entire time, adding in his comments for almost every note. She didn't need him literally breathing down her neck but the more he said, the more she realized it was nervous energy that was making him act that way.

"D-rock, what does this say?" Claire pointed to an unidentifiable scribble on the page.

"Hmm…" He leaned in even closer. "Forte."

She lifted a brow.

"Or maybe decrescendo?" he said, his face scrunched up.

"Neither of those things look like this scribble," she said. "And neither fit this part of the music."

He shrugged. "Okay, so skip it and move on. It's probably not important."

Her eyes widened briefly as he waved a hand. She looked back down at the scribbled writing, most of which was barely legible to her.

"At least we know it's not you," she muttered to herself.

"What's not me?" he asked.

"Oh, umm…" Now why did she bring that up? Chloe probably wouldn't want D-rock to know but…what was the harm? "Okay, don't say anything, but Chloe's been getting these anonymous letters. We're pretty sure they're from a boy, but the writing is so neat, and proper and…almost kind of fancy."

D-rock snorted. "I only know one boy who's neat and proper and almost kind of fancy."

"What do you me—" Claire gasped sharply. "*No*. You don't think…?"

"No, I don't," he said firmly.

"What are we gonna do about this?" she asked, her eyes wide.

He frowned at her. "Nothing. Let's just pretend we don't know."

"Aw, come on," she said. "Can't we at least slip in some romantic lines for them to play or something? Please?"

"Oh, Claire… Here, let me take a turn."

Her shoulders drooped in disappointment, but she turned the laptop towards him anyway. For a few minutes, she just watched D-rock work on her laptop, adding notes here and there. He turned to her with a smile, his green eyes sparkling.

"What do you think of this?" he asked, before pressing the play button.

As she listened, a new melody, mixed in with the other, caught her ear.

"Is that—" She put it back and listened one more time. "You goofball, is that 'Black Is the Color of My True Love's Hair'?"

His eyes twinkled with mirth. "I honestly didn't expect you to recognize it. Do you think they'll notice?"

"Yes!" She smacked her forehead. "You said you *weren't* going to write them something romantic."

"Yeah, well, I changed my mind."

"Could have picked something less obvious," she said.

"But it fits so nicely with 'Nothing Else Matters.' Don't you think?"

"Yeah, it really does," she admitted. She turned the laptop towards herself. "But we should at least add more to this so it feels intentional."

"Intentional matchmaking," he said. "Mmhmm, let's do that."

"You started it."

For a few minutes, she worked on adding a couple more instruments to carry the rest of the tune. Then she let D-rock write some harmonies while she got up and started poking through the cupboards. Maybe it was rude, but this much creativity required sustenance.

After she'd opened and closed three cupboards, D-rock said, "Try the freezer. Mom keeps all her good chocolate in there."

"Ohh." Claire went straight to the freezer and sure enough, there were some high-quality chocolate bars in there. "You sure she won't mind?"

"Nah." He flicked his hand. "Help yourself."

"You sure know how to treat a birthday girl," she said as she took one of the chocolate bars out.

He turned to her sharply. "Is it your birthday?"

"Mmhmm." She unwrapped the chocolate bar, broke it in half and then held out half to him.

Confused, he took it but placed his piece on the table. "Why didn't you say anything? You didn't have to come over. You could have done something fun."

She chuckled. "This *is* fun. Besides, my aunt already took me out for lunch and my parents sent me a gift a couple weeks ago. Honestly, I think they just don't remember the *exact* date of my birthday, but at least they sent it early."

D-rock watched her for a moment as she ate his mom's chocolate. "Is that supposed to make me feel better?"

"It's not my job to make you feel good," she said with a coy smile. "Thanks for the chocolate."

"You're welcome." He turned back to her laptop and picked up the half a chocolate bar she gave him. Shoving it into his mouth, he said, "Do you want to listen to this?"

"Do you want to maybe chew and swallow first?" was her answer. She sat next to him while he chewed noisily with his mouth open as if to demonstrate. "And yes, of course I want to listen."

D-rock played the piece back and when Claire heard it, her heart melted.

"Okay, that is *so* good. I love this. I can't wait to play it with everyone."

He smiled, but he still felt bad that he hadn't done anything to make Claire's birthday special, especially since she'd just turned 16.

The next morning, D-rock went to school and headed straight to Amber's locker. If there was anyone who could make a girl happy, it was definitely her.

"Hey, Amber," D-rock said as soon as she got there. She gave him a bright smile. "Did you know it was Claire's birthday yesterday?"

"Aw, no, I didn't," she answered as she opened her locker.

"Okay, well can you do something nice for her?" He put his hand through his hair. "I feel bad she spent her whole evening with me. And I didn't even know until the end."

"Oh, *no*," she said dramatically, whirling around with her hands over her heart. "Claire had to spend her birthday with a cute boy who's nice to her? She must be *so* traumatized!"

D-rock's eyes narrowed as she giggled. "Get off the ship, it's never gonna set sail. Please just do something for her."

Amber pressed her lips together to keep from laughing more. "Okay," she said lightly. "You don't have to beg me to be nice to my own friends."

"Thank you."

Just as he turned to go, she said, "Never say never," in her perky, cheeky voice.

He just rolled his eyes and tossed a wave over his shoulder.

Amber could joke all she wanted, but she took her job as a friend seriously. And if D-rock wanted her to make Claire's birthday special, that was what she would do. At lunchtime, Amber raced out of her classroom to wait by the cafeteria doors for her. When Claire came by, Amber linked her arm with Claire's. Claire raised her eyebrows in surprise but smiled anyway.

"Hi, Claire." Amber looked her up and down. Claire had put on an orange sweater dress and fawn-coloured leggings and the fall colours were really nice on her. "You're looking so sweet and…sixteen today!"

"Oh," Claire said with a half smile. "D-rock told you."

"Yeah." Amber led her towards the table she shared with Rach and Meg. "He felt real bad you didn't do any celebrating."

Claire shrugged. "It's fine. I don't really do much for my birthday anyway. Normally, I like to decorate for Christmas, but I did that a few days early because I was bored."

"Aw." They'd reached Rach and Meg, and Amber gestured to them as they sat. "We could still do something together, though."

"Do what?" Rach asked, having missed their whole conversation. "I don't trust you to organize another girls' night. Sorry."

Amber frowned. "It was Claire's birthday yesterday."

"Aw, happy birthday," Meg said before they started arguing. "You should've told us."

"It's really okay," Claire said as she took out her lunch. "I spent it doing what I like."

"Hanging out with D-rock?" Amber asked.

Claire held up a finger. "Writing music. Which you'll be playing tomorrow. You're welcome."

"Christmas music?" Meg asked.

Claire paused and shook her head. "I'll have some of that soon. Harmony and I are working on it. D-rock doesn't care for it."

"Hmm." Amber's frown deepened. "Well, can you tell him I at least tried to get you to do something fun?"

"Sure," Claire said with a smile. "And I appreciate the effort."

For a few minutes, they ate quietly. Rach nudged Meg and said, "You know you can eat with Trey, right? You don't have to stay here."

Meg's gaze flicked briefly across the cafeteria where Trey was sitting with his friends. "It's fine. I don't really fit in with the jocks."

"You're *dating* a jock," Amber reminded her.

Meg smiled. "I didn't say I don't fit with him."

"Shut *up*," Amber said. "That's so precious."

Meg's smile grew as her cheeks went pink. The truth was that she probably would sit with Trey if his friends weren't quite so…loud and boisterous. She preferred sharing lunch with her girls.

When Meg went to her locker after lunch, she remembered exactly why she didn't always want to hang out with Trey's friends. Because some of them gave her the same vibes Chad did.

And there he was, leaning against her locker with his arms crossed and looking bored. His eyes locked on to hers and for a moment, she was frozen. He waved his hand impatiently, beckoning her closer, while his lips remained thinly pressed together.

She was tempted to look around her, just in case Trey—or literally anyone else—was around to fall back on. But she wouldn't. She could handle Chad.

When she was finally brave enough to draw closer, he said simply, "Hey."

"Hi," she said on a sigh. "How's your shoulder?"

He shrugged and winced. It was enough of an answer.

"Can I get to my locker?" she asked.

"Yeah." He pushed off her locker so she could open it but didn't leave.

"What's up, Chad?" she asked, avoiding looking directly at him.

For a long moment, he didn't say anything. She chanced peeking at him, and he was staring at her, the frown still there. "I'm here to apologize," he finally said.

"You are?" she asked in surprise.

"Yeah." He dropped his gaze, and she went back to looking into her locker. "I was too pushy with you. Maybe I was even being a jerk. So…I'm sorry."

"Okay," she said barely above a whisper.

"Okay?" he asked in a confused voice.

"Yeah, you're forgiven." She took a textbook out of her locker and shoved it into her backpack. But Chad still stood there.

"Can you call off your dog, then?" he said.

She looked over her shoulder at him. "*Pardon?*"

"*Trey.*" He shook his head. "Can you tell him I said sorry?"

"Sure."

She zipped up her backpack and still Chad didn't take the hint to leave.

"You could have just told me it was about him," he said.

She could hear the insecurity in his voice. She should have let it go. But if he was going to bring it up, then maybe it was time to clear the air.

"That what was about him?" she asked to clarify.

"That you didn't want to go out with me because you're into him," he said. "It's not like you guys are keeping it a secret that you're dating."

Meg slammed her locker shut harder than she meant to and whirled to face him properly. "I don't know how to say this and still spare your feelings, but it *wasn't* about him. It was about *you*. I wasn't interested in going out with you. When I said no twice, you should have let it go. I don't even know you that well. And honestly? I don't know why you chose me when you could have lots of other girls. Do you understand?"

He licked his lips, staring down at his feet. "Yeah," he said loosely. "I get it."

"Thank you for the apology," she said. The bell rang. "I hope you never treat anyone else that way again."

He nodded and then left without another word. Meg let out a long breath, expelling the tension from her body. Hopefully he would go back to ignoring her for the rest of the year.

Chapter Seven

Hacks ran his fingers along the piano at Sunny Meadows, the local retirement community. And while he did, his mind was far away, still working on his most recent programming project. Funny how when he played he thought of programming and when he was programming he thought of playing. There was probably something wrong with that scenario, but he wasn't going to overanalyse it.

Mr. Johnson came by and rumbled something to him over the sound of the piano. Hacks wasn't playing loudly, but the acoustics in their dining hall were perfect for carrying the sound to the far reaches while the residents ate.

Still, he'd always had good hearing and had gotten used to the way most of the residents spoke. Hacks smiled pleasantly and nodded before transitioning into "How Great Thou Art." They sure did like their hymns here.

Hacks played until the last resident had finished their dinner and left the dining hall. When he'd signed up to volunteer for Sunny Meadows, they had been happy to have him for half an hour. And he'd done that at the beginning. But seeing how much they loved listening to him play had encouraged him to stay longer and longer and now it had become his custom to leave after they had.

Just as he was getting up to leave, Mari, the nice programs coordinator, approached him. She leaned on the piano in a way that he hated but he smiled anyway.

"That was such beautiful playing tonight," she said.

"Thank you," he answered politely. He could have played better if he hadn't been running calculations in his head, but he didn't mention it.

"So, I had an idea," she said, the corners of her eyes crinkling with her excitement. "What if you came and played a special Christmas program?"

"Oh."

"Yeah! Instead of the half attention you get during dinnertime, you can have a whole hour to yourself in the main entertainment hall." Mari smiled bigger as she stared at him expectantly.

"Oh, I, um…I like the half attention," he said.

Mari's smile fell. "Pardon?"

"I just…I like playing like this," he said, gesturing to the dining hall. "In the background, without too many people noticing me."

"Oh." She looked down at her feet and he could tell she was disappointed.

He licked his lips. "But, uh, you know…I play in this band, and they might like that. Do you think we could all come play?"

Mari pursed her lips, cringing a bit. "Are they as good as you?"

"Oh, better!" Hacks said quickly. "Trust me, you won't be disappointed."

"Well…" Mari fluffed up her bleached curls. "Okay. I'll trust you, Hacks. Find out if your band is available December tenth and get back to me."

"The tenth," Hacks said, his heart dropping. "That's really soon."

"It's the only Friday night I haven't filled with a holiday activity," she said. "So if you could let me know by the end of the week, that'd be great."

Hacks nodded. "Sure, I can do that."

As he left, Hacks debated asking in the group chat. But he hated getting drowned out by a million replies—especially since some of them only communicated in emojis—so he decided to leave it for tomorrow night instead.

♪ ♫ ♪

The next day at school, Max came right up to Hacks with his ever-pleasant smile on. "I have a favour to ask."

Normally, a phrase like that would send Hacks running because it usually meant his classmates wanted "help" with homework and tests. But Max wasn't like that, so Hacks motioned for him to go on.

"I really want to synchronize my lights to music this year," Max said, clasping his hands together in excitement. "And I was thinking you could—"

"Say no more," Hacks said, his mind already running through the possibilities. "I already have the perfect program template for it. I'll even do your wiring for you."

Max's eyes lit up. "Really? That's awesome. Hacks, you're the best!"

"In some ways, yes," he said.

Max just chuckled.

Later that day, Hacks went to Max's house early to show him what he could do with Max's setup. After he'd uploaded his program to Max's computer, he explained to him how the program worked to control the lights.

"The best part about this program is that it analyses sound waves and syncs to those," Hacks explained. "So you can play any song you want, and it'll still work."

"Wow," Max said, staring wide-eyed at his laptop.

"Yeah," Hacks said. "Theoretically, you could even do this with a live band if you had the proper mic setup."

"A live band? That would be amazing," Max said.

"It would be," Hacks said. "Unfortunately, we're not accustomed to the proper techniques and using the equipment it would take to do that."

Max smiled. "You're so practical, Hacks."

"Thank you."

Hacks went back to looking through his program while Max bit back a smile. He could mean that as a compliment if that's how Hacks wanted to take it.

Soon enough Chloe arrived, followed by the others. By the time Amber and Bryan showed up, Hacks had gotten so amped up for Christmas that he could barely contain his excitement. When he told them about Sunny Meadows, they were all very excited. All except D-rock, but no one seemed to notice his silence.

When they'd finally calmed down, D-rock asked, "Does anyone want this new music or not?"

That got them excited all over again and they clamoured for the music. Bryan took his and frowned at the exquisitely written piece.

"I can't play all this," he mumbled.

"Then give it back," Claire snipped, holding out her hand towards him.

"No, seriously," he said, though he held onto the sheets. "This is…this is a lot. I'm not the guitar player you were looking for when you wrote this."

"Didn't you say you wanted Metallica?" she asked.

"Yeah, but—"

"Bryan," Amber said in the most annoyed tone. "Stop fishing for compliments and just play it."

He rolled his eyes at his sister but placed the music on his stand anyway.

"It's a shortened intro anyway, Bryan," D-rock said. "And actually, Hacks will play two bars before you and Claire and I will be playing background chords. Then the violins come in and once the main melody starts, everyone else will come in. No sweat."

"Yeah," Bryan said, still sounding uncertain. "Go ahead, Hacks."

Cool as ever, Hacks played the opening bars. And despite his protests, when Bryan came in, he played the melody as if he'd done it a hundred times before. D-rock smiled as he placed his bow to his bass. His band was far better than they thought they were.

The melody of the verse was shared between the woodwinds culminating into a stronger sound with the brass during the chorus. There was a musical interlude in the middle of the song which should normally have been played on the guitar. But while Bryan played, Max and Chloe chimed in with a new song—the "secret" D-rock and Claire had added in.

Though it wasn't a part of "Nothing Else Matters," neither Max nor Chloe seemed bothered by it as they played their harmonies beautifully. The piece ended with them trading off melodies with the rest of the band.

When they'd finished, Bryan turned to Claire with a huge smile. "That was *so* perfect."

"For once I agree with you," Amber said. "I loved that."

"Also," Chloe said, lifting her bow into the air. "'Black Is the Color of My True Love's Hair?' I love that song! And it fit so nicely."

Max threw a sharp glance at Claire and then D-rock, who looked a bit guilty but smiled anyway.

"Wow." D-rock swallowed hard. "You know that song? I didn't think anyone would recognize it if I slipped it in."

"I mean, everyone has a cover of it," Harmony said.

"Yeah, it's pretty much everywhere," Corbie added.

"Cool," D-rock said, nodding. "Cool, cool."

Claire nudged him with her elbow, and he nudged her back. "Let's just play it again," she said. "It sounded nice. You're all lovely."

Max bit his tongue and kept quiet until it was time for everyone to leave. He'd recognized the song too and thought it was maybe a coincidence. But when D-rock gave him side-eye as they played it a second time, he knew they'd done it on purpose.

As everyone packed up to leave, Max went up to Claire and D-rock with a polite smile. "I have some suggestions for you two if you want to stick around for a minute."

"Sure, Max," Claire said as she loosened the hairs on her bow.

Max waited while the others said goodbye and left. When they'd all gone, he turned back to Claire and D-rock with a scowl on his face. "Very cute. Who told?"

"Who told what?" Claire asked innocently while D-rock stared at his feet.

"'Black Is the Color of My True Love's Hair?'" Max said emphatically as he crossed his arms.

D-rock pointed at Claire, and she swatted his hand away. "*Technically*," she said, "he figured it out. But you—" she stopped to smile at Max "—were the one who confirmed it."

Max pulled on the knot of his tie as if he suddenly couldn't breathe. Pinning Claire with a look, he said, "Why do girls always have to say *so* much? Would it have killed you to keep it to yourself?"

Her eyes widened innocently, and she put her hands up. "All I said was that I noticed D-rock's handwriting is terrible compared to…well, everyone's but especially some really lovely writing I've seen recently. D-rock—"

"Hey," D-rock cut her off. "I didn't explicitly say that it was Max's writing. I just said I could only think of one person who matched that kind of writing. Your name never even came up in conversation."

"And that song?" Max asked irritably. "The one you *slipped in* that is specifically only played by two violins that you were *sure* no one would notice?"

Claire and D-rock gave each other contrite looks. Claire's shoulders drooped and D-rock let out a disappointed sigh.

"I'm sorry," D-rock said. "It was my idea."

"But I helped," Claire said softly.

Max threw his hands in the air. "What's it going to take to keep you quiet?"

"What?" Claire asked, her eyebrows drawn in.

"We're not gonna say anything," D-rock said. "We were just having some fun with the music, okay? I didn't know it would bother you that much."

"I promise," Claire said. "We won't say anything."

"And no more meddling," Max said firmly.

Claire and D-rock nodded, both of them feeling bad over what they'd done. They started heading up the stairs but then Max said in a soft voice, "Thanks for the new music. It's really pretty."

D-rock smiled at him, but Claire just nudged him forward. Sullenly, they walked up the stairs and left Max's house. Claire pulled out her phone as D-rock placed his bass into the back of his mom's van.

"Tell me you're not ordering an Uber," he said.

"Of course I am," she said.

He picked up her cello without asking and lifted it into the van next to his bass. "Just get in," he said irritably.

Glaring at him, she shoved her phone in her pocket. Then she got into the passenger seat and slammed the door shut as hard as she could. D-rock put the van into gear before Claire had even buckled up but to her surprise, he pulled out onto the street at a respectable speed.

"You could have asked," she said quietly.

After a momentary pause, D-rock mumbled, "Do you want a ride home?"

Claire just sighed. "I live on Hampton."

D-rock nodded and then fell silent.

"Is there any chance you'll want to come to Sunny Meadows with us?" she asked softly.

D-rock shook his head.

"So, I guess you don't want to look at the music Harmony and I wrote?" she asked hopefully. When he didn't even acknowledge her question, she said, "Look, Harmony's really smart and it's nice music but it's missing that...spark that's always there in your arrangements."

"The last time I added spark to something, I got yelled at," he said bitterly.

"Max didn't yell at us," she said. "He just doesn't want us telling everyone his secret. Please."

D-rock's face softened as he turned onto Hampton Avenue. "Where's your house?"

"Two up on the right," she answered.

Silently, he pulled into her empty driveway, parked, and got out. He took her cello out of the back of the van and handed it to her.

"Send me the midi files and I'll..." He stopped and sighed dramatically. "I'll listen for your missing spark."

Claire smiled. "Thank you! And thanks for the ride."

He mumbled something, got back inside the van, and drove off before she'd even made it into her house.

Chapter Eight

Bryan impatiently finished cleaning out the change rooms at the community centre. Was he anxious to get to Max's house and help decorate? Nope. But he didn't want to keep Harmony waiting too long for him since she seemed so excited about it.

He hadn't fully acknowledged how much he liked seeing her every Saturday after her orchestra rehearsal. But when he finally stepped out into the foyer and she smiled brightly at him that's when he knew—it was bad. Far worse than he'd ever intended.

He nearly ran right out the building without her.

He got in his car and put the heat on full blast. As she buckled up, he said, "Straight to Max's house?"

"Shouldn't we pick up Amber first?" she said.

"Right," he said. "Yeah. Amber."

"Are you guys fighting or something?" she asked.

"No," he answered. In fact, he and Amber hadn't gotten along this well in years. But he didn't know how to admit that, in Harmony's presence, he'd briefly forgotten about his own sister's existence. So he said nothing as he drove home.

In the driveway, he honked the horn and kept the car idling. Amber came out with a frown on her face, no doubt from the rude way Bryan had of letting her know he was here to get her. But when she saw Harmony in the front seat, her mouth turned up into a coy smile.

She opened the door and said, "I didn't know you were getting Harmony first."

"Oh, we just came from the community centre," Harmony said. "Did you want the front seat?"

Bryan pulled out of the driveway before Amber could answer. She'd barely even shut the door and certainly wasn't buckled in.

"You were both at the community centre?" Amber asked as she hastily did the buckle.

Harmony turned in her seat to look at her. "Bryan works there while I'm in orchestra rehearsal. He drives me home every Saturday. Did you not know that?"

Amber's mouth dropped open and then she smiled. "I was unaware. Tell me more!"

"There is no more," Bryan said, cutting off whatever Amber thought she was going to get out of them.

"Well," Harmony said. "That's not true. *Sometimes* he slows down when I ask him to."

At that comment, Bryan pushed harder on the gas, making both girls squeal. He couldn't help smiling. At least now they'd stop talking about him and Harmony. Since there was no him and Harmony.

When they got to Max's house, they found several of their bandmates there already. Chloe, TK, Trey, Meg, and Rach were sorting through boxes of lights and other decorations. Max, Hacks, and Claire were bent over a mixing board.

Corbie and Marty came right after Bryan had parked and got out of an old beat-up van. They waved to Marty's mom before approaching the double garage doors that had been left wide open.

They all headed over to where the others were sorting. But not Bryan. His eye had caught sight of a classic car inside the garage, and he couldn't help taking a closer look. As soon as he approached it, his eyes grew wide, and he sucked in a sharp breath.

"Max!" he shouted, rushing back out to find him. "Max!"

Max turned, startled by Bryan's shouting. "Yes, what is it?"

"Is that a sixty-seven Impala?" Bryan asked.

"Yes, and don't touch it," Max warned, his eyes flashing. "My dad would never let you come back."

"Well, can *you* touch it and pop the hood?" Bryan asked hopefully.

Max shook his head vehemently. "Absolutely not."

"Is your dad here?" Bryan asked.

"Dude," TK called out to him. "Max owes you literally zero favours. Leave him alone."

Ignoring him, Bryan clasped his hands together and gave Max his most pitiful look. "*Please*, Max. I'm never going to see another car like this again in my life."

Max chewed his bottom lip. Although TK was right, he could tell Bryan was genuinely interested. Wordlessly, he waved his hand and led Bryan inside the house. Bryan followed with a certain bounce in his steps. After calling for his dad a couple of times, Max found him in his office. Just because it was a Saturday didn't mean he wouldn't be working.

"Hey, Dad," Max said. "Remember Bryan?"

His dad nodded, though he looked confused. "Guitar, right?"

Bryan smiled and nodded.

"Bryan's wondering if he can look at your Impala," Max said quickly, as if to get it out of the way.

"Oh!" Mr. Ford's eyebrows inched up his forehead. He looked at his watch and frowned. "Yeah, I could take a break." He rose from his chair and turned to Bryan. "You like cars?"

"No, sir," Bryan answered. "I *love* them. Like, even more than my guitar or girls."

Max rolled his eyes, but his dad just laughed. They went back outside where everyone else was pretty much just goofing off. Max, who had never been interested in his dad's car, left them there to begin the decorating process.

"Here you go," Mr. Ford said as he lifted the hood. "It's kind of a mess, but I guess that's why they call it a work in progress."

Bryan didn't think so. In fact, he thought it was a gorgeous engine, but he didn't say so because he didn't want to seem too excited.

"I haven't worked on it in a while," Mr. Ford continued, heedless of Bryan's silence. "I need to replace the crankshaft but who knows where I'll find one?"

Bryan took a close look at it. It was rusty and a couple of the spirals were bent. "I saw one just like it last week."

"You're kidding," Mr. Ford said. "Where?"

"At this scrapyard outside of town." Bryan shrugged. "Don't know if it would fit perfectly or if it even works, but it looked like it was in better shape than this one."

"If you see it again, will you bring it to me?" the older man asked. "I'll pay you for it."

Bryan shrugged again like it was no big deal, though he was very much looking forward to having a chance to go to the scrapyard again—and possibly seeing the Impala. "Sure."

"Thanks." Mr. Ford closed the hood and then clapped Bryan on the shoulder before leaving.

Reluctantly, Bryan went out to the others. Max had more or less planned out where he wanted all his lights to go, and they had already begun stringing them up.

Feeling grateful, Bryan approached Max and said, "Hey, how can I help?"

Max looked over to where Marty had taken a string of lights and was climbing a ladder while Corbie held on to the lights. "Go hold that ladder. I don't trust those two at all."

Chuckling, Bryan did as Max asked. With a lot of coordination on Max's part and effort on everyone else's part, their vision for a music-themed house slowly came to life. Lights were strung around every outline on the house, including the gables, windows, and doors. A string of red and white lights ran the perimeter of the circular driveway. In the centre of the front lawn were sprays of lights that resembled fireworks.

The pièce de résistance was the speaker setup. Two large subwoofers accompanied by six smaller speakers sat next to the porch on a raised platform. They were covered by a sealed plastic coating that would protect them from the elements. But they would still be loud enough to be heard by passing cars.

Hacks had completed his necessary wiring and all his preliminary tests on the programming were working. The sun had just gone down by the time they had finished putting everything into place. The only thing left to do was plug everything into the main power.

Holding the extension cord in one hand and the first string of lights in the other, Max turned to Chloe. "Did you want to do the honours?"

Her eyes lit up brighter than he knew his lights would. "Really? Sure!"

She took the two cords and without delay or warning plugged them into each other. The lights nearly blinded everyone and Chloe laughed. It was beautiful.

"Okay, Hacks," Max said.

One tap of a button and the music started, and with it the lights started changing, pulsing and strobing to the beats.

"Yes!" Hacks shouted. "It works!"

Everyone cheered and enjoyed the show before heading home. And while Max loved the end product, it was really his friendships he enjoyed the most.

♪   ♫   ♪

Although D-rock hated the holiday season, it was at least a good time of year to pick up a temporary job and make some extra money. There were usually a few places around that would take the extra help in stocking, sorting, or other random jobs that regular employees couldn't or wouldn't handle. And it wasn't the worst way to spend a Sunday.

He looked around at the department store stockroom that was overflowing with cardboard boxes, half of which were open with product spilling out. He'd done this before...a year ago. But that didn't make it any better. Where would he even start?

"Hey, a seasonal help buddy!" said a sassy voice from behind him.

He breathed a sigh of relief and turned to face none other than Chloe. "Oh, thank God. I thought I was going to get stuck with someone incompetent."

She cringed looking around. "This is my first time, so no promises."

"At least I know I can tolerate you," he said, turning back to the mess.

"Careful, D-rock," she said as she put her long hair up into a messy bun. "Any more compliments like that and I might think you're coming on to me."

D-rock laughed out loud, probably harder than he should have, and she frowned at him. "Sorry. You're lovely. Here, let's just get to work. And see if we can...manage this."

"Okay, what are we doing here?" she asked. "They told me you'd tell me what to do."

"Oh, great." With a deep sigh he went farther into the room. "We're sorting through returns. Anything packaged or with tags still on can basically go right back onto the shelves. Anything without tags is a different story, but we'll start by looking for tagged stuff."

She rubbed her hands together. "Let's get to it, then."

Together, they worked in a companionable silence, emptying cart after cart of product. It was a huge department store, and they could hardly believe the sheer amount of stuff that got bought and returned within days. D-rock didn't mind the tedious work because it meant he didn't have to be at the till watching the madness that was holiday shopping. Chloe didn't seem to mind either, if her lack of complaints was any indication.

He glanced over at her, only to find her "taking a break" near a pile of men's clothing. She had a dark blue tie around her neck, and she was running her thumb along the pattern of white dolphins.

Coming closer, D-rock asked, "Are you thinking of trying a new fashion trend?"

She smiled shyly. "No. It's just…this tie makes me think of Max."

"Oh." He sat next to her. He wanted to keep his promise to Max but wasn't going to pass up this opportunity. "He does really like ties, doesn't he?"

"I've never seen him without one," she said, shrugging.

He took the end of the tie and looked at the tag. There were three red stickers on it, discounting the tie to a ridiculously low price. "This tie is so on sale I'm pretty sure no one would even notice it missing. You know…if you wanted to give it to him."

She chuckled as her cheeks went pink. "I'm not gonna steal a tie. I could buy it. But…don't you think he'd find that weird?"

"*Whaaat?*" He flicked his wrist in an exaggerated manner. "No. Of course not. Max really likes...*ties*. He just likes them so much."

"Yeah, we established that." She took the tie off her neck and folded it up.

"Well, I bet he'd also really like knowing one of his friends is thinking about him," he said in a more serious voice.

"You're right," she said. "Okay, I'll get it. Thanks for convincing me. It's only two-fifty after all. Wow, I am so cheap."

"No, you're not," he said, standing back up. "You're resourceful."

"Ah, the story of a poor kid's life," she said.

He winked and she laughed.

As Chloe went back to work, D-rock decided to take a break himself. He put his headphones on and listened to the tracks Claire had sent him. There was absolutely nothing wrong with them—save for the fact that it was all Christmas music—but there were little things that he might have done differently. And like he'd promised, he wrote down anything he might change if he'd been the one writing it. Starting with taking the bass out.

Chapter Nine

Claire marked off another day on her calendar. 24 more days and her parents would be home. She wasn't *excited* per se, but she would be happy to see them. Being alone all the time sometimes took more energy than living with others. And of course, she did miss them. They were her parents after all.

24 days felt like it would take forever.

As she walked to school, she had to admit that for the first time in her life she didn't feel nearly as lonely as she always had. Less than Perfect had filled that void. Especially the girls, who had all been so sweet to her. And yes, even D-rock.

At lunchtime, when she caught sight of Amber, Rach, Meg, and Chloe all sitting together she knew they would have space for her. And she also knew she didn't have to wait for them to approach her first. Sure enough, as soon as she came forward, they all greeted her, and Rach slid an empty chair over to their table.

As they ate and talked, D-rock approached their table but didn't sit. Instead, he placed a small stack of papers in front of Claire. "Here you go," he said reluctantly. "I tried to write as neatly as possible."

"Oh!" she said, glancing down at the top sheet. It was an itemized list, and the writing was indeed more legible. "You were serious."

"Yeah." He looked at the other girls, gave them a small smile, then waved. "See you tomorrow night."

As he walked away, Amber asked, "What is it?"

"Notes on the Christmas music Harmony and I did," Claire said. There were 11 items. The last one simply read: **TAKE OUT THE BASS**. Claire rolled her eyes at that.

Chloe's eyes widened and she leaned in to look at the list. With a sigh she leaned back out.

Claire smiled sympathetically. "He's not the one."

"That's okay," Chloe said with a shrug. "*The one* stopped leaving me letters a couple weeks ago anyway."

Amber's eyebrows drew in deeply. "He did?"

Chloe nodded.

"Wonder why," Rach said.

"Probably got bored," Chloe said with a forced indifference.

"I doubt that," Meg said kindly.

"Maybe he ran out of stationery." Claire bobbed her eyebrows.

Chloe laughed. "Yeah, maybe. Anyway, it's not a big deal. What's in the notes?"

"A lot of stuff he said he wouldn't do," Claire mumbled.

D-rock had gone through each song to make suggested changes and had even notated some of the more complex ones. He may have "hated" Christmas music, but even that couldn't stand in the way of his passion.

♪　　♫　　♪

D-rock would never admit it, but he'd spent hours going through that music for the band, making what at the time felt like minor changes. But he knew those little tweaks would make a big difference in the way the band sounded. And that still mattered to him, regardless of what they played.

Since he suspected the one suggestion Claire wouldn't take was to remove the bass, he got ready for another Less than Perfect night. And he knew tonight it would be all Christmas music. There was no getting around it now.

As he closed his case, his mom came up behind him to…say goodnight? He turned around only to find her in a black dress she hadn't worn in ages, silver dangling earrings, and her hair perfectly curled into soft waves.

"Another date?" he asked, trying to sound neutral.

"Yeah." She smiled. "He's picking me up so you can still use the van tonight.

D-rock nodded. "Are you going to tell me who it is?"

She hesitated and then finally said quietly, "It's Ed."

"Ed who?" he asked.

"Ed…Ritz."

The name clicked quickly in his head. "Meg's dad?" he asked.

She nodded and he floundered around for words. Since when did she even know Meg's dad? And what was he supposed to do with this information?

"Okay, look," she said, putting up her hands. "I'm at the grocery store a few weeks ago, right? And I run into Ed, who I haven't seen in years. But since you and Meg are in Less than Perfect together, I think maybe I'll stop and say hi. And then we get talking, and he's looking *hella fine*, so obviously he's been taking care of himself, and in a moment of weakness I forgot all men are terrible and I asked him to have coffee with me, and now we're on our third date."

D-rock stared at her as she finally stopped to take a breath. He put his hands up to his face and then dropped them.

"Okay…okay," he said.

"I was going to tell you," she said. "I just…I didn't know how far this would go."

"It's fine, Mom," he said, his voice cracking. He cleared his throat. "Totally fine."

Her eyebrows drew together in concern. "You're sure?"

"Of course." He nodded a little too much, but his mind was reeling. "But just, please never call anyone hella fine ever again."

"Well…" She looked away, a little smile on her face. "You haven't seen him recently, have you?"

"*Mom*," he breathed.

"I'm sorry." She opened her mouth to say more but the doorbell rang. "That's him. You going to be cool?"

"Of course," D-rock said with forced nonchalance.

But still, he raced to the door before his mom, who would never be able to keep up in her high heels. He got to the door and as soon as he opened it, Mr. Ritz lifted his eyebrows. But then he smiled.

D-rock looked him up and down. He looked perfectly normal to D-rock, certainly nothing to write home about.

"Hello, Derek," Mr. Ritz greeted pleasantly.

"Hi, Mr. Ritz," D-rock said. "Where are you taking my mom tonight?"

"To The Blue Rock," Mr. Ritz answered.

"Uh huh." D-rock crossed his arms. "And when will she be home?"

"Meg gets worried if I stay out past midnight." Mr. Ritz glanced past D-rock and his smile grew as he focused on D-rock's mom. "But I could let her worry tonight."

D-rock took a deep breath, biting his tongue as he considered his answer. But he never got the chance. His mom sidled past him, patted him on the cheek, and told him a firm goodnight.

As soon as they'd shut the door, D-rock immediately pulled out his phone and called Meg. She answered pleasantly, though she did sound a little surprised.

"Did you know our parents are dating?" he asked without preamble.

"Well, yeah," she said.

"Does Trey know?"

She hesitated before saying, "Yes…"

"Why did no one tell me?" he whispered.

"Oh, D-rock," she said in a sympathetic voice. "I thought you knew, and you just weren't saying anything because you were cool with it."

"Well, I—I—"

Meg waited for him to find his words and when he didn't, she said, "Do you want to talk about it at Max's house?"

"Sure."

Though what good that would do, he didn't know.

♪　♫　♪

Max looked at the blank card in front of him, pen poised just above it. He'd been trying to write Chloe something meaningful for a while now, but it was a struggle. Not only did he not know how many eyes would see his next letter, but he didn't know how to say what he really wanted to say. "It's me, Max" felt simultaneously too easy and too hard.

The doorbell rang and Max put his stuff away, having still written absolutely nothing. He knew Chloe would let herself in, so he took his time making his way down to the basement from his bedroom. For a moment, he listened at the top of the stairs as Chloe tuned her violin. Letting out a deep breath, he went downstairs.

She smiled and turned to him as soon as he sat next to her. She leaned down towards the violin case at her feet while he watched curiously.

"I found this tie at work, and it made me think of you." She pulled a nicely folded tie out of her case and held it out to him. "So, here you go."

Max's heart skipped a beat as he took the dark blue tie with the white dolphins. "Dolphins," he said, instead of asking why she'd gone out of her way for him. "Because I like swimming so much?"

She raised her eyebrows in surprise. "Do you actually?"

"Yeah," he said. "I'm a lifeguard. I guess technically when I'm working, I don't really swim much and just watch other people swim."

"I had no idea." Her face split into a wide grin. "It's actually just because dolphins are so smart and pretty."

He laughed, his face growing warm as she picked up her violin again.

"Anyway, it's probably the cheapest tie you'll ever own," she said. "And I totally won't be offended if you don't wear it ever."

"I'm already putting it on," he said.

She looked up and watched as he loosened his tie. His face heated even more, spreading to the tips of his ears. Feeling terribly vulnerable, he turned around to finish taking his tie off. Then he replaced it with the dolphin tie, doing it up as fast as he could, and turned back around.

"It looks good on you," she said.

The heat from his face filled the rest of his body until he felt like he was on fire. "Thank you. This is a really great gift."

"You're welcome," she said.

She finished tuning her violin while Max fumbled over a million words in his head. He gathered up all his courage and said, "Chloe, I, um—" The doorbell cut him off and he breathed out a ragged breath. "I'll get that."

As he rushed away, he could hear Chloe play "Black Is the Color of My True Love's Hair" and it nearly tripped him up his own stairs.

D-rock was at the door, looking flustered. Max let him in and after taking a close look at him, D-rock said, "Nice tie."

"Thanks," Max said, grasping it lightly.

"I'm just going to wait up here for Meg."

"Alright…"

Max went back downstairs. Harmony arrived and let herself in. Meg, Trey, and Rach came soon after. When Meg saw D-rock, she smiled softly and told the other two she'd be down in a minute. They stood off to the side so they wouldn't be in the way while the others came in.

Meg took one look at D-rock and said, "So, you're not okay."

He shoved his hand through his hair and shook his head. "It's not because of your dad…"

"I know," she said quickly.

"Are *you* okay with it?" he asked.

She looked down, chewing on her lip, and paused for a long moment before answering. "My dad's been alone for a long time," she finally said. "He deserves to be with someone nice. Like your mom. But I still…"

She stopped as tears rose to her eyes. D-rock's heart fell. He would never understand what it was like to lose a parent forever and he felt selfish for making a big deal out of this.

"You still miss your mom," he said softly.

She nodded and then dabbed at her tears before they could fall. "I do. But if my dad's ready to move on, then I have to be, too."

He nodded, understanding the implication. He had to accept it like Meg had. "I get that."

She patted him on the arm and smiled through her tears. "It could be worse, right? They could be dating way worse people. Your mom is really great."

He nodded again. "I'm sure your dad is great, too. My mom thinks he's really attractive."

"He *has* been working out," she said.

"Yeah, I noticed," he said lightly. "I guess you and my mom have a type."

Meg chuckled and ducked her head shyly. "Hey, I...I told Trey I was okay with it, because I mostly am. So, it wouldn't technically be a lie if you just...didn't mention the other stuff to him."

"Don't worry," he said, looking into her concerned eyes. "I got you covered."

"Thanks." She smiled again. "Are you coming downstairs to play with us, or did you really expect Claire to remove you from the band?"

He rolled his eyes. "No, I'm coming."

Chapter Ten

By the time Meg and D-rock went downstairs, everyone else had arrived and were already warming up. There was fresh music on everyone's stand, including D-rock's. He didn't say anything about it, but when Claire saw him, she took the music off his stand.

"My bad," she said. "This actually belongs in the garbage."

"Technically you should recycle it," he said lightly. Gently, he took the music back from her and replaced it on his stand.

"Thank you for your help," she said in a more serious voice.

He just nodded as he got his bass ready. There were five pieces in total, and everyone had started looking through their music, playing bits and pieces of it.

"Okay, problem," Marty said. "This says sleighbells and I don't own sleighbells."

D-rock reached into his backpack and pulled out a set of sleighbells, holding the stick by its handle. "Catch," he said.

He tossed them over the drum set and Marty's eyes lit up as he caught them. "Problem solved," Marty said cheerfully.

Claire and Harmony had picked out five different Christmas songs: "White Christmas," "Winter Wonderland," "Joy to the World," "Little Drummer Boy," and "Mary Did You Know?" They were easily recognizable and weren't overly complicated to play, so they whipped through the first three with no problem.

At that point, Hacks stopped them and said, "Five songs won't be enough to fill the whole hour. But it's okay, I can just play hymns in between."

"Hymns?" TK asked as if it were a foreign language.

"Yes, hymns." Hacks lifted an eyebrow. "Old timey churchy music. The residents really like them."

"Well, if you'd told me that, I could have arranged some hymns," D-rock said, shaking his head. "What do you want, Hacks? Never mind, we'll talk about it later. Let's just finish up the last two songs."

"Okay, I have a question about 'Little Drummer Boy,'" Marty said.

Claire turned towards him. "What is it?"

"There are a bunch of empty bars in the middle of the music, and it just says 'Marty, do whatever you want,'" he said.

"What's the question?" Claire asked. "Don't you read English better than you read music?"

"Yes..." he said uncertainly.

Harmony chuckled. "The rest of us are going to vamp for a bit while you do...you know..." She waved her hand at the drum set.

"Oh, it's a solo," Marty said, a smile growing on his face. "Ohhh."

Hacks stood from the piano so Marty could see him clearly. "Please keep in mind some of the residents are literally on pacemakers. So, try not to overdo it."

Marty lifted a sassy eyebrow. "But how good is their hearing?"

Hacks opened and closed his mouth a few times. "Just...be considerate."

Marty winked and Hacks shook his head but sat back down anyway. Despite Hacks's reservations, when it came time for Marty's solo, he played something that was not only a respectable volume but fit the rest of the music well. They weren't quite all sure when he'd finished his solo, but Hacks did a good job of bringing them all back in.

Once they'd finished, Claire turned to Marty with a smile. "That's why we left half your music blank."

Marty grinned back at her. They finished off their rehearsal with "Mary Did You Know?" When they'd written this one together, Claire could tell it was one of Harmony's favourites as she'd put so much more thought into the arrangement. Slow and soulful, it built its way up from a soft melody to a passionate anthem.

While they played, D-rock noticed his parts were greatly simplified and he wondered if that was because Claire didn't know what he could handle or if she thought he'd bail at the last minute and not leave too much of a gap. He glanced at her while they played. She looked up at him and they both faltered in their playing and quickly readjusted.

No, she knew him well enough by now. She had given him an out if he didn't want to perform with them. But even though the music brought pain to him, something about the way they played it wasn't...terrible. There. He could admit it wasn't awful to suffer through Christmas music for Less than Perfect.

After they'd finished playing through all the songs, everyone slowly packed up, taking their time to have conversations. Max didn't mind at all. It was far better than having to rush them for fear that his parents would catch them. Now that they'd given their okay, Max was happy to let his friends hang out as long as they wanted.

Though he did have a slight misgiving when Bryan approached him.

"Hey, Max, is your dad home?" Bryan asked. "I have that part he asked me for."

"Oh, right." Max waved at Harmony as she went through the front door. "Yeah, let me go find him."

Amber stayed and chatted with Hacks in the front hall while Bryan went out to get the crankshaft. When Bryan came back, he put his hand on Hacks's head and nudged him out of the way.

"Stop talking to my sister," he said gruffly. "Your mom's outside."

Hacks sighed but after he'd walked past Bryan, he rolled his eyes at Amber and she giggled. Bryan waited patiently for Max to return with his dad.

"Here you go," Bryan said, holding out the crankshaft. "Hope it fits."

Mr. Ford's eyes lit up as he took the part. "Wow, thanks so much, Bryan. Here."

He held out a few bills. Bryan took them and his eyes widened.

"Oh, no, Mr. Ford," he said as he tried to hand them back. "This is way more than I paid for it."

Mr. Ford shrugged. "Finder's fee."

Bryan wasn't going to argue with that. He quickly pocketed the money. "Thanks."

"Have a good night," Mr. Ford said.

"You, too," Bryan said.

After Mr. Ford had walked away, Max said, "I'm so glad you had the opportunity to bond with my dad."

Neither Bryan nor Amber missed the hint of bitterness in his voice. But they weren't quite sure what to say.

Bryan shrugged uncomfortably and said, "Okay. See you next week."

As he started to walk away, Amber said, "Oh, I left something downstairs. I'll be out to the car in a minute, Bry."

He shrugged again and left the house. Amber turned back to Max and crossed her arms.

"What?" he said, crossing his arms back at her.

"Bryan's not trying to steal your dad," she said.

"Of course he's not," Max snipped. "He'll just weasel his way in and take my dad's money."

She sighed. "That's not what he's doing." Max lifted his eyebrows in a look of disbelief. "Look, our dad treats Bryan and Bryan's stuff like his own personal property. I think your dad is the first grown-up who's actually shown an interest in something Bryan *really* likes. That's all it is, okay?"

He dropped his arms, his face softening. "Okay. I'm sorry. I'll try to be cool."

"That's a good boy." She patted him on the shoulder. "And really, the last thing Bryan wants is another father figure." A horn honked outside, and she cringed. "Although maybe if he did have a good one, he'd know not to honk at girls from the driveway."

Max's eyes flashed. "*Maybe...*"

Amber chuckled as she headed to the door. "By the way," she said demurely, "Chloe thinks you're bored of her."

At first, Max's eyebrows drew in but then when he realized Amber was referring to the anonymous letters, he rolled his eyes. "Do you want your sockets and video game or not?"

"Yes, please," she said pertly.

"Then stay out of it," he said as he opened the front door for her.

Bryan honked the horn again just as she was stepping out the door. She frowned. "You boys are all alike," she muttered as Max closed the door behind her.

♪   ♫   ♪

Rach was just putting books into her locker when she could sense someone come up next to her. She'd always been taught to have a pleasant manner anytime someone approached her, which was difficult when half the school made fun of her. And when it turned out to be baby-faced Cameron, she couldn't conceal her cringe.

"Hey, Rach," he said with a boyish grin.

"What do you want, Cam?" she said, turning back to her locker.

"I kinda want to decorate you like a Christmas tree," he said.

She slammed her locker shut and whirled around to glare at him. "Is that an insult or a pickup line?"

His smile grew. "Yes."

"Wow, negging. Classy." She took a step closer to him and stared down into his eyes as his smile fell. "First of all, you're far too short for me. Second—"

She took another step closer and Cam dropped the binder he'd been holding, spilling papers everywhere. She bit her lip to keep from laughing.

"You're way too clumsy," she said. "And also, unless your voice drops another octave, I'm never going to be interested in you."

His face scrunched up as he stared at her. "Drops a what?"

Rach blinked at him, blindsided by his absolute ignorance. "Never mind. This conversation is literally not worth it."

She brushed by him, just close enough to nearly knock him over. As she did, he asked, "So is that a yes?"

"*Maybe*," she tossed over her shoulder, just for the fun of confusing him further.

Rach went around the corner to Amber's locker and sighed heavily clear above Amber's head. Amber patted down her hair as if Rach had actually disturbed it.

"What's the matter, Rach?" Amber asked.

"Cam just offered to decorate me like a Christmas tree," Rach said bitterly.

Amber smiled up at her. "Oh, my gosh, that would be so cute!"

"Amber, *no*," Rach said. "Not cute. Also, have you met me? Cute isn't exactly my aesthetic."

Amber calmly closed her locker and then picked up her backpack. As she led the way to their social studies class, she said, "Honestly, I don't know what your aesthetic is. But I do know that you could be having *way* more fun than you currently do."

Rach sighed again. "I don't want to dress up like a Christmas tree, or the CN Tower, or a skyscraper, okay? That doesn't sound fun."

"Well, it does to me." Amber shrugged. "If we could switch bodies for a day, there are so many things I would do! Like steal stuff off the top of people's fridges, and smack some annoying guy in the back of the head, and buy one of those dresses that only fits a model's body because they're all tall and willowy and gorgeous like you."

Rach half smiled. "If we switched bodies for a day, you'd find out how not fun it is to be me. And I don't want people's fridge junk. But I'm totally game because I would love to have a normal, adorable body like yours."

Amber looked down at herself. "You think I'm adorable?"

"Doesn't everyone?" Rach huffed.

"Well, did you know all the girls are jealous of you because you're so pretty?" Amber said. "And all the boys are intimidated because they think you'll reject them, which… You do always reject them, don't you?"

Rach hesitated. "Maybe…"

Just before they reached their classroom, Amber stopped and turned to her. "Rach, I sincerely hope you learn to appreciate what you have and *own* it. You could have it a lot worse, you know?"

Rach chewed her lip thinking about it but had no answer for Amber. When they walked into their class and someone immediately started humming "The Imperial March," Rach lifted her eyebrows at Amber as if to point out just how fun it was.

"See?" Rach said, gesturing to a snickering group of kids at the back.

"Yeah, you get your own theme song!" Amber said cheerfully. "I hope they roll out the red carpet next. You deserve it, girl."

Rach laughed as she headed to her favourite desk at the back of the classroom. Amber followed her, but when she passed by Stacey and caught her mockingly laughing at Rach, she stopped.

"Hey, Stacey," Amber said in her nice voice. "I don't know if you've heard, but being a little brat will cause premature aging and wrinkles in all the wrong places."

Stacey narrowed her eyes to tiny slits. "Watch yourself, Amber. I hear ugly is contagious."

"Then I should probably get away from you," Amber said before skipping off to the desk next to Rach.

Stacey crossed her arms and shot one more glare over her shoulder at both Rach and Amber before Mr. Duncan called their attention.

Chapter Eleven

For the next couple of weeks, the band practised the songs for their first ever gig. None of them seemed to care that it was for elderly people, or that they would be squished into a small programming room, or that they were playing Christmas music and hymns. They were just happy to have the chance to share what they could do with other people.

Claire and D-rock wrote two more simple arrangements: "How Great Thou Art" and "In Christ Alone." They wrote them quickly and hoped the band could learn them just as quickly. Hacks hadn't given them very much time to practise, but D-rock and Claire had gotten accustomed to how fast they caught on to a new piece.

Amber and Bryan practised together during times when their parents weren't home, to avoid having to play loudly over any anticipated arguing. When there were arguments, they found other places to go. Amber went over to Claire's eerily quiet house while TK was more than happy to let Bryan hang out with him and jam. But he made Bryan promise not to tell Hacks since they practised during times TK should have been studying.

Hacks, for his part, was far more excited than he'd let on. He had even pushed aside some of his own homework in favour of rehearsing. He would give nothing but the best to his fans. And he was happy to share those fans with his band.

Harmony, though she had other concerts to prepare for, still found herself more drawn to Less than Perfect's arrangements. And it wasn't because she'd had a part in writing them this time. They were just as special as the other pieces they'd played so far.

Trey was more than happy to "need" extra practise time at Meg's house, and he wasn't even mad when Mr. Ritz burst into the sunroom to let Trey know he was playing out of tune. Trey just laughed him off while Meg rolled her eyes. Though they noticed her dad had no problem with Corbie and Rach also coming over to play with them—and they definitely hadn't bothered tuning first.

And while Chloe practised over and over at home, ignoring her rude neighbours who occasionally told her to be quieter, Max begged all of his friends to come over and play with him. He hated how his violin echoed around his empty house. Although some of them joined him, Chloe never did take him up on the offer, preferring to still come on just Tuesday nights.

Marty, of course, had no other choice since his drums now lived at Max's house. Not that he minded, since it meant he always had someone else to play with, too.

♪ ♫ ♪

Hacks went early to Sunny Meadows to meet with Mari and start setting up for the others. The programs room would be full for their performance, but Hacks didn't think the others would mind. Marty was the first to arrive since he had so much to set up. Harmony came soon after and went straight to the piano.

She pressed a few of the keys on the piano, her eyebrows drawing in tightly. "Hacks," she said. "This piano's out of tune."

"Slightly, yes," he said as he continued arranging chairs to suit Less than Perfect. He'd been sure they would all fit in this space, but now that he was seeing it with all these chairs while Marty set up the drums, he became unsure.

"No, not slightly," Harmony huffed. "Listen to this." She played two notes an octave apart. They should have matched in pitch, but the cringey warbling tones proved her right.

He looked over at her worried face. "You're right, Harmony. I guess I never notice when I'm playing on my own. And it doesn't bother anyone around here."

"But how are we supposed to play with this?" she asked. "What do we tune to?"

"I'm sorry, Harmony," Hacks said, putting his hands up in surrender. "It was an oversight, but I don't think it needs to ruin our night."

She sighed heavily and looked towards the door just as Bryan and Amber came through. Amber lifted her eyebrows and asked how setup was going.

"Well, look at that," Harmony said, putting a hand on her hip. "Hacks did something dumb, and you guys are on time for once. Am I in an alternate universe?"

Bryan slung his guitar off his back and exchanged a quiet, confused glance with Amber.

"Okay," Amber said slowly, "I'm going to ignore how rude that was because you seem really frantic. What's wrong?"

"The piano's out of tune!" Harmony threw her hands in the air.

"It's not that bad," Hacks said, placing down one last chair.

"Yes, it is." Harmony went over to the piano. "Listen to these Cs."

While Amber cringed, Bryan nodded and said, "Yeah, that's bad. But it's not that big a deal, right?"

"It *is* a big deal," Harmony said, verging on frantic. "How can we stay in tune with this piano?"

"Honestly, Harmony," Bryan said, brushing past her to where his seat had been set up. "You're being a bit of a music snob."

Amber gave a short bark of laughter. "That's rich coming from a guy who wouldn't date someone because she doesn't listen to music."

"That's different," he said. "People who don't listen to music, whether it's in tune or not, are clearly psychopaths. Plus, you agreed with me!"

"Yeah, but I'm not the kettle calling the pot black here." Amber turned to Harmony. "You're right, it kind of sounds bad. But I doubt it'll be all that noticeable with the rest of us playing. Hacks, have the residents ever complained about the piano?"

He pushed his glasses up his nose and then wrapped his arms around himself. "Only two. But one likely won't come today and the other…passed a few weeks ago."

"Oh," Amber said sadly.

He shrugged uncomfortably and turned to Harmony. "And for the record, I didn't do something dumb. I just didn't think of it because I genuinely love playing this piano. I'm only human," he whispered the last part.

Harmony's face fell and she came closer to him. "I'm sorry," she said softly. "I didn't mean to… That was mean of me. I'm sorry."

He shrugged again. "It's fine. I usually avoid the worst keys on the piano, anyway."

"Good call." She sighed again as she looked around. "It's going to be tight once we get the stands in."

"It's okay, I don't need my music," Marty piped up.

Harmony bit her lip as some of their bandmates arrived. When Rach walked in and saw how close they would be sitting, she raised her eyebrows, but didn't say anything. Max walked in and stopped in the doorway, looking around.

"Well," he said, stepping farther in. "What a wonderful day to be elbowed by Chloe."

"I'm sorry," Hacks said, putting his hands up. "I admit that spatial ability isn't my strong suit."

"I don't mind," Max said graciously.

Bryan sat in his chair, looked out at the empty room with rows of seating waiting for the residents, and then immediately stood. He turned around to face Amber, who always sat behind him. "I don't want to sit here. Switch me."

"Can't," she said as she put her clarinet together. "You're part of the strings *and* the rhythm, remember?" She smirked up at him.

Bryan scowled and looked around. D-rock approached and said, "Aside from the piano…and the lack of space…and Marty not wanting to use his music…is there another problem here?"

"Yeah, I don't want to be front and centre," Bryan said quickly. "Switch me."

D-rock snorted. "With my bass? And this body?"

Bryan and Amber both looked D-rock up and down. He was wearing dark slacks and a black button-down and had combed his hair nicely.

"Yup, right in the middle," Bryan said.

Amber smiled. "You do look very nice."

D-rock shook his head. "I don't even want to be here. And we're not rearranging the band just because you suddenly got self-conscious. Suck it up, Bryan."

"Oh, very Christmassy of you," Bryan said sourly, even as he took his proper seat.

Harmony leaned in close to him and said quietly, "No one's going to notice you with the tuning on that piano."

Bryan looked up, down, and then up into her eyes again. "They also won't notice me if you keep leaning over in that dress like that."

With a gasp, Harmony straightened, clutching the neckline of her dress. She scoffed as she scurried past him to her own seat. Bryan chuckled and couldn't resist looking over his shoulder at her. The green knit dress brought out the lighter flecks in her brown eyes, but it was the annoyed scowl that he liked most. She rolled her eyes and started warming up her flute.

The rest of the band got settled and once they'd sufficiently warmed up, Claire suggested they tune. Harmony tried not to sound judgmental when she asked to what, exactly, they would tune.

"Chloe," Max said, pointing to her. "She's always the most in tune."

Chloe turned a bright smile at him. "I was going to say you!"

He smiled but didn't get the chance to say anything when Harmony cut them off. "One of you just pick and we'll tune to you, okay?"

Max motioned to Chloe, and she got up to stand in front of them. "I've never gotten to do this before," she said. "So fun. What should I play?"

"B flat, C, and then D," Harmony said immediately. "If you could."

Chloe played the notes slowly, one at a time for her bandmates and listened to them tune. Chloe could tell where the dissonances were but Harmony took it upon herself to tell everyone how to tune. Which was just fine with Chloe, since some of them seemed to not quite appreciate Harmony's direction.

The program room doors opened and some of the residents were ushered in. Chloe turned back to everyone and said, "Sounds good. Let's play."

"But—" Harmony cut herself off as people made a beeline for Hacks.

"Hi, Joe!" one old man said as he tried to amble over to Hacks with his walker.

"Joe!" an old lady with rosy cheeks called out. "Joe, you're here!"

Hacks rose and quickly went in front of the band so that they wouldn't disrupt their careful seating plan. His band watched in utter fascination as Hacks greeted every single person who came in by name, offering some of them hugs, some of them handshakes, and even some of them his cheek to be kissed. They all, without fail, called him Joe before finding a place to sit.

Hacks finally turned around only to find his band staring at him wide-eyed. "What?" he said, his hands up. He looked straight at Harmony. "Are you ready to go?"

She nodded. "Yes, but are you going to introduce us?"

"Oh, yes, of course." Hacks smiled and waited for the residents to settle down and stop their chatting. "Hi, everyone."

A chorus of "Hi, Joe," came back to him, making his smile grow.

"This is my band, Less than Perfect."

"Oh, Joe's Band!"

"Hi, Joe's Band!"

"Is Joe's Band going to play for us?"

"That's right," Hacks said cheerfully. "We're going to play for you for a bit. I hope you like it." He looked right at the woman sitting front and centre. "Maybe turn down your hearing aids, Ethel."

She smiled and touched her ears. Finally, Hacks was able to make it back to the piano. He nodded to D-rock, who nudged Claire, who then looked at the whole band. They were staring back at her. They hadn't once considered what to do without a conductor, though Claire did admit to herself that normally she took the lead on getting their songs started.

But then she got cold feet and turned to Marty, who she knew was already comfortable playing front of people. "Marty?"

He smiled, winked, and flipped one of his sticks in the air. Then he started the beat for "Little Drummer Boy," and Claire was immediately put at ease. She could handle this if everyone else could.

And in fact, it only took them a few bars to settle into the song and when they did, they played beautifully. Despite the out-of-tune piano and their nerves, when they played together, they were unstoppable.

In between their pieces, Hacks played hymns that, to his band's surprise, the residents all sang along to. It was hard to tell by looking at him how Hacks felt about it while he was playing. But when they'd finished their mini concert and the residents very affectionately thanked "Joe" with their kind words and hugs, his smile shone bright.

As the band packed up their instruments, Corbie asked Hacks, "Why do they all call you Joe?"

Hacks leaned on the piano he loved so much and shrugged. "It's easier for them."

"So many identities." Corbie shook his head and popped the mouthpiece out of his trombone. "I don't know why you can't just stick to Fabiano."

Several gasps were heard, and the others turned to Corbie as Hacks straightened up. Hacks pursed his lips and TK put his hands up in a what-are-you-doing gesture.

"*Corbie*," Amber said, her eyes wide. "I can't believe you did that."

"What?" A second later, Corbie's hands flew to his mouth and he looked straight into Hacks's unimpressed eyes. "I'm *so* sorry. I totally forgot you didn't want anyone to know."

"We all know his real name," Rach said flippantly. "We just don't use it out of respect."

"I'm sorry," Corbie repeated.

Hacks rubbed his eyes under his glasses and shook his head. "It's fine. It's just a terribly awkward name when you're not even Italian. And especially when you don't look like the model on a Harlequin."

"Oh, Hacks." Amber patted him on the cheek. "Let's get you out of here before the residents hear and decide to call you that instead."

Chapter Twelve

Before they all left, Max told them that his parents were allowing him to have them over for a Christmas…get together. Not a party, because they didn't like the idea of them "partying" in their house. But if the band wanted to spend next Friday night together at a respectable volume, then they were welcome to do so.

"And just to be clear," Max said, turning to Amber and Bryan, "it's just *you guys*. Just the band. No one else."

Bryan cast a sidelong glance at Amber. "Why is he looking at us like that?"

She rolled her eyes. "Oh, I *wonder*, Bryan. Thanks, Max. We'll be there. Just us."

"We will?" Bryan said, his lips curled in disgust.

"Yes, oh, my gosh. Bye, everyone."

As they walked away, Chloe leaned close to Max and said, "Are you sure you want to invite them?"

He shook his head with a tiny smile. "Yes. I want you all there. If you want to come."

She put a hand on his shoulder and smiled. "I'll be there. Sounds fun."

"I'll probably skip out," D-rock said as he closed his bass case. "Thanks anyway, Max."

"I understand," Max said, nodding at him. "You're always welcome if you change your mind."

D-rock smiled, grateful for such a gracious friend. But it was unlikely he'd want to change his mind to celebrate something that brought him such pain. He went over to the piano, which Hacks was still leaning against, and played a few notes.

"I could probably help you tune this," D-rock said, gesturing to the piano.

Hacks frowned thoughtfully. "It hadn't occurred to me to do that myself. Do you think we can?"

"Yeah, if we get the right tools," D-rock answered.

Hacks smiled. "Thank you. I would appreciate that."

D-rock nodded and grabbed his bass. He scooted out of the room behind Claire. Before she could even pull out her phone, he said, "Don't call that Uber. I'll drive you."

She rolled her eyes. "I can take care of myself, you know."

"But you don't have to." He grinned. "Because I'm here."

She shook her head but followed him out to his van anyway. She wasn't going to say no to the free ride if she didn't have to.

After dropping her off, D-rock went home, where his mom was waiting for him. She seemed happier than usual as she asked how the band did.

"It was good," D-rock said. "They're, like…really good musicians. You know? Really good."

Dawn's smile widened even more. "That is so nice, Derek. I'm glad you have…a new group of friends to spend time with."

"Yeah, I know, Mom," he said, suppressing a sigh. "I should have listened to you about Ted and G a long time ago."

She shrugged, but her smile was still in place.

"What are you so happy about?" he asked.

She opened her mouth, hesitating. "Ed invited us to have Christmas dinner at his house."

"Oh."

Her smile turned sympathetic. "I won't force you to go. But I didn't say no."

He nodded. "I'll think about it."

She squeezed his shoulder and still her smile never left. He was glad, at least, that she had something to smile about.

♪　♫　♪

Harmony never told Less than Perfect that the youth orchestra had a performance the day after Sunny Meadows. As soon as she got home, she went straight back to rehearsing. Maybe it was overkill, but she wanted to be ready and not let the orchestra down.

She was only slightly nervous as the lights at the Bridgetown Performing Arts Centre beat down on the young musicians. At least she wasn't near the front like the cellos and violins. It didn't seem to matter how many times she'd performed in front of other people; she always got nervous.

But as soon as she lifted her flute to her mouth, her nerves disappeared, and her confidence grew. And just like all her other performances, this one seemed to fly by. Even her piccolo parts in "The Magic Flute" weren't nearly as daunting as they'd been a few weeks ago. She played a wrong note, but just had to remind herself not to dwell on it and that likely no one else would have noticed.

Afterwards, when her parents and younger brother, Cody, met her, they seemed so proud. Obviously they hadn't noticed the wrong note...which she definitely wasn't still thinking about.

Just beyond her family, she could see another lone figure. Black slacks, a white button down, and even a nice jacket. He had his hands in his pockets and was glancing over at them shyly. Which was the last word Harmony would ever have used to describe Bryan.

"Hey," she said, coming over to him. "What are you doing here?"

He shrugged as a small smile lit his hazel eyes. "I was bored," he said loosely. "Hey, Mr. and Mrs. Franco. Cody."

"Uh, Mom, Dad, this is Bryan." Harmony gestured to him. Why did he have to look so good? She wasn't expecting this. "He's in Less than Perfect, too."

"Oh, very nice," Mrs. Franco said, extending her hand. "What do you play?"

"Guitar," he said as he shook her hand. He shook Mr. Franco's hand as well and then turned to Harmony again. "You did really great."

"Thank you," she said. "I don't even know how you knew the concert was today."

"Well, the signs were plastered all over the community centre, so…" Bryan shrugged again. "I just really wanted to know how much fancier the orchestra is than Less than Perfect. I mean, there is a reason we call ourselves that."

Harmony giggled. "We're a really good band. Never doubt that, Bryan."

Bryan nodded, his smile growing the tiniest bit. "Yeah, I guess you're right. Anyway, it was nice to see you."

"You, too," she said.

She would have said more except he gave a quick wave and then left without another word. Her mom gave her a questioning look, but Harmony was just as confused as she was. Maybe Bryan had been serious when he said he had just come out of curiosity. Either way, it was still nice of him to stop and talk with her, no matter how briefly.

♪   ♫   ♪

It was a cold, snowy Monday morning that Chloe and June were forced to walk through to school. At least Chloe had replaced the zipper on June's coat so she didn't have to hold it closed anymore. But that didn't keep June's teeth from chattering. She could have been wearing a scarf and hat like Chloe, but June was too concerned about her hair, apparently.

After seeing June off at the elementary school, Chloe continued down the street to Bridgetown High. As soon as she got in, she was greeted by a sight that made her heart drop to her stomach. If it had been anyone else holding hands with Alyssa, leaning close to her against her locker, Chloe wouldn't have cared. But no—it had to be Jaden.

With a heavy sigh, Chloe scooted past before they could see her and practically ran to her locker. As if her day couldn't get any worse, there was *another* black envelope. It had been an entire month since she'd heard from him. Why now? She'd already decided to let go of her mystery guy, but this new envelope gave her reckless hope all over again.

She took the envelope and ripped it open. Feeling bad over her carelessness, she carefully took out the card. Inside was a smaller envelope and that beautiful, familiar writing.

You and I are two rivers,
One running north and south,
The other east and west.
The point at which they converge
Is where I want to be.
With you,
Always.

Chloe's heart had run away with her brain, and she could barely breathe. She recognized these words but couldn't think of where she'd heard them before. That became clear when she opened the smaller envelope.

Inside were two tickets for Skipping Stations, a local band who were well on their way to making it big time. And now she knew the words in the card were lyrics from their song "Rivers." Whoever this guy was had great taste—and not just in girls. The tickets were closer to the stage than Chloe could ever imagine being at a concert.

"And what am I supposed to do with this extra ticket?" she mumbled to herself.

She looked around but there was no one nearby. The tickets were for New Year's Eve, so who would even go with her? The petty part of her didn't want to ask one of her friends. Especially not Jaden now that she'd seen him and Alyssa together. Maybe someone from Less than Perfect? One of the girls would surely go with her.

At lunch, she chose to forgo her normal group in favour of sitting with Amber, Meg, Rach, and Claire. She showed them the concert tickets and told them who they were from but didn't show them the card.

"Are any of you free?" Chloe said. "I don't know who to take with me on such short notice for New Year's Eve."

"Oh, Bryan and I are visiting with our grandparents," Amber said quickly. "Sorry."

"And my parents have been gone for so long," Claire said. "I wouldn't feel right ditching them on New Year's Eve."

Chloe turned to Meg, who said, "I'm doing New Year's Eve with Trey's family."

"Well, I'm free," Rach said.

"No, you're *not*," Amber said, elbowing her hard. "You have a family thing, remember? Out of town? We were just talking about that."

Rach's face scrunched up. "We were?"

"*Just* being a loose description," Amber added. "I'll remind you of the conversation later. In any case, Chloe, it looks like you'll have to ask someone else. Sorry."

Chloe shrugged but was still somewhat disappointed. "Maybe I'll ask D-rock. They seem like the type of band he would like."

Amber nodded slowly as she pulled her phone out of her pocket. "Mmhmm, try D-rock."

Amber sent a frantic message to D-rock.

Amber: idc what you're doing on nye, you are BUSY. do you understand?

D-rock: ummmm k

Chloe looked around the cafeteria and found D-rock eating by himself as he often did. "Oh, there he is. I'll go ask him."

D-rock, who'd been minding his own business, narrowed his eyes as more messages came from Amber, all reminding him just how busy he was for New Year's. He didn't even care much for it, so he didn't know why she was being so weird.

"Hey, D-rock."

He looked up at Chloe, who smiled and showed him two really amazing concert tickets.

"Do you know Skipping Stations?" she asked.

"Yeah, they're great," he said as his eyes lit up. "Where'd you get those from?"

She shrugged. "I have no idea. They were a mystery gift. Do you want to go with me?"

D-rock's phone pinged again and he gave the girls' table a furtive glance. "Ah. Well, that's really nice of you to ask me, but I, uh…have plans already. Sorry, Chloe. I'm sure you can find someone to go with you, though."

"That's alright," she said lightly. "I've got more options." She paused a moment then asked, "Are you coming to the party on Friday?"

"Maybe," he said, staring down at his lap.

She nodded and left. As soon as she was gone he looked back down at his phone. It took some scrolling but he finally got past Amber's million messages.

D-rock: i would have really liked that concert. what are you gonna do make sure everyone in the world is busy on nye except max?

Amber: HOW DO YOU KNOW ABOUT THAT

D-rock: with the way info spreads i'm surprised she doesn't know about it. stop meddling.

Amber: i am not meddling i'm aligning the stars.

With a sigh, D-rock rose and headed straight for their table. He tapped Amber on the shoulder and nodded to the cafeteria entrance. She rolled her eyes but followed him out anyway.

"What?" she said as soon as they'd passed through the doors.

"Stay out of Max's business," he said under his breath.

"Okay, Dad." She crossed her arms. "I was just trying to help."

"Well, don't," he said. "You can't force something to happen that should happen naturally."

Amber threw her hands in the air. "How can you be so unromantic?"

"Unromantic?" He put a hand over his heart as if affronted. "Who do you think put 'Black Is the Colour of My True Love's Hair' in 'Nothing Else Matters'? And let me tell you, Max did *not* appreciate it."

"Oh," she said. "Well, how was I supposed to know?"

"You're not," he said firmly. "Just act like you don't know like I'm doing, okay?"

She dropped her arms and looked down. "I was just trying to help. They'd be so cute together."

"Look, I totally agree," he said in a nice voice. "But Max needs to deal with that on his own. Without help."

"Okay, you're right," she said.

"Those are awesome tickets," he said, putting a hand through his hair. "I'll never be that close to the stage at a concert."

She smiled up at him. "You should be *on* the stage at your next concert."

A slow smile grew on his face. "Stop. Flattery will get you nowhere."

Chapter Thirteen

If Max could have gotten away with only inviting *one* of his band members to his Christmas party, he would have done it. Not that he didn't care for the others, but he'd been hoping that maybe this would be the night he could finally tell Chloe about...everything.

He put his tie on and looked at himself in the mirror. Black dress pants, a red shirt, greenish tie. His hair was perfect, but he couldn't get his hands to be still today. Not that she would notice at all.

He went down to the living room where he had a variety of snacks and drinks—all pre-approved by his parents. They were home tonight but had retreated to their own corners, supposedly to give them their space. But truthfully, he wondered if they still didn't trust him and were secretly watching.

Max was surprised when the first people to arrive were Bryan and Amber. Clearly, they loved a good party more than playing music, but Max wouldn't mention it.

Bryan slung his guitar off his back and said, "We brought each other. Is that okay with you?"

"Yes, that's perfect," Max said graciously. "You can put your instruments downstairs if you'd like."

Bryan grunted as he passed by him, but Amber just smiled and looked Max up and down.

"Is that mistletoe on your tie?" she sassed.

He glanced down. "Maybe."

Her smile widening, she lifted the tie up and kissed him on the cheek. Then she let the tie drop while Max rolled his eyes.

As she passed by him, he mumbled, "It wasn't for you."

She just laughed and he wiped her kiss off his cheek. The doorbell rang again and he opened the door for Harmony. She took one look at his tie, laughed, and also kissed him on the cheek.

"Nope, not you, either," he whispered.

More Less than Perfect members came in, most of them making mention of his very obvious tie. When Chloe got there, he smiled brightly at her. She waved and brushed past him so she could chat with the other girls. Wasn't it *such* a good thing he'd spent so long trying to look good?

He followed Chloe into the living room and paused as he passed by Trey in an overstuffed chair with Meg sitting on his lap. "I apologize for the lack of seating in my...gigantic house," Max said.

Meg blushed, but Trey grinned cheekily and tightened his hold on her. "I could get rid of more chairs if you think it would help," he said.

Max chuckled. "No, thank you, Trey."

Trey's smile grew and he nodded at Max. "Nice tie."

Max just rolled his eyes and went to answer the door once again. Everyone else had already arrived, all bringing their instruments with them, so he shouldn't have been surprised to see D-rock.

"Oh, you're here!" Max said.

D-rock gave him a tight smile as he pulled his bass inside. Then he flicked Max's tie. "Trying too hard, dude."

Max sighed heavily. When they went back into the living room, he said, "Alright, last call for this tie because I'm taking it off."

Marty jumped up off the couch where he'd been sitting next to Corbie. He rushed over to Max, kissed him on the cheek, and then laughed as Max's face went bright red. Everyone else laughed while Max turned and strode out of the living room. He knew he shouldn't have put this tie on.

Claire came over to the doorway of the living room where D-rock was hanging back, still holding on to his bass. "Hey, you came," she said.

"Yeah…" He looked around at his friends happily chatting with each other. Even Bryan seemed like he was in a good mood. "My mom made me come," he whispered to Claire.

"I'm…so sorry?" she said lightly.

He looked down into her amused eyes. "Okay, yeah, I guess I could be doing something worse on a Friday night. Like…playing my bass all by myself. Actually, no, that sounds better right now."

"Gonna be like that tonight, eh?" she said. He just shrugged. "Well, at least there are fancy rich people snacks."

"Oh, not a total loss, then," he said. "I'm gonna take my bass downstairs."

Claire smiled and went back into the living room.

Meg had yet to move from Trey's lap and when Max came back into the room with a new tie on, she leaned close to Trey's ear. "How long is it going to take him?"

"What?" Trey asked, surprised.

Even quieter, she said, "How long is it going to take Max to just tell Chloe?"

A slow smile spread across his face, making butterflies take off in her stomach. "Are we making bets?"

She smiled back at him. "January twenty-first."

His brow furrowed. "No way. Valentine's Day."

She held out her hand. But instead of shaking it, he kissed her.

"You're on." He looked around and his smile fell. "Did D-rock leave already?"

"I think he went downstairs," she said.

"I'm gonna go check on him," he said.

She smiled and kissed his cheek quickly before getting up to let him up.

Trey crept quietly down the stairs and found D-rock sitting on his stool. His bass was out, but he wasn't playing it or even pretending to. He nodded at Trey who nodded back and took Claire's seat next to him.

"Are you alright?" Trey asked.

D-rock nodded. But his hands were clasped tightly together, and his shoulders were hunched. He swallowed hard. "You don't have to be down here."

Trey leaned back, crossing his legs at the ankle and putting one arm over the back of his chair. "Nah, it's nice and quiet. Do you know how much quiet I get? It's not a lot."

"Well, at least you have Meg's house, right?" D-rock said.

"Yeah." Trey looked at D-rock as he deflated some more. "Come on, man, I'm trying to be your friend. Talk to me."

D-rock put his hands up. "I just *hate* this time of year. There's no joy in it for me. And the whole world has a tendency to make it last as long as possible and it's just torture."

"If you feel that way, why did you come to the party?" Trey asked as gently as he could.

D-rock forced a shrug. "My mom convinced me to. I think she just wanted to be alone with Ed."

"Ah." Trey nodded. "Does it bother you that they're, you know, together?"

D-rock dropped his gaze to his lap. "It would be selfish to say yes. This is the happiest I've seen my mom in a long time."

"He's a really nice guy," Trey said. "He's only threatened me once so far."

D-rock let out a humourless chuckle. "Well, I'd like to threaten him many times, but Meg very politely asked me not to."

Trey's lips curled into a goofy smile. "And it is pretty hard to say no to her. But just think, if your parents got married, you'd get a totally awesome sister."

"And I'd hate to have to threaten my new sister's boyfriend, too," D-rock said wryly.

"Oh, dude, you wouldn't last two seconds in a fight with me." Trey lightly punched D-rock's shoulder as if to demonstrate.

D-rock didn't take the bait. Instead, he looked down again and scratched the back of his neck. "You know, I actually have two little sisters."

"Really?"

"Yeah." He dropped his hand and shrugged again. "I've never met them. They're seven and five. I guess after the second one, my dad finally realized he'd rather raise them than…me. Guess I just wasn't worth it."

"Dude…" Trey paused for a moment. "That's really heavy."

D-rock let out a shuddering breath and when Trey looked at him, he could see tears in his eyes. After a moment of internally debating what to do, Trey reached out and squeezed D-rock's shoulder, shaking him lightly.

"Your dad screwed up," Trey said. "But that's not about you. That's about him. You shouldn't be walking around feeling like you did something wrong just because your parents couldn't figure it out."

D-rock sniffled and nodded.

"I think it's trash that your dad left you at Christmas," Trey continued.

"But you're gonna live a long time. Are you gonna let that ruin every single Christmas for the rest of your life? Or do you want to move on with your new family?"

D-rock looked into Trey's kind, sympathetic eyes, his own red and watery. He swallowed hard while Trey gave him a soft, encouraging smile.

"I want to move on," D-rock whispered.

Trey nodded, his smile widening. "Good. I like that idea."

"It was your idea," D-rock said with a little laughter in his voice.

"Oh, I know," Trey said, his smile turning cheeky.

D-rock shook his head and brushed the remainder of his tears away. "Please don't tell anyone I was down here crying."

"As long as you don't tell anyone I gave yet another cheesy pep talk," Trey said as he stood up.

"We're pretty used to those by now," D-rock teased.

Trey put his hands up in surrender. "I'm gonna go back upstairs."

"Thanks, dude."

Trey left him there and found the others had nearly finished polishing off a brand-new tray of cookies. He grabbed two before they were gone and went back to his spot with Meg.

As the rest of them talked and enjoyed their evening, Claire sat quietly. A melody caught her ear and she frowned. It was deep, low… She got up and inched towards the doorway to get a better listen.

"Hey, guys, shh for a second," she said, holding up a hand. When they had more or less quieted down, she said, "Is that…D-rock?"

Amber came next to Claire and squinted, listening as well. Sure enough, they could hear the clear strong lines from "What Child Is This?" echoing up from the basement. The girls crept towards the basement stairs and one by one the others followed on their heels.

"What should we do?" Marty whispered.

Claire glanced at him over her shoulder and shrugged. "Accompany him?"

Everyone stood still for a moment, not knowing what the best thing would be.

Finally, Hacks said, "I'll go down."

He crept down and a minute later had joined D-rock in the song. Amber nudged Claire and motioned for her to go. But Claire, being too shy, took Amber's hand and brought her along. They picked up their instruments and as soon as they'd begun to play, the others trickled in after them.

"I'll just tidy up and be right down," Max said to the remaining few.

Max started stacking dishes and when he heard a clinking sound behind him, he turned to find Chloe doing the same.

"You don't have to do that," he said.

She shrugged. "It's fine. I don't mind. To the kitchen?"

He nodded and led her to the kitchen, both of them holding their own stack. Once there, he started rinsing off the dishes so he could put them in the dishwasher, assuming Chloe would leave. Instead, she just waited and watched him, making him feel terribly awkward.

"So, I was given these really awesome concert tickets for a band called Skipping Stations," she said.

He tightened his grip on a slippery plate and in the calmest voice he could muster said, "Oh?"

"Yeah, and I was wondering if you wanted to go with me," she said. "I doubt you've seen them since they're pretty new and underground still."

Startled, he whirled around and said, "*Me?* You want *me* to go with you?"

She nodded. "To be honest, I did ask a couple of other people. But it's on New Year's Eve and everyone already has plans."

"Well...what about the person who gave you the tickets?" he asked.

"Oh, well, if I knew who that was, I would absolutely go with them," she said. "But I don't know. And I never will. So I might as well enjoy it with someone who's not afraid of me."

Max swallowed hard and turned back to his dirty dishes. If that wasn't a slap in the face, he didn't know what was.

"Ah, you've probably got some fancy party to go to," she said, mistaking his silence.

"No," he said quietly. "My parents throw one every year. But from what I gather, it's a lot more fun if you're an adult who can drink." Taking a deep breath, he turned back to face her. "I'll go with you."

"Yeah?"

"Yeah. Sounds like a fun night."

"Awesome." She smiled brightly at him. "That's great. It's downtown Toronto and I was thinking I'd head to Nathan Phillips Square for the countdown after."

"Even better," he said, trying to calm his racing heart.

Chapter Fourteen

By the time Max and Chloe had come downstairs, their band had moved on to a different song. "Let It Snow" filled the basement as they grabbed their violins and hastily joined in. It had been weeks since they'd played by ear off the tops of their heads, and it wasn't perfect, but none of them seemed to mind.

When they'd finished the song, D-rock turned to them all and said, "You know, for a band with no director, we're really good!"

Harmony chuckled. "We've literally all been following your lead."

"What?" he said, his eyebrows drawn.

"Yeah, we have a director," she said to him. "It's you."

"You big goofball," Amber said, her eyes dancing. "Did you not know that?"

"No?" he said. But his heart filled with warmth when the others all agreed with her. "But I'm not like...your conductor. Plus, I've been following Claire the whole time."

"Yeah, and I always wait for you before I start the songs," Claire said with laughter in her voice.

"And you're always counting with your head." Marty bobbed his head as if to illustrate. "And if my downbeat doesn't match whatever your head's doing then you stop and start again. It's actually kind of hilarious."

"I…wasn't aware," D-rock said. Now that everyone had turned their attention to him, he ducked his head, trying to hide behind his bass. "Let's just play another song."

They ended their night doing what they really loved—gossiping in between musical interludes. By the time they'd decided to call it quits, everyone was in a lighter mood.

Claire watched D-rock put his bass away. He got distracted several times by their friends trying to say goodbye to him, but finally he got the bass packed up. When he turned to her, she smiled.

"What's up, Claire?" he said.

"I'm waiting for you to boss me around until I get into your van," she said.

He stared at her for a moment before bursting out laughing. "Would you like a ride?"

"Yes, please," she said pertly. She turned to Max. "How'd your night work out for you?"

He smiled, whimsically if she weren't mistaken. "Pretty well, actually. Thanks for coming."

"Thanks for having us," she answered.

"Yeah, thanks, Max." D-rock patted Max's shoulder.

A chill wind whipped around them as D-rock led Claire down the street to his van. She got in while he hefted both of their instruments into the back. As he drove, she smiled at him, though he couldn't even see it.

"You know what I think?" she said out of the blue.

"What?"

"You should play the melody more often."

He just shook his head.

"No, seriously," she said. "You play *so* nicely. And you never feature yourself. You know how hard it is for me to slip in extra melodic lines for you without you noticing?"

"I *do* notice," he said as he took a left turn. "And you don't have to do that. Really. I like blending into the background. It's what I'm good at."

"That is absolutely incorrect." Her phone vibrated and she pulled it out of her pocket. "But to each his own."

"I'm just saying. The bass is just meant to *be there*. You know? It's not supposed to stand out. I'd rather…"

D-rock's voice grew distant as Claire read her mom's message a third time.

We'll be home after New Year's. Love you.

No explanation. No ETA. Just Claire, alone again, this time for Christmas.

As D-rock pulled onto her street, she sank into herself and stared out the window at all the colourfully decorated houses. She had spent so long making her house look perfect. And for what? It wasn't like anyone would see it now.

"Claire?"

How could they do this to her? They'd already been gone for seven months. Did they really need an extra two weeks away from home? From her? They'd extended tours in the past but never for that long and it had never bothered her as much as it did this year.

"Are you okay?"

She shook her head as D-rock pulled into the driveway. Woodenly, she got out of the van before D-rock had even put it into Park. She trudged up to the front door, her cello all but forgotten. She barely registered the sound of D-rock opening the back of his van and rushing to catch up to her.

"Claire," he repeated as she went through the enclosed porch. "Don't you want this?"

She pressed the numbers on the keypad outside the front door and swung the door wide open, letting it bang satisfactorily against the inner wall. "I guess," she finally answered him.

"You guess?"

After a moment's hesitation, he followed her in and set her cello by the door. His eyes widened as he looked around. There were decorations *everywhere*. Two wintery paintings hung on the wall next to him. The staircase that led upstairs had tinsel wrapped around the banister. Lights were strung along the top of the wall, leading the way to other parts of the house. There was even a mini-tree taking up a corner of the front hall.

"*Whoa*," he breathed. It was everything he hated. Or so he'd thought before he'd seen it all at her house.

His gaze fell to Claire, who had finally bothered with her cello. She tried to pick it up while also dabbing at her eyes with the sleeve of her sweater. When she nearly dropped the cello, D-rock reached out to grab it.

"Hey, what's wrong?" he asked softly.

With a long sigh, she showed him the text message. She hadn't even responded to it because she had no idea what she was supposed to say. He squinted at her phone and then his eyebrows rose sympathetically.

"Aw, Claire, I'm so sorry," he said. "That sucks."

"No, what sucks is that this is my favourite sweater," she said, practically shoving one of the sleeves in his face. "And this mascara isn't supposed to get wet. Look at this!"

He glanced briefly at the darkened patch on the cuff of her sleeve. "Then why are you wearing it?"

"I didn't expect to be crying tonight!" A sob punctuated her statement and D-rock's heart plummeted.

"I'm sorry."

"It's not your fault."

"Do you…want a hug or something?"

Her lips trembled as a trail of mascara ran down her cheek. She stepped forward and leaned her forehead against his chest. He patted her back as she let out another sob.

"This is so dumb," came her muffled voice. "I don't want to cry over them."

"It's okay to cry," he said softly.

She pulled back, her eyes narrowed to tiny slits. Another tear ran down her face. "No. I'm not doing this."

She put her hands up, but D-rock caught her wrists before she could reach her face. "Don't forget about your sweater. At least get a tissue. They can ruin your Christmas, but you don't have to let them ruin your clothes."

She scowled and tried to pull her hands closer to her face, but he just gently lowered them. Then he wiped her cheeks off with his own sleeves while her frown deepened.

"Well, now it's all over your shirt," she said.

"That's okay," he said. "It's black anyway. Plus, it doesn't even look good on me."

She let out a strangled chuckle. "No, it kind of doesn't." She turned to her cello and grabbed the handle. "Thanks for the ride, D-rock."

"You're welcome," he said as he stepped back towards the door. "Don't ruin that sweater."

"Alright," she snipped.

♪   ♫   ♪

Since Amber and Bryan's dad was working late and their mom had shut herself away in her room, Amber had decided on other plans for Christmas Eve. So what if their parents didn't care about them or each other? Amber had plenty of other people who *did* care and she'd rather spend her time with them.

So she put on a pretty dress and wiped away her tears. After doing her makeup, she knocked on Bryan's door. There was no heavy music today since there was no fighting to drown out, but she knew he was in there. He still didn't answer, though.

"Bryan, can you give me a ride to church?" Amber called through the door.

He opened the door, his eyebrows nearly touching his hairline. "What?"

"Can you drive me to Bridgetown Community Church?" she repeated.

"Is this a trick?" he said.

She shook her head. "No. It's Christmas Eve and Hacks told me he's playing for the church's choir and Corbie's in the choir, and I want to go see my friends and be somewhere where people actually care."

"You obviously haven't been to many churches," he snarked.

She put a hand on her hip. "Be nice. I just want a ride. Please?"

Instead of answering, he glanced down at her dress. "Shouldn't you wear something a little more conservative?"

Admittedly, her dress had thin straps and a low-cut neckline. She cringed. At least it went down to her knees. "I'll go put on a sweater."

He sighed. "I guess I'll get my keys."

They left without saying goodbye to their mom, who didn't seem interested in the company anyway. It wasn't a long drive to the church and when they got there, Bryan parked and then looked at Amber expectantly.

"You're not coming in?" she asked.

"I knew this was a trick," he said as he put the car back into gear.

"Wait, no, Bryan." She put her hand on his arm to stop him from actually driving away. "It's not a trick. It's just half an hour. What, are you too busy or something? You got plans tonight?"

He grunted but turned the car off anyway. After opening the door, he said, "Are we going or what?"

She smiled and hastily followed him out. Inside the church, they were greeted by an usher in a stiff black suit and a pleasant smile. He directed them into the sanctuary that had been brightly decorated. At the front of the platform was a life-sized nativity scene, complete with an angel hanging overtop and some plastic animals.

Amber started walking up the aisle, but Bryan took her elbow and shook his head at her. "We sit in the back," he said under his breath.

She rolled her eyes but complied anyway. She waited patiently for the service to start while Bryan bounced his leg. His arms crossed and a frown on his face, he slunk down into the pew as soon as the pastor came onto the platform to start the service.

After a short greeting from the pastor, the choir went onto the platform and Hacks headed to the piano. Amber smiled as Hacks started an introduction for their first song.

Bryan leaned towards her and whispered, "Which of these guys do you have the hots for?"

She elbowed him. "Neither."

"So, both?"

"Stop that."

They fell into a reverent silence as they listened to the choir sing. Bryan's frown eased as Amber's smile grew. Yes, this was definitely better than being at home feeling sorry for herself.

When the service ended, Amber rose quickly and said, "Okay, let's go before he sees me."

"Who?"

"*Hacks.*"

Bryan's eyes widened and he laughed. "You *do* like him."

"No, I don't," she said quickly. "I just don't want him to feel weird."

Bryan grinned. "Well, I'm not ready to go yet. I want to say hi to my friends!"

"*Friends…*" she muttered, crossing her arms.

She had no choice but to wait as Bryan made a beeline for Hacks. Not wanting him to say something he definitely shouldn't say, she caught up quickly just in time to hear him saying hello to Hacks's entire family.

"I'm Bryan," he said in a charming voice as he shook Mr. Ackenstein's hand. "This is my lovely sister, Amber. We're *very* good friends of Fabiano's."

Amber just shook her head, but Hacks caught her eye and smiled. "It was nice of you to come," he said.

"Amber couldn't *wait* to see you," Bryan said.

"Okay, thanks so much, have a good Christmas," Amber said quickly. She tugged on Bryan's arm and pulled him away as the family said a confused goodbye to them. "Do you mind?" she snipped at him quietly.

"No, I don't," he said in a cheeky voice. "Hey, there's Corbie. Let's go say hi to him, too."

There was no stopping him. All Amber could do was follow and make sure he didn't say anything dumb. He greeted Corbie's family in a similar fashion and Amber made sure to say goodbye before he got too far in conversation with them. Corbie gave her a hug—which Bryan smirked at—but she would never not return a hug from a friend.

Finally, she managed to coax him out of the church he hadn't wanted to go into in the first place. Bryan was still smiling as they got into the car, so at least he was in a better mood.

"That was fun!" he said. "We should go to church more often."

"Maybe *you* should," she mumbled as she buckled in. After Bryan had gotten back onto the road, she asked, "Do you think Dad's still working?"

Bryan snorted. "No. But I don't think he's home, either, if that's what you meant."

Amber frowned. "You don't think he's home? It's Christmas Eve. It's late. What could he possibly be doing?"

Bryan hesitated. Snow had started to fall, and he took a long time finding the perfect setting for the windshield wipers. Finally, he said quietly, "I mean he's probably…hanging out with some friends. Or something like that."

"Hanging out with friends on Christmas Eve?" she said. "What are you talking about?"

"I mean, he might be hanging out with one…specific friend…" Bryan glanced at her quickly, but she still wasn't getting it. "Might be a female friend, but I could be wrong."

Amber gasped sharply and Bryan flinched. He probably shouldn't have said anything, especially not today of all days.

"You don't think…"

"I don't know."

"I don't know how to feel about that," she said slowly.

"Just don't think about it," he said quickly. "I'm probably wrong anyway." He turned onto their street and their house came into view a few seconds later. "Look, there's Dad's car. Obviously, I was wrong."

Amber relaxed but when they got inside, they could hear their parents having yet another argument. Amber didn't want to listen. She tried to rush past the living room, but she couldn't help catching the words she didn't want to hear. Her mom asking why he couldn't give other girls a break tonight, why he had to go sneaking around.

Bryan was right.

Chapter Fifteen

"Alright, Dad," Meg said. "The table is set, your turkey is *gorgeous*, and your hair looks great!"

Mr. Ritz patted the top of his head. "Thanks, sweetheart."

When he started wringing his hands together, she put hers on top of his. "Are you nervous?"

"No," he said, though he took her hands and gripped them a little too hard. "Men my age don't get nervous anymore. Especially not over a woman."

She smiled. "Okay, so yes, you're very nervous. Now I see where I get that from."

"That's true," he said, nodding. "Your mother was the picture of confidence. She always knew where she was going and what she was doing. And I literally tripped over my own feet on our first date."

Meg laughed. "And she still married you. So there you go."

"Even still…" He patted her on the cheek, giving her a soft smile. "You remind me so much of your mom."

Biting back tears, Meg shook her head. "Dad, don't do this today. Your girlfriend's gonna be here in, like, ten minutes."

He sniffled and dropped his hand. "You're right. It's not a good time to be sentimental."

"Christmas *is* a good time to be sentimental," she said, shaking her head. "But really...your girlfriend is coming. Be sentimental about her."

He lifted an eyebrow. "How many times are you going to refer to Dawn as my girlfriend?"

"She *is* your girlfriend, is she not? Or are we just having Christmas dinner with a random friend who you definitely don't have feelings for?" She smirked at him.

He shook his head and let out a little chuckle. "I just...feel too old to have a girlfriend."

"So, call her your lady friend or your partner." The doorbell rang and Meg smiled. "Wow, early. I'm starting to like her more and more."

Mr. Ritz opened the door and smiled brightly at Dawn and D-rock. Well, mostly at Dawn, but he did graciously hold out his hand to D-rock after he was done staring at Dawn.

"Hey, Ed," D-rock said as he shook his hand. "Merry Christmas, Meg."

She smiled at him and took the pie plate he was holding. "Do you want to come see my practice room?"

"Definitely."

They went first to the dining room to put the pie down. Then D-rock followed her through the house, leaving their parents behind to do...who knew what? He didn't want to dwell on it.

Meg led him to the sunroom where she spent so much of her time. "This is it," she said, sweeping her arm across the room. "A place just for me."

D-rock took in the plants that lined several of the floor-to-ceiling windows, the small table with his own musical arrangements stacked neatly in one corner, and the two trumpets with two music stands next to them.

"All for yourself, eh?" he said, gesturing to the trumpets.

She giggled. "Well…I can't remember the last time he took his trumpet home. But he does practice, I promise. See?"

She gestured to the music on the stand. D-rock smiled. They'd been playing "Secrets." "Not that I'm grading him, but I can tell you guys practice. He's gotten a lot better since the beginning of the year."

"I know!" she said. "I keep telling him that, but he doesn't believe me. He'd believe you, though. He thinks you're an amazing musician."

"Oh," he said, surprised.

"Which you are," she added hastily.

"Thanks." He went over to the tall windows and looked out at the snow covering the backyard. "Alright, how long are we supposed to leave them alone?"

"I don't know," she said with laughter in her voice. "Maybe not too much longer. My dad's super nervous." When he just nodded, she asked, "Are you okay? Everything okay today?"

"Yeah, it's fine," he answered, still looking out the window. "My mom told me I could stay home but I don't really want that. Trey was right… It's time for me to move on. Could be worse, right?"

"Well, when your standards are set so low…"

He shoved his hands in his pockets. "My standards are always set low, Meg."

She chuckled. "Are you sure about that?"

Turning to her, he lifted an eyebrow. "What do you mean?"

"Have you seen the music you and Claire write?" she said. "It's set at a much higher level than most of us think we're capable of playing."

He frowned. "And yet, you pull it off every week. So what's your point?"

"My point is your standards aren't low," she said. "You just don't pay attention to the things you don't care about."

"Okay…" He chuckled. "Thanks, Mom."

She laughed, too. "I'm just saying."

"Mmhmm." He turned back to the door. "Okay, they've had enough time. I'm hungry and whatever you guys made smells delicious."

She smiled and shook her head but led him to the dining room anyway. They sat down for the meal, which was just as delicious as D-rock expected it to be. And even though he had turkey and several helpings of the sides, he still left room for his mom's pumpkin pie.

As they were enjoying dessert, D-rock's phone vibrated and without thinking he pulled it out of his pocket. There was a message from Claire, asking if he'd checked his email today. He frowned. He hadn't checked his email in weeks, let alone today.

He opened his email and the most recent one popped out at him. "A Gift From Your Friend, Claire." In the email was a download link for the same music writing program Claire used on her laptop. But…it was so expensive. There was no way she'd bought him a copy, right?

"Derek," his mom said lightly.

He looked up at her and she held out her hand.

"We're at the dinner table." She waggled her fingers at him. "Give me your phone."

He handed it over and watched her read what was on the screen. He'd never had anything to hide from her before and this was no exception. Her eyes widened.

"Oh, wow, what a nice gift," she said, apparently having forgotten her own rule.

"What is it?" Ed asked.

Dawn leaned towards him to show him the phone, which D-rock felt was a little unnecessary. "His friend Claire bought him a music writing program. They're always writing music together."

"Well, not always," D-rock mumbled.

"Aw, that *is* nice," Meg said.

Dawn looked back at D-rock. "Did you get her anything?"

He put his hands up in surrender. "No, obviously not. I wasn't expecting anything, and she knows I…hate Christmas."

His mom gave him a look he easily interpreted. Obviously, he needed to fix that.

"I guess I could take her some leftover pie," he said, gesturing to the half-eaten pumpkin pie.

"Oh, very generous," Dawn said as she passed his phone back to him.

Meg smiled at him. "I'll go with you if you want, D-rock. I feel bad she's all alone."

"She's alone?" Dawn said in a concerned voice. "Why didn't you tell me?"

He shrugged. "She didn't want to make a big deal out of it."

"Well, what are you waiting for?" Dawn waved at them. "Get out of here."

He smiled and came around the table to give her a hug. Then he whispered, "Very subtle."

She turned to him and patted his cheek with a smile. "About as subtle as buying an expensive gift for your *friend* who's bringing you half a pie."

He just shook his head and left the dining room with Meg following. When they got outside, D-rock headed to his mom's van but stopped when he noticed Meg staring longingly down the street. At Trey's house, no doubt.

"We can ask him to come if you want," he said.

"Okay!" she said happily.

D-rock chuckled as he followed her down the street. He stayed on the sidewalk while she went up to the house. One of Trey's brothers answered the door and a minute later, Trey came out. He put his arms around Meg and pulled her in for a kiss while D-rock wished he had opted to just go alone.

Trey waved at D-rock then turned his attention back to Meg. A conversation that should have taken 30 seconds took much longer when it included so much kissing. Finally, Trey came out of the house in his coat and boots and headed towards the sidewalk with Meg on his arm.

As D-rock trailed behind them, he said, "Wow, you guys talk so quietly you have to be lip to lip to hear each other, eh?"

Trey tossed a smile over his shoulder. "I can show you and Claire how it's done if you want."

D-rock bit his lip. He'd walked right into that one. "Hard pass."

"*Hard?*" Trey said incredulously.

"Yup." D-rock jogged up to the van, unlocked it, and got in before they could say anything else.

Meg got into the front seat, and he passed her the pie. Claire lived across town, which was plenty of time for Trey and Meg to carry on a mushy conversation about how much they had missed each other in the two days they hadn't seen each other. D-rock was happy for them, though.

When he parked in Claire's driveway and then just looked at Meg, she gave him a small smile.

"Did you want me to ring the doorbell?" she asked.

"Yes, please."

Trey and D-rock stood behind Meg as they waited for Claire to answer the door. Trey whispered, "Dude, why are you being so weird?"

"I'm not," D-rock whispered back.

Claire opened the door, a surprised smile spreading across her face as she made eye contact with each one of them. "Hey! What are you guys doing here?"

"We came to wish you a merry Christmas," Meg said kindly.

"And we…brought you pie," D-rock said, holding it up.

"Aw…" She opened the door wider. "Come in."

They went in and took their coats and boots off. D-rock looked around and noticed that most of the decorations had been taken down. He felt bad but chose not to mention it. She led them to the kitchen.

"Sorry it's already half-eaten," D-rock said as he held out the pie. "I just…wanted to come say thank you for the gift."

"Oh!" Her smiled brightened up the whole room. "I was wondering what was taking you so long to answer."

She set the pie down on the table and went to the cupboard for some plates.

"Claire, don't do that," Trey said. "No need to dirty plates. Just get some spoons."

She furrowed her brow at him. "Okay…" she said with laughter in her voice.

She passed out the spoons and then they dug in as they chatted. Meg had a few bites and Claire thoroughly enjoyed a healthy chunk, too. But the boys ate like they hadn't just had huge holiday dinners less than an hour ago. D-rock graciously allowed Trey the last bite, after which Trey patted his stomach.

"Okay, now I gotta walk that off," Trey said. He smiled at Meg. "You coming?"

"Sure," she said.

After they'd left, D-rock said, "Do you ever wonder what it must be like to be Trey and just eat whatever you want and walk it off and then just be athletic and awesome all the time?"

Claire laughed and shook her head. "Do you?"

He put his hands up in surrender. "I mean…sometimes?"

"You don't need to be Trey to be awesome all the time," she said.

When she didn't elaborate, he lifted an eyebrow and changed the subject. "Thank you so much for your gift. But…that's too much."

"No, it's not," she said firmly. "I have like five free codes for it and exactly one friend who would use it as much as I do. And now you can finish that piece you're working on without needing my help."

He nodded. Was she trying to get rid of him? He didn't exactly want that either. "Well…I might still need your help anyway. A little bit."

She smiled. "I'm more than happy to. I can't wait to see the spark you'll put in it."

Smiling, he ducked his head. He was pretty sure she thought more highly of his writing than anyone else. "Are you going to be okay here this week? You know, till your parents come home?"

Her smile fell and he wished he hadn't brought it up.

"I'll be fine," she said sadly. "They've been gone so long, it's not like I can't handle a few more days."

He nodded. They heard the front door open and happy voices drifted over to them. D-rock picked up the pie plate and went over to the front hall.

"Thank you so much for coming to see me," Claire said.

"It was Meg's idea," D-rock said quickly.

Meg's eyebrows drew in, but she didn't correct him. Instead, she leaned forward and gave Claire a hug. "Merry Christmas. We'll see you soon."

"Merry Christmas," Claire said.

Trey hugged her, too, nearly picking her up off the ground while she laughed. D-rock didn't offer her a hug, though. The one from last week was already too much.

As they drove back to Meg's house, she asked, "Why did you lie to Claire and tell her it was my idea to come see her and not yours?"

D-rock shrugged. "I didn't want her to feel awkward."

"You don't want her to feel awkward...because you care about her?" Meg asked.

"Yeah."

"You think it's awkward if your friends think you care about them?" she pressed further.

"Well...no..."

"You do it, Trey," she said, putting her hands up.

"Dude," Trey said, leaning forward between the front seats, "why don't you just tell her you like her?"

"See, this is what I mean," D-rock said. "Look, Claire is one of the best friends I've ever had, and I don't need other people ruining that by trying to make things romantic between us. So, if you could just, like, *not* do that."

Meg and Trey shared a secret glance, after which she said, "Alright, D-rock. We won't make things awkward."

Chapter Sixteen

After spending three hours shopping Boxing Day sales with Amber and Chloe, Rach was done with a capital D. She'd never in her life spent that much time going in and out of clothing stores at the mall. She didn't even know they had that many! And there certainly weren't many that had clothes that properly fit her very tall frame.

But Amber had insisted they be thorough, and Chloe was confident she could help Rach tailor *anything* to make it look good. And although Rach had to admit that Chloe's upcycled wardrobe was adorable, she wasn't so sure Chloe would be able to pull off that same magic on Rach. Amber, on the other hand, was magical in just about every way imaginable.

And after all that, they still had to lug all their millions of bags up five flights to Chloe's apartment. She apologized a few times, but Rach couldn't even answer as out of breath as she was.

"I don't remember these stairs being so bad last time I came over," Rach complained.

"Well, we did just spend hours walking around the mall," Chloe said.

"Shouldn't you be better at this?" Amber tossed a teasing grin over her shoulder. "I mean, you have tuba lungs!"

"Yeah, yeah," Rach huffed. "And in fact, they're larger than yours simply because of my height. But I'm also just...*very* out of shape. Maybe I *should* play basketball."

Chloe snickered. "I really can't imagine you doing that."

"Good," Rach said. "Since everyone else seems to be able to."

Finally, they reached the fifth floor and Chloe opened the door of the stairwell. "Don't worry, you'll always be a tuba player to me."

Rach smiled. Having someone see her as just a tuba player was her ideal aesthetic. Now all she had to do was convince everyone else around her of the same thing. Which would be hard, since hardly anyone even knew she played.

Chloe led them inside her apartment, which she discovered was empty. "Oh, good, we've got the place to ourselves. Love my sister, but she's pretty much always in the way."

They went into Chloe and June's room and tossed their bags onto the bed. Chloe, for some reason, had Rach and Amber stand next to each other while she grabbed a measuring tape.

"You guys are the *perfect* height difference," Chloe said as her gaze roved over their legs and hips. "Like this is total friendship goals."

"Really?" Rach asked as she looked down at their legs.

"Totally!" Chloe measured the distance between the top of Rach's hips to the top of Amber's hips. Then she measured their inseams and their waists while they stood there waiting for more instructions.

"I'm going to take the extra fabric from the bottom of Amber's pants and put it on Rach's pants." She dumped out the contents of one of the bags onto her bed and moved on to the next bag. "Trust me on this, it's gonna be great!"

"What about the shirts?" Rach asked. "I mean, Amber's fit her just fine."

"*Um,* except that I don't fill them out half as nicely as you do," Amber protested. "Have you seen my chest? Like, when is puberty gonna hit me?"

"Amber—"

"You know you're both perfectly formed, right?" Chloe said, flicking her wrist dismissively before going back to rifling through the clothes they'd bought.

They both stared at her long enough that she noticed their silence and turned to them. "What?" she said.

"Says the girl with the perfect hourglass figure," Amber said. "Look at you!"

"Yeah, you've got it made everywhere, Chloe," Rach added. "Even your arms. I mean...honestly!"

Chloe looked down at herself, then back at them and smiled. "You guys are nuts. We're all gorgeous, okay? Let's just alter the clothes and you'll see what I mean."

They dropped their complaints—and their compliments—and started going through the clothes. True to her word, Chloe showed them how she could take extra fabric from Amber's clothes to put on Rach's. She adjusted shirts for both girls to show that it didn't matter what their body types were so long as their clothes fit in a certain way.

Rach and Amber were totally mesmerized watching Chloe expertly run her mom's ancient sewing machine. Watching her play violin was one thing—but this was amazing!

"See, Rach?" Chloe said, holding up a checkered green and white shirt. "You thought I was crazy for picking this out of the men's section for you but try it on now."

"I didn't think you were crazy," Rach said as she removed the shirt she was currently wearing. "Just that I'm tired of literally having to wear men's clothes and don't think any of it will actually look good on me."

She put the shirt on and buttoned it up then looked at herself in the mirror. Her eyes grew wide and her jaw dropped. The shirt gave her boobs! And a waist! And didn't look like it had been intended for a man at all.

"*Rach*," Amber said, her eyes wide.

"Okay, I take it back," Rach said quickly. "Chloe, you're magical and I love you."

Chloe laughed and then tossed another shirt to Amber. "Here, you try this one, too."

Amber put it on as quickly as humanly possible and then stood next to Rach, who was still admiring herself in the mirror.

"Chloe, you *are* magic! Thank you."

She went over to Chloe and crushed her in a hug while Chloe just laughed some more.

"Oh, before I forget," Rach said. She pulled something out of her purse and handed it to Chloe. "This was a gift from my grandparents and there's no way you'll make it fit me. Plus it has way more of a Chloe vibe, so it's yours if you want it."

Chloe took the shirt and her eyes lit up. It was grey, with a dark-tone rainbow on the front. The words "let your rainbow shine" ran across the top of the rainbow.

"I love this!" she said. "But are you sure? I could totally cut off the bottom and make it a crop top for you."

Rach scowled. "No, thank you. Keep it."

"Thanks!" Chloe didn't waste any time putting it on. "Oh, this'll be perfect for the concert."

"Hey, did you find someone to go with you?" Amber asked.

"Oh, yeah, Max is going with me," Chloe said nonchalantly as she took the new shirt back off.

"Oh!" Amber was surprised and pleased but tried not to show it. "Wow, that's so nice."

Rach's face scrunched up. "Don't you think he could have afforded a ticket on his own if he wanted to go to a concert?"

Chloe chuckled. "Of course he can. Remember his wall of tickets?"

"But you're taking him anyway?" Rach said, confused.

"Yeah."

"Come on, out with it, girl," Amber said. "Why'd you ask him?"

Chloe shrugged. "I like him." When Amber squeaked, Chloe put up her hands. "I mean like enough to give him my extra concert ticket. Not like...like how you like every boy you see. He's my friend."

"Uh huh," Amber said. Nothing could wipe the smile off her face, though. "Yeah, okay, you like him as a friend."

"Exactly," Chloe said. "And I think...he's kind of lonely, you know? Like he told me all he does for New Year's Eve is go to his parents' party and that it's only fun if you can drink and he sounded kind of sad about it? So, I'm glad I asked him."

"Because you like him," Rach repeated.

Chloe sighed. "In a very friendly way. Like I like you guys."

"You called us gorgeous a little while ago," Amber teased.

"Because you *are*," Chloe said with a huge smile. "Now, stop bugging me about it. You both had the chance to go with me, too, you know."

Amber bit her lip and decided to take D-rock's advice to not meddle. "Well, I'm glad you found someone to go with you. I'd be worried about you being downtown Toronto all by yourself."

Chloe smiled gratefully. "I'm sure it'll be fine. And this shirt really is perfect. I was going to wear these leggings, but wasn't sure what to pair them with yet."

She pulled out a pair of black leggings with rips in them from her dresser.

"Oh, those are so cool!" Amber said. "Where'd you get them?"

"I've had them for a long time," Chloe said. "They're my favourite pair and they got a little tear in them. I was disappointed and then thought…eh, why not? Ripped some more holes in 'em and now they're even better."

"You are the coolest person I know," Amber said.

"Like, actually," Rach added. "You're the poster child for 'if life gives you lemons…'"

Chloe laughed. "I hate lemonade. But I'll take the compliment."

♪   ♫   ♪

"I still can't believe you're making me do this," TK said, resisting the urge to crumple up his math workbook. "It's New Year's Eve, dude."

"Exactly," Hacks said patiently. They were sitting on his bed, TK's math textbook on Hacks's lap and TK with his workbook. "I want you to start off the new year on the right foot. And I know if I make you study now, you'll feel so much better about going out later."

TK rolled his eyes, but he'd gotten used to Hacks's methods and he knew his friend was right. TK had vastly improved his math grade simply by forcing himself to do it before rewarding himself with something he actually liked doing. And it *was* satisfying to see that most of his workbook had been completed and had the correct answers in it.

But as they studied, even Hacks seemed distracted. There were several times when TK knew he'd gotten something wrong and Hacks had just shrugged it off.

"What's up with you today?" TK finally asked.

Hacks shook his head. "I have six months left."

"What?" TK said. "Are you…dying?"

Hacks gave him a withering look. "No. I would have told you by now if I were fatally diseased."

"Six months till what, then?"

"Graduation!"

"Yeah, you and me both," TK said. "So long as I pass math."

"You will," Hacks said confidently. "I'm still trying to figure out how to cram in as many high school experiences as I can before I'm gone."

"You really need to stop talking like you're dying, my guy," TK said. "I mean what is even left for you to do? You have the highest grades ever, you've got your hours and extra-curriculars covered and...you already got an acceptance to university, didn't you?"

"I did," Hacks said plainly. "But I feel like I'm years behind my peers. I still can't ask a girl out without having a panic attack. How am I supposed to..."

"Supposed to what?" TK pressed. "Oh...are we having...*the talk*?"

Hacks's face scrunched together for a moment and then he rolled his eyes. "No, TK. I don't need the talk. I don't expect that to happen...for a long time. I just meant I don't know what I'm supposed to do when I'll soon be going to school with girls who are much older than me."

TK's eyes widened. "Maybe you *do* need the talk."

Hacks rolled his eyes again. "Okay, thanks for your help. Let's get back to statistics."

TK closed his workbook. "No, no. I'm sorry. What can I help you with?"

"How do I ask a girl out?" Hacks said.

"Okay, try this. Close your eyes." TK waited until Hacks's eyes were closed. "Now repeat after me. Do."

"Do."

"You."

"You."

"Want."

"Want..."

"To."

"To…"

"Go."

Hacks's eyes flew open. "Yeah, there's no way it's that simple."

"It definitely is." TK waved his hand dismissively. "Trust me, I've asked out lots of girls."

"And how many rejected you?" Hacks asked bitterly.

"Most of them," TK answered, his mouth twisted up. "What's your point?"

Hacks just sighed.

"Okay, we're going to get you through this," TK said. "Pick the hottest girl you know and you're going to ask her out the next time you see her."

Hacks chewed on his lip. "I can't ask out Amber. I doubt she'll give me another pity date."

TK resisted the urge to roll his eyes like Hacks had done five times already. "Okay, pick the second hottest girl you know."

Hacks hesitated and then shook his head. "I don't think Max would appreciate that."

TK pursed his lips, but Hacks was right. "Okay…who's the third?"

"Oh." Hacks laughed as his cheeks went red. "Yeah, I don't exactly want to get beat up by Trey."

"*Hacks.*" TK shook his head even as he laughed. "Okay, let's just go back to Amber. There's always a chance she'll say yes and not out of pity."

"How are you always so confident?" Hacks asked.

"It's really not about that," TK answered, his brown eyes going serious. "It's just about knowing that even if you do get rejected, it's fine. Like, think about it. You have *so* much else going for you. Having one or even a few girls turn you down, for whatever reason, isn't the end of the world."

Hacks stared into TK's eyes for a moment. "What's the likelihood I'll get rejected?"

"Hmm…" TK scratched the back of his head. "Like I said, I've asked out a *lot* of girls. And I'd say I've got one yes for ever five girls I've asked. And yes, you're a lot younger, but you're very sweet, so I'll bet you have the same odds. Twenty per cent chance?"

Hacks smiled and TK smacked his own forehead.

"Wow, I cannot believe you made me do that," TK said.

Hacks's smile grew. "I do wager that statistics is your strongest math discipline."

"Ughhh, whatever," TK said as he picked his workbook back up.

Chapter Seventeen

Meg knocked on the door of Trey's house. She'd learned the hard way that ringing the doorbell would get their two dogs far too excited. And as much as she loved dogs, she didn't need them to be all over her like last time.

One of the twins answered the door. As soon as she saw him, she said, "Hey, Clay."

Clay's eyes widened. "How'd you know it was me?"

Meg laughed. Clay and Hayden were 10-year-old identical twins, but Meg had learned the difference between them a while ago. "I have superpowers," she stage-whispered.

"Hayden!" Clay shouted as he retreated through the house. "Meg has superpowers!"

Meg laughed and let herself in. She took her coat off and as she was looking for a hook that wasn't too full of coats and scarves, Trey finally came to the door.

"Sorry," he said. "I was helping Dad with…"

She turned her head to him. "With what?"

He shook his head and smiled. "You look so nice today."

"You said that yesterday," she teased, though the compliment warmed her from the inside out.

"You look nice every day," he said seriously.

Having finally hung up her coat, she turned and put her arms around him. Trey was the one who always looked good, but she didn't need to say it…again. He sure smelled good, too, like…

"Apple crisp," she said. "Were you helping your dad make apple crisp?"

Trey's eyes lit up. "Yes! And you're just in time to have some before the boys eat it all."

Meg smiled and followed him to the living room. May was curled up in a corner of the couch with earbuds on, her phone in her hand, and a cat on her lap. She greeted Meg with a wave before returning her hand to the cat's back. The boys ran into the room and stopped in front of Meg. When she saw them, she looked at Clay and laughed.

"Changing your clothes isn't going to change who you are, Clay." Then she looked at the other boy. "Hi, Hayden."

Now both of them were staring at her while Trey laughed. He put his arm around Meg and squished her to himself.

"Nice try," he said to the twins. "But Meg's too smart for you."

Trey gestured to the couch, telling Meg he'd be right back with a plate of apple crisp for her. She sat next to May and immediately noticed a French horn nearby, sitting on its stand next to some music.

Gesturing to it, Meg said, "You've been playing?"

May took out one of her earbuds. "Yeah. I was inspired."

"You mean, Trey's been making you?" Meg said.

May smiled. "Yeah…he really wants me to join your band, but I'm totally not good enough for that."

"You don't have to be good enough," Meg said. "All our music is handmade for us. We'd just have to ask D-rock and Claire not to make it crazy like they do for the rest of the band."

"Thanks, but…" May's face scrunched up. "I think I'll stick to playing on my own for now."

Trey returned and handed Meg a plate before sitting next to her. His parents joined them a minute later and they both greeted Meg kindly. While they ate the apple crisp, Mrs. Donnelly asked about the band and Mr. Donnelly asked about her dad.

The band was good. Her dad was out with Dawn. They didn't seem surprised to hear that bit, so Meg assumed Trey had already told them about her dad and D-rock's mom. She didn't mind. She knew he had a close relationship with his parents, and he obviously trusted them enough to talk about her with them.

"Did the boys show you their Christmas gifts?" Trey asked, one eyebrow lifted high.

Meg shook her head. As soon as he said it, Clay and Hayden jumped up and ran off. They returned a moment later, one of them carrying an electric guitar and the other an electric bass, both with a wide grin that reminded Meg of Trey.

"Grandma and Grandpa got us these," Hayden said proudly.

"Wow!" she said. "Those look fun."

"They're loud," Trey mumbled into her ear.

A pleasant shiver went down her spine, but she ignored him as the twins showed her what they'd already learned—which wasn't a lot. But that was okay. She could tell they already loved the instruments enough to spend a lot of time with them.

After a few minutes, they switched instruments and Meg chuckled. Trey put his free arm around her and squeezed. She smiled at him. He might have thought his family was loud and he probably got very little privacy. But they were also loving, and it was clear he loved them, too.

"Okay, I need a walk," Trey said as he took Meg's empty plate. "You coming?"

Meg had quickly learned that Trey taking walks—which he did often—was his way of getting out nervous energy. And Trey had learned to slow his walking pace for her after the first time when she'd nearly had to run to catch up to him.

As they walked up the street past her house, Trey took her hand and tucked it into his coat pocket. "I'm really glad you came over tonight. My parents love seeing you."

"Oh, your parents do, eh?" she couldn't help teasing him by saying.

He chuckled. "Well, obviously I do, too. I've just never been with or even met another girl who fits in with my family like you do."

She stopped walking to stare into his sweet blue eyes. "I love you."

He took a deep breath and let it out in a "Huh?"

She felt her cheeks warm but at least the air outside kept her cool. "I love everything about you and that includes your family. They're wonderful and every girl who passed on that is seriously missing out."

He wrapped his arms around her, drawing her close so he could kiss her in that way she really loved, too. "Meg—"

"You don't have to say it."

"Oh, but I'm going to."

"You really don't have to."

"Stop. I love you, too."

Those words melted her heart. She clutched the front of his shirt and pulled him close again while his hands tangled up in her hair. She couldn't think of a better way to end the year.

♪　　♫　　♪

Amber spent most of her New Year's Eve in her room, by herself. Her parents had gone out—separately she guessed, since both of their cars were gone. Bryan's car was also gone, and she hadn't asked him where he was going. She only regretted not going out with Chloe a tiny little bit. She was happy to let Max have that one, but she was also thinking he seriously owed her—and not just sockets and a video game this time.

She heard a car pull into the driveway and she checked her bedroom window to see which of her parents had come home. But to her surprise, it was Bryan. She went downstairs to see what was up and why he'd come home when it was barely 10 p.m.

He shrugged and headed to the kitchen. "I was at a party, but it was super lame, so I came home."

"Were you drinking?" she asked as he rooted around in the fridge.

He scowled at her. "I drove home, didn't I? I'm not gonna ruin my car like that."

Amber rolled her eyes because Bryan wasn't always the most careful driver. But inwardly, she was glad he had the good sense not to drink and drive.

"There's a pie in the freezer," she said.

"Oh, good," he said eagerly.

She turned the oven on to a low setting while he took the pie out. Once it was in the oven, they sat at the kitchen table together. With a frown, Bryan shoved some of the stuff on the table to the side so they'd at least have a place to eat... Together, she assumed.

"So, what about you?" he asked. "Why didn't you go out tonight?"

"Just didn't feel like it," she said. "But now that you're here, we can work on our resolutions together!"

He groaned. "I don't want to do that. I'm not doing that."

"Oh, come on," she said, pushing him. "This year, I'm going to be nicer to people."

He stared at her for a moment. "Amber...that's literally the laziest resolution ever. You're already the nicest person."

"No, I'm not." She shrugged. "I could totally be nicer. Your turn."

Bryan rubbed his chin, which could have used a good shave. "Okay, I'm stealing that. I'll be nicer, too."

"What?" she said, her eyes narrowing. "You can't steal a resolution."

He laughed. "Yes, I can. Also, everyone's always telling me what a jerk I am and how I should be nicer. So, this year, I'll be nicer. Aren't you happy?"

She opened and closed her mouth a few times. "That's—fine. Fine. We'll do the same resolution. But don't be surprised when I do it better."

He pursed his lips. "Is this a resolution...or a competition?"

"I guess that depends on how you treat it." She stood up and went over to the oven. "Let me get you some pie."

"No!" He hurried over to the oven and pushed her out of the way. "Let *me* get *you* some pie."

"Bryan." She chuckled, putting her hands on her hips. "The new year hasn't even started yet."

"No time like the present," he said as he took the pie out.

She shook her head but said no more. If he wanted to be a nicer person, she wasn't going to stop him.

♪　♫　♪

The shirt Rach had given Chloe really was perfect for the Skipping Stations concert. The only thing that could complete the look was some dark eye makeup and bright red lipstick. But...was it overkill? Would Max think she'd put way too much thought into her appearance tonight? Or would he just literally not care or notice, like every other boy Chloe knew?

It didn't matter. She wanted to look good for herself. Not for a handsome rich boy who had no business invading her thoughts. Oh, why had she asked Max to go with her?

Chloe was just finishing off her New Year's Eve look when someone knocked on the half open bathroom door. She looked over at June and smiled at her.

"What do you think?" Chloe asked.

June gave her a small smile. "You look great."

Chloe tilted her head. "It's too much, isn't it?"

"No, no." June stepped into the bathroom. "Really, you're so pretty, Chloe. I'm going to beg Mom to let me do makeup like you."

"Soon, kiddo," Chloe said. She turned back to the mirror and wondered if she had time to wash it all off to tone it down.

"Um, Chloe?"

"Yeah?"

"I wanted to give you this."

June stuck her hand out in front of Chloe. Chloe looked down, only to find several dollar bills neatly folded up in June's hand. Frowning, she turned to her little sister.

"What? Why?" Chloe asked.

June shrugged. "Just…in case you need some money tonight. Like, if you wanted to use this or need some money."

"June…" Chloe hesitated. "Where did you even get all that?"

June shrugged. "It's birthday and Christmas money from my dad and grandparents. I've been saving it."

"Well, that's really sweet of you to offer it to me, but I don't need money. I've got my own."

"I know, but—" June huffed and refused to lower her hand.

"What's going on with you?" Chloe asked gently.

"I broke your bow!" June's eyes filled with tears at the admission.

Chloe wasn't exactly surprised, though it was a shock to have her admit it like this right now.

"I broke it," June repeated, her voice cracking. "All the hairs came off it and I didn't know what to do and I knew you'd be mad so I took it straight down to the dumpster before you or Mom could see. I thought it would be okay since you showed up with another bow."

Chloe took a deep breath. Instead of telling June that breaking the hairs on the bow would have been a fixable mistake, she said, "I've...been borrowing my friend's extra bow. Why are you telling me about this now?"

"Because I feel terrible." June shook her head, trying to shove the money at Chloe. "I should have just told you what happened. I'm so sorry. This is all the money I have, please take it."

Chloe wanted to get mad all over again. Not only had June needlessly thrown out her bow, but she'd let Chloe get grounded over it. But as she looked into June's eyes, she knew she truly felt bad over it. And she was only nine, after all. Chloe could see that the guilt eating away at June for all these weeks was punishment enough.

"Do me a favour," Chloe said, wrapping her hand around June's. "Put this money somewhere safe and tell Mom I was right."

"Really?" June said. "That's it? You're not mad anymore?"

"Oh, I am." Chloe turned back to the mirror to make sure her makeup was 100 per cent flawless. "But I'm not going to take your money. We're turning over a new leaf, okay? Don't ever lie to me again. And definitely don't touch my stuff without asking me."

June was silent for a moment before throwing her arms around Chloe and squeezing hard. Chloe laughed and patted June's back. With June's confession and Max's bow indefinitely in her possession, Chloe would be just fine.

Chapter Eighteen

Max looked out the window of his dad's car as they drove to the train station. His stomach felt unsettled, and he was about two wayward thoughts away from an asthma attack. But he tried his best to act like everything was fine.

"You doing alright?" his dad asked. Because of course his dad knew he wasn't quite himself tonight.

"I'm fine," Max said. "Thanks for the ride."

"You're welcome," Mr. Ford said. "I'm just surprised you wouldn't rather be home tonight. Don't you like our New Year's Eve parties?"

"Yeah, of course," Max said. It was only a half-lie.

"And you're sure you'd rather go to some random concert?" his dad asked.

"Absolutely," Max answered. "I wouldn't miss this concert for the world."

His dad frowned thoughtfully. "You like this band that much?"

Max nearly choked. He hadn't told his parents much about what he was doing tonight, except that he was going with a friend to downtown Toronto to see Skipping Stations. They hadn't been too bothered with him going to Toronto for New Year's Eve, knowing he'd have the means to get home whenever he needed to. They had barely asked for extra information after confirming where exactly he'd be and roughly when he'd be home.

Now he found himself admitting, "It's not about the band."

"Oh?"

It was all the encouragement Max needed to tell him the rest. He half turned in his seat and said, "My friend who invited me—Chloe… I gave her the concert tickets."

His dad's eyes widened. "Well, I guess I'll know what to expect on your next credit card bill."

"No," Max said. "I already paid it off out of my allowance."

"Okay, so why are you telling me that, then?" his dad asked.

Max bit his lip. "I gave her the tickets anonymously, so she has no idea. But then she turned around and asked *me* to the concert. And now I just—" He sighed and put his face in his hands.

"Ohhh." His dad took a left turn into the parking lot of the train station and found a spot to park. "You like her?"

"Very much."

"Why don't you just tell her you gave her the tickets?" his dad asked.

"Because…" How could Max even explain his convoluted actions now? "I gave her the tickets as a *gift*, so she would have something fun to do tonight. I'm worried if I tell her, she'll just think I'm trying to buy her. I don't want that."

Mr. Ford turned his sympathetic gaze to his son. "I understand. But she did ask you to go with her, right?"

"Yeah," Max said. It gave him the smallest hint of hope. "But I wasn't her first choice."

"Regardless," Mr. Ford said, "you should be honest with her. And if when you tell her she thinks your intention was anything less than honourable, then she's not worth your time, son."

"Yeah, I was worried about that, too," Max mumbled.

"Hey." Mr. Ford stretched his arm across Max's shoulders and gave him a loose hug. "Call me if you need *anything*. Okay? Anything at all. I know I'm old, but I still know a thing or two about women."

Max smiled. "Thanks, Dad."

He went into the train station and nervously adjusted his tie, straightened his shirt, and then shoved his hands in his pockets. He glanced around but Chloe hadn't arrived yet. Which was understandable since he was a good 20 minutes early for their train. He fiddled with his hair, touched his tie again, and then put his hands back in his pockets.

He had no reason to be nervous. It wasn't like this was a date. Chloe had simply asked him to come because no one else could. He was literally her last option.

But he had a hard time convincing his brain of that when he finally saw her step through the doors of the train station. She was wearing stylishly ripped black leggings, a dark shirt with a rainbow on it, and the coolest black vintage bomber jacket he'd ever seen. Her dark eye makeup made her brown eyes look more serious and...well, he wouldn't even think about her bright red lips. When she smiled at him, he wished he'd brought his inhaler. He would just have to remember to take deep, calm breaths.

"Hey, do I look okay?" she asked when he'd stared too long.

"Yeah, you look great," he said. "You ready to go?"

"You didn't already buy my ticket, did you?"

He shook his head.

"Great!" She headed towards the ticket booth.

"Do you want me to—" Max cut himself off at the look Chloe gave him. Nope, he definitely would not be buying her train ticket.

Chloe bought her own ticket and Max got his. They went outside to wait for their train on the platform and Max did everything he could to not constantly stare at her. When they got onto the train, Chloe chose a seat facing backwards, which worked just fine for Max since he was already feeling sick enough to begin with. Chloe looked out the window as the train started up. Max watched her from under his eyelashes.

"Have you listened to Skipping Stations before?" Chloe asked.

Max hesitated. He should have just told her right then and there. But instead, he said, "Well, I just binged them in preparation for the concert."

She smiled, still looking out the window, her chin resting in her hand. "I'm surprised. I didn't really think you'd be into indie folk rock."

"What do you think I listen to?" he asked.

She shrugged. "Classical?"

"Do I look like Harmony to you?"

She turned to him and took in his entire outfit. The white vans, dark jeans, and brown suede jacket. The tie she'd given him and his nicely combed hair. She reached out and loosened the tie a bit, then tousled his hair.

He raised his eyebrows. "Better?"

"Hard to improve on, but yes." She smiled as his cheeks went pink. "So, what *do* you listen to?"

"When my parents are home, I listen to jazz because in their minds that stimulates the brain waves." He rolled his eyes and she giggled.

"And when you're alone?"

Looking right into her eyes, he said, "Rap."

"Are you kidding?"

He laughed and held up his hands. "Okay, I admit it, I have no idea how to do this whole teenage rebellion phase thing. And I don't relate to the lyrics in rap music at all, but I kind of…still…love it?"

She burst out laughing and he couldn't help laughing with her. "Wow, there is so much more to you than I first thought."

He nodded. "I'm going to take that in a good way."

"It's a very good thing," she said.

She fell silent and looked out the window again while he tried not to stare at her. Which was hard when she'd done her best to look absolutely stunning tonight. Not for him, he was sure.

Chloe, however, was keenly aware of how Max's eyes hadn't left her since he'd seen her inside the station. Granted, she didn't normally get this dressed up for a regular Tuesday night rehearsal. But his attention was starting to make her feel shy. Had she overdone it? It was too late to change that now.

The concert was in a small theatre a few blocks away from Union Station. It was an unseasonably warm evening for December 31, even though a few snowflakes fell on them as they walked. The streets were busy with people trying to get to their party destinations.

At the theatre, they were asked for ID and their tickets, after which the usher marked each of their hands with a black X. Then they found their seats, which were only a few rows back from the front. Max had almost splurged for front row but then thought that would be too obvious. If he'd known Chloe would take him, he might have reconsidered that.

Chloe shoved one of her hands in Max's face and said, "You could have stayed home and snuck some of your parents' alcohol."

He laughed. "I'd rather be here."

"That's fair," Chloe said. "These are *amazing* seats. I feel like I'm going to be able to see the sweat on Elliott's face."

"Elliott?"

"Yeah, the bass-slash-singer," she said.

"Ah."

The concert itself was just as thrilling as Chloe knew it would be. For such young musicians, Skipping Stations's stage presence and musical chemistry was amazing. Not once did they falter. Though at one point, Elliott forgot the lyrics and laughed into his mic, joking about how easy it was to forget the lyrics you wrote yourself. It just made their performance that much more authentic and endearing.

When the opening chords of "The Emma Song" started, Chloe reached over and gripped Max's hand so hard he winced. But he wasn't about to let go either.

"This is their best song," she said right into his ear.

While he agreed internally that this was probably the band's best song, he couldn't focus on it at all. Not with Chloe still leaning close to him, holding tightly to his hand. He had to tell her. He couldn't keep it inside anymore.

He turned to her but stopped when he saw her quietly singing. Okay, he would tell her when she wasn't singing along to her favourite song at a concert. So he let the rest of the concert slip by without saying a single word to her.

When the concert ended, Chloe could not stop talking about every aspect of it. From the music, to the lyrics, to the performance itself, to the clothes they'd worn, everything was interesting to her. She didn't seem to mind that Max had very little say and filled in the silence for him as they made their way to Nathan Phillips Square for the New Year's Eve countdown.

He was surprised she even had any voice left after all the cheering and singing she'd done during the concert. He cleared his throat and nodded. "Yeah, it was amazing. Thank you so much for taking me."

As they got closer to the square, the streets got more and more crowded. Chloe wasn't bothered and easily weaved around people. But when she noticed Max having a hard time keeping up, she looped her arm through his and pulled him closer.

"Come on, I don't want to lose you," she said.

"Never," he said too quietly for her to hear.

"What?"

He just shook his head and tightened his hold on her arm. He let her lead him to the heart of Toronto, where people were clustered around a huge outdoor skating rink. Near the two tall buildings that made up town hall, a stage had been set up where a DJ was playing house music. The TORONTO sign was lit in blue while the maple leaf next to it was red.

As they passed by it, a cheer went up throughout the crowd. They looked over at the big screen at the back of the stage. One minute till midnight. Then Chloe's carriage would turn into a pumpkin and Max would lose his princess.

They finally found a spot to stand where they could see the countdown and also not be jostled by other people. Not knowing what to do with himself, Max pulled back and put his arms around himself. Chloe was turning in a circle to take in every detail, and he couldn't help smiling.

"They're starting the countdown," he said.

She whirled around to face the stage just as the crowd shouted, "Ten! Nine!"

She looked at him with a sassy glint in her eyes. "We can't not kiss."

He lifted an eyebrow. "We can't?"

She dropped her gaze. "Unless you really don't want to kiss me."

"Three!"

Max smiled…

"Two!"

Tilted her chin up…

"One!"

And put his lips on hers as fireworks roared overhead. Placing a hand on his chest, she leaned into him. For a moment, time stood still as the wind curled around them, bringing in a fresh newness.

Then a guy shouted, "Woohoo!" right next to them and Max abruptly pulled back. He dropped his hand, his gaze flicking from her soft red lips to her beautiful brown eyes.

"Happy New Year, Chloe."

Chloe momentarily forgot how to speak. She hadn't expected Max to take her up on the offer, but she wasn't exactly mad about it either. She cleared her throat, trying to hold his gaze.

"Happy New Year, Max."

I know. What a terrible place to leave you. I'm sorry; you'll just have to wait. Volume 2 will be out later this year and will contain:
Less than Perfect Wedding
Less than Perfect Prom
Less than Perfect Summer

Less than Perfect

Volume 2 – Books 4-6

A NOTE FROM THE AUTHOR

Thank you so much for reading *Less than Perfect: Volume 1*! If this is your first introduction to Less than Perfect, then I hope you loved it. Whether you did or didn't, will tell you me what you thought and review it?

If you've totally fallen in love with at least half these characters, check out my website. I have lots of fun stuff there, including character bios and even a quiz to see which one you're most like.
www.natasjaeby.com

Stick around for Volume 2. You won't be disappointed!

—Natasja ♥

OTHER SERIES BY NATASJA EBY

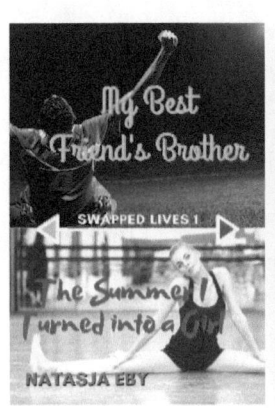

ABOUT THE AUTHOR

Natasja is a librarian and the self-published author of the Swapped Lives series, the Knockout Girl series, the Onepian Chronicles, and the Less than Perfect series. She is an avid fan and participant of NaNoWriMo and has completed several novels over the past few Novembers.

In 2019, Natasja received two Indie Original awards for *Knockout Girl*, one for Best New Author and the other for Best Young Adult Novel.

When she's not working on her many unfinished novels, she can be found playing video games with her husband and two kids, singing, or curled up with a good book. Natasja lives just outside of Toronto—close enough for good shopping and far enough to avoid the traffic.

Follow her on social media!
https://www.natasjaeby.com/
https://www.facebook.com/Natasja.Eby/
https://www.instagram.com/natasjaeby/
https://twitter.com/NatasjaEby